WITCH ALONE

A WITCH ALONE

RUTH WARBURTON

Hodder
Children's
Books

A division of Hachette Children's Books

First published in Great Britain in 2013
by Hodder Children's Books

1

A Catalogue record for this book is available from the British Library

ISBN 978 1 444 90471 0

Typeset in Berkeley by Avon DataSet Ltd, Bidford-on-Avon, Warwickshire

Printed and bound by CPI Group (UK) Ltd, Croydon, CR0 4YY

The paper and board used in this paperback by Hodder Children's Books
are natural recyclable products made from wood grown in sustainable forests. The
manufacturing processes conform to the environmental regulations
of the country of origin.

Hodder Children's Books
a division of Hachette Children's Books
338 Euston Road, London NW1 3BH
An Hachette UK company
www.hachette.co.uk

For Ian, for everything

CHAPTER ONE

It was dark, but I could tell someone was there as soon as I opened the barn door.

'Hello?' My voice echoed in the rafters. 'Hello?'

I waited for a moment, listening. Nothing. But I wasn't alone. I didn't need witchcraft to tell me that; someone was there – a living, breathing someone – and the knowledge made the hair on the back of my neck prickle.

A long shriek broke the silence and I jumped, but it was only the barn door slowly swinging to behind me, the damp wood groaning as it went. Then it clunked shut and darkness engulfed the vast space.

I wasn't afraid. If I was blind, so was he. I stood, waiting.

The blow hit me like a blindside, slamming into me so hard I staggered and saw stars. I stumbled against a wooden beam and clutched at it, holding myself upright as I tried to gather my wits for a counterspell.

'Sl—' I tried. But the blast of lightning came too quick, sending me sprawling to my knees in the straw.

In that brief, blinding instant I saw him, standing on a rafter in the centre of the room. It was a vantage point, but a dangerous one. For a minute I lay face down on the filthy barn floor, trusting that he'd be pulling himself together, readying himself for another go.

Then I leapt up.

'*Ábréoðe!*' I yelled.

There was a deafening crack from the beam he was standing on – then a bone-breaking crunch and a cry of pain as a body hit the floor.

I stood, panting, waiting to see if he got up. He didn't, and for a moment I felt triumph. Then a suffocating web of threads began to drop from the darkness, sticking to my hands, my eyes, my mouth. The more I struggled the closer they clung, like a giant spider's web, binding me in their grip. In a panic I struck out, useless curses right and left, countercharms that did nothing but singe my skin and rip my clothes. I heard laughter, mocking laughter, shiver through the dark and fury rose up in me.

'*Unwríð!*'

The bindings sizzled into shreds and I concentrated all my rage into a spear of anger and flung it through the darkness in the direction of the laughter. It hit – I heard his cry of pain.

Now it was his turn on the defensive. I pushed home my advantage, hitting him again and again, punching him with every ounce of magic I could muster.

But I was tiring and he wasn't. I could feel his energy and the strength of his magic as he pushed back my blows. Then he began to force his way across the floor of the barn towards me. I was concentrating not on hurting him, but on keeping him back. And I couldn't. He forced me back, back, until my spine was against the rough wooden wall of the barn. He was so close I could feel the crackle of his magic, the heat of his skin, smell his sweat.

'No!' I panted.

But it was too late – I was trapped in a corner and he was inches away, crushing me. I felt him lean in, closer and closer in the hot blackness. It was all over. He'd won.

'OK,' I said, my voice shaking with exhaustion, 'OK, I—'

His hand closed on my shoulder, the other gripped my hair, and he kissed me.

For a minute I couldn't think – I just stood, shattered, all my defences down, and let him. All I could think about was the soft heat of his mouth, the hard strength of his body, the harshness of his unshaven skin against mine. For a long, long minute I did nothing, just stood and trembled as he kissed me.

It was only when I felt his hand slip beneath my shirt that clarity broke through. A vicious blast of magic shook the barn. His body was flung backwards, crashing against the opposite wall with a terrible cracking sound. And then there was silence.

'Oh God, Abe!' My hands trembled as I tried to remember the lamp-charm my grandmother had taught me. '*Loet* – no, *léoht* . . . Wait, oh God. *L-léohtfœtels-ábíed*!'

The room suffused with a bright glow and there was

Abe, lying quite still against the far wall with something ominous and dark pooling on the straw. I ran to him, my heart in my mouth, and knelt beside him on the dusty floor, cradling his head.

'I'm so sorry. Are you OK?'

He coughed, spat blood on the floor, and then heaved himself to a sitting position against the barn wall.

'Jaysus, woman.' His voice was hoarse. 'A simple, "Thank you, but I've got a headache," would've done.'

'Abe!' With the knowledge that he was alive, all my anger came flooding back, sharper for being mixed with relief. 'You're supposed to be training me, not sodding goading me into GBH.'

'Had to.' He spoke shortly around a mouthful of blood, then spat again with a disgusted look. 'You weren't going to pull your finger out otherwise, were you? *Yeuch*, why does blood always taste so rancid?'

'Are you OK? Should we go to A&E?'

'A&E – you're joking, right? I'm fine. It's just a nosebleed, it'll stop in a sec. You could help instead of standing around like the shy girl at the disco.'

'Oh shut up,' I said, but I put my hand to his cheek and did my best to help his body heal itself. The blood flow stemmed a little and I added, 'Anyway, what do you mean, you *had* to? I was doing my best.'

'No you weren't.' Abe grabbed my arm to haul himself stiffly to his feet. There was straw and blood on his ripped jeans. 'You were faffing around with those sodding charms your grandma's so keen on. You weren't going to let go until I made you – so I did.'

'You didn't have to sexually assault me,' I said grumpily, as we hobbled out into the chill night air.

'Best way I could think of, off the top of my head.' Abe gave me a wicked sideways grin. 'Win-win scenario – if you didn't enjoy it then you'd unclamp enough to actually do some damage, and if you did enjoy it – well, bonus situation for both of us.'

'Shut up,' I growled. Perhaps the anger in my voice got through to him, for he fell silent.

We walked slowly through the moonlit woods to his car and I felt my cheeks cool and my anger fade. After all, it wasn't Abe's fault that my heart was still so bruised that the lightest touch made me curl into a hedgehog ball of prickles. It wasn't Abe's fault that I still couldn't fully access my magic without raw emotion ripping it from me. And it wasn't Abe's fault that I was starting to enjoy our practice fights a bit too much. I didn't like to analyse the fierce snarling joy that had filled me when I sent his body flying through the air to smack into the wall of the barn.

Guilt made me stretch on tiptoes to brush Abe's cheek as he stopped by the car, groping for his keys. He turned, his face naked, surprised.

'What was that for?'

'For putting up with me. I know there are probably more fun ways to spend your Friday night.'

'Hmph.' He stuck the car key into the lock, then folded

himself painfully into the driver's seat. 'Well, I wouldn't be here if I didn't want to be, trust me.'

'I know.' I climbed in the passenger side and shut the door gingerly. Too hard and the handle came off in your grip. 'But I'm still . . . you don't have to do this – help me, I mean. I'm grateful. I wish there was something I could do for you, in return.'

'I don't want your gratitude.' His voice was irritable. I said nothing while he did a fast, bad-tempered three-point-turn towards Winter. But as the road rolled away beneath the tyres and the silence stretched, taut with unspoken feelings, I couldn't stop myself.

'So what *do* you want?'

He said nothing, only turned to look at me in the shifting, flickering dimness of the car, his black eyes fixed on mine in a hard stare that left me first uncomfortable and then, as the seconds ticked out, frankly panicked.

'Abe, look at the road,' I said at last. 'Abe . . .' Then, 'Look at the damn road!'

'Fine.' He turned his gaze back to the winding forest road, staring into the darkness.

It wasn't until we came out of the trees on to the coast road that I realized how the weather had changed. It had been a cool spring evening when I entered the barn. Now fog was rolling in from the sea and unseen waves crashed against the foot of the cliffs. A blank whiteness began to press against the windscreen, reflecting the car's headlights back at us. When I turned to look out of the rear window, the wall was red as a hellmouth, flickering as Abe's foot hovered over the brake, slowing the car as the mist thickened.

I watched as the speedometer dropped to thirty, then twenty, and then below even that. The road ran right along the cliff-edge. It'd be all too easy to miss one of the tight turns in the fog and hurtle into the sea. I'd survived two drownings, but even a witch's luck had to run out sometime.

'What a foul bloody night,' Abe said at last, and I was relieved to hear the anger was gone from his voice. 'It's not normal, this weather.' He wriggled his shoulders uneasily inside his jacket. 'It's all wrong. It – it goes against the grain of normal weather somehow. Can you feel it? Like the fog, with this wind. It shouldn't—'

He broke off as a mournful echoing bray split the night air, booming against the cliffs and making me jump. I felt the car give a nervous stutter as Abe's foot jerked reflexively on the brake and then he laughed.

'Bloody foghorn. I've lived here eight years now and it still gives me the heebie-jeebies. It sounds like a giant cow dying in the throes of labour.'

The sound came again, a long lowing wail that sent a shiver up my spine. I thought of all the fishermen out there, bent low over their flickering GPS displays, peering through the murk towards the safety of the port. I thought of . . . but I pushed that thought away. Not now. Not here in the car with Abe. I couldn't.

'Want to meet up tomorrow for a rematch?' Abe asked,

breaking into my thoughts. I shook my head.

'I can't. I'm going up to London.'

'Huh. Seeing Granny, eh?'

'Yes, if you must know.'

'You're a sandwich short of a picnic, messing with that crew.' He shook his head and the moonlight glinted off his eyebrow ring as he frowned.

'It's none of your business,' I said shortly.

'You're right.' His voice was rigid. 'I have no say. Doesn't stop me from caring whether you get made into witch-meat.'

'Look, I have no choice.'

'Because you're related to the old bag?'

'No, because . . .' I found I was breathing fast. Why was I even bothering to justify myself to Abe? Why did I care what he thought of me? 'Because I – I've decided to do something. I'm tracking down my mother.'

Abe's head turned sharply.

'Is that a good idea?'

'I have to try!' The desperation in my own voice surprised me. 'I *have* to. I can't go through my whole life not knowing if she's still out there, if she died, if she killed herself even.'

'What makes you think you'll do any better than your dad and your grandmother and all the other people who tried to track her down? If she's out there, she doesn't want to be found, that's pretty clear.'

'I've got more information than either of them. They each had only half the picture. I know much more – for

8

example, I know that she returned to the Ealdwitan headquarters, after she was supposed to have gone missing.'

'Are you sure?' Abe's voice showed his scepticism. 'She was running from them like her life depended on it, from all you've told me. Why the hell would she go back to their HQ?'

'I don't know,' I said. 'But a passer-by saw her jump from St Saviour's Dock a few days after she disappeared. They thought suicide, of course, and dredged the river, but no body was found. But I looked at a map and I realized—'

'That St Saviour's is where the Neckinger enters the Thames,' Abe finished. 'One of the entrances to their headquarters.' His fingers tapped the steering wheel with restless energy. 'But that still doesn't answer why.'

'I know. That's why I have to go there again. They must have some kind of records – some kind of witch equivalent of CCTV. I've got to get access to their files. Find out what she did.'

'You're nuts,' Abe said shortly. 'Anna, for God's sake don't do anything stupid. Nearly getting yourself killed by them once was enough. If you get caught going through their papers . . .'

'I won't,' I said. 'But I've got Elizabeth on my side now, don't forget. If it comes to the crunch, I'm pretty sure she'll protect me.'

'You reckon blood's thicker than water?' He turned to look at me, his eyes dark and unreadable. Then he turned back to the road, the dim light illuminating his grim, uncompromising profile, the hard set of his mouth. 'I wouldn't rely on it, Anna. Not as far as the Ealdwitan are concerned, anyway.'

'Did I hear a car?' Dad came out of the kitchen as I slammed the front door behind me.

'Yes, Abe dropped me,' I said.

'Hmm.' Dad withdrew without further remark. I knew what he was thinking. Abe wasn't exactly the boy next door. He smoked, drank, and swore, and tried only half-heartedly to hide those facts when he was around my dad. He was also – well, I wasn't quite sure how old. It wasn't really surprising that Dad wasn't keen. But at the same time, Abe had played a big part in keeping me sane after . . . after Seth left.

Even thinking his name still caused a tearing sensation inside me, as if small unhealed stitches were ripping open. It was hard to believe it was – what? Eight, ten weeks since he'd left? Two months. It felt like forever, and yesterday, both at the same time.

Dad had made my favourite food and refrained from telling me to woman up and get over myself because he'd been through the same thing, only twice as bad, when my mum left. Instead he'd just comforted, and cooked, and let me take my own time getting over it. And Em had jollied, and joked, and propelled me round school with sufficient force to stop my grades completely collapsing. Between them, they'd got me through. But Abe – Abe had made me angry. He'd made me laugh. He'd made me *feel* again. And Dad knew that.

A delicious smell was coming from the kitchen and, when I pushed open the door, the air was heavy with the scent of something rich and mouthwatering. Dad was bent over the stove, stirring, and the smell of butter and spices rose up to greet me.

'Wow, what's in there?'

'Moong daal. Thought you'd be pleased.'

I was. It was one of the few things that I still really, really missed about London. Winter had a Chinese takeaway but no Indian, and there were times when I yearned for our old curry house in Notting Hill.

'That's nice. What are we celebrating?'

'Oh, nothing much. Friday, the weekend, end of school. What are you up to tomorrow? Would you like to come into Brighthaven with me? I'm driving over to pick up some things for El—' He stumbled and finished, 'A friend. Would you like to come?'

I sighed.

'It's all right, Dad. You can say her name, you know.' There was enough in Winter to remind me of Seth, and it wasn't like Dad tiptoeing around Elaine's name made it any less obvious. Besides, I liked Elaine. I knew she worried about Seth as much as I did. I liked to hear Dad talk about her.

'OK. Sorry. Anyway, do you want to come? You were saying you needed some new jeans.'

'I do. But I can't. I've arranged to see Elizabeth this weekend – I'm staying the night, remember?'

'Oh.' Dad's expression turned closed, reserved. He looked down at the bubbling pan. I knew it had been hard for him to forget past wrongs and accept my grandmother in my life. There was a lot to forget; she'd cut her daughter off when Isla fell in love with my outwith father. 'Now you mention it you did say, but I forgot to write it on the calendar.'

'I'm sorry, only . . .' I trailed off and Dad gave a slightly forced smile.

'Don't apologize! It's nice that you're spending time with Elizabeth. I still feel guilty that you lost out on eighteen years of each other because of—'

'Dad . . .' I put my hand on his. 'Please, don't. It wasn't your fault. I understand, truly.' Dad had been bound, barely able to speak my mother's name, until the charm wore off when I turned eighteen. I knew that now. What I still didn't know was why.

After supper I helped Dad clear and wash up, while he chatted about his plans for the weekend. I couldn't concentrate though; the lowing moan of the foghorn kept breaking in on my thoughts.

Abe was right. There was something unnatural about this fog, the way it groped its way through the trees and huddled up against the house. I glanced at the thick white blanket pressed up against the kitchen window and shivered, thinking of the sailors out in it, thinking of . . .

No. I pushed that away, dried my hands, then filled a glass of water.

'Dad, do you mind if I go up? I'm shattered and I need to pack.'

It was true. My practice with Abe had taken it out of me, and my grandmother would probably want me to do more tomorrow, although her approach was almost the polar opposite of Abe's – all rote learning and books and memorizing. She'd taught me how to scry, how to divine, the difference between a charm and an incantation. She'd made me learn every one of the Given Runes. She'd rehearsed me in the Bright Invocations and the Dark Invocations, the spells to protect and safeguard, and the spells to blast and break and maim.

She believed that the best magic came from books and learning. That you could swot your way out of trouble. Whereas Abe felt that magic came from inside, that instinct was better than memory, that if you couldn't come up with the spell yourself, you shouldn't rely on it in a tight place.

They both agreed on one thing, though: I had eighteen years of neglect to make up for. I had power, but power alone couldn't make you powerful. For that you needed control and confidence, and I lacked both, a problem which had almost proved fatal a few months ago. Both Abe and my grandmother were determined that if another crisis evolved, this time at least, I'd be able to look after myself.

13

Dad was looking at me with concern.

'You do look tired, sweetie. Have an early night. Want a lift to the train station tomorrow?'

'Sure? I'm going early,' I warned him. 'I told Elizabeth I'd be up in London mid-morning, so I'll have to be at the station by eight-ish at the latest.'

'That's fine. I'd rather get to Brighthaven before the parking fills up anyway. I'll drop you off and then carry on to . . .' He faltered, but then carried on bravely, 'To the Anchor to pick up Elaine.'

'Oh, you're going with her?' I was surprised.

'Well I thought I might, since you can't come. It'll be more companionable with someone else and if I go early she can be back before the pub opens for lunch.'

'Good.' I tried to smile. 'Great idea. Give my love to Elaine. Ask her . . .' I stopped. But Dad knew what I'd been going to say.

'Yes, I'll ask her for any news.' He kissed my forehead. 'Goodnight, sweetie. Sleep well.'

The concern in his face stayed with me as I climbed the creaking stairs and pushed open the heavy oak door to my bedroom.

He worried about me. Worried about what I did all night, holed up in my room. He would've worried even more if he'd known the truth.

The bedsprings squeaked as I sat, but I didn't get undressed, not yet. Instead I spread my hands on my knees and looked at my seaglass ring, smoky amethyst in the light from my lamp. The foghorn boomed again and, suddenly, pulled by a temptation too strong to resist, I wrenched off the ring and picked up the polished wooden bowl that sat on my bedside table.

For a long minute I just sat on the bed, holding the bowl in my lap and the ring in the palm of my left hand, my breath coming fast. Then, with a quick movement, I emptied my glass of water into the bowl, dropped in the ring, and put my face down inside, so close to the surface of the water that my reflection became broken and meaningless, a collection of choppy refracted lights, too close to focus into a single image.

As I gazed the waters seemed to shimmer and move, rippling with the grain of the wood, with the trembling of my hands, with each breath I exhaled. Small waves sprang up, lapping at each other, chasing a fleck of light across the bowl. Then, gradually, clouds began to gather, the waters darkened, and the fleck of light dwindled and resolved into a tiny boat racing across the sea, trying desperately to keep ahead of the huge waves that threatened to overwhelm it. Nearly all the sails had been stripped away, until the boat was scudding under almost bare poles. I could see a figure at the tiller, lashed by rain and wind, struggling to keep the prow pointing into the oncoming waves.

And I could do nothing. Nothing but watch the silent struggle, the figure alone in the dark, in the middle of this vast hostile waste of ocean.

I watched, until I could bear it no longer. Then I sat

upright, ripping myself bodily out of that storm-racked, lonely world.

My neck was so stiff I could hardly straighten it. I rubbed slowly at the cramped muscles while my eyes got used to the light of the lamp, so warm and soft after the harsh blackness of the storm.

I fished the ring out of the bottom of the bowl and poured the water on to my African violet, feeling a mixture of fear and disgust. Fear for Seth, and disgust with myself, for spying on him like this.

I'd watched him obsessively at first. It was part of what had worried Dad so much after Seth left; my habit of keeping to my room, with a charm-locked door. But I wasn't moping or crying or tearing Seth's pictures out of my photo album. I was scrying. Fruitlessly at first and then, after I used the seaglass ring to focus my attention, with better and better accuracy. I never knew *where* Seth was exactly – what coast he was sailing past, what quay he was moored at – but I could always find his face. And it became an obsession: watching him sail, and eat, and sleep, and cry. And, one horrible night, bring a woman back to his boat. She was beautiful, with hair like polished mahogany, and as she walked down the steps to the cabin I saw the tail of her sarong as it fell to the ground. And then I saw Seth, as he turned to follow.

I threw the bowl out of the window that night and vowed never to spy again. I felt degraded by what I'd done, and by what Seth had done, even though he owed me nothing. Not now. Not any more.

Tonight, though, with the fog so low – I wasn't spying, only wanting to make sure he was OK. Wasn't that different?

Maybe. But I still wished I hadn't. What would Seth think of me using my power like a peeping Tom? And what good did it do? I couldn't help him. I couldn't change a thing. I could only watch as he battled his demons alone – and I battled mine.

CHAPTER TWO

*K*iller *Fog Claims Three!* screeched the billboard, as I came up the steps from the tube, my nostrils still filled with the warm, sooty air. *South Gripped by Death Mist* the banner headline read and, underneath, *Three dead in freak fog.* Their faces stared up at me from a discarded newspaper; an elderly Essex man who'd tumbled down some steps in the mist and a young couple whose car had ploughed into the central reservation of a lonely motorway. No news about ships. But a year of living in Winter had taught me that sailors' deaths weren't usually reported, unless they were well-to-do day-trippers. Real sailors – professional fishermen and skippers – no one was interested in the risks they took.

The last of the mist still curled thick and strange about the streets as I walked quickly through Pimlico. Perhaps it was the fog, but London looked somehow unfamiliar. It was hard to believe that I'd walked these busy streets every day, that the stink of car exhaust and the warm gush of air from the tube vents had been more familiar than the smell of the sea and of oyster pots drying on the quay.

I felt a fierce stab of longing to be back in Winter – but I pushed the thought down and turned on to Vauxhall Bridge Road, trying to ignore the growing sense of foreboding about what was to come.

I hadn't been back since my first disastrous visit – first and last. My grandmother had come to Winter and I'd visited her house, but every time she'd asked me to come to the Ealdwitan headquarters, I'd refused. I'd made my peace with my grandmother, but I'd never be able to forget the Ealdwitan's actions last year, not with Bill's memorial stone still clean and white in the Winter churchyard.

But the fact was, if I wanted to find out the truth about my mother and myself, I had to go back there. When I'd first suggested it to my grandmother, it hadn't seemed like such a big deal. But now . . .

I stood on the parapet of Vauxhall Bridge looking at the silky swirl of the grey waters beneath and my stomach did a little flip.

'Come on you bloody coward,' I whispered to myself, steeling myself for the leap. Buses thundered up and down the road and there was a ferry passing beneath, so I murmured a few words and then looked down at my feet to check the invisibility charm had worked.

'Houston, we are go,' I muttered. And then I jumped.

The smell hit me first, like the memory of a nightmare. As I opened the door, the rich air flooded into the small anteroom, laden with the scent and feel and taste of magic, like a thousand spices crushed underfoot. I flinched.

Don't go in! every bone in my body screamed. I stood, with my hand on the reinforced steel door, and the man at the desk looked at me quizzically. I desperately wanted to turn and flee. But instead I found myself taking a step forward. Back into the heart of the Ealdwitan.

Inside, the atmosphere closed around me like a thick blanket. I felt the layers of charm and countercharm, magic and deception, settle like a physical weight upon my shoulders.

'Good morning.' The man at the desk gave something that was probably supposed to be a smile, if you gave him the benefit of the doubt. 'Can I help you?'

'Um . . . thanks. I'm here to see my grandmother, Elizabeth Rokewood.'

'Of course.' He barely thawed an inch. Must be one of the rival factions. There were five Chairs and, from what I'd heard from my grandmother, no more than two were generally on speaking terms with each other. Their camps followed suit.

I signed in at the book on the table. The office behind him was shadowy, but I could just make out rows of shelves, each stacked with dozens upon dozens of similar leatherbound tomes, and a thought struck me.

'Do you keep these sign-in ledgers? Old ones, I mean.'

'Of course.' He gave me a hard stare.

'What's in them?'

'A list of all the visitors each day and an account of any noteworthy occurrences and meetings.'

'And can . . . um . . . can people see them?'

'Certainly not.' His stare deepened into a frankly suspicious glare. 'Why do you want to know?'

'No reason.' My heart was thudding. Just as I was wondering what to say next, I heard a voice I recognized and turned to see my grandmother walking briskly down the long, carpeted corridor, dictating to her secretary as she went.

'. . . in light of this a security reassessment is essential, underlined, comma, including the withdrawal and reissue of all current passes and security clearances stop. New paragraph— Anna! . . . No, Miss Vane, of course that wasn't part of the memo. We'll resume later.'

I felt her thin, jewel-laden hand close on my shoulder as she kissed me lightly, once on each cheek, and I inhaled the scent of her bitter perfume.

'Hello, darling. I'm afraid I'm going to be rather busy today. It's fortunate you suggested meeting here, as I would have had to come in anyway.'

'What's happened?' I asked. She grimaced, her skin stretched tight over the bones of her face, and we began to walk down the corridor towards her office, the velvet *shushing* beneath our feet.

'A long story. Security issues, combined with some recent worrying events. We're having an emergency meeting about it today and I would like you to attend.'

'Me?' I gulped. 'But—'

'Anna, I realize this is throwing you in at the deep end. I didn't want to introduce you to the Chairs like this. But just now everything is in flux. The Chairs are panicked; I think this could be the moment.'

'The moment?'

She looked up and down the corridor and then drew me inside her office and shut the door.

'For holding Thaddeus Corax to account.'

Thaddeus Corax – who had ordered the attack on Winter; who had sent his servants to terrorize me and my friends; who, according to my grandmother, was to blame for everything that had happened in Winter one year ago. She'd promised me that we would confront him one day and prevent him treating anyone else the same way. But now? So soon?

Elizabeth must have read the doubts flickering across my face, for she spoke decisively.

'Thaddeus has been destabilized more than anyone by these events, Anna. If we have any chance of damaging his authority, it is now.'

'So what . . . You want me to talk about – about last year?'

'No, at least not at the moment. I taxed him a few months ago with his actions in Winter. His stance is unwavering and his account unchanged; according to him, he sent a party of people to investigate you and to try to persuade you to stop practising magic unguardedly. They

22

became carried away and operatives on the ground exceeded their responsibilities, entirely unbeknown to him. It's very hard to prove either way.'

'Then – why? Why do you need me?'

'Because, Anna, you are the last of the Rokewoods.' Her dark eyes were unfathomable. 'And I am old. Because Corax is holding on to his mortality with a tenaciousness that frightens me, using methods I cannot bear to think of. And because when I am gone – and if Corax has his way that may be sooner rather than later – the Chair will fall to you.'

'No!' I took a step back, crashed into an ornate coffee table. 'No! I don't want it. I don't *want* it!'

'You *must* seize it. Or Corax will install one of his camp and all will be lost.'

I shook my head, imagining myself entombed in this underground maze for ever, chained to a Chair I didn't want, enslaved to a duty I never sought. I imagined the weight now on my grandmother's shoulder's settling on mine.

'You are a Rokewood.' My grandmother's voice was harsh.

'I'm not, I'm a Winterson.'

'You are a Rokewood – and Anna, whether you choose to believe it or not, there are greater evils than Thaddeus Corax out there.' My grandmother's voice was grim. 'Right now, the Ealdwitan, imperfect though we may be, is what stands between your friends and that evil.'

23

My heart thudded in my chest. But there was no way back. There never had been, not since I first opened the pages of the Grimoire. I could only press on, blindly.

The chamber was domed, with a vaulted roof studded with ornate bosses. It was late afternoon by my watch, but there were no windows in the hall and by the shadows in the rafters it might have been midnight. The witchlights in the sconces around the walls flickered softly, casting an uneven light on the stone walls and the carved backs of the five imposing chairs arranged in a circle at the centre of the room. Four of them were already occupied; these people must be the famous Chairs, representatives of the most important witch clans in Britain.

Around them, at their backs, were ranged their followers, clustered into little camps on the high, tiered benches. I was seated behind the empty chair, with my grandmother's secretary, Miss Vane, and a number of others whose faces I didn't know.

'Who are the people in the middle?' I whispered, under cover of the general rustling as people settled themselves, spread papers, took out pens and plumped cushions.

'The lady sitting opposite us, the young one, she's Margot Throgmorton,' Miss Vane whispered back. 'She's deputizing for her husband, Edward Throgmorton, who's very elderly and too ill to attend at present. If he dies, no one knows what will happen. Margot will try to seize the chair, I'm sure, and she will probably have support from Erasmus Knyvet – they're said to be lovers.'

I looked down at the beautiful, vivacious face of the woman Miss Vane had indicated and I wasn't surprised at the rumours. She couldn't have been a day over forty, even allowing for a witch's habit of smoothing away wrinkles. As I watched her, I noticed something coiling sinuously around the legs of her chair – an animal too large to be a cat. A flash of red and I recognized it: a fox. Margot Throgmorton's hand crept down and scratched the creature behind the ears, and it writhed with pleasure before vanishing in the shadows under her seat.

'Knyvet is the man next to her,' Miss Vane continued. 'He's very proper, very traditional. His wife –' she nodded subtly towards a very pregnant woman high on the benches at the back, '– is due in May with his eighth child.'

Eighth? I looked from the grey, drawn face of the woman opposite, down to the thin foxlike visage of Knyvet. He was leaning in, speaking confidentially to Margot Throgmorton, every line of their bodies exuding mutual amusement.

'Next in the circle is Charles Catesby,' she nodded down at a leonine man, with a grizzled mane of hair and a blond beard streaked with white. 'He's an old friend of your grandparents.'

'And the last man?' I asked, my throat dry. Miss Vane shot me a look.

'Yes. The last man is Thaddeus Corax.'

I looked down through the dimness of the chamber at the back of his head. He was small, wizened, impossibly old. I'd hated him, feared him, for so long. And now here he was.

As I stared, he turned, as if he could feel the intensity of my gaze. Two hooded eyes swept the chamber and I glimpsed yellowed teeth, a beaklike nose, a face so graven with lines he looked carved from stone. Then he ducked his head with a curious bobbing motion and turned back to the circle.

Last to be seated was my grandmother, and I watched as she moved to take her place, a strange suffocating feeling in my chest. It felt like . . . affection. Love, even. But that was impossible, surely. How could you love someone as hard, as indomitable as my grandmother?

Perhaps it was because she looked – strangely – frail. She was old. Sixty, even seventy perhaps. And there wasn't an ounce of spare flesh on her bones. Her wrists were skin and sinew, her rings hung heavy on her thin fingers. Her still-black hair was scraped into an immaculate chignon so heavy it seemed impossible that her neck could support it. She'd been a hard mother, I knew that. Hard on her daughter. And she'd be hard on me too, if I let her. But now, seeing her bow her neck beneath the weight of all this authority and malevolence, I could see she'd been harder still on herself.

'The meeting will come to order,' Thaddeus Corax said in a harsh, croaking voice which rang through the chamber – and silence fell.

'Now, as you know,' he continued, 'we are here to

discuss the attack on our shores which took place last night.'

'Attack?' I whispered to Miss Vane.

'The fog,' she whispered back. 'Shh.'

'We believe the fog was a test mechanism,' Corax was continuing, 'a precursor, if you will, for a future attack which might cause more damage. As far as we can tell, the fog itself did no harm. But its very presence is of the utmost concern – it should not have been able to penetrate these shores. A thousand years of spell and counterspell ought to have repelled it. These spells, for whatever reason, failed.'

'And what reason can my fellow Chairs suggest?' It was Knyvet who spoke, his voice smooth as oil.

'Treachery!' boomed Charles Catesby, his voice echoing around the rafters and making the spectators jump. 'Treachery! Betrayal! A spy within the camp.'

'Hold, hold, Chair Catesby.' Corax raised a hand. 'We do not yet have proof of this. But it is true that the fog seems to have concentrated on every weak spot in our defence – and that is extremely worrying. It is almost as if the sender had access to privileged information on those defences and was able to fashion and direct a weapon to penetrate them.'

'Almost?' Margot Throgmorton's sultry voice purred across the chamber. 'Why "almost", Chair Corax? I understood from the briefing that it's not merely a question of last night's fog. It seems that papers have gone missing, confidential spells have been breached, messages have been intercepted and never reached their recipient. I am –' she lowered her eyelashes, '– only a deputy, but it seems as clear as day to me. Yet you don't believe in the existence of this spy?'

'Forgive me . . .' For the first time Corax seemed to grope for words. He raised his eyes, looking around the chamber as if in bewilderment. 'Forgive me, madam, if I find it hard to believe in the treachery of one so close to this circle that they know the secrets of power. Forgive me, for being an old man, trusting in my friends.'

Trusting? I nearly let my breath hiss through my teeth. Thaddeus Corax looked as if he'd never trusted anyone, man, woman or child, since the day he was born.

I could see my grandmother was struggling with the same concept. Her mouth was pressed into a thin, bloodless line and her ringed hands were locked in her lap so tightly that the knuckles shone white.

'It would have to be a very strong motive, Chair Corax.' She spoke for the first time, her voice grim. 'A very strong motive indeed. For someone at the centre of so much power, to risk so much, to gain – what? Safety, from a challenger perhaps?'

Her eyes bored into his, but he did not flinch.

'Or help, to topple an adversary perhaps, Chair Rokewood?' His reply was cold. 'There are many possibilities.'

'Friends, friends . . .' Knyvet's voice was smooth, insinuating. 'We must not quarrel among ourselves. United we stand, divided we fall – is that not how the saying goes?'

'Indeed, dear friend.' Corax put his hand in Knyvet's and his graven face creased into something I suspected was meant for a smile. But my grandmother didn't smile and when Corax held out his free hand, she didn't return the gesture.

'Our house is already divided,' she said coldly. 'The only question is where this invisible fissure lies. Friends or not, we have been betrayed; there is a crack in our very foundations which will split us in two. And until we know where that crack lies, how can we protect ourselves?'

'What do you propose then, Chair Rokewood?' Margot Throgmorton's voice was less sultry now, and there was impatience in her tone. 'Instead of prophesying doom, perhaps you could tell us what course of action you advise?'

'Lock down,' my grandmother said shortly. There was an immediate hubbub around the chamber, but her voice rose, ringing above the chorus of disapproval and consternation. 'We revoke every pass. We cancel every security clearance. We reissue them one by one, on a strictly need-to-know basis. And we watch to see when the leaks recommence.'

'This is absurd,' Knyvet said impatiently. 'Chair Rokewood, you would have us waste time quarrelling among ourselves instead of looking to the true enemy.'

'And who is the true enemy, Chair Knyvet?' my grandmother demanded.

A hushed silence fell over the chamber. I had the

impression that everyone was waiting – waiting for a hammer to fall.

But before Knyvet could answer, an enormous explosion shook the chamber.

The witchlights in their sconces guttered suddenly, dwindling to threads, as if a terrible blow had been struck at the source of their power, and for a moment I heard a thunderous rush of water around us, as if the rivers were pressing very close, straining to break their chains and reclaim their powers. The chamber was a dark, flickering cavern filled with screams and whimpers.

In the middle of the floor the Chairs jumped to their feet, gazing wildly around.

'Everybody, please be calm and keep to your seats!' Thaddeus Corax barked in a harsh voice. His words were ignored. All around, people were running.

Miss Vane stood, biting her lip, then she put her hand firmly on my shoulder.

'Anna, stay here, do you understand? Stay here until I'm back. I'll only be five minutes but I must check – I have to find out what's—'

'Go,' I said. 'I'll be fine.'

'I'll be five minutes,' she repeated firmly. And then she was gone, clattering up the steep steps to the door at the edge of the chamber.

For a moment I sat, my ears still ringing from the blast. Then I ran after her.

CHAPTER THREE

The corridor was almost deserted but from far away, deep within the labyrinth, I could hear shouts and the thunder of spells and charms. The strange feeling of an illusion worn thin persisted – I felt as if I could press my hand through the red damask wallpaper in the corridor, plunge my arm shoulder-deep into the river's filth and silt.

Miss Vane was disappearing at a ladylike run around the curve of the corridor to my left. I waited, pressed against the wall, until she'd gone and then I turned right.

I hoped to God I could remember the way. The Ealdwitan's HQ was a maze and I'd only the faintest recollection of its layout. I passed two rooms I recognized and for a moment started to feel cocky – and then I came to a dead end. There were two great glass doors in front of me; inside was a vaulted glass cathedral – a giant hothouse filled with tropical plants and trees.

Damn, damn. I turned around, feeling sweat trickle down my back, and hearing again Miss Vane's firm 'Five minutes'.

I began to run.

After what felt like a lot longer than five minutes I found myself at the reception desk, facing the ledger I'd signed so recently. And, as I'd hoped, the desk was unmanned, the office behind shadowed in darkness and empty.

My heart was thudding in my throat, so hard that for a minute it was hard to breathe. But I ignored it and clambered awkwardly over the polished wood of the reception desk, whacking my ankle painfully as I did so. I stifled a yelp, then ducked into the shadowed cave beyond.

The room was dark – very dark – and I looked for the light switch before I remembered where I was.

I stretched out my hand and drew a deep breath, trying to calm myself.

'Léohtfœtels-ábíed!'

A cool white light flickered on my palm, illuminating the room.

Ledgers were stacked all around me, piled haphazardly on shelves, tables, stacked upon the floor . . . Where to begin? 'Five minutes' was echoing in my head as I began to scan the spidery writing on the spines.

Day Ledger 1808, *Day Ledger 1809* – much too old. Then *1947* caught my eye on a dusty shelf – at least that was closer. I looked further down the row . . . *1968* . . . A little further . . . Damn! *Day Ledger 1716*. Hadn't they heard of order?

Sweat trickled into my eyes and the witchlight in my palm flickered and dwindled. I swore, glaring at my palm, and it blazed into light again.

Day Ledger 1978 – OK, good! *1979 . . . 1981 . . . 1992 . . .* and suddenly there it was. I snatched it off the shelf with eager hands and let the witchlight flare up again as I opened it, trying to keep my palm angled to illuminate the page. January, February . . . I counted on my fingers. Six weeks from my birthday, so that was the sixteenth of January . . . One, two, three . . . The first week of March, near enough. I flicked forward in the ledger and scanned down the lists of names. Nothing. Nothing I recognized.

I was about to slam the ledger down in disgust when a shadow suddenly passed across the lamp in the corridor and my breath caught in my throat. The witchlight in my palm guttered and died abruptly, and I shrank into the corner of the room, holding my breath.

But the passer-by continued on their way and I let out a great shuddering gasp. Then suddenly an idea struck me.

'You idiot,' I whispered under my breath. Of course – when my dad had said six weeks, he'd meant six weeks from my *real* birthday, not my fake one. Six weeks from the sixth of January. That meant – the third week of February.

My hands were shaking so hard that the witchlight in my palm cast flickering shadows across the thick paper. I turned back sheet after sheet . . . The twenty-first of February, nothing. The twentieth of February, nothing. Next I ran my trembling finger down the column of names for the nineteenth: *Franklin, Adelstrop, Restorick, Vandellen,*

Menton, Vane, Ayckbourn . . . Rokewood.

My finger stopped. She'd been here.

I. Rokewood. 11.45pm, Neckinger entrance.

And then a note at the foot of the page, before the new day's entry for the twentieth of February began: *Today a most regrettable disturbance in the library; the vandalism of one of our most valuable tomes, the* Codex Angelis. *An entire page, 'The Riddle of the Epiphany', was torn out. It is very hard to believe that one of the members present on this date was responsible for the destruction.*

Coincidence? The thought hung in the air as the witchlight flickered and waxed high in my palm. Impossible.

Then a shadow fell over the page and an accusing voice came from behind me.

'Who are you and what are you doing here?'

I jumped and let the ledger fall from my hands with a sound like a clap of thunder.

'I—'

Light flooded the room as the stranger cast his own witchlight, engulfing mine in a blaze of brilliance.

'You!'

We both gasped.

It was a man – a boy, really, just a few years older than me – wearing an immaculate grey suit. His smooth chestnut hair gleamed in the witchlight. And I knew him. A few months ago he'd saved my skin – and I had no idea who he was, beyond his first name.

'M-Marcus?' I managed.

'Get out,' he said harshly. 'The archivist is coming. You do *not* want to be found here.'

'Thank you!' I gasped.

'*Go!*' he hissed.

I didn't need to be told again.

I ran.

'Anna!' Miss Vane looked furious but relieved as I sank into the seat next to her, trying to suppress my panting. 'Where have you been? I was beside myself! I told you to stay here – what possessed you to wander off? Especially today of all days.'

'I'm sorry,' I said. My voice was as even as I could make it. 'I needed the loo and I got lost.'

'Oh.' She looked slightly mollified. 'Well it looks like the meeting is breaking up in any case. Chair Rokewood –' she turned as my grandmother wearily ascended the steps towards us '– is the meeting closing?'

'Yes, it seems so, for the moment at least.'

'Do they know what caused the explosion?'

'Not yet. There was no physical evidence of a disturbance – but the sound would seem to indicate that one of the wards was compromised. We're not certain if it was merely some activity of the outwith which impinged on one of our security measures. If they dig too close to the rivers it can destabilize the foundations, though the wards are supposed to prevent that. But whatever the cause, it's worrying that the shields were so badly affected. The Keepers are working now to reinstate them and we've agreed to adjourn the meeting until they're fully operational. I think the only thing to do is seize the opportunity to take some supper. We'll dine in my office please, Miss Vane.'

My grandmother sank into an armchair in front of the fire and passed a weary hand over her face. She looked several hundred years older than this morning. Then with a sudden, angry movement she picked up the briefing notes from the table in front of her and threw them savagely into the grate, her face stern in the flickering firelight as they blazed up.

'Damn Corax,' she said at last. 'He had the meeting by the throat. Doesn't he *care* there's a spy in our midst? I know the leaks are coming from within his camp, I *know* it.'

'Grandmother . . .' I stopped and then, screwing up my courage, I carried on. 'What did you want Knyvet to say – before the explosion?'

'I don't know, child.' She passed a weary hand over her face, her rings glittering in the candlelight. 'But there is a spy – and that spy is acting for someone. The best-case scenario is that they are acting for one of the other Chairs.'

'And – the worst?'

'They are acting for another country.'

'Another *country*?'

'Yes. Did you think we were the only ones of our kind in the world? Our people exist in every corner of the globe,

36

from the poles to the equator. And wherever our kind gather, we love order and ritual and hierarchy. And feuds. Other countries have their councils: Les Viseurs. El Circulo. The Nodus. The Sistren . . . Some are very like the Ealdwitan, as old or even older. Some are very different. The lust for power, the search for knowledge – those forces are the same, wherever they arise. But the methods . . .'

She stopped and then said, with a harshness in her voice that sounded almost like pain, 'Anna, I know you have experienced the worst of the Ealdwitan. But we are not the worst of all. Good God no, we are not the worst. The others—'

She broke off, at the sound of a knock at the door.

'Come in, Miss Vane.'

'It's not Miss Vane,' said a voice – a male voice, low and amused. The door opened and the visitor walked into the room. My heart did a horrible flip, like missing a step on the escalator and I scrambled to my feet, ready to flee.

Something flickered in his eyes, but his face remained a polite mask as he turned to my grandmother.

'I'm sorry to interrupt, Chair Rokewood, but I wondered if I might have a quick word.'

'Of course, Marcus. Have you met my granddaughter, Anna? Anna, this is Marcus Corax.'

'We've met,' he said. Something tugged at the corner of his mouth.

'Really?' My grandmother looked surprised. 'How?'

'Oh, on Anna's last visit here. I was able to assist her

37

with some directions.'

I remembered my naked desperation, running for my life to get out of the mazelike corridors. Marcus had shown me a way out.

'And more recently,' he continued, 'didn't we bump into each other at reception?'

'I – I'm not sure,' I said. My heart was still thumping and I gave him a sharp look – was he laughing at me? The thought made me angry and stiffened my nerve. 'But thank you for the directions last time.' Somehow I kept my voice steady. 'I never had a chance to say.'

'No need for thanks.' He held out his hand. I hesitated for a moment and then I put mine in his. Who was he? Why had he saved me, twice? His hand was strong and immaculately manicured. But as we shook, something in my grandmother's introduction scratched at me like a snagged nail. Marcus Corax. *Corax?*

He was already speaking to my grandmother.

'I wanted to apologize. For my father. You're right and he's wrong – I don't know why he refuses to see it.'

'Because he doesn't want to admit I'm right? Because revoking all security passes will be costly, disruptive and extremely political? Or because he is protecting the spy?' My grandmother pinched the bridge of her nose and then sat back with a weary sigh.

'Not that!' Pain crossed Marcus' face and he sat too, hitching his beautifully pressed trousers to preserve their crease. 'I'm certain of that.'

'I wish I could be so sure,' my grandmother said. 'But you may be right. Well, will you do what you can to persuade him, Marcus? We vote tomorrow on rescinding the passes and we must get it through. Without revoking security clearances we really have no idea where the leaks are coming from.'

'I will try, ma'am, but as you know, I'm not in my father's best books at the moment. Since he knows I'm taking your side on this . . .' He trailed away and then seemed to steel himself. 'But I'll try again. What other votes do you think you can secure?'

'As to that, I'm not sure. Your father has Knyvet's vote in his pocket, we're all aware of that. Catesby will back me, or at least I hope he will.'

'And Margot Throgmorton?'

'Ah. There, I really don't know. Properly, of course, the vote is Edward's. But I doubt he's well enough to understand the question, let alone express a view. Normally I would say her inclination would be to side with me – she has no affection for your father and her words today make me think that she is fully alive to the dangerous reality of this spy. But her relationship with Knyvet compromises matters. I don't know how far she will go along with him. She may abstain and, if she does, that means an even split.'

'W-what happens then?' I found myself asking nervously. 'Does someone have a casting vote?'

'No.' My grandmother sounded weary. 'In the event of an even vote, the chamber empties and we Chairs are locked in without food or water until someone cracks and changes sides. It's an archaic practice and never pretty.'

Hmm. She wasn't really selling this 'inherit the Chair' business.

'Marcus,' my grandmother was saying, 'will you stay and dine with us?'

'I'd love to. I asked Franklin to take dinner to my office but I'll ring down and let him know I'll be eating here.'

Suddenly I felt a lot less hungry.

Just then Miss Vane bustled in with a covered trolley and, a few minutes later, a tall man in a black suit appeared, carrying a tray which presumably contained Marcus' dinner. They moved around the room efficiently rearranging the furniture, set out the crockery, and then melted away.

'Ma'am?' Marcus pulled back my grandmother's chair and she sat. Then, 'Anna?'

My cheeks flamed and I sat, awkwardly and too soon, so that I was marooned several feet from the table and I had to stand again and shuffle forwards with the chair following me.

My grandmother raised the silver cover of her plate.

'Lamb. Very good.'

'Wine, ma'am?' Marcus raised the bottle and my grandmother nodded.

'Well here's to . . .' She raised her glass and paused. 'What shall we drink to? Family ties, perhaps.' She smiled, and drank, and then said casually, 'You two are – well, cousins of a sort, did you know that, Anna?'

Cousins? With a Corax? My face must have shown my astonishment, because my grandmother and Marcus both laughed and my grandmother patted my hand.

'You will learn soon, my dear, that family relations among our kind are never simple. My younger sister, Catherine, was Marcus's mother. I'm not sure exactly what that makes you two, but some form of second cousin, I imagine.'

A cousin. This smooth, enigmatic man was my cousin.

'I never had a cousin before,' I said slowly. 'My dad's an only child.'

'I have dozens,' Marcus said. 'My father is one of twelve, so as you can imagine we're quite a clan. But one more is very welcome, especially one so lovely and accomplished.'

The line would have sounded hopelessly cheesy coming from anyone else. If Abe had said it I would have rolled my eyes and snorted, but somehow Marcus pulled it off. I found myself blushing furiously and glanced at my grandmother, hoping she hadn't noticed.

Luckily she was preoccupied with her cutlet, but before she could raise the fork to her lips the telephone on her desk shrilled out.

'Oh, how vexing.' She sighed. 'Hello? No, don't worry, Miss Vane, that's fine. Yes, I see. Still, it can't be helped. Yes, of course. Five minutes.'

She put down the receiver with an irritated click and turned back to me and Marcus.

'I'm sorry, my dears, this can't wait. Please eat and, if

Franklin comes to clear, tell him to take my plate.'

She hurried out and Marcus and I were left looking at each other. He raised the bottle. 'Wine, Anna?'

'Yes, please.' I felt I'd probably need it.

There was silence for a moment as he filled our glasses and then raised his.

'Well, to echo your grandmother – to family.'

'To family,' I said. The wine was bitter and caught at the back of my throat and I coughed. I was half expecting him to challenge me – to ask me about what I'd been doing in the archives. But he said nothing, only sawed meditatively at his cutlet. When he raised a mouthful to his lips he made a face.

'Ugh, cold.' He let his hand hover over his plate and I averted my eyes. It wasn't any different to microwaving your dinner to warm it up, not really. But Maya's frugality with magic had rubbed off. I could never imagine myself using my power so casually.

I put a piece of cutlet in my mouth and chewed, but it seemed to stick in my throat. I couldn't relax – I wanted to run after my grandmother and force her to explain. Who *was* this man? Why was a *Corax* eating food with us? And – most puzzlingly of all – why had he helped me, twice now? I owed him – and I didn't like it. And I didn't know why.

'I knew your mother, did you know that?' Marcus' voice broke in on my thoughts. My fork clattered to my plate as he took a mouthful of lamb and chewed thoughtfully. 'Only as a very small child of course. But my mother died

42

when I was two and Isabella was very kind. She'd been close to my mother, so she understood my grief when my mother died and she comforted me. God knows my father didn't, so I suppose I clung to her in lieu of any real parent. I missed her, after she left. I still do.'

I found myself staring at this stranger, who must have grieved for my mother as I never could. Then I dropped my eyes.

'How awful. I'm so sorry.'

'I never knew what happened to her.' He looked away, at the fire, his face unreadable. 'I knew that she'd disappeared with your father and that no one had been able to trace her from there. She became a taboo subject around here, completely unmentionable. The one who'd done the unthinkable: put her outwith lover before her family and her duty. But I never forgot her. I always hoped that she might come back. As did you, I'm sure.'

'N-no . . .' I said uncertainly. 'I never did. At least . . .'

At least, not exactly. But the more I found out, the more I realized there was no reason for my mother to have killed herself. I didn't hope that she would come back, but I had started to hope – what? That *I* could find *her*?

'You're very like her,' he said abruptly. 'That's one thing I remember clearly – how beautiful she was.'

My cheeks flared up again, as scorching hot as the flames of the fire at my side. I dropped my eyes to my plate and fumbled taking a sip of wine. My hand shook and drops spilled on the cloth like a bloodstain.

'Damn,' I said under my breath, scrabbling for a napkin. '*Damn*.'

'Anna . . .' Marcus put his hand over my wrist. For a moment we were motionless, his warm brown eyes locked on mine. Then I pulled my hand away and the wine drops were gone, the cloth flawless white again.

'See?' He gave a charming smile. 'No use crying over spilled wine.'

'Marcus,' I said desperately, 'why—?'

'Presumably you've got a lot of catching up to do on Ealdwitan gossip, so why don't I fill you in?'

As we finished our meal he chatted easily, telling stories about the Ealdwitan that made me see another side entirely from the fierce cut-throat politics that preoccupied my grandmother – funny anecdotes about old retainers and accounts of the dazzling parties held in the underground ballroom and tea-dances in the conservatory.

'Ballrooms, conservatories, libraries – what isn't down here?' I asked.

'Mmm . . . good question. There's no swimming pool, as far as I know. Ironic really, considering the whole thing is rooted in river-water. But yes, it is a warren. I've been exploring these corridors all my life and I still find myself lost every now and again.'

'Did you live here? Growing up?' I wasn't sure if it was a stupid question, but I honestly didn't know.

'No, not in the sense of sleeping here. This is an office building – we all have homes above ground. For a while, after my mother died, I ran wild here in the day while my father worked. But then my father noticed I was becoming – hmm, shall we say, a bit feral. So he sent me off to boarding school. I was there from seven to fourteen.'

Seven. The word was like a slap. *Seven.* But I only asked, 'Why did you stop boarding?'

'Oh, it became awkward, you know. When my magic started to come in. It was all right at first, I practised in the holidays and tried to keep it under wraps at school. But there were a few slip-ups.' His knife screeched on the plate, and he winced and then gave a rueful laugh. 'I don't mean to start special pleading – I mean we're all in the same boat as regards secrecy – but believe me, a dormitory full of twenty outwith boys can be a tough place to come into your powers.'

I tried to imagine – and failed. God, it had been hard enough becoming a witch in Winter, let alone in the unrelenting hothouse of a boys' boarding school.

'Were there any others like you?' I asked. 'I mean, at your school?'

He shook his head.

'No. None. So it was quite a relief to come back here. But enough of me – what about you?'

'Oh . . .' I looked down at my hands, wrapped around the crystal stem of the wineglass. The seaglass ring winked in the candlelight. What to say? 'It's – it's complicated. My mother left and my father – well, as you know, he's an outwith.'

'So what happened?' Marcus looked at me, his brows drawn together into a frown. 'That must have been very difficult to negotiate?'

'Yes and no. My mother . . .' I bit my lip. Was this very, *very* stupid? I had no idea whether I could trust him. He was an Ealdwitan. *And* a Corax. But on the other hand, my grandmother seemed to trust him – and really, what did I have left to hide? If I wanted answers to my own questions, I had to start talking. 'My mother left a charm that kind of crippled my magic until I was in my late teens. So it wasn't something I had to deal with until I was quite old.'

'Really?' Marcus put his chin on his hand and stared at me across the table. Little candle-flames flickered in his chocolate-coloured eyes. 'And why did she do that?'

I shrugged helplessly.

If only I knew.

Later, much later, Franklin had cleared the dinner plates and brought us coffee and petits fours, and there was still no sign of my grandmother.

'You should go home.' Marcus looked at me. 'It's late. You look very tired. I think the Chairs have been called back to the chamber.'

'And what does that mean?'

'A very long wait until they come out. I assume you're staying with your grandmother – do you have a key?'

'No, I'll just wait. I'm fine, honestly,' I said. Then I spoiled the remark by failing to suppress a huge yawn.

'You're dropping on your feet,' Marcus said. He stood and picked up the telephone on the desk. 'Hello, Miss Vane. Yes, she's still here but she needs to go home. Is there anyone who can let her in? OK, no problem. Thank you.'

He put the phone down and began searching for something in a stand on the wide oak desk.

'There's a spare key apparently – should be . . . Aha! Here we are.' He held out my coat, helped me into it, and then began shrugging into his own jacket.

'Are you going home too?' I asked, stifling another yawn.

'No, I'm walking you. No!' He held up a hand. 'I know what you're going to say, but it's very late and I'm – well, old-fashioned. Humour me.'

'I used to make my own way home through London all the time,' I protested. 'I think I can manage a stroll through Knightsbridge.'

'I said, humour me.' He took my elbow. 'Anyway, how will you find your way out of here?'

OK. That was a good point.

Marcus led me through a warren of corridors, rooms and chambers, until we came to a small panelled door between two potted palms. When he opened it the chill, damp smell of the river wafted out. I stepped through and found myself stumbling on to the hard concrete of a pavement beside Hyde Park.

The night was cool and the streets were still unbelievably busy. It was hard to believe that it was getting on for eleven. There were more people out and about than in Winter

47

town centre on a Saturday morning. Marcus took my arm and we walked along the dusty pavement past Harrods, beautifully brash in the darkness, towards Kensington Road.

'Where do you live?' I asked, more to make conversation than anything.

'I'm up at Cambridge at the moment,' he said. 'Christ's College. But it's the Easter vac so I'm staying with my father. He has a flat just off Piccadilly.'

The phrasing struck me; the way he said 'I'm staying with my father' rather than 'I've come home'. I couldn't ever imagine just *staying* with Dad.

'Do you . . .' I paused, suddenly not sure if I was overstepping the mark. 'Do you get on with your father?'

'Frankly? No.'

Something in Marcus' voice made me glance up at him, trying to see his expression, but he was facing down the street, not looking at me. His profile, in the shifting gold light of the street lamps, was uncompromising and I could see his brows were drawn into a deep frown.

'I'm sorry,' I said meaninglessly. He let my arm drop and rubbed his forehead, as if trying to smooth away the frown into something more sociable.

'Truly, don't worry, Anna. It's no secret. My father's old and for a long time he's considered himself the most important member of the council, though by tradition there's no hierarchy among the Chairs. I'm his only son – his only child in fact – and he's beginning to recognize the fact that his Chair will, one day, pass to me, no matter what he does to prolong his life. And that fact is causing . . . tension. For both of us. He wants my support, but he wants it unconditionally, without listening to my opinion and, frequently, without telling me even what I'm supporting. And I won't do that.'

'Marcus . . .' I gulped. This was a leap in the dark. Maybe a suicidal one. 'Did you know your father tried to recruit me? That he threatened to kill my family?'

'Yes, I do know that – now.' He looked at me, as if trying to read my reaction. I kept my expression as even as I could. I didn't want the murderous hatred I felt for Thaddeus Corax to spill out between Marcus and me. 'But I didn't at the time,' he said. 'Your grandmother was very angry when she found out and she kicked up a huge dust at the council meeting. I'm very sorry – if I'd known . . .' He took my arm again as we crossed the road.

'It's OK.' I'd never forgive Thaddeus Corax, but I didn't see why Marcus should be punished for his father's actions. 'But why did your father want to recruit me so badly? It's something I've never worked out.'

'I don't know.' He looked at me again. 'But if I can find out, I'll—'

He broke off. A girl was standing in front of us, her hands to her mouth in exaggerated shock.

'O. M. G! Anna Winterson!'

I blinked. The girl flung her arms out, looking like she expected – what, a *hug*?

49

'Anna!' she said. 'It's me – Lauren, for goodness' sake!'

'Lauren!' I looked closer, almost unable to believe my eyes. Lauren? Here? Somehow the coincidence seemed crazy, impossible. And yet – we were only a few hundred metres from my old school. 'Lauren!' I dropped Marcus' arm and ran forwards to give her a hug. 'I can't believe it – I nearly didn't recognize you with the new hair. How are you?'

'I'm good! And blimey, mate, I don't need to ask how you are, you look a-bloody-mazing!' She held me at arm's length and gave me an admiring once-over. 'Has your dad won the lottery? Where did you get that fantastic dress?'

'Oh . . .' I realized I was wearing clothes my grandmother had given to me. They were, as ever, ridiculously fancy designer pieces, totally unsuitable for wearing to school or anywhere useful. How could I explain that – explain everything that had happened in the single short year since I'd left London?

'Long story,' I said at last. 'It was a present.'

'And I suppose you must be Seth.' Lauren smiled flirtatiously at Marcus, looking up at him from under her eyelashes. 'You're every bit as good-looking as Anna said.'

It was like a kick to the stomach. I felt suddenly sick, faint with the unexpectedness of the blow.

Marcus waited for me to reply and then, realizing that for some reason I couldn't, he stepped in.

'Actually no, I'm Marcus.'

'Oh!' Lauren was taken aback. She looked from me to

Marcus, then back at me, clearly wondering what she'd said. Then she smiled. 'Well, nice to meet you anyway. How do you know Anna?'

'Family friend. We've been out for the evening and I said I'd walk Anna back.'

'Quite the gentleman! I'd walk with you, but I'm going the other way – I'm out clubbing. Fancy coming along? Shame to be all dressed up and nowhere to go!'

'Sorry.' I had to force out the words. 'I'm shattered. Maybe . . .'

'Yeah, maybe another time. Gotta run anyway, we were meeting at eleven and I'm already late. Lovely to see you! And great to meet you too, Marcus! Anna, we *must* catch up – I'll call you, yeah?' She blew air kisses at us both and trotted off down the road.

As the sound of her heels tapped into the distance, I leaned against a wall, trying to catch my breath.

'Anna,' Marcus put a hand on my back, 'are you all right?'

'Yes,' I managed. 'Just – she hit a nerve. I can't—'

'It's OK, no need to explain,' Marcus said quietly. We walked in silence the rest of the way to my grandmother's.

At the house, Marcus waited politely while I fished in my pocket for the key.

'Well, goodbye,' I said awkwardly.

'Wait.' Marcus put his hand on my arm. 'Just a second. Listen, if there's ever anything I can do . . .' He fumbled in his jacket pocket for a pen and then looked around for something to write on. 'Damn, where's a receipt or something when you need it? Hang on.' He put his hand inside his jacket and took out a beautiful linen handkerchief. Before I could protest, he'd written a number across it, in old-fashioned looping handwriting.

'This is my mobile. If you need anything – well, there it is.'

'Marcus . . .' I took the handkerchief and bit my lip, looking down at the number. 'I mean – thank you. But – but why? Why do you keep helping me?'

'It's only a mobile number,' he said lightly, an amused smile at his lips. But then his brown eyes met mine for a moment and there was something else there – a sadness. 'I loved your mother. She was the closest thing to a parent that I can remember.'

I wanted to say something – but no words came.

'Well, there you go,' Marcus said. 'Please keep the number. If you need it.'

'Thank you,' I said. He bent and kissed my cheek. Then he was gone.

CHAPTER FOUR

The hall clock was chiming midnight as I closed the door carefully behind me, then locked it with the unwieldy key. Wearily, I kicked off my shoes and climbed the stairs to the second floor, where the little white spare room awaited. This was 'my' room when I stayed – and I should have walked thankfully inside and flopped onto the narrow white bed.

Only – for some reason – I kept climbing. Up into the darkness.

The bulb had gone at the top of the stairs and, as I climbed, the shadows closed around me. By the time I reached the top floor it was almost completely dark and I had to feel for the doorknob by touch. I didn't know what was inside. But I could guess.

I turned the knob, the door swung open, and I stepped inside my mother's bedroom.

It was a teenager's room, but a teenager of decades ago, frozen in time the day she'd left it.

There were fading posters on the wall: bands I'd never heard of, plays that closed decades ago, gigs in venues long since disappeared. A timetable for A-level revision was pinned over the desk, giving me a guilty twinge about my own revision, which was somewhere around the bottom of my list of priorities.

Photos were stuck around the frame of the mirror: laughing girls, groups of friends, their arms slung around each other. I looked carefully, but didn't recognize anyone. No, that wasn't true. There was one face I did recognize. A girl with long dark hair and smoky blue eyes, laughing at her friend. It could have been me, but it wasn't. It was my mother.

Suddenly there were tears in my throat; hot, painful tears that lodged hard in my gullet like a sharp piece of bone. My limbs were shaky and I sat down hard on the bed. Her bed. The covers were rumpled. The last person to sleep here had been . . .

I lay down, very carefully, feeling as if I was disturbing a museum relic. And then I turned my face to the pillow and breathed in the smell of my mother, the scent of her hair, the ghost of her perfume.

'Please,' I whispered to the silent house, to her ghost, 'help me.'

But only the night-sounds of London answered me.

When I woke up I was stiff and cold, and my mouth felt acid and hungover, though I hadn't drunk much at dinner. I looked at my watch. 4.10 a.m. Yuck.

Something about the quiet of the house told me that my

grandmother was still not home. I made my way stiffly down the stairs and sure enough the door of her bedroom was still gaping wide, the bed covers smooth and flat in the grey dawn light.

In the spare room I pulled on a jacket and scribbled a quick note.

Dear Grandmother,
I'm sorry, I had to leave unexpectedly. I hope the meeting goes/went well. Call me when you have time.
Anna x

Then I walked out into the pale, sour dawn and began the long trudge towards Victoria Station and the first train to Winter. I wanted to be out of London. I wanted home. I wanted . . . The answer as it came to me, surprised me.

I wanted Abe.

'Abe!' I yelled through the door again. Surely he wasn't out?

He wasn't. As I was just about to knock again, I heard a coughing shuffling sound from inside and the lock clicked. A tousled head, face crumpled on one side from the sheets, peered blearily around the door.

'Anna – what are you doing here? I thought you were in London?'

'I was. I had to come home. Can I come in?'

'Sure, yeah. Sorry I'm a bit . . .' He opened the door wider and looked down at himself. He was wearing stubble, a towel slung around his waist, and not much else.

I don't know why, but I flushed red. A smile twitched at the corner of his mouth and he shrugged.

'I wasn't expecting guests at the crack of dawn. Wait a sec.'

'It's hardly dawn!' I called down the corridor towards his retreating back. For answer, he stuck his middle finger in the air and I grinned and made my way to the kitchen. The other thing I wanted was coffee. And lots of it.

By the time Abe came back, his black hair still tousled but now damp as well, and wearing jeans and a heavy jersey, I was sipping a cup of coffee strong enough to take the enamel off my teeth.

'Make yourself at home, why don't you!' He sat down at the counter beside me and poured himself a cup too.

'Sorry for dropping in unannounced. D'you mind?'

'Do I get much choice?' he said. But his voice, muffled by his coffee mug, had a smile. 'Christ, this is strong enough to strip paint.'

'Sorry,' I said again. 'I needed it.'

'Hard night? Grandma bit of a partygoer is she?'

'Yes – and no.' I told him about my discovery at the Ealdwitan headquarters and his mouth thinned.

'What?' I said at last, as I finished. 'I thought you'd be pleased? It doesn't tell me a whole lot more, I agree, but it feels like a step closer, don't you think?'

'Two things: one, I don't like you going to that place.' I wasn't sure if he meant my grandmother's, the headquarters, or just London in general. Possibly all of them. 'And two, are you short of a screw, trusting that Corax bloke? What do you know about him, apart from the fact that his dad's a bastard?'

'He seems OK,' I said, and then held up my hands at the sight of Abe's expression. 'I know, I know. But honestly, I really don't think he likes his father a whole lot more than I do. They seem to have some *serious* issues.'

'Anna, I've got serious issues with *my* family. Doesn't mean Jesus wants me for a sunbeam.'

'That's not what I meant,' I said crossly. 'And you know it.'

'Well I don't see your logic. The guy sounds a total sack to be honest.'

'For your information, he saved my skin. Twice.'

'Probably to get into your—' He broke off, seeing my face, and amended: 'Good books. His dad clearly thinks you've got something he wants; maybe Marcus is just handling his end of the campaign with a bit more tact.'

'He helped me long before he knew who I was,' I said shortly. 'And how am I supposed to get answers about my mother without going through the Ealdwitan?'

'I don't know.' His face was troubled. 'But she went to hell and back to try to keep you a secret from them. And now you're throwing all that away. It seems kind of . . . stupid.'

'I'm not throwing it away, because the advantage disappeared the second I left London – can't you see that? They *knew* where I was straight away. Whatever protection

57

my mother gave me, I lost it when I moved to Winter. They know where I am – and I'm pretty sure some of them at least know *who* I am. And I don't. I've got to get that information. Otherwise I'll never know.'

'Know what?'

'Who I am.'

'Who you are? What do you mean?' His face was confused, frustrated.

'No, I don't mean that. I mean – what I'm capable of. What I can do.' I felt panic rise inside me.

'What the hell are you on about? Surely you just do stuff and see what happens? No one ever told me what *I* was capable of. You're a witch, not a bloody sports car. You don't come with horsepower, nought to sixty, and instructions for how to operate the sunroof. You want to do something? Try it. See what happens.'

'No!' My voice was a cry, almost a shout. 'I can't. I can't risk it.'

'Anna, what are you on about?' Abe put his hands on my shoulders and turned me to face him. I tried to look away, but he touched my cheek, forcing me to look at him. 'What's the matter?'

I took a deep breath.

'Look; Emmaline, Maya – everyone's always assumed that whatever it was about me was something good, something desirable. But what if it's not that?'

'What do you mean?' Abe's expression was wary.

'What if . . .' Words rose in my throat, choking me. I'd

never admitted these fears to anyone, never said them aloud, not even to Seth. 'Abe, what if I'm . . . evil?'

His eyes widened and he opened his mouth, but I hurried on, not yet ready to let him speak.

'Maybe I should have been . . . destroyed. Maybe that's what was supposed to happen. Perhaps that's what my mother was doing; protecting her child at a cost to everyone else. But she couldn't cope with what she'd done, so she fled.'

For a minute Abe was silent. Then he started shaking his head, more and more vehemently.

'No.'

'It makes sense.'

'No. No, no, no. You've no proof of any of this.'

'I have no proof of *anything*. It's as likely as anything else.'

'It's not. What the hell d'you mean, *evil*? You're a good person.'

'I hurt people, Abe. Even when I don't want to.' I thought of Seth, in pain a hundred times because of me. Because of my hands burning his flesh, because of storms I'd conjured to harm his family and wreck his home. Because of his love for me. A love that had twisted and maimed until we were both scarred by it. 'That's why I can't risk it,' I said. There was a lump in my throat. 'I can't just *see* what happens. What happens might be . . . death. Worse. So I have to know what my mother found out about me that set her running.'

59

Abe didn't answer. But, still in silence, he put his arms around me. I let my forehead rest on his shoulder, hard and muscled beneath his T-shirt.

He said nothing, just sat and held me. But I felt his magic wrap around me, more tender and more urgent than Abe himself would ever let on. I remembered again the fierce, burning exhilaration I'd felt when Seth had injected me with Abe's magic. I remembered it coursing through my veins, filling me with Abe's power and passion for life.

There was no going back from that. I could feel his life inside me – and I knew that he could feel it too.

As I trudged up the long, rutted drive to Wicker House, I was thinking of only one thing: firing up my laptop and doing some digging. There had to be a copy of the *Codex Angelis* somewhere. The British Library. Google books. *Somewhere.*

Failing that, maybe 'The Riddle of the Epiphany' would bring up some hits. Or perhaps Caradoc would know something.

It was a lead, anyway. At last I felt like I had something concrete to get started with.

But when I opened the front door Dad was in the hall, lacing up his walking boots and humming to himself. He looked like he'd had Prozac for breakfast.

'Anna!' he said as he caught sight of me. 'You're back early. Fancy a walk?'

I bit my lip.

'I'd like to . . . but . . .' I scrabbled for an excuse. 'I should be revising.'

'You've been revising too hard.' Dad straightened up and wagged his finger at me. 'You're looking positively peaky – Dr Winterson prescribes a pub lunch. Come on – it's a gorgeous day and I've hardly seen you all week. Give this old man a bit of company for a change. I was going to treat myself to a roast at the Cr—' He broke off and covered his tracks awkwardly. 'We could drive out somewhere,' he finished, looking down at his walking boots slightly wistfully.

I sighed.

'How about we walk to the Crown and Anchor, Dad? Then we don't have to drive anywhere and you can have a pint with lunch.'

'Sure?' Dad looked uncertainly at me. 'I don't mind a spin down the coast if you'd prefer that.'

Yes, yes, I'd prefer that. To be honest, I'd prefer rancid chips on Brighthaven pier. The thought of sitting in Seth's pub, with his mum waiting on us and being lovely, made me want to stick knitting needles in my eyes.

But I had to get over this. Winter was a small town. The Anchor was one of the few places that did a decent meal. And there was no point in punishing Dad and Elaine with my pain.

'Honestly, Dad, it's fine. I'll enjoy the walk.'

* * *

'Anna!' Elaine looked up from the bar as we entered and, for a minute, her expression was complete shock. Then she recovered and came out from behind the bar smiling, kissed me on both cheeks, and showed us to a sunny table by the open window. 'And Tom. How nice to see you both. Lovely weather, isn't it?'

'Very summery,' Dad agreed, spreading his Gore-Tex out on the polished oak bench. 'We celebrated by walking over the cliffs. It was fantastic wasn't it, Anna?'

'Beautiful,' I agreed. And it had been. The walk had blown away the shadowy fears from earlier and reminded me exactly how lucky I was to live in a place like Winter.

'Well, I'll get you some menus and leave you to it,' Elaine said. 'But I will tell you that the roast lamb is particularly good – it's from Jenks' farm, and it's absolutely delish.'

'Lamb it is for me,' Dad said. 'And a pint of Old please, Elaine.'

'Lamb for me too, then,' I said.

'Any drink for you, Anna?' Elaine asked.

'Just water please.'

'Okey-doke. See you shortly.'

Dad watched as she made her way back to the kitchen and then turned to me.

'Sure you don't want anything more exciting? It's a special occasion, after all.'

'Is it?'

I ran through the possibilities in my head, silently

panicking that I'd missed something vital. It was only April – Dad's birthday wasn't until August. Mine had been and gone. I had no idea when my mother's birthday was and Dad had never marked it, nor his wedding anniversary. What could it possibly be?

'Today, my dear, it is exactly a year since we moved to Winter. Remember our first night cuddled up with the spiders and mice? Seems a long time ago, doesn't it?'

It felt like a *lifetime* ago.

A year. A year to the day since I'd moved to Winter, discovered the truth about myself, met Emmaline, met Seth . . . How had so much happened since then, how had everything gone so right, and so wrong?

'I know you didn't choose to leave London and it wasn't the best time, what with me being fired and so on, but are you glad we moved?'

I looked out of the window at the children playing in the beer garden while I thought about that. Was I glad? What a question. I was a different *person* because of Winter – my old life in London seemed impossibly ordinary, stiflingly safe. Would I change anything, if I could? Give up all the terrifying and wonderful and heart-wrenching things that had happened to me in Winter?

'Yes, I'm glad.' I said at last. 'There's lots I miss about London but – yes. I'm still glad.'

'Good.' Dad patted my shoulder. 'I've always loved Winter, right from the first time your mum and I saw it. Somehow it always seemed like a place I could call home.'

The word 'mum' still gave me a little jolt. Dad's eighteen-year silence had broken on my birthday, three months ago, but I still wasn't used to hearing that word on his lips. It took a minute before the little shiver of surprise subsided and I realized what he'd actually said.

'Hang on.' I interrupted something he was saying about the house. 'What did you say? You first came here with my *mum*?'

I didn't ask: *How come you never told me?* I knew the answer to that: a charm that had silenced his tongue as brutally as a knife. But surely Dad could have told me he'd been here before?

'Did I never tell you that story?'

'No,' I said, astonished that Dad could even ask.

'We came here on honeymoon. We were supposed to be going to Russia – St Petersburg, I think it was – and then at the last minute your mum had problems with her visa and we cancelled and decided to stay in the UK. So we were flicking through a guide to romantic B&Bs and your mother saw a listing for a fisherman's cottage in Winter. And she said instantly that *that* was the place we absolutely must go, it was a sign – because she was about to become Mrs Winterson, you see.' He paused as a waitress put a pint in front of him and a glass of water for me, and then added, 'It's a tea room now, that one up past the library, on the cliffs.'

'So – that was why you came here, when it all fell apart in London?' I asked. Dad rubbed the side of his nose.

'Well, if you put it like that, I suppose perhaps yes. It was one of the last places I'd been completely happy with Isla, before – you know.'

I nodded. I knew. Before she got pregnant with me, and the paranoid delusions started, and they had her sectioned and drugged.

'Because it wasn't long after that – well . . .' He laughed and picked up his pint. 'Let's just say, there's a strong chance that you were conceived in Winter. In fact, pretty much a certainty. Isla gave me the news virtually the day we got back to London.'

'Ew, Dad!' I groaned. It wasn't like I could have got here *without* Dad having had sex. But I didn't really want to hear about it. I was very used to Dad being comfortably single and that suited me fine.

'Sorry, sweetie.' He raised his glass, drinking to hide his smile. 'Let's change the subject to something more suited to your delicate sensibilities. Oh hello, Elaine.' Elaine bore down on us with two plates of roast lamb. 'You're just in time to save Anna's blushes.'

'Anna's blushing?' Elaine put the plates down. 'Something I should know?'

'No, no.' Dad grinned. 'Just me trying to embarrass her. Have you got time to sit down for a drink?'

'Well . . .' Elaine looked at the bar, 'Not really. But I haven't had a break this morning. Ange!' she yelled across the bar. 'Can you manage for a tick? I'm just going to have a quick sit down.'

'Yup,' Angelica called back. 'No probs.'

'OK, I'm officially on a break.' Elaine sat gratefully on a bar stool at our table and kicked off her shoes. 'How are you two?'

'Oh fine,' Dad answered for both of us. 'Anna's supposed to be home doing her revision, of course. But aside from that . . . How are you, Elaine? Any news on Bran?'

'News?' I looked from one to the other. Elaine sighed and ran her hand through her hair, in an echo of Seth's characteristic gesture that tugged at my heart.

'Dad's not so good. I was telling your dad yesterday. He's in Brighthaven Infirmary. They don't think he'll be coming out. And he's asking and asking . . .'

'For . . . Seth?' I concentrated on chopping up a roast potato to avoid her gaze.

'Yes. But Seth's in the middle of nowhere on some boat. What can he do? He's turned back, but I really doubt he'll be in time.'

The meaning of her words hit me suddenly. Bran was so ill that he was probably going to die before Seth made it back to Winter.

'What's funny,' Elaine went on, 'well, you'll laugh . . .' She looked like laughter was the last thing on her mind. 'He – he asked for . . .' She looked down at her hands and then took a breath. 'He asked for you.'

My fork fell from my fingers.

'*Me?*'

'Yes. Funny, isn't it?' Elaine said in a flat, hollow voice.

'But – why would he ask for Anna?' Dad said confusedly. 'He always seemed quite . . . um . . . resistant.'

Resistant was the understatement of the year. *Full of bitter hate*, was the phrase I'd have chosen. Elaine spread her hands.

'I know. What can I say. I was surprised too. But don't worry, Anna – I'm not telling you this to make you feel that you have to go. I wouldn't put you through it – it's not like he's ever done anything to deserve your compassion now. And I don't think he's entirely lucid anyway, to be honest. He's asking for all sorts of people – people from the past. People I've never heard of. Last night he was raving about someone called Isla. God knows who that could be – I've never even met an Isla.'

'Isla?' I choked. I could see from Dad's face that he was as shocked as me.

'Yes,' Elaine looked from me to Dad and back again. 'Sorry, do you . . . ?'

'Anna's – her mum was called Isla,' Dad managed at last. He reached for his glass and his hand shook. 'Funny coincidence, that's all.'

I picked up my fork again and put the potato to my lips, chewing mechanically. But it was suddenly impossible to swallow.

CHAPTER FIVE

As soon as we got back from the pub I disappeared upstairs, muttering excuses about revision. As I peeled off my walking socks I mentally promised myself that I would actually *do* some revision, so it wasn't completely a lie. Only – after some extracurricular research.

But two hours later the internet had thrown up nothing. There were lots of hits for *Codex Angelis* but nothing that looked remotely right and 'The Riddle of the Epiphany' didn't return a single hit.

Next I checked the Winter library catalogue and then, when that turned up nothing, the British Library online catalogue. Nothing.

At last I clicked on my email browser and started a new email.

Dear Caradoc,

I hope you're well and Jonathan too. It would be lovely to come up to London to see you some time.

But I'm afraid I'm emailing to ask a favour; I'm trying to trace a text called 'The Riddle of the Epiphany', from a book called the Codex Angelis. *The book is in the Ealdwitan library – but their copy was defaced and the page with the riddle in was torn out.*

Do you know anything about the book? Might there be another copy in existence? I can't find any record of it, but I wondered if you might have other avenues.

Any suggestions would be very welcome.

Much love,

Anna

Then I closed down the email and opened up my neglected file of revision notes. Today, according to the timetable above my desk, I was supposed to be doing Maths practice papers.

The first one said fifty-five minutes and I set my alarm clock and got down to it. But I'd barely got halfway through the first problem when my email pinged. The harder I tried to ignore it, the more it niggled at the edge of my consciousness, stopping me from concentrating. At last I gave in – it'd be better just to check the sender and then, when it turned out to be something boring, I could go back to the exam paper.

But it wasn't boring. It was from Caradoc.

I clicked it open, ignoring the ticking clock. Had he found something so soon?

Dear Anna,

How delightful to hear from you – and with such an intriguing question too.

I know of course the volume to which you refer. The Codex Angelis, named for the illuminated angel on page two, is a tenth-century collection of Anglo-Saxon riddles, prophecies and poetry. Much of the mundane content is similar to that in Codex Exoniensis *and the* Vercelli Book, *but it is a shadow volume – that is to say, unknown to the outwith world, hence your difficulty with the British Library – and the prophesies are, as far as I am aware, totally unique. I know of only one copy in existence: that which resides in the Ealdwitan library.*

Your quest to find the text of this missing riddle will not be simple. My cursory researches have turned up a mention of a translation dating around 1570, but the reference is to a copy in the library of Peter the Great, the Tsar of Russia, and I can find no mention of the work since that date.

However, I will make enquiries and will be in touch as soon as I have any news to convey.

Your most affectionate friend,

Caradoc Truelove

Somehow it didn't sound too positive and I typed a quick thank you then turned back to my Maths with a sigh.

The alarm pinged for the final time to say that my time was up again and I set the last practice paper on the floor and stretched my tired back, before turning off the timer. It was nearly quarter to ten. No wonder I was knackered.

I could hear faint film music filtering up the stairs and I guessed that Dad was probably snoring on the sofa. He always flaked out if he drank at lunchtime.

Maybe it was doing the practice papers tonight, but all of a sudden the exams felt terrifyingly close. How many weeks were left? I wasn't certain, but I had a horrible feeling that it might be down to single figures.

As if in time with my thoughts the wind groaned in the chimney and I went to the window and looked out. There was something wrong about the weather again, the same false note Abe had mentioned the other night.

But the air outside was sharp and cold, not a wisp of fog to be seen. So it wasn't that. There was a storm building though. I could hear it in the howl of the wind and the crash of the surf against the far-off cliffs. The sky was clear overhead, but away out to sea I could see rolling black shadows, building and boiling in the distance. A crow wheeled and cried in the darkness, its wingspan a star-blotted blackness against the dark of the night sky.

And then the phone started ringing.

Automatically I looked at the clock. 9.50 p.m.? Who'd be ringing now? I clattered down the stairs to grab the phone before it rang out.

'Hello?'

'Anna?' The voice at the other end was strange: croaky and hoarse, like someone who'd been crying.

'Um . . . yes . . . ?'

'Anna, it's me – Elaine.'

'Elaine! What – what's happened? Are you OK? Is Seth—?' I stopped. I couldn't speak. My hands were cold and numb against the phone. I thought of the storm, of the distant boiling clouds in the black night, of a small boat, horribly fragile . . .

'Seth's fine,' Elaine said, but her voice was cracked and odd, and there was an echo on the line. She wasn't phoning from the pub. 'Anna, I'm really sorry to ring so late, and I'm really, really sorry to ask you this . . .'

She stopped and I swallowed against the fear and said, more harshly than I meant, 'Elaine, please, you're scaring me. Just say it.'

'Anna, it's Bran,' she gulped, and there was a sob in her voice. 'He's d-dying. I really think he's dying and so do the doctors. And he's raving and sobbing and c-crying out – for Seth, but also for you. And I can't do anything about Seth, he's stuck in some port, trying to get a visa. And I know I have no right to ask you this, p-please believe me I do know that. You don't owe him anything. But I thought—'

'I'm coming,' I said.

Even as I spoke, getting the right department and ward, I was shrugging into my coat.

Elaine was wrong. I owed Bran. And I owed this to Seth.

'Dad,' I called as I ran into the night, 'Dad, get your keys.'

'Anna!' Elaine jumped up from the side of the bed as I entered. Her face, even in the soft, low light from the bedside lamp, was grey and drawn.

'Elaine.' I kissed her. 'You look . . . tired.'

'I am tired.' She passed a hand over her face and it trembled. 'It's been . . . Oh, I can't bear it.'

It hurt to see her like this, her face so raw and naked, and so alone. Seth should have been here, helping her. And he wasn't.

'Is there anything I can do?' I asked in a whisper.

'Well . . . I hate to ask . . . but could you sit with him for a few minutes while I go to the loo? I didn't want to leave him before, but he's asleep now so I think he'll be fine for a while. They gave him something to help. You know, with . . . with the pain . . .' she put a hand to her face.

'Of course.' I swallowed. 'It's no problem, I promise.'

'OK,' Elaine nodded and drew a deep breath. 'Thank you. I'll feel better knowing you're here and can ring the bell. Just to warn you –' she took another shaky breath '– he's not very . . . lucid. He's on very strong pain medication. He might not recognize you if he wakes, but maybe . . .'

She stopped. I knew what she was thinking. Maybe that would be for the best.

'It'll be fine,' I said. 'I'll get one of the nurses to call you if he wakes up, I promise.'

'Thanks, Anna.' She gave me a watery smile and I watched as she walked, slow and stiff, away down the corridor.

When she'd gone I turned to Bran.

He lay under the sheets and his body was as thin and

frail as a ten-year-old child's. It was impossible to believe that this was the same man who, just a few months ago, had been hobbling around his island kingdom, fishing off the rocks, cackling and swearing and imposing his will on everyone.

Now he lay completely still, his skin sunken around the bones of his face, his clawed hands slack against his chest. There was rheum around the edge of his mouth and at the corners of each eye. As I watched he seemed to shiver and I saw his eyes move restlessly beneath the paper-thin lids. Then he gave a gusting, weary moan that made my heart wring.

'Seth . . .' It was almost impossible to make out the word, but I caught it – just a whimper, the sound of someone keening for their lost child.

'Oh Bran,' I couldn't help it. The words slipped out and I took his fragile old hand and pressed it to my cheek.

'Eh . . . ?' He gave a croaking sigh and his eyelids opened. I let his hand drop and steeled myself for his reaction, but it didn't come. His filmy eyes searched the room. 'Who's there? Elaine?'

'No, no, Bran.' I leaned closer, so that he didn't have to strain to see me. 'It's me, Anna. Elaine said that you were asking for me.'

'Asking . . . yes, I was asking. For my grandson. Do you know him?' His voice was piteous. 'Do you know my grandson, Seth?'

'Yes.' My throat hurt. 'Yes I know him.'

'He's a good boy,' Bran said with a weary sigh and the ghost of a smile cracked his lips. 'The sins of the fathers . . . but he's a good boy. And who're you, again?'

'I'm Anna.'

'No you're not.' He lifted his head from the pillow, shaking with the effort, and for a moment his eyes were as piercing as before and the grey flashed an impossible fire. 'I know you, I *know* you!'

'I'm Anna,' I repeated. 'Anna Winterson. I go – I used to go out with Seth.'

'I did you wrong.' His hand suddenly clutched mine. 'Didn't I? When I turned you away. And you turned your vengeance on me, with your curse.'

'I don't know what you mean,' I said uneasily. His grip was hard, his nails digging into my skin.

'You poor bitch, God knows your load was heavy enough, and I should have helped you, you and your child, but your curse took everything from me, everything. My life, my livelihood. When you crippled me, did you know what you did? I know it was aught but what I deserved, I know that now.' His breath reeked on my face. 'But don't make my grandson pay for my mistake. Don't pass the curse to him, I'm begging you.' Tears flooded suddenly from his eyes, running down the lines graven in his cheeks. 'I'm begging you!'

'Bran, I don't know what you mean!'

'Say you won't,' he wept. 'Don't harm my grandson. And for my part, dear God in heaven I'm sorry – every day since, I've rued the night I spat at your feet and turned you away into the night. But don't harm my Seth!'

'I won't!' I said, bewildered but desperate to comfort him. 'I promise I won't – I love him. I love Seth. I'd never hurt him.'

'Eh?' He blinked and seemed momentarily confused, then he sighed. 'Oh, aye.' He gave my hand a feeble squeeze and lay back against the pillow. 'Child, I'm sorry.'

'Sorry?'

'Aye, sorry. Sorry can't undo the wrong I did your mother, I know, but that lies a score of years back.'

'My mother?' I found I was standing, my breath coming fast. 'Bran, who do you think I am?'

'Who are you?' His eyes shifted from side to side and then he frowned. 'Aye, who are you? Where's my daughter?'

'She's gone for a coffee, but Bran –' I found I was nearly weeping '– you said something about my mother. Did you know my mother?'

'Know her?' His eyes welled with tears. 'No. I met her but once. And then I failed her, drove her to her death, and she cursed me for it, damn her for a cold-hearted witch. Ahhh . . .'

A horrible groan of agony bubbled from his lips and he clutched at his side, then jabbed frantically at a red button on a wire. A nurse came hurrying through the door, holding a tray of tablets and vials.

'Mr Fisher, are you in pain?'

'Aye.' He was white and sweating. 'A bad go just now.'

76

'Would you like some more morphine? It's past time, if you want it.'

'Aye.' He nodded gratefully. 'Morphine. Yes.'

I watched as the nurse administered the dose, then helped Bran to sip a little water. Then he sank back on the pillows and his lids fluttered closed.

The nurse gave a sigh.

'He'll do now for another few hours. It's very sad when they get to this stage. Are you all right dear?' She turned to me. 'It's very upsetting seeing them in pain, I know, but he'll be comfortable now for a while.'

'I'm OK,' I said huskily.

She nodded, then said, 'Well, I'll leave you be.'

After she went I took Bran's hand and sat, holding it very gently and listening to his harsh, rattling breaths. His hand was thin and brittle in mine, and I closed my eyes.

When I opened them he was looking at me, his grey eyes, so like Seth's, filled with tears. He seemed to beg me to understand something – his lips moved, but no sound came out.

'I can't hear you Bran,' I said. His grip tightened and he took a painful breath and tried to speak again, but the words were just sighs and rattling clicks. His face twisted, full of effort, and then his lids drifted closed, but his grip on mine was hard, as if he was trying to communicate his message through touch alone.

I thought of Em and the way we spoke to each other in our heads, mind to mind.

I thought of my promise never to interfere with an outwith again, never to cast a spell on an ordinary person.

And then I thought of Bran's agonized eyes, begging me to understand something he couldn't say, begging me to help him before it was too late.

I took a breath, closed my eyes, and touched my fingers to Bran's temple. Then I waited.

It hit me like the buffet of a wave – the smell of the quay, the howl of the wind, and the woman standing in front of Bran, her black hair whipping in the wind, her face white in the darkness, her coat clutched around her huge swollen belly.

What do you mean, no? Her voice trembled.

I said no. Bran's voice – but not his voice. His voice as it must have been twenty years ago, strong, sure, above the crashing waves and shrieking wind.

But I've come all this way – you don't understand. You'll be condemning us to death – me and the baby. The prophecy said you would save her – that you'd give your life for her.

I'll not give a brass farthing for her, or you, or any of your kind. Understood? You and your talk of prophecies – what do you know? My will is my own.

Her face twisted. She took a step forwards, towards him.

I've read the prophecy a hundred times – it can't be wrong. A man of the sea – the Fisher King's line. It's you – it must be you. I scryed a hundred different ways and every way – the water, the rods, the bones – they all led me here, to Winter.

And I will drive you away, back where you came from, witch. He spat at her feet, a gob of filth on the quayside, and she staggered back, her hands over her belly. *I'll die meself before me or my kin helps your kind. Understood?*

She looked at him. Her blue-grey eyes were full of tears and hate, and her voice, when she spoke, was a hiss.

Then I curse you, Bran Fisher. I – Isla Winterson – I curse you for what you've done to me and my child. I curse you to limp through life a broken man, chained to the sea, your life in its grip. That wound you got in the war will fester, you will die a little more each time your foot hits solid land, and every tide that pulls away from the shore will take a little of your strength, a little of your life, a little of your hope. You will walk in pain every day until your death, and when you die the curse will pass to every son of your line, until they die themselves.

She turned and began to walk into the storm-drenched night, her coat flapping in the wind.

Don't you dare walk away from me, you bitch! Bran shouted. He began to walk after her and then he stumbled, his foot hitting the ground in such a way that pain shot up through his knee and thigh and hip, a piercing pain from his old war-wound. He let out a groan, but forced himself on, after Isla's retreating shadow. *Get back here!* The pain stabbed again, crueller, harsher than before, and he fell to the ground, clutching at his hip, and lifted his voice in a roar of inarticulate rage. The sound rose above the storm, echoing around the empty quay. Then it faded slowly into the noise of the hospital monitors bleeping and the sound of laboured breathing. The morphine took over and Bran drifted into a drugged and dreamless sleep.

I sat holding his hand very gently, until Elaine came back.

'Was everything OK?' she asked in a whisper.

'He woke up,' I said slowly, still trying to process what I had seen and heard. 'But . . . he didn't really recognize me. The nurse gave him some more morphine.'

'Oh good.' Elaine gave a relieved sigh. I didn't know if she was relieved about the morphine or his lack of recognition. 'Thank you. For coming, I mean. I really appreciate it. Even if Bran doesn't exactly remember, I think somewhere he'll know. I just wish . . . I wish Seth . . .'

She stopped. I nodded, and we both stood, dry-eyed mirrors of each other's pain.

'I'm sorry,' I said. I hoped she knew what I meant. For Bran – for Seth – for everything.

Bran died that night, in his sleep. The funeral was three days later, at the small stone fishermen's church on the cliff, with the granite memorial to all the townsmen lost at sea over the centuries.

Dad parked on the verge and we walked slowly along the cliff path, the wind whipping at my black skirt and flinging Dad's funeral tie irreverently over his shoulder.

'Do you know who's going to be there?' I asked. I thought my voice was convincingly level, but Dad wasn't fooled.

'Lots of townspeople, I'm sure. But Elaine's very upset because it looks like Seth won't make it. She was thinking of postponing, but no one could guarantee when he'd be allowed to fly out.'

'Oh.' I closed my eyes for a moment and some strong feeling washed over me like a wave. I wasn't sure what it was. Relief? Disappointment? My cheeks felt hot in the cold sea wind. 'What's the problem?'

'Apparently he put into some port he didn't have a permit for, because he was trying to get back quickly. It backfired and he ended up mired in red tape and without an exit visa, so they wouldn't let him fly. Elaine got the embassy involved, but last I heard it wasn't going to be resolved this week.'

Poor Seth. Poor Elaine. We walked in silence until we reached the graveyard, where townspeople were milling around the door of the church, smoking last-minute cigarettes and chatting with an air of grim concern.

'Tom!' someone called and Dad was absorbed into the crowd. It struck me for the first time what a part of this community he was now, how easily he fitted in.

Someone passed me an order of service and I glanced at it. On the back was printed a poem.

> *Death is nothing at all*
> *I have only slipped away into the next room*
> *I am I and you are you*
> *Whatever we were to each other*

That we are still

Life means all that it ever meant
It is the same as it ever was
There is absolute unbroken continuity
What is death but a negligible accident?
Why should I be out of mind
Because I am out of sight?

I am but waiting for you for an interval
Somewhere very near
Just around the corner
All is well.

Canon Henry Scott Holland

The lines were familiar but strange – and they gave me a little prickle of anger I couldn't put my finger on. Then I realized. They were the same lines my mother had used in her last note to me, only longer. More of the poem was here. But something – something was missing . . .

'Hey,' said a familiar voice at my elbow and I looked up in surprise.

'Abe! What are you doing here?' It wasn't only his presence that shocked me. He was barely recognizable. He still hadn't shaved, but he was wearing a beautifully ironed white shirt and a black tie, and an impeccably cut black suit that I suspected belonged to Simon. He looked – well, he looked hot, if I was being honest. I pushed the thought away, disgusted with myself, hoping

Abe couldn't read the flush on my cheeks. Hoping no one could read it.

'I'm here with Maya and the gang.'

'But Bran – you know . . . He hates, I mean he hated . . .' The word 'witches' hung in the air, like an unspeakable swearword. Abe shrugged.

'We still owe him respect. He was a powerful man.'

'And he saved Emmaline's life, don't forget.' Maya came up at Abe's side, with Emmaline behind her. 'He was a good man, Bran Fisher. Whatever he thought of us, I admired him and I owe him a great deal.'

'Well, I'm glad you're here.'

I took Emmaline's arm and we walked together into the church, Maya, Abe, Simon and Sienna bringing up the rear. Dad was still chatting to his friends in the porch and I touched his arm as I passed, telling him that I'd be sitting with Emmaline. He nodded.

Inside, the church was very cool and I couldn't suppress a shiver as we moved down the aisle, looking for a free place to sit.

'Cold?' Abe asked me, as Maya led the way into an empty pew.

'I'm fine,' I said and ruined it by shivering again as I sat down between Abe and Emmaline. Abe pulled off his suit jacket and slung it round my shoulders. 'I'm *fine*,' I said more crossly. There was something unbearably intimate about the gesture, with the jacket still warm from his body and faintly scented with his aftershave.

'Suit yourself,' Abe said casually. 'Keep it on, take it off. Take everything off if you like, I don't care.'

'Shh,' Maya said severely and I saw the minister had entered and was making his way to the pulpit. It seemed easier to subside and accept the damn jacket.

'Friends and parishioners,' he began. 'Let me welcome you here today, to celebrate the life of our friend Bran Fisher, well-known to us all in the town of Winter.'

The service wasn't long. Elaine spoke briefly about Bran's life. His naval service in the Second World War, where he sustained his war-wound. His time on the fishing boats in the Fifties and Sixties. His semi-retirement as lighthouse keeper on Castle Spit; and then, as the light went automatic, his true retirement, to eke out his life on his war pension, in the cottage leased to him for life by the lighthouse trust.

Then we sang 'For Those in Peril on the Sea' and then the minister got up, I assumed to close the service. But no.

'And now, for the final reading before we make our way to the graveside, I would like to invite Bran's old friend, Reginald Markham, to read part of psalm one hundred and seven, sometimes known as the Sailor's Psalm.'

An old, old man got up from the front of the church and made his way, very slowly, up the steps of the pulpit. Then he raised his head and began to speak, his old cracked voice reaching to the back of the silent church.

'They that go down to the sea in ships, that do business in great waters;

'These see the works of the Lord and His wonders in the deep.

'For He commandeth and raiseth the stormy wind, which lifteth up the waves thereof.

'They mount up to the Heaven, they go down again to the depths: their soul is melted because of trouble.

'They reel to and fro, and stagger like a drunken man, and are at their wit's end.

'Then they cry unto the Lord in their trouble and He bringeth them out of their distresses.

'He maketh the storm a calm, so that the waves thereof are still.

'Then are they glad because they be quiet; so He bringeth them unto their desired haven.'

He stopped, and bowed his head for a moment, rubbing his old eyes beneath their glasses. 'My friends, we can be glad that Bran Fisher has reached his haven.'

And suddenly I was crying. I wasn't the only one, but I felt the most hypocritical. I'd hated Bran. I'd hated him and ranged myself against him in a fight for Seth's love. And we'd both lost, only Bran had lost his life too. He'd died without ever saying goodbye to his grandson. The last words between them were full of bitterness and hate, because of me.

I found I was sobbing and I stood, blind with tears, as the pallbearers moved to take their places at the corners of the coffin.

Abe put his arm around me and for a minute I shook

my head, blindly resisting his comfort, trying to pull away, but he hugged me close and it felt so good to have a shoulder beneath my cheek.

Then, through the swimming tears, I saw the pallbearers heave the coffin to their shoulders and I stood up straighter, Abe's arm still comfortingly around me, and faced the aisle to pay Bran the respect due to him on his final journey.

The coffin moved slowly, even more slowly than was customary. As I swiped away my tears, I saw that one of the bearers was moving awkwardly, his leg dragging stiffly as he walked, and the others were matching their pace to his painful limp.

But it wasn't until they drew level that I saw his face.

It was Seth.

He turned and, as our eyes met, his blazed into fury. I suddenly saw the scene as it would look through his eyes – me wrapped in Abe's jacket, leaning into his casual embrace, Abe's arm protectively around me. As if . . .

'Seth . . .' I managed, though my throat was raw with tears. I pushed Abe's arm away and stretched a hand out past Emmaline and Sienna. 'Seth!'

For a minute his face burned with some emotion so strong it was impossible to read; the white face, blazing eyes – they could have meant anything from hate, to a kind of bitter, searing love.

Then he ripped his gaze away from mine and continued his painful progress up the aisle of the church, out to where the open grave was waiting.

I should have been watching the minister, or the coffin, or Elaine as she threw the first handful of earth into the grave. But I couldn't tear my eyes away from Seth.

He stood on the opposite side of the grave from me, just feet away, and the tears streamed down his face. There was no other sign that he was crying; he made no sound and his expression hardly changed from a kind of blank deadness. Just his eyes carried on spilling over and over, betraying his grief. Every part of me wanted to reach out across the void and comfort him. But of course I couldn't. I couldn't, because no one could soothe away a grief like that. And I couldn't, because I no longer had the right.

At last the service was finally over, the sexton started filling in the grave and the crowd began to disperse. For a long moment I just stood, ignoring Emmaline and Maya's discussion behind me about whether to go for fish and chips or cook. I was torn between the need to speak to Seth and the knowledge that it would be a very stupid thing to do. He began to walk away. My insides were screaming to run after him. But I held fast. Until, at the lychgate, he turned and, for a second, his eyes flickered towards mine.

'Seth.' It was like a charm was broken and I began to walk, and then to run, towards him. 'Seth, wait.'

He quickened his step but with his limp he couldn't hope to outpace me and I caught up with him halfway down the path to the cliffs.

'Seth!'

I put out a hand and he turned abruptly.

'What?'

The hostility in his voice was like a slap in the face and I flinched. Where had this anger come from? Our parting had been brutal, but Seth was the one who'd broken it off.

Following him had been a huge mistake. I turned away. He made a small, bitter sound, like a snort of disgust, and I rounded on my heel.

'What does that mean?'

He shrugged, his lip curling into an expression that needled at me even more. 'I didn't say anything. If you've got a guilty conscience . . .'

'Guilty conscience? What the—'

'It didn't take you long, did it? From my bed to his.'

'Shut up!' I was suddenly furious. 'How bloody dare you, Seth. You know nothing, *nothing*.'

'Nothing? So, let me see, wearing his clothes . . .' He flicked a contemptuous finger at Abe's jacket, still slung around my shoulders. 'Letting him fondle you in public, cuddling up to him at my grandfather's *funeral* . . .' He was suddenly white with anger, a cold, still fury that made me flinch. 'While I had to stand there and *watch* the two of you petting. All that was nothing, was it?'

'He gave me a hug, you – you stupid, fatuous, nasty-minded *bastard*.' I was choking with hot anger, almost unable to speak. But Seth – Seth was infuriatingly cold. He watched me for a minute, his face set into lines I hardly recognized. Then he seemed to shrug and began to limp away down the hill.

'Stop it,' I shouted, enraged beyond reason. 'Stop right now, we are *not* done here, Seth.' And then, as he carried on his slow, painful progress, I spat it again, putting all my power into the words this time. '*Stop!*'

He stopped, dead, his feet glued to the path. For a minute he seemed unable to believe it. I could see the tide of blood flooding the back of his neck as he put all his strength into ripping himself from the ground. Then he turned to face me and his expression made me quail. There was something close to hate in his eyes.

'Let. Me. Go.' He spat the words very slowly, like the worst swearwords imaginable. 'Or you'll regret it, witch.'

'I'm sorry,' I covered my mouth in horror and then loosed the charm, so abruptly that he sprawled to the ground, stones cutting into his hands and knees. 'Oh my God, I'm so sorry, please, let me . . .' I put my hand to his shoulder, trying to help him up, but he threw my arm off so violently that my own hand caught me across the mouth, splitting my lip along the old scar where Caroline had slapped me, so long ago.

I cried out with pain and suddenly there was blood in my mouth and Seth had his hands to his face. His cold vicious calm was broken and he began to sob – great tearing sobs that seemed to be ripping him apart from inside.

'Anna!' he choked out, and then we were in each others

arms, our limbs locked, my feet lifting from the ground, his cheekbone crushing so hard against mine that it hurt. There was blood on my lip, and in my mouth, and on his collar, staining the crisp whiteness of his shirt with scarlet blossoms across his shoulder and chest.

'Anna,' he sobbed again and I was crying too.

I don't know what the others thought. But no one came to disturb us, though we stood for – I don't know how long. They left by the other gate and Seth and I stood, clinging together like survivors of a shipwreck, while the church bell tolled out the strokes of Bran's long life and Seth's heart beat beneath my cheek. He felt real in my arms, thin and hard, but real – his skin hot beneath his shirt, his heart strong and quick.

At last the churchyard fell silent and I lifted my face from Seth's shoulder to find the sun was setting in the west, red and bloody. Seth limped to the church wall and we sat, watching, as it sank into the dark clouds at the horizon, leaving the graveyard bereft and shadowy.

'Seth, what have we done?' I asked. I turned to look at his face in the twilight. It was thinner and there were shadows under his cheekbones that shouldn't have been there and new scars I didn't recognize: bruises and half-healed cuts.

'I don't know,' he said at last. He ran his hand through his hair, his expression utterly defeated. 'We can't go back, there's no way back, but I feel . . .' He closed his eyes and my heart ached. 'I feel broken.'

'What happened to your leg?' I asked in a low voice.

'Stupid accident. I slipped, in a storm a few weeks back. Cracked my hip and thigh on a bulkhead. I thought it was just badly bruised and it seemed to be getting better but – well, these last few days it's got worse.'

'Will you see a doctor, while you're here?'

'I'll have to. But I don't know what they'll say. Probably, rest up and don't do anything strenuous. And that's not really an option.'

'Why not?'

'Because I've been paid to transport a boat to Helsinki by a set date and if I don't show up on time I'll lose half my wages – I'm already behind. I've put into a strange port without any kind of entry visa or paperwork and then left the boat. None of this was part of the plan. And the boat, it's not my property, I have to go back and retrieve it, pay the fines, try to get back on schedule . . .' He sighed and rubbed his face wearily. 'I'm sorry I was such a shit to you. I'm just – tired and in pain. The flight didn't help – eight hours crammed into an economy seat. I could hardly walk at the end.'

'Seth . . .' I couldn't help myself – I reached for his hand, but he flinched away.

'Don't.'

I bit my lip and watched as he pushed himself upright, favouring his good leg.

'Goodbye,' he said with finality.

'Don't, wait . . .' I begged, but he turned away and I blurted, without thinking, 'Stop!'

I winced as the words left my mouth, wishing I could snatch back the reminder of what I'd done, but he stopped – of his own free will, this time. He stood with his back to me, not moving, his silhouette long and lean against the twilit sky.

'Don't go, not yet. Will you – can we walk down to the town together?'

'You're going the other way.'

I want to go with you, I wanted to say. But I bit back the words and only shrugged, trying to pretend an indifference I didn't feel.

'I don't mind. I need a walk.'

'OK,' he said, almost angrily. 'But it'll be bloody slow. I can't go at more than a hobble with this leg. Don't blame me if you're late home.'

We walked in silence down the hill, side by side, my arm sometimes brushing his when trees and bushes narrowed the path, or when one of us stumbled over a tussock in the darkness. Once his knuckles grazed mine and I had to fight the temptation to catch up his hand, hold it in mine.

Then, as we came out on to the cliff top, he spoke, unexpectedly, his face turned back towards the churchyard.

'My dad's buried there too, over by the far wall. His funeral – it wasn't like this. It was winter, lashing rain. I remember being glad because the rain ran down my face and none of my mates could see I was crying.'

A lump rose in my throat and I couldn't speak.

'Dad . . . Grandad . . .' he said. I wasn't sure if he was talking to me now, or himself. 'Poor Mum. She's got no one left to lose now – except me.'

'Seth, don't.' I couldn't help myself – I took his hand and he stopped, his face pale in the gloaming. 'Don't talk like that.'

'Like what?'

'Like . . .' But I couldn't finish. Like he was next, was what I meant. But I couldn't say it. My mouth tasted of blood and the salt of tears on my lips.

His fingers closed around mine and for a moment we just stood. Seth closed his eyes and I saw the salt-streaked paths where the tears had dried on his cheekbones. Then he turned, his hand still in mine, and slowly we walked the last few hundred metres to the quay, where the boats bobbed and the rigging sang a strange metallic song.

At the jetty we stopped.

'You should go,' Seth said. 'It's getting late. Your dad'll be wondering . . .'

I nodded and drew a shaky breath.

'Goodbye . . . I'm sorry about your shirt.'

He looked down at the stains of blood and tears spread across his chest and shoulders.

'It's all right – I've had worse . . . I'm sorry about your lip.'

'I've had worse,' I echoed, with an attempt at a shaky laugh. 'Seth, do you . . .' I tried to swallow away the tightness in my throat. 'Do you think we'll ever stop hurting each other?'

He looked away, past the boats and the harbour, out to sea and the unending, unfathomable dark. I couldn't see his face. But I heard him swallow and when he spoke there was a catch in his voice.

'No. I don't think we ever will. We should have listened to Bran. Some things – some things just aren't possible.'

His fingers tightened around mine, just for a moment. His hand was cold and the skin felt rough; weathered and scarred. Then he let go and turned to walk away.

CHAPTER SIX

'Anna.' The voice was insistent, sharp. 'Anna!'

And then suddenly Mrs Finch was standing in front of me, tapping at the page with her finger.

'Anna Winterson, for heaven's sakes. I've asked you three times to please read the next passage. What's wrong with you recently?'

'I – I'm sorry,' I shook myself out of my stupor. 'I've not been . . .'

She bent down and put a hand over mine, her face softening.

'Anna, are you OK?' She lowered her voice and said quietly, 'I know this has been a tough term for you, but—'

'I'm *fine*,' I snapped. The last thing I wanted was Mrs Finch's pity. I'd had enough of people's concern when Seth left the first time.

Mrs Finch put up her hands and took a step back.

'Very well! Look, if you want to discuss anything, stay behind. But now, could you please read the next passage?' She sighed as she saw my blank expression. 'The one beginning, "It is often suggested . . .". And this time *please* try to pay attention.'

I tried. And I tried at home too, ignoring Dad's concerned expression after Seth left for the airport. I'd ignored his footsteps outside my room at night, checking to see if I was sleeping. I'd ignored his veiled hints about dropping an A-level, if everything was getting on top of me. I even did my best to ignore Emmaline and Maya's worried looks. But I couldn't ignore Abe. At least, I tried, but Abe made himself unignorable.

'Knock knock,' his voice startled me out of my evening Maths revision, so that I dropped my pen, then hit my head with indescribable force on my desk as I bent down to retrieve it. When he opened my bedroom door he found me curled with my forehead to my knees, clutching my skull.

'What in God's name are you doing, woman? Is that some new yoga position designed to get blood to the brain?'

'Shut *up*,' I groaned and then sat up, rubbing my scalp. 'Ow. Ow, ow, ow . . .'

'What did you do?'

'What does it look like, you dick?'

'Don't take it out on me!' His face was amused, but he came to sit beside me on the bed and put his hand gently over the bruise. I felt his magic prickle through my skin and the aching muted to something more bearable.

'Better?'

'A bit.' I pulled away and sat up straighter. 'What are you doing here?'

'I've come to take a look at you.' He eyed me as if judging what tack to take and then said bluntly, 'Emmaline's worried about you.'

'Why? What business is it of hers?' I was still snappish from the pain in my head.

'That's a nice thing to say of a friend!' Abe pretended to look shocked, but I knew he wasn't really. 'You know why, anyway. Because you're having some kind of minor breakdown, only you won't admit it.'

'I'm not,' I said stubbornly. 'I'm coping.'

'Really? Tell me what you got in your last piece of Maths coursework.'

That was easy. I'd handed it in before Christmas.

'An A,' I said smugly. 'Thanks for checking.'

'And what did you get in your last practice paper?' he said pointedly. My face fell. Emmaline really had been snooping.

'Shut up.'

'Come on, what?'

'I'll get it together.'

'How many hours did you sleep last night?' he pressed.

'Eight.'

'You're lying.'

Damn him.

'OK,' I said shortly. 'I'm lying. I've been finding it hard to sleep. So what?'

'Because you're going quietly nuts! Anna, you're doing too much. Searching for your mum, keeping up with school, trying to cram eighteen years of magical education into a few weekends – honestly, do you think you can keep up the pace? And now loverboy waltzes back, splits your lip, and screws you up all over again.'

'Hey!' I jumped up from my seat. 'Leave Seth out of it. He's got nothing to do with it.'

'Really? What were you thinking about last night, when you couldn't sleep?'

He stood too and we stared at each other. Abe's eyes were black, angry, and his breath was coming fast. I didn't know what to say. He was right – of course he was right. But . . .

'It's not what you think,' I said at last.

'What I think? What *do* I think?'

'Seth. The reason I've been worrying . . .'

'Yes?'

I felt sick. I had barely started to process what had happened with Bran, but maybe, maybe Abe could help . . .

'Oh, Abe –' suddenly it was a relief to say it, and the words came tumbling out '– I've been so worried. Seth's leg – I've got a horrible feeling . . . I think it's to do with my mother. She cursed Bran – cursed him to limp. And I think the curse . . . I think with Bran's death . . . the curse – it's passed to Seth.' I stopped, staring into Abe's dark, frowning eyes. 'Is that even possible?'

'Yes,' he said slowly. He sat down on my bed again

and chewed his lip. 'It is possible. But what made you think of this?'

I told him about Bran and what he'd shown me. I told him about Seth's limp, about his pain and bitterness, so like Bran's. And the way that the two incidents had slowly coalesced in my mind, into a cold, hard certainty.

'She thought that Bran could protect her – I don't know why. But she was very knowledgeable about prophecies; it was the subject of her dissertation. I think she found something that made her think Bran would help and so, when the Ealdwitan were on her trail, she turned to Bran. But she was wrong – he didn't help. He turned her away.'

'So she cursed him – and his descendants,' Abe finished. I nodded.

'You said Seth had screwed me up – and it's true, he did. But everything that happened was my fault. I started it and, although I'm hurt, I'm going to be OK. I'll cope. But I screwed Seth up too and I'm afraid he's *not* going to be OK.'

I thought of Bran, bitter and twisted, marooned on his island. He had predicted that the move to Winter would kill him, that he could never live so far from the sea. And he'd been right.

'If the curse has passed to Seth,' I said slowly, 'how would I go about undoing it?'

'It depends,' Abe said. 'It depends if the witch who set the curse is still alive.' He looked up at me, his black eyes very direct. 'Is she?'

I walked to school the next day more tired than ever, having spent a sleepless night running over everything in my head. Speaking to Abe should have made me feel better. It hadn't.

But I'd had three large cups of coffee and I was determined to keep it together today. I'd done my English homework, I'd prepared for the Classics test. Well, *ish*. And there were only a couple of weeks left until the end of term. After that it was the Easter holidays and then it was study leave until exams began. I could hold it together for two weeks. Couldn't I?

I was barely out of the trees when my mobile phone beeped. YOU HAVE ONE NEW VOICEMAIL MESSAGE said the text. I dialled in and listened as I walked.

'Hello?' The voice somehow managed to be both croaky and yet chocolate-smooth. It was Caradoc and he plainly hadn't quite got the hang of answerphones. 'Hello? Is this Miss Winterson? . . . What?' By the sound of it, that was over his shoulder to someone else. Then a tut. 'Oh, a recording. Very well. Um, message for Anna Winterson.' He spoke very clearly, as if giving dictation to the hard of hearing. 'Caradoc Truelove speaking. I have found the text we were discussing, but I don't really want to give too many details over the phone. We don't want this translation going the same way as the original. Would you come to the shop and we can talk in person? Please call me. Thank you. Goodbye. Is that it? Oh, I have to press this . . .'

I rang back, my fingers shaking, but the shop answerphone picked up in Jonathan's voice.

'Hello, and welcome to Truelove and Fox. Our opening hours are ten a.m. to five p.m., Tuesday to Saturday, and by appointment only on Mondays and Sundays. If you are calling outside these hours please leave a message. Thank you.'

'Hi,' I said, my words falling over each other. 'Jonathan, I just got Caradoc's message. I'm coming to London. I'll be with you –' I looked at my watch '– Elevenish. See you soon.'

Looked like that Classics revision was going to be a wasted effort after all.

The train was slow. The tube was slow. I ran from Leicester Square tube station through the slow crowds of slow people, slowly milling around. But at last I turned into Cecil Court and made my way across the stone flags, trying to calm my heaving chest. *Truelove & Fox* read the modest grey sign on the farthest shop and beneath, in smaller text, *Antiquarian Book Sellers*.

The bell above the door jingled as I entered and I called, 'Caradoc! Jonathan! It's me, Anna.'

No one answered.

I stood for a moment at the counter, looking at the beautiful gilded grimoires in the locked display case, and then, feeling like an intruder, I stepped around the counter and put my head into the back room. There was no one there either, but a cup of black tea stood on the sideboard, curls of steam rising in the air.

Odd. But at least it meant someone was here. They wouldn't have gone out without locking up. Perhaps they were downstairs?

Beneath the floor was a second room of books; a secret area for shadow books, known only to witches. It was accessed by a hidden door which I'd managed to find once – though whether I'd opened it by sheer willpower, or whether Caradoc had helped, I'd never known. I had no idea how to open it now. The floor was shining wood, without any obvious joins.

'Caradoc?' I called hopefully and then knelt on the floor, cupping my hands to the boards, 'Caradoc, can you hear me? Can you open up?'

And I heard – I don't know what I heard. Something. A sound so faint it was hard to put my finger on. But suddenly my stomach was a tight knot and I knew I had to get into that cellar. I just had to.

I backed against the wall and searched my memory for a spell.

'Ætýne!' I called, tentatively. A dark crack appeared in the middle of the shop, a sliver of blackness hanging in thin air, and a breath of air gusted out before the door blew shut again with a bang. My stomach clenched. The air smelled of . . . blood.

'Ætýne!' I shouted and the door flew open with a sound like a clap of thunder, leaving a gaping black rift in the centre of the shop, with stairs leading down into darkness. I put my hand to my mouth, stifling a cry. The stench of blood was stronger than ever.

'Caradoc!' I called, trying not to let my voice shake, 'Caradoc? Jonathan?'

Silence. Broken only by my trembling breathing and the creak of the stair treads as I began to descend towards whatever was in that cellar.

I could see almost nothing in the blackness, just something on the floor, glinting with a dull lustre. Then my groping hand found a switch on the wall and dim bulbs flickered out across the basement, one after the other, glinting off the pool of liquid at the foot of the stairs.

Blood. I pressed my hand hard over my face, keeping out the butcher's smell, pushing back the cry that wanted to erupt at the sight of the crimson pool. So much. Nobody could lose that much blood and live, surely?

I followed the slick, liquid trail along the floor between the stacks of bookshelves. I was terrified at the thought of what lay at the end, but I couldn't turn back.

The tide lapped round the corner of a huge shelf-stack. I turned too – and a scream ripped from my mouth.

There was blood – blood everywhere, sprayed on the books and the walls, even spattered on the light-fitting.

And in the centre, Caradoc, lying as peacefully as a child asleep, with his throat slit from ear to ear.

'Caradoc!'

I fell to my knees in the sticky crimson pool and then

– I couldn't stop myself, I knew all about crime-scenes and forensics, but I couldn't stop myself from putting my hand to his cheek. His throat had been slashed just above his cravat and the fabric was soaked through and through with blood, until it looked as if his whole chest was gaping open.

'Caradoc . . . Oh my God, oh Caradoc . . .'

And then I heard, quite distinctly, the sound of footsteps in the shop above.

I didn't think my body could produce any more adrenalin but, before I could think, I was on my feet, my heart hammering. Should I call out? Hide?

Before I'd decided, a cry floated down the stairs.

'Caradoc!'

I stood, frozen. It came again.

'Caradoc, I've got the milk. Will you drink yours up here or shall I bring it down?'

'Jonathan!' I scrambled to the cellar steps and began to claw my way up, my shoes and fingers slippery with Caradoc's blood. 'We need – the police – oh God – Caradoc – he's—'

There was a crash as the tea cup Jonathan was holding fell to the shop floor, shards of china and drops of tea flying across the little space.

'Anna, what . . . ?' He stood in the doorway, his face ashen, turning to blank horror as he took in my bloodstained clothes and hands. 'Sweet Jesus, what—'

'Call the police!' I stumbled towards him, but he took an

involuntary step back and I grabbed at the counter to steady myself instead. 'We need an ambulance. It's Caradoc, he's—'

'Let me see . . .'

He ran to the cellar steps, but fell back as he saw the lake of gore.

'Oh Christ! Oh help . . .' He put a hand to his mouth as if pressing back vomit and then managed, 'But what – what's happened? Anna, what's happened?'

His face was white, with spots of red high on each cheekbone, and his eyes were wide and wild.

'He's dead,' I choked out. For a second everything seemed to swim and I gritted my teeth, trying to keep it together.

'He's dead?' Jonathan seemed unable to process it. 'But – how?'

'His throat's been cut.' I felt bile rise in my own throat and my ears suddenly sang. I hardly heard Jonathan's questions as I shook my head, trying to swallow down my own nausea. 'Call the police,' was all I could manage.

'We can't,' Jonathan said angrily. 'He's in the forbidden part of the shop. We can't have outwith police tramping around down there.'

'Damn the outwith!' I sobbed. 'What does it matter?'

'It still matters!' Jonathan shouted back. His face was contorted with agony and he sank down slowly against a bookshelf, his hands over his face. 'Oh God, Caradoc! Oh my darling . . .'

105

'What can we do then?'

'We'll have to move him. Up here.'

'No!'

'You don't understand.' He spoke very slowly, his teeth clenched. 'It would be more than my life's worth, and yours, to have outwith cops clumping around down there.'

'But it won't make any sense up here. The crime scene – there'll be no blood. And how could anyone have done it up here without being seen?' I gestured to the street.

'We'll have to persuade the police.' His face was grim. 'By one means or another. Now are you going to help me, or not?'

Jonathan was sick as we wrestled Caradoc's body up to the ground floor and sick again as I tried to lay his body as close to how I'd found him as possible. It was as I was putting his hand across his breast, just as it had been downstairs, that I noticed the tiny scrap of paper between his clenched fingers.

I pulled it out and smoothed it. It was a corner, no more, printed in heavy black-lead type, of the sort used in Victorian novels. Beneath the bloodstains, it read:

A Rydelle
A childe shalle be born on the feaft of Kings
A childe of the Rook tho
And t

'What is it?' Jonathan asked, wiping his eyes with his sleeve.

'I think,' I swallowed against the sharpness of the grief in my throat, 'I think it's what they came for. A riddle. And it's gone.'

'A riddle?' Jonathan raised his eyes to the ceiling and his face twisted into an expression of such heartbreak that I looked away. 'Oh Caradoc, you gave your life for a bloody riddle.'

And then he began to sob – huge, heavy, tearing sobs. I tried to comfort him, but he put out a hand.

'Go. Just go, Anna.'

'But – the police . . .'

'Just go.' His voice was rough and torn. 'You can't help. It's better not to complicate things any more. I can just say I found him.' He pulled out the cash drawer of the till and threw the contents on the floor, the coins skittering towards the exit. 'There. It was a burglary. Now, I'm calling nine-nine-nine, so go.'

'But – but my clothes. They're all covered in blood.'

'You're a damn witch,' Jonathan cried. 'You sort it out.'

He sank to his knees on the shop floor, while I crept away.

The bloodstains were gone by the time I reached the main road.

The tears on my face took longer to dry.

I trudged aimlessly, trying to walk away the dread and agony. Leicester Square, Soho, Oxford Street, Regents Street, Piccadilly, Bond Street – I zigzagged across London, the pavements hard beneath my feet, the outwith parting before me like gusting leaves. My feet were throbbing, but the feeling somehow kept the memory of Caradoc at bay, and I kept putting one foot in front of another, until I ended up in Green Park.

And there – bizarrely, inexplicably – Emmaline was standing on the path in front of me, her face full of fury and shock. She ran towards me, gripping my arms with painful intensity, and then threw her arms around me.

'Thank God! What happened?'

'What do you mean?' I asked dully.

'Abe heard you – I don't know how. He heard you screaming and he rang me at school. And that was when I realized, you hadn't come in all day. So I went to your house and you were gone – what the hell are you doing here?'

'I came . . .' I sank to the grassy verge and drew my knees up to my chin. 'I came to see Caradoc.'

'And? Anna, what's wrong? You look like you've seen a ghost.'

It was too close to the truth. I shut my eyes, pressing my palms to my face. The words swelled and choked inside me, lodging in my throat like stones. 'Caradoc's dead,' I managed.

'*Dead?*'

'I asked him to trace a text, a riddle, that my mother stole from the Ealdwitan. And he found it and called me to tell me. But he was killed before I could get to him.'

'Oh my God.' The colour had drained from Em's face

and she sank to the grass beside me. 'This is serious, isn't it?'

'Caradoc should never have been involved!' I cried. 'It's all my fault – I *asked* him to look for that riddle. I should have known!'

'How on earth could you have known? This is *not* your fault.'

'So people keep saying – not my fault . . . not my fault . . . None of it's ever my fault – Bill's death, Bran's death, now Caradoc's death. I didn't kill them – but they died because of me, Em. Not my fault? Really? What else do you want?'

'They died because of something far bigger than you. And the fact that you're caught up in it too doesn't make you responsible. You're in this trap just as much as the rest of us. It could have been you.'

'Who's next? Who's going to be next?'

Em only shook her head, while hideous pictures flashed through my head: Emmaline, Abe, Seth, Dad . . . I shut my eyes, unable to bear it, but the images only burned brighter in the darkness.

'It's Thaddeus Corax,' I said at last. 'I know it is. He was responsible for Bill's death. He *must* know whatever my mother was trying to hide. He knows – and he doesn't want me to find out.'

'It could be,' Em admitted, though there was something reluctant about her expression. 'But what are you going to do?'

'I'm going to confront him.'

'You're crazy.'

'No, it's the only way. If I keep digging around in the dark, more people are going to get hurt. This way—'

'This way the person who'll get hurt is *you*!'

I just nodded.

'No,' Em said. She grabbed my arm. 'No! Don't be stupid, this is *not* the way.'

'It's the only way.' Suddenly I was calm. 'I'll visit him at his office. I'll make an appointment. If it's all out in the open, what can he really do?'

'You've just finished telling me that you think this guy had Caradoc Truelove *killed*. And you're asking me, what can he *do*?'

'He's not going to have me killed. He wants something – something I've got. I'm just about the only person he *can't* get rid of.'

'You're crazy.' She pushed her glasses impatiently back up her nose and began digging for her mobile. 'I'm calling Abe.'

'Call who you want. I'm calling Marcus.'

'Who the hell's Marcus?'

'Marcus is my cousin. He's Thaddeus' son.'

I could hear Emmaline frantically jabbing buttons on her mobile as I picked up mine and fished Marcus' thick, expensive handkerchief out of my pocket. I felt suddenly completely calm, completely sure.

He answered on the first ring.

'Hello?'

'Hello, Marcus? It's Anna – Anna Winterson.'

'Hello, Anna. How lovely to hear from you.'

'I'm not calling for a chat, I'm afraid. I need a favour. I'm sorry.'

'Don't be. What's the favour? I can't promise I can grant it, but if I can help . . .'

'I want to see your father.'

'Oh.' There was a silence at the other end of the line.

'Marcus?'

'I'm sorry, I don't think that will be possible.'

I bit my lip.

'I don't want to be pushy – but it's really important. I could come and wait – I don't care how long it takes.'

'His appointment diary gets booked up weeks in advance.'

'Couldn't he fit me in between meetings? Or over dinner? I'm sorry, Marcus, but this is urgent. If I have to I'll just turn up and sit outside his office until he comes out. I'd rather not make a scene about it, but if I have to I will.'

'It's that important?' Marcus asked.

'Yes.'

There was another silence, as if Marcus was wrestling with something, making up his mind. Then he said. 'Hold on. I'll speak to his secretary and see what can be done.'

There was another silence, punctuated by a door shutting and the sound of muffled voices. Then Marcus came back on the line.

'You're in luck, he's just had a cancellation. He was supposed to be meeting your grandmother actually, but she had an emergency call and had to hurry off. Some old friend's had an accident, I believe?'

Caradoc – oh Caradoc! I shut my eyes at the thought of my grandmother, heading towards the hideous waiting news.

'Yes,' I said. I didn't try to disguise the bleakness that had crept into my voice. 'It's part of the reason I need to see your father.'

'Your grandmother's meeting with him was at four. Can you make it for then?'

'Yes, I'll be there. Goodbye, Marcus.'

'Goodbye, Anna.'

And he was gone.

As I put the phone away I heard Emmaline's panicked voice and imagined Abe's sarcastic tones on the other end of the line.

'Yes, completely nuts . . . That's what I'm telling you . . . Well of course I did, but failing that, what can I do? You tell me . . .' There was a long silence and then Emmaline nodded. 'OK, I'll try . . . OK . . . Bye.'

She looked up at me, then shook her head.

'He's coming. He says don't get killed before he gets here.'

CHAPTER SEVEN

'Lovely to see you again, Anna.' Marcus kissed me carefully on both cheeks and then looked past me at Emmaline and Abe, both standing in attitudes of furious tension by the reception desk. 'Won't you introduce me to your friends?'

'Marcus, this is Emmaline Peller. Emmaline – my cousin Marcus. And this is Abe Goldsmith.'

'Pleased to meet you.' Marcus shook hands with Emmaline and then put out a hand towards Abe. Abe only stared at it, as if he'd never heard of such a bizarre custom as 'shaking hands'. There was a brief silence and then, after a moment, Marcus gave a shrug and dropped his. I thought he'd be offended, but when he looked at me there was a small smile at the corner of his mouth.

'Well, quite the happy party. Are you all seeing my father?'

'No,' I said, at the exact same time as Abe said, 'Yes.'

We glared at each other.

'Oh, I'm sorry,' Abe said. 'Do you and Thad need some time alone together to catch up on old times? Or were you going to regale him with your girly secrets?'

'I didn't ask you to come,' I snarled.

'No, my role as a human shield is in a purely voluntary capacity,' Abe spat back.

'I'm sorry?' Marcus looked from me to Abe with a puzzled expression and suddenly I was too tired to fight it out any longer.

'Come if you want,' I said. 'I really don't care. Just leave the talking to me, OK?'

'OK,' Abe said meekly.

We set off down the long velvet-carpeted corridor and behind me I could see Emmaline gazing around with a mixture of horrified wonder, taking in the flickering witchlights, the huge domed chambers that led off to the left and right, and the pulse and flow of power beneath our feet, as the rivers chained to this place twisted and writhed to be free.

'This is too much,' she whispered. 'I can hardly breathe – it's putrid with magic.'

I knew what she meant – the heaviness of power in the air was almost overwhelming. But, as I saw it through her eyes, I had the strangest sensation that the spells holding the place together were buckling, no longer effortless, but perhaps even inadequate. I felt as if I was watching a dyke holding back the sea and had seen a single pebble roll down the face: the warning of a deluge.

'Here we are,' Marcus said, and we stopped outside a carved oak door, black with age and deeply polished. He knocked and waited for a moment. No answer.

'Hmm.' He looked at his watch. 'He should be there – he's expecting you.' He knocked again.

'Oh for God's sake.' Abe reached for the handle. 'He's probably fallen asleep.'

'There's no point trying the door,' Marcus said. 'My father has enchantments twelve-deep on that—' but his voice broke off as Abe turned the handle without effort and the door swung wide.

It seemed that Abe had guessed right; Thaddeus Corax was not at his desk, but lying on the sofa in front of the fire. The sofa back was between us and him, but I could see his head, lolling against the arm, and his eyes were closed.

'Father,' Marcus said, walking briskly over. 'Father, your four o'clock . . .'

He stopped. For a moment I couldn't understand why, then as I drew level and saw over the back of the sofa, I realized.

The carved bone handle of a sword stuck straight up between his ribs.

Thaddeus Corax was dead, stabbed through the heart.

Before I had time to do more than gasp, there was a terrifying rumbling roar, the red damask wallpaper split like wet tissue and the walls of the room caved in.

I caught sight of Marcus, his arms outstretched towards his father; Abe, his face blank with terror; Emmaline, frozen in a scream – and then the waters crashed in. Above the roar and thunder I heard Marcus bellow an incantation and a huge shield sprang out to encompass his side of the room

– but before it could reach me the current snatched me.

Somewhere in the muddy swirling crash of waters, I felt a hand grip my wrist, fierce with strength.

'Don't let go,' Abe's voice roared in my head, and I didn't. He pulled me towards him in the buffeting torrential rush, his arms around me, his shield reaching out to cover us both. I knew I should be trying to help him, but the force of the water was crushing us together, crushing the breath out of my body, and then the waters crashed over my head and it was all I could do to keep myself alive.

I was on a beach, if you could use that word to describe a mud-flat beside a filthy river. And I was covered with stinking black silt from head to toe. There were cold pebbles beneath my cheek and around me were strewn empty drinks cans, clogged plastic bags, a used condom. I sat up, spitting filth and grit, and looked wildly about, trying to figure out where I was.

For a minute I was totally disoriented – then I saw the familiar pyramid-topped tower of Canary Wharf in the distance. I must be on the eastern stretch of the Thames – but how? And where were the others?

There was a coughing sound to my right and I looked down to see Abe curled on the mud.

'Abe!' I hugged him fiercely and he gasped, coughing up river-water.

'Go easy,' he said hoarsely, but his fingers squeezed my wrist. I felt a hot rush of relief that he was alive.

'Are you OK?'

'No, I'm lying here dead,' he croaked, hauling himself into a sitting position. 'You're just hallucinating me hacking up phlegm like a sixty-a-dayer.'

'Stop it,' I choked, and he put his arms gently around me, filthy and stinking as I was. My fingers clenched his mud-matted hair and then we both pulled back, looking at each other's stained and muddied faces.

'What the hell just happened?' Abe asked.

'I don't *know*.' I tried to make my battered, waterlogged brain work properly. Then, as I began to realize the full horror of what had happened, I shut my eyes. 'Christ, he's dead. Thaddeus Corax is *dead*.'

'Why do you care?' Abe asked.

'He knew . . .' I said slowly. 'He was the only person left who knew the truth about me. Everyone who gets close is getting picked off. But I thought . . . I thought . . .'

'You thought he was behind Caradoc's killing,' Abe finished. 'Maybe he was. But then, who killed him?'

'Was it the spy?' I stared at him. 'What's happening?'

'Anna, this is pointless.' He stuck out a mud-streaked hand and hauled me to my feet. 'We're not going to get any answers here. And we've got to find Em.'

Emmaline. Oh God. I tried to think back, to remember if Marcus' shield had had time to reach her – and I couldn't. My only comfort was that she was a powerful witch in her own right. If magic could save her, Emmaline would be all right.

'Let's try ringing her,' Abe said. But our phones were blank and dark, waterlogged to the point of death. Even when we tried breathing magic into them nothing happened.

'Arse,' Abe said. We both stared at each other for a while and then began the trudge back towards London.

We fell into silence after the first mile or two, so that when Abe's wordless exclamation broke the relentless beat of our footsteps, I looked up, startled.

'What?'

For answer he pointed at the gap in the Wapping warehouses which had opened up to show the Thames.

I stifled my own gasp.

The Thames was running red with blood.

A great swathe of gore was flooding out from the south bank into the river, turning the water into a churning cauldron of red. On the wind floated the sound of sirens and a faint hubbub of voices.

'We've got to get across,' Abe said. 'How? Come on, you're the Londoner – isn't there a bridge?'

'Yes,' I said. 'That way.'

Abe grabbed my wrist again and we ran.

I could hear the shouts and sirens wailing as we pounded along Shad Thames towards St Saviour's dock, and all the time the flood of gore kept pumping into the river like a slashed artery. What *was* it? Where was it coming from?

'Stand back,' shouted a policeman as we approached. He flung his arms out, barring our way. 'We've had a building collapse. No access until the area's been cleared.'

'Oh you bastard,' Abe panted. He pulled me around the corner behind a building and said, 'Invisibility. Pronto.'

Then he disappeared. If it hadn't been for the feel of his hand still gripping my wrist, I wouldn't have even known he was there.

'Come on,' said his voice from close beside my ear. 'What are you waiting for?'

I was shattered; cold and bone-tired, both physically and magically. I'd seen two dead bodies since breakfast – it felt like I'd lived a hundred years since I listened to Caradoc's message.

I couldn't feel a single scrap of power left inside me, but Abe had managed, and I was damned if I was going to ask him for help. From somewhere I scraped together a little magic and muttered the charm my grandmother had drilled into me.

'Did it work?' I asked.

'Not completely.' Abe's voice was appraising. 'I can see your outline, like a ripple.'

I gritted my teeth and repeated the incantation, forcing power out of every muscle, feeling it shudder across my skin like goosebumps.

'Better,' Abe's voice said. 'Come on, while you can still keep it together. Hold my hand so we don't lose each other.'

We ran silently back past the policeman and round the corner, almost bumping into another policeman who stepped into our path, unable to see us coming. Then we were teetering on the edge of St Saviour's Dock, almost in the water, staring open-mouthed at the ruins of a huge warehouse near the head of the docks. The foundations seemed to have crumbled from underneath, bricks and chunks of concrete were piled in the water, and from beneath came the gouts of pumping blood, mixed with swirls of something black and viscous – like tar. Currents boiled beneath the surface, as if some sinuous giant creature were writhing in the depths. There were dead birds in the crimson water: crows, three of them. Real birds – or witches, trapped in their changed state and unable to get out? A woman's designer shoe floated past on the swirling current. It looked a lot like the ones worn by my grandmother. I felt nausea suddenly rise up, overwhelming, and put my hands to my mouth, pressing it back as a cold sweat prickled over my skin.

'Anna!' I heard Abe's sudden, urgent hiss and I realized to my horror that I'd flickered into view.

'No!' He grabbed my arm as I gabbled the spell again. 'Don't make it worse – oh you've done it. You idiot, there was a policeman watching.'

'I'm sorry, I didn't—'

'Never mind, just stay invisible now and let's get out of here. We need to find Em.'

'And Marcus,' I whispered.

'Screw Marcus,' Abe said harshly. He pulled me roughly towards a gap in the warehouses – and then we both stumbled into something hard and invisible – something that gave a yelp of shock and pain.

'Argh!' Abe bellowed and he came abruptly into view, as if a switch had been flicked. One hand was outstretched, feeling for the invisible obstacle. The other was pressed to his nose, which was running scarlet with blood. 'For crying out loud, not my nose again!'

'Your nose!' Emmaline was suddenly standing in front of us, clutching at her forehead with both hands. 'What about my head?'

'Is your head broken? I don't bloody think so.'

'Oh Abe!' She dropped her hands from her head and flung them around him, hugging him so hard that he gasped. 'I was so worried. Where were you? Where's Anna?'

'I'm here!' I stepped towards her and then realized from her wild gaze that I was still invisible. 'Here!' I shrugged off the spell impatiently. 'It's me!'

'Anna!' Em flung her arms around me. 'Thank God. What happened?'

'I don't know – we ended up somewhere near Canary Wharf, miles away. What happened to you?'

'We washed up near Westminster. We did the only thing we could think of and followed the river down – then we saw this.'

'We?' Abe asked sharply.

'Me and Marcus,' Em said. A few feet away there was a sudden ripple in the air, like a heat haze, and Marcus shimmered into view. He was dry. Immaculately dry. So was Em, I realized.

I looked down at my own soaked clothes, drying into stiff, mud-crusted creases.

'Marcus shielded us,' Emmaline said sheepishly, interpreting my gaze. 'So we didn't actually get wet.'

'But no matter,' Marcus said. 'We can fix that.' He pointed a finger at my feet and murmured something under his breath, drawing a line up the centre of my body from my feet to the top of my head. When I looked down, my clothes were dry and clean. No illusion – actually clean.

'Wow!' I gasped. 'Why didn't we think of that, Abe?'

'Seems like most people would be more worried about finding their friends than drying their clothes,' Abe said sourly. 'Forgive me if I had something else on my mind.'

'You think I didn't?' Marcus crackled with sudden anger. 'Are you forgetting we saw my father's body shortly before his office was blasted to smithereens?'

'If you're bothered, you've got a funny way of showing it,' Abe spat back.

'My father is *dead*. Murdered. How dare you presume to know anything about my feelings on the matter!'

There was a sudden spitting sizzle in the air between the two men and a feeling of silent tension, as if some great unseen struggle was taking place. Abe's fists clenched and I saw a vein was standing out on Marcus' forehead. The air seemed to ripple with fury and then, just as suddenly, they both turned away.

I looked from one to the other, trying to work out what had just gone on. Abe's face was twisted with disgust but there was a tiny, cruel smile at the edge of his mouth. Marcus looked as if nothing had happened, but his breath was coming fast; I could see his chest heaving beneath his snowy shirt.

'If you two have quite finished swinging your dicks around,' Emmaline said furiously, 'maybe we could try to work out what the hell just happened.'

What *had* just happened? Suddenly the horror of it all washed over me. Two elderly men, butchered like pigs. And the only thing that linked them was a knowledge of my past, my true identity, and the fact that I'd used them – or tried to – to find out the truth. Then something else occurred to me.

'Elizabeth. What if she was in there?'

'I don't think she was,' Marcus said. 'But either way, she'll have returned now. They'll have summoned her back.'

'Which entrance would she use?' I asked. 'She was going to Charing Cross.'

'I'm not sure.' He rubbed his temple. 'It'd be a toss-up between the Fleet entrance and the Effra entrance from there. She uses the Effra more. I think that's where she'd try first. I'll come with you – I need to get back there, find out what's happened.'

'Thank you,' I said. I looked at him, his white, worn face, the blue shadows beneath his eyes. I wanted to hug

123

him, to promise him it would be OK. But I didn't know him well enough – and anyway, that was a promise I had no right to make. His father had died. Nothing would ever be OK for him again.

Instead I turned to Emmaline and Abe. 'You two don't have to come. I don't know what we'll find. I don't want—'

Abe shook his head, his jaw set.

'If you're going back, I'm going too.'

I looked at Emmaline and she raised one eyebrow.

'What? And stump back to Winter on my tod? Not likely. Looks like it's a cab for four.'

We stood on the parapet of Vauxhall Bridge, peering into the dark, swirling waters.

'No blood,' Abe said. 'Looks all right.'

'There's only one way to find out,' Marcus said. 'Well – who wants to go first? Shall I?'

'No,' I said. 'I'll go first.'

'Anna –' Abe put out a hand '– wait!'

But I knew if I waited I'd lose my nerve. I jumped. Abe's voice disappeared as I fell, and then the waters closed over my head and I was tumbling towards oblivion.

I landed with a crash and a sudden sense of foreboding. I was in the familiar concrete vestibule, like the lift shaft of an underground car park – but the reinforced steel door stood open and the smell that came out was not the rich scent of heavy magic, but a stink of river mud, blood and filth. Before I could do anything there was a series of crashes and Emmaline and Abe tumbled on to the concrete floor beside me. Last of all, Marcus touched gently down. As he saw the open door his face paled, but he squared his shoulders and together we led the way into reception.

No one was there but from further down the corridor I could hear shouts and the stench of river mud grew stronger as we began to walk in the direction of the noise. The witchlights in the sconces along the walls were burning so low they cast only a flickering grey light as we passed and the red damask walls were stained and blotched with river mud. There was a sound from above our heads and I looked up to see a crack zig-zagging across the ceiling above us, splintering through the cornicing like icing on a cake. Black water began to drip through, spattering us as we ducked beneath.

We turned a corner, heading towards the main debating chamber, and the corridor forked.

'Which way?' I asked Marcus.

He opened his mouth to reply – but the answer never came.

'Watch out!' Em's cry cut across whatever he might have said. 'The wall!'

I turned sharply. The wall to our left was bulging, splitting like an overripe fruit. As I watched in horror, a giant rent appeared in the paper.

Marcus shouted an incantation and his forefinger

drew a lightning-fast symbol in the air. The characters glowed bright for a second before exploding in a firework flash. The wall shuddered, and seemed to heave itself back into place for a moment, but then with a crash like a waterfall, it exploded, silt and mud and water gushing through the split.

We ran for our lives along the narrow corridor, Marcus hurling charms over his shoulder, the waters snarling and roaring behind us, like some vast beast that had slipped its chain and rampaged out of control.

My breath was tearing in my chest and I stumbled as the water snapped and spat at our heels.

'In here!' Emmaline yelled.

She flung open a door and we scrambled inside, slamming it shut just as the torrent crashed against the wood. The door groaned and Emmaline slapped a hasty charm across it and then looked at me, her face ashen.

'What in the name of all that's crazy is going on out there?'

'The place is falling apart.' Marcus had his back to the door and I could see the strain in his muscles as he forced all his magic into trying to keep the water at bay. 'The rivers are breaking loose.' There was sweat on his forehead and he closed his eyes, concentrating on keeping back the waters.

'What are you waiting for?' Emmaline snapped at me and Abe. 'Help him!'

I shook myself and put my hand against the door,

feeling Abe's magic flowing into the wood along with mine.

After a few moments the din subsided and we all looked at each other.

The wave had retreated, leaving the corridor ankle-deep in Thames mud. There were strange things coiling in the ooze. I tried not to look at them as we picked our way carefully through. Instead I kept my eyes on the walls and ceilings.

We'd only gone a few yards when I heard a familiar voice filtering from an open door.

'Miss Vane, lock down the Fleet entrance – we must keep all traffic to one entrance for the moment. Partridge, get the word out to the other Chairs, tell them to alert their camps. And will somebody *please* find Ratzinger and get the Effra entrance secured and manned!'

'Grandmother!' I ran, slipping in the filth, slimy creatures thrashing underfoot as I sprinted along the corridor to the open door. 'It's me!'

I burst into her office and she looked up from the desk she was standing at. She was immaculate as ever, not a hair out of place. But the room was a wreck. The silk sofas and brocade hangings were spattered with mud. Dirty water swilled in the grate where a fire should have burned. Her desk was cracked down the middle, a great charred slash as if a burning beam had fallen on it. But it was still standing – just – and it was spread with grimoires and antique spell books from the Ealdwitan library, each with quills and markers sticking out of pages, as though she had been desperately seeking a remedy for the chaos unfolding all around.

For a moment her face was blank – then she stumbled out from behind the desk, her arms outstretched.

'Anna – darling . . .'

I scrambled across the silt-strewn floor and into her arms.

'Thank God – when I heard . . .' Her fingers clutched me, painfully hard.

'What happened?' I asked.

'I have no idea. That's the terrifying thing.'

'Corax is dead, did you know?'

'I know he's dead, but not how. No one seems to know if it was an accident or something worse.'

'It was murder.' Marcus' voice was level, but the words cut like a knife. 'He was stabbed.'

'Stabbed?' Elizabeth's face was a mask of shock. She turned from me to Marcus, and then back again. 'You saw this?'

'We saw his body,' Marcus spoke like an automaton. 'He'd been stabbed in his office, with a sword.'

'His *office*? Then it must – it must have been someone known to him.' My grandmother's face was grey. 'One of us.'

'They'd breached the wards,' Marcus said. 'The door was unlocked.'

'My God,' my grandmother whispered. She stumbled to a chair and sank on to it, hardly seeming to notice that the velvet upholstery was soaked through with mud. 'I thought . . . Oh my God, Thaddeus – how I wronged you.' She put her face in her hands, the stones in her rings winking in the dim light. But when she raised her head, the steel was back; her expression was hard. 'We will find his killer and punish them grievously. Marcus, will you gather who you can of your father's camp? Bring them here.'

'What can I do?' I asked. Everything felt suddenly unreal.

Elizabeth shook her head, her eyes bright.

'Thank you, my darling, but the best thing you can do is to go home. There is no time to teach you what you'd need to know to be of use here – that goes for your friends too. And I would worry. You're safer in Winter. I will call you tonight.'

'Do you promise?' I asked as she kissed me on each cheek.

'Yes, I promise. Now, go. It's late. Your father will be worrying.'

Dad. It was like a cold slap. Of course – he'd have been expecting me home hours ago. What could I say? How could I explain?

'Marcus,' my grandmother was saying, 'will you show Anna and her friends out?'

'Of course,' Marcus said.

We walked in silence along a maze of corridors, until we reached the door between two palms. They were dead now, crushed to splinters.

'Are you sure there's nothing I can do to help?' I asked. 'I don't want to leave you like this.'

'Look, just go. Your father . . .' He put a hand to his temple as if crushing down something he couldn't bear to think about. 'Honestly, go home.'

'You'll be all right?' My heart wrung at the sight of his face. He was so self-contained, so reserved, it was hard to remember that he had lost his father today, on top of all this terror and destruction.

'Of course. Truly, go. I need to do something – to work . . .' Some shadow of a very strong emotion shivered over Marcus' face and I had the feeling that he was close to breaking down. 'I *need* to work.'

He'd lost his father. He had lost everything.

We walked through the door and, as I let it close gently behind me, I had the feeling of a traitor, shutting him in, abandoning him to his grief and the blood-soaked waters.

CHAPTER EIGHT

'Are you sure you won't come in, Abe? You look like death. You too, Anna.' Maya put her hands on the open car window, her face white and worried beneath the street lamp. Inside the car the hazard lights blinked, striking a staccato ruby fire off Abe's eyebrow ring.

Abe rubbed his face tiredly, but shook his head.

'We can't stop. I've got to get Anna home.'

'Did you reach my dad?' I asked anxiously.

Emmaline had managed to breathe a bit of magic into her mobile and had spoken to Maya on the train, but between the crackles and cut-outs it was hard to know how much Maya had understood. Then the phone had died completely and we'd been left hoping that Maya would pass on a message.

Maya nodded.

'Yes, but I didn't really know what to say – I wasn't sure if you'd come here first or go there, so I didn't want to contradict whatever you might tell him. He knows you're alive – but that's about it. I think he's a bit . . .'

'I'll stand well back,' Abe said dryly.

'He was pretty angry,' Maya said apologetically.

I held that thought in my head as we drove in silence along the coast road and tried to work out what I could say.

As he pulled into the drive Abe's headlamps swept the front of Wicker House, coming to rest on Dad, his arms ominously folded, standing outside the front door.

'Anna Winterson,' he cut in before I'd even got out of the car, let alone started speaking, 'there had better be a bloody good explanation for this.'

'Dad—'

'You weren't at school, apparently.'

'How did you know?'

'I thought better of you, honestly, Anna.' His face twisted. 'I mean, cutting school – OK. Honestly, I'm not impressed, but there's not much I can say. But leaving me until –' he looked at his watch '– until eleven p.m. without a word, when you knew, you *knew* I'd be frantic—'

'Look,' Abe broke in, 'don't blame Anna. It wasn't her fault.'

'You!' Dad spat. 'Mind your own business.'

'You're being unfair – Anna wasn't to blame, she—'

'Who *was* to blame then?' Dad snarled. 'You ought to be ashamed of yourself – she's half your age. You should be letting her get on with her schoolwork, not dragging her off to—'

'Dad, stop it,' I said. 'Abe didn't drag me anywhere. If you must know, he came up to London to get me back.'

'London! What in God's name were you doing in London?'

'Does it matter?'

'Yes, it matters! For goodness' sake, Anna, what's wrong with you?'

'Look,' Abe said in a low voice, 'she's had a long day and she's been through a lot. Can't you just let her go to bed and leave this for the morning?'

'Thanks,' Dad said furiously, 'but I'm not quite reduced to taking parenting advice from someone who . . .' he stopped, biting his tongue.

'Who . . . ?' Abe said dangerously. 'Go on?'

'Stop it, both of you,' I cried. 'Dad, stop taking it out on Abe. It was nothing to do with him. And Abe, just go. You're not helping.'

'OK,' he said. 'OK. I'm going.'

He turned, but then, as if thinking of something he'd forgotten, he stopped and put a hand on my shoulder.

'Anna?'

'What?'

He bent and kissed my cheek, his lips soft and warm, the gesture unbearably tender.

Then he turned away to the car, the door slammed, and the engine revved with its throaty, choking roar.

Dad stood and watched in stiff fury as the car bumped up the track and out of sight, and then he let out a great gust of breath and some enormous tension seemed to roll off his shoulders.

'Anna, I'm your dad,' he said as we turned to the house. 'I don't want to police your life, but didn't it occur to you that I'd be beside myself with worry? Couldn't you have called?'

'Of course it occurred to me,' I said wearily. I put a hand to my aching head, trying to remember when I'd last had food or drink. It must have been – breakfast? 'I tried to call, Dad. Really I did. But – stuff happened.'

'What kind of stuff?' Dad asked.

The memory of Caradoc's broken, bloodied body rose up in front of my eyes like a waking nightmare and I put my hands to my face, pressing back the sobs that were suddenly threatening to break free.

'I saw . . .' I tried to think of something that was true, but bearable for Dad. 'I saw an accident, in London. It was horrible. Someone died.'

'Oh love.' Dad's anger ebbed. He'd never been able to stay cross with me for long. He pulled me into his arms and I pressed my forehead to his shoulder, wishing there was some way I could explain what had happened today. But Dad didn't ask any more questions and at last I stood stiffly, wiping at my cheek with my sleeve.

'D'you mind if I go up now, Dad? School tomorrow . . .' I said it with a laugh, trying to make it a joke, but my voice faltered and it sounded more like a sob. Dad only nodded, soberly, and watched as I walked slowly up the stairs to my room.

Upstairs, I stripped off my clothes. Even though Marcus

had made them clean, I couldn't shake the feeling of the river silt ground into my hair and skin, and I went and stood under the shower for a long time, trying to think of nothing at all – not of Caradoc, not of Thaddeus Corax, most of all not of Marcus' white, stark face as he turned back to the horror and the mud.

We'd both lost our mothers, too early to remember, and we'd had that great aching absent loss in common, but now Marcus had gone beyond. He'd lost both parents. He was a true orphan, no longer a child in any sense. I couldn't begin to imagine his loneliness tonight.

Before I went to bed I checked my email. What I saw made my heart leap, chokingly, into my throat.

From: Caradoc Truelove. Sent: Today, 10.33 a.m.
Subject: Further to my call.

For a moment my hands shook so badly I couldn't work the mouse, and I had to stop, take a deep breath, and wait for the trembling to subside. Then I clicked on the header and the email opened.

Dear Anna,

I imagine by the time you read this, you will probably have received my telephone message and will know that I have managed to track down, not the original, but the translation I spoke of in my message.

In view of the 'accidents' with previous versions of this

text, I thought that it might be wise to send you an electronic copy – attached herewith. Dear Jonathan has gone out for a moment so this is my first experiment in using the scanner – I hope it succeeds!

In brief, it is a Victorian reprint of a sixteenth-century translation of the original. As you will see, it has been rather inelegantly transmuted into a form of sonnet which is certainly not an accurate reflection of the original poem. Without access to the Anglo-Saxon text it is very hard to know what is pure invention and what is original material, but I'm sorry to say that much of it appears to be, at best, a creative interpretation. Some of it is almost certainly entirely fabricated to fit the requirements of the sonnet form. Some parts are not even sixteenth century, in my opinion, but Victorian insertions.

I am sure you will appreciate the significance of some of the elements, but I'm afraid I write in haste – dear Jonathan has run out for milk and a customer has just come into the shop above – so I must leave you for the moment, but perhaps you could call me when you are at leisure and we can discuss it in greater detail then.

Your affectionate friend,
Caradoc Truelove

I should have cried myself dry today – but the tears threatened to overwhelm me again as I closed down the email, Caradoc's distinctive chocolate-dark drawl still echoing in my head, and clicked on the attachment. For the longest time I could see nothing – nothing but swimming patterns of black and white and blue, though I scrubbed angrily at my eyes, drawing great shuddering breaths in an effort to calm myself.

At last the screen swam into focus – the secret that had cost Caradoc his life. And it was blank. A beautifully rendered scan of a blank sheet of yellowing paper, with a few fly spots and marks and, very faintly through the thick paper, the heavy black type of the poem showing through the other side, utterly unreadable.

He had scanned the wrong side of the page.

He'd been so close to sending me the information – and then he'd put the paper in the scanner the wrong way up and, in his haste, never checked.

I put my head in my hands, the water from my damp hair running down my wrists like tears.

I woke with a jolt and a beating heart to find myself slumped uncomfortably over my desk, the wood damp and warm beneath my cheek. The phone downstairs was shrilling out in the darkness, and the clock on my computer screen said 5.43 a.m.

I shut the laptop with a click and ran down the stairs, trying not to trip over my towel. Still the phone shrilled as I stumbled to the ground floor. Then I stood in the hall for a brief moment, trying to gather myself, face the worst.

I picked up the receiver.

'Hello?'

'It's me.' It was Marcus' voice, low, full of weariness.

'Are you all right?' Stupid question. As soon as the words fell from my lips I wanted to hit my head on the oak beam in front of me. His father was dead. Why would he be all right?

'I'm OK,' he said, though his voice didn't sound it. 'But your grandmother asked me to call – she wanted you to know that she hadn't forgotten her promise, but she couldn't get away. She sends her love, she's sorry she can't talk to you at the moment but she's very – they're all very busy. Trying to sort things out.'

'What – what *happened*?'

There was a pause, as if Marcus was weighing up what he could say, and then he sighed. 'You may as well know the worst. There's no sense in hiding it now. The Neckinger has broken free.'

'What?'

'Oh, I keep forgetting – you wouldn't know.' He drew another deep breath and I could feel his intense fatigue, even at a distance of a hundred or more miles. 'The Ealdwitan headquarters draws its power from the lost underground rivers – did you know that?'

I nodded, forgetting that he couldn't see me, but he continued, 'The rivers each have a spirit – a demon we call them when they're chained. They're very old spirits, older than witches or men, and very powerful. It's part of the role of the Chairs; they each control a demon, keep it bound, keep its power and will tied to the foundations of the headquarters. My father's death gave the Neckinger the chance to get free.'

'And?'

'It was always a black river – one of the hardest to chain. Now it's free, there have been collapses all throughout south London. The tap water is running red, like the Thames, and it tastes of blood. Water's spraying up through the foundations of buildings, cracking the street tarmac. Underground warehouses and car parks have been flooded—'

I closed my eyes, imagining the blood-soaked streets.

'The remaining Chairs are trying to contain it. It's our fault after all – a thousand years of servitude builds a powerful resentment.'

'But what will happen? Can it be recaptured?'

'In theory – yes. But with so few Chairs . . . That's why your grandmother couldn't take time to call.'

'And you –' I hardly dared ask, but I needed to know '– will you become Chair now, Marcus, in your father's place?'

'I don't know.' I heard a rasping sound at the other end and guessed that he was wearily rubbing his unshaven face. 'It depends on my father's will – and we haven't found it. Everything is in limbo until then.'

'Marcus, you sound dead on your feet.'

'I'm . . .' he stopped. I felt his despair as if he were standing next to me. 'I'm very tired. I'm very, very tired. I don't know what to do.'

'Go to bed,' I said.

I wanted to say, 'It'll all be better in the morning,' but that wasn't true. Nothing would be better. His father would still be dead. We would still be under attack from a strange, faceless enemy.

'Go to bed,' I repeated, hopelessly. There was silence on the other end of the line and then I heard his breath shudder.

'Goodnight, Anna.'

'Goodnight, Marcus.'

The phone clicked.

CHAPTER NINE

Maya's kitchen was a warm fug of hot tea, hot cake, and hot beeswax. She was standing at the kitchen stove, dipping candle-wicks into a vat of melted beeswax. Abe was sitting at one end of the table, frowning over Emmaline's laptop. Emmaline, Simon and I were at the other end, looking at the bloodied fragment of paper I'd taken from Caradoc's dead hand.

I hadn't wanted to bring the poem round to Maya's – even such a small scrap seemed tainted by the deaths it had caused. But, as Emmaline had pointed out, there was safety in numbers. As long as only one or two people had read it, they were vulnerable to the same fate as Caradoc. But whoever was behind this couldn't very well pick off the entire Peller family, plus in-laws. According to Em, anyway. I hoped she was right.

We sat in silence, staring at the lines of writing, and listening to the drip, drip of wax falling back into the pot and Maya's slow, purposeful movements as she dipped the wicks, patiently building up layer after layer.

'I can see why it gave Anna's mother the shivers,' Simon

said at last.

'Child of the rook, I got that,' I said bleakly. 'It's me, right? Rokewood comes from Rook.'

'I'd say so. And were you born on the Feast of Kings?'

'I've no idea. Is that a festival?'

'Yes, also known as the Epiphany. Hence the title given to the original document, I presume. It's celebrated on the sixth of January by western churches.'

Something cold trickled up and down my neck. So that was why my mother had changed my date of birth. Not just to hide my identity, but to obscure the link with the riddle.

'Yes,' I said in a low voice. 'Yes, I was.'

Simon turned away from me to look again at the scan on Emmaline's laptop. Abe had spent an hour on Photoshop, sharpening up the image and increasing the contrast in an attempt to get the writing to show through, but nothing had worked.

'It's definitely the same piece, isn't it?' Simon asked Abe.

Abe nodded. 'Yes, the first few lines are showing through – you can see the word "Kings" quite clearly and something about fowl on the next line. But further down the page it's still too faint to see.'

'Anna, can I forward this to myself at work?' Simon asked. 'I'd like to show it to a couple of people at the university. It's possible they could get more out of it than we can.'

'Sure,' I said, at the same time as Abe said, 'D'you have to?'

'What's the problem?' Simon asked, looking from me to Abe and then back again.

'Well, I'd say it's fairly obvious,' Abe said impatiently. 'Anna's mother went to great lengths to keep this hidden. She may have had a reason for that. Don't you think?'

'I think it's gone beyond that, Abe,' Maya said. '*Someone* clearly knows about this – they've already made the connection to Anna, so the damage is done. Now the secrecy isn't protecting Anna any more, it's a danger to her. And to us, if it comes to that.'

'I agree,' I said. 'And it's my email, so I think I get the final say.'

'I know what you're doing.' Abe turned to me angrily. 'You think you're protecting the rest of us at a cost to yourself. If we keep it a secret then we're in more danger from whoever is picking people off. If we tell lots of people then *you* may be in more danger, but we're safer. Well I'm sorry, but I'm not going to save my own skin at a cost to yours.'

'Who's to say my mother was right, Abe? Maybe she had it wrong altogether. Maybe she had her own agenda!'

'Like what!' Abe's face was frankly disbelieving.

'She ran away. Don't you think that's kind of worrying? What if—'

'She did it to protect you!' Abe cried. 'Can't you see that?'

'We don't know that. We don't know anything for sure. No.' I was suddenly coldly, flatly certain that this was right.

'I'm fed up with secrecy and hiding. It'd be better to know. Anything would be better than this – this looking over my shoulder all the time.' I leaned across the table, clicked forward on the email, and typed in Simon's university address. Then I pressed send.

Simon stood up and picked up his coat.

'Thanks, Anna. For what it's worth, I think you're doing the right thing. Your mother clearly wanted to protect you while you were too young to fight, but I think her plan B was always to arm you to defend yourself.'

'What do you mean?'

'Well, her protections only extended so far, didn't they? She must have known you'd move out of Notting Hill eventually. And she deliberately limited the curb on your dad's tongue to let him give you his side of events when you turned eighteen. I think she saw this coming, or saw that it was a possibility at least. She was never trying to keep this under wraps for ever – she knew she couldn't. All she was trying to do was give you enough time to grow into your powers. Enough time to fight back.'

He shrugged himself into his coat and added, 'I'm sorry I have to run off. But I'm supposed to be at the hospital with Sienna in half an hour.'

'Hospital?' I said in surprise. 'Is something wrong?'

'Wrong? No. Quite the reverse.' Simon's face was suddenly pink above his black beard, a rosy blush tingeing his cheeks. 'We're – well, she is – having a baby.'

'Oh, Simon!' I felt my mouth spread into a huge, wide,

involuntary beam. 'I'm so pleased!'

Impetuously, I flung my arms around him and he laughed and squeezed me back.

'Thank you. We're pleased too. Obviously. Anyway I must run or I'll be late for the scan. Do you want a lift? It's not too far out of my way.'

'Don't worry,' Abe said abruptly. 'I'll drop her.'

'No, don't be silly, it's nearer my route than yours.'

'I said, I'll drop her. Sienna will perform a blunt-spoon vasectomy if you're late for the scan, and I'm assuming you want more kids, so leave Anna with me.'

'Fine!' Simon threw up his hands. 'Good Lord, far be it from me to try to do anyone a good turn around here. Goodbye all.' He kissed around the group and then left, and Abe picked up his keys.

'Coming?'

'D'you know what?' Em said. 'I'm going to *walk* Anna. Since she is *my* friend and all. Bye, Abe.'

And she seized my arm and pulled me out of the flat and down the stairs.

Out in the street, the air was blustery, the wind riffling our hair and plucking at our clothes. Emmaline set a brisk pace that had me struggling to keep up. As we turned the corner down to the harbour she gave me a look, not quite hostile, but something close to it.

'What?' I asked. Then, as the silence stretched out, '*What?*'

Emmaline only shook her head and we continued in

silence down past the quay. But then, as we began the climb up the coast road, she suddenly burst out, 'What's going on with you and Abe?'

'Me and Abe?' I was startled. 'Nothing!'

'Well what happened on that Friday then?'

'Friday?' I struggled to cast my mind back. 'Which Friday?'

'Couple of weeks ago. He turned up at ours in a weird bloody mood – said you'd broken his nose. And then, when Sienna asked how, he snapped that he was sick of the sound of your name. Then he got disgustingly drunk and Simon had to drive him home.'

'Oh.' I remembered our fight in the barn. It seemed like a hundred years ago. Then I thought of the kiss and my cheeks flamed scarlet. 'Nothing. Nothing happened.'

Em gave me a look.

'Nothing, really? Is that why you're impersonating a tomato? Come on, Anna. I'm not ten. Neither is Abe.'

'What's that supposed to mean?'

'I mean, that you can act like he's the brother you never had and all that bollocks, but he's not. He's—'

She broke off.

'He's what?'

'He's not your brother. He's . . . Oh, you know what I'm talking about. Stop acting like a nun. Look, you and he want very different things, and I think you're being—'

'What?' I was angry now, really angry, though I wasn't sure if I was cross with Em, or with myself. 'Why is it always the girl's fault? He knows what I want. I've been completely honest with him.'

'And you know what he wants,' Em said shortly. 'So try being honest with yourself.'

'He's not . . .' I pressed my hands to my eyes. 'It's not *like* that. But . . .' My cheeks flamed again and I was suddenly unsure how to talk about this – this unbearably, achingly intimate thing Abe had done. 'Ever since he gave me his magic – you know . . . It's been . . . there's something. I can't explain it.'

'There was something long before that,' Em said. 'And if you really *were* being honest with yourself, you'd admit it.'

'There wasn't.' I shook my head vehemently. 'Not for me anyway. It was always Seth.'

But Seth wasn't here now. The fish-hook in my heart twisted.

Emmaline didn't answer. We walked on, shoulder to shoulder, listening to the sound of the keening wind and the sea.

CHAPTER TEN

'Can I speak to you for a moment, Anna?'

I looked up from shoving books into my bag, startled.

'Me, Ms Wright?'

'You are the only Anna in the class, yes,' Ms Wright said dryly.

Emmaline gave me a slightly alarmed look and I shrugged. Ms Wright perched on the edge of her desk as the class filed out, tapping her heel on the lino. Emmaline was the last to leave, reluctantly trailing out of the door and, as she did so, Ms Wright edged it shut with her elbow and came over to where I sat.

'Anna, is everything OK?'

'Have you been talking to Mrs Finch?'

'Yes, actually. And Mr Henderson. They're both concerned.'

I didn't say anything – I couldn't think what to say. Ms Wright pulled up a chair.

'Look, I know you've had a tough term, what with Seth leaving—'

'You don't understand.' My throat was suddenly tight

and sore and it was hard to speak.

'I know it's impossible to believe at your age, but I do, I really do. I may be pushing thirty, but I remember my first break up like it was yesterday and how completely agonising it was. I understand what you're going through – but you *can't* throw away all your hard work.'

Throw it away? I looked at her, my face stony, and she bit her lip.

'OK, maybe throwing it away is a bit unfair – but you were set for As across the board a few months ago. Now, if you scrape Cs and Ds it'll be solely on the marks from your earlier modules. Your last essay was a shambles and in class you look like you're barely here. You're going to end up in resits at this rate. Is that what you want – to lose out on university and spend a year packing fish and doing retakes?'

I sat in silence. There was nothing I could say. Nothing she'd believe, anyway. She looked at me, her eyes full of mute exasperation.

'Is there something wrong at home? Or something else? Whatever it is, please talk to someone. Me if you like – or your dad. Or your GP, maybe. Whatever's going on, it's solveable, somehow. I promise it is. You don't have to deal with it alone.'

I let my fingers close on the edge of the desk, my nails biting into the soft, frayed wood, and tried to tune out her attempt at understanding, her impossible, ignorant kindness. Since Seth left I'd had my magic under control – mainly – but I felt close to losing it now.

'Anna,' she said at last, her voice mixing sympathy with exasperation, 'are you even listening? Do you realize how serious this is – what it means for your grades if you don't pull things together? I just . . . I hate to see someone with your promise throwing it all away for the sake of some worthless bloke.'

Worthless. I put my hand to my eyes, closing them, closing out her concerned face and the incomprehension in her bright blue eyes. I pushed my fingers against my lids, pushing back the unfairness of it all, the rage that roared inside me, the howling loneliness.

There was silence, and I felt her waiting presence, waiting for me to say something. Then, with a creak of the chair, she stood and I heard her heels click away. The classroom door opened and swung closed again. And at last I was alone.

The magic boiled and roared and rose inside me, suffocating me. I swallowed, tried to breathe, tried not to lose it.

At last, when I could finally trust myself to speak, I got out my phone.

'Again,' I shouted, and a stunning spell hit me like a punch, sending me sprawling into the pine needles. But it didn't matter, I was conscious and not bleeding from any important places. Being flat on my face didn't matter. This had been by far our most successful session; I'd been matching Abe blow for blow ever since I'd opened fire with a blinding volley of illusions.

Now we were doing basic charm-and-defence work –
let the other person hit you as hard as they could with a
spell and try to repel it.

I scrambled to my feet, sweating and shaking.

'Again!'

'No.' Abe shook his head, his chest heaving. 'You've
had enough.'

'You mean, *you've* had enough.'

'OK, if it makes you feel better, I've had enough.'

'Fight me.' I slapped him with a stinging blast of magic
and he staggered, but shook his head again.

'Stop it.'

'Fight!' I flung out again, smashing him sideways into
the trunk of a pine tree. He gasped and sank to his knees,
and when he stood there was blood on his cheek.

'Stop it! I'm not going to fight you when you're like this
– you're shaking with exhaustion.'

'How can I improve if you never push me? Stop being so
bloody gallant. Fight me properly – I have to know how to
defend myself. Fight dirty!'

'You've had *enough*.'

'Don't tell me when I've had enough!' I shouted.
Electrical sparks crackled across my skin and I pointed my
finger at Abe. 'Or are you just afraid?'

'Try me,' Abe snarled.

A stab of electricity crashed, white and blue, across the
clearing, scorching the pine-needles beneath Abe's feet –

151

and then suddenly Abe was gone. In his place cowered my dad, crouched like a frightened child, his arms curled above his head. His clothes were scorched and burnt and there was smoke coming from his hair.

'Anna!' he cried, his voice cracked with terror and pain. 'For God's sake, what are you doing?'

'Dad!'

I ran across the clearing and fell to my knees in the soft forest debris, still hot and scorched from my blast. Dad trembled as I prised his arms away from his head, holding him, searching his face for injuries.

'Oh, Dad! Are you hurt?'

His face was blank and stiff with uncomprehending fear and I flung my arms around him, burying my face in the crook of his neck.

'I'm sorry,' I gasped. 'I'm so, so sorry.'

'You should be,' said a voice. I stiffened. Something was wrong. Instead of the familiar scents of woodsmoke, soap and cooking, Dad smelled of – Abe.

I lifted my face.

It *was* Abe. Abe's body I was wrapped around. Abe's face, two inches away, his expression twisted in a grim smile.

I leaped to my feet, a tide of blood flooding up from my heart.

'Hey.' He held up a hand, reading the fury in my eyes. 'You asked me to play dirty. You want to be prepared? You *can't* be prepared. I can't put you through what they will

– because I won't inflict that on you. I *can't*.'

'You bastard.'

'This is nothing. *Nothing*. Don't fool yourself.'

'Is that what you think? That I'm fooling myself that I can find my mum?'

'No.' His grim expression faded and he looked suddenly very tired. The blood on his cheek stood out, raw and livid. 'I think you can probably do anything you set your mind to. I just think you may not be prepared for what you find.'

We sat down beneath a tree and Abe pulled out a bottle of water and took a long swig. He passed it to me, and I drank thirstily and then passed it back, and we sat in silence for a while, listening to the sounds of the forest returning to tranquillity after our fight. A wood pigeon crooned somewhere deep in the woods, its woodwind coo a strange background to my tumbling, churning thoughts.

'I'm starting to think I may never find her,' I said, the words harsh in the soft, sunlit quiet. Abe turned to look at me, his eyes an unfathomable, unreadable black.

'You're giving up now? After all this?'

I knew what he meant. After all the deaths, the destruction, the horror upon horror – if I gave up now, all that would be for nothing. Seth would live his life in pain, chained to the sea and a crutch. And I would live my life in the dark for ever, always wondering.

'I don't know where to go, what to do next. I thought the riddle would tell me something – show me where to go next – but I can't even find that.'

'Where does the trail stop?'

'After she returned to the Ealdwitan headquarters to steal the riddle. That was when I was six weeks old. After that, the trail goes cold. I have no idea where she went – she just disappeared. Maybe she did commit suicide.'

'The more I hear about your mother,' Abe said, 'the more I'm convinced that the one thing she'd never have done is kill herself. Anyway, it seems to me that you do know where she went next – you've forgotten one thing.'

'What?'

'The charm under your step.'

'It was in Russian,' I said slowly. 'But that doesn't mean she went to Russia, does it? Maybe she met a Russian witch in London.'

'Not possible.' Abe said shortly.

'Why not?'

'Jeez, you know you need to do a course in witch history so we can stop with the bloody lectures.' He sighed and then said, 'Look, the Russians used to be one of the most powerful witch-clans in the world – and one of the most ruthless. They did some dreadful things, practices we've completely outlawed here . . .' He grimaced and then seemed to force himself on. 'By the turn of the century their leader pretty much controlled everything – he had the tsar and tsarina in the palm of his hand and, through them, the whole of Russia. But they pushed too far. They brought down . . .'

'Revolution,' I said, suddenly understanding. Abe nodded.

'The witches were sent to the salt mines along with the rest of the ruling elite. We heard rumours. Rumours that they were still there, that they'd been living and breeding and feeding off each other. But behind the Iron Curtain, no one knew.'

'And when the Iron Curtain fell?' I asked. Abe shrugged.

'If they're there, they're biding their time. I've never met a Russian witch, never known anyone who has. The legends live on, of course. The things they used to do, the excisions, the transfusions, the puppet-armies . . . but they themselves are silent.'

'OK . . .' I said slowly. 'So my mother went to Russia then. But perhaps she went before I was born. That's equally possible, right?'

'I don't think so. Look, she didn't show any paranoia, any worries until she was pregnant with you – right? Whether she stumbled on the prophecy while she was pregnant, or whether she knew about it before and only clicked to the meaning later, I don't know. But it sounds like it was quite sudden. From your dad's account, she spent nine months getting more and more desperate, trying route after route to protect herself and you – but that's quite a narrow window for her to fly to Russia. I think your dad would have noticed if she'd left the country. No: I think it was quite late on that she decided she couldn't protect you herself and she turned to the Others.'

'The others?'

'That's what the Ealdwitan have always called them – the Other side. As if they were the only other witch-clan in the world that mattered. And for a long time they were – the Ealdwitan and the Others. The two most powerful witch-clans in the world.'

'The Others . . .' I whispered. Something jangled in the back of my head, like a chord with a strange, false note. 'The other . . . side . . .'

My school bag was hanging from a branch and I stood up, scrabbling inside for my purse, suddenly feverish with urgency. The piece of paper was folded into quarters, tucked inside the space meant for notes and business cards. I pulled it out, trying not to tear the worn paper.

'This is a note she left.' I held it out to Abe. 'The only note she left for me. Read it.'

'Anna, are you sure—'

'Don't be stupid!' I snapped. 'This is important, read it!'

I watched as his eyes skimmed down the page, down to the poem.

'Read it aloud,' I said.

'"Death is nothing at all",' Abe quoted. '"I have only slipped away into the next room. I am but waiting for you for an interval. Somewhere very near. Just around the corner. On the other side. All is well".'

He frowned at the paper and then looked up at me, 'Hang on, I've read that poem somewhere recently, haven't I?'

'Yes, it was on the back of the order of service at Bran's funeral, a longer version. But one line was missing from Bran's version: "On the other side". The original version of the poem doesn't contain those words. I thought she'd just misquoted. But now . . .'

'Now, I'd say it's pretty clear.' Abe looked at the page, his black brows drawn into a scowl. There was something in his expression that made me shiver.

'What? Why are you looking like that?'

'Well, first of all, it looks like the Russian witches are back. And for a group that was once the most powerful witch-clan in the world, I don't think they'll be planning to sit at home making tea and cakes. Second, they gave your mother quite a lot. Some pretty strong charms, for a start. Shelter. Asylum from whoever was following her. Anonymity. The question is, what did she give them?'

We both looked at each other and I could see my own thoughts reflected in his black eyes. I could see again the dagger in Thaddeus Corax's back. Hear the roar of waters as the Neckinger slipped its chains and threw off the enchantments of centuries. Feel the fear in the heart of the Ealdwitan.

Someone had betrayed them.

My mother had betrayed them.

CHAPTER ELEVEN

I didn't sleep that night. I didn't try to. I sat with my duvet hunched round my shoulders, staring into the wooded dark and listening to the far-off crash and roar of the waves breaking against the cliffs.

I had answers now – to some of my questions at least. But one question was still gnawing at my insides.

Who could I trust?

My mother had given up everything – any hope of a happy life with her husband and child – to keep me safe. She'd turned traitor; betrayed her parents and her country to secure my safety. And I no longer knew what I should be running from.

I thought of Simon's words, his idea that she'd always meant to arm me to defend myself. She'd limited her enchantments so that one day I could leave, one day I could fight. But fight who?

Words chased themselves around my head, twisting and coiling and twining into impossible contradictions. The words of my mother's letter, the words of the riddle, the words of the charms. All wreathed in smoke and mirrors and slyness. I'd never met a witch who could answer a straight question with a straight answer – apart from Abe, perhaps.

A cool greyness tinged the sky over the east of the forest and I knew that dawn wasn't far off – and with it Dad, and school, and everything mundane and lovely and comforting.

But none of it was for me.

There was no way back. There was *never* a way back, never a way to unlearn what you'd learnt, to un-be what you were.

I thought of Seth, setting sail halfway across the world to try to escape his demons, and I knew, achingly, how he felt. But when I left, I would be taking the demons with me. Because the demons were in me, and always would be, until I found the truth. And the truth lay in Russia, I was sure of that now. And my mother was in Russia. Dead or alive, she was there.

There was no way back. I could only keep going. Into the shadows.

The thought should have terrified me – but instead it gave me a strange peace. No more running. No more hiding and pretending. Whatever lay out there, waiting for me, I would face it. I would fight.

I couldn't escape my destiny – but I could run to meet it. Instead of being backed into a corner, I could choose my own ending to all this – even if it was still an ending.

It was with a strange lightness in my heart that I lay down, pulling my duvet over myself. The grey light pooled on the floor beneath my window, cool and calm, as I closed my eyes and slept at last.

I told Emmaline first.

'You're mad.' She put her knife and fork down with a clatter on the canteen table, her pale face suddenly spotted with pink, high on her cheekbones.

'It's the only way.'

'But *now*? What about your exams? You'd throw all that away?'

I laughed – it was so comically close to my conversation with Ms Wright.

'I've thrown all that away already, Em. I'm not going to pass at this rate – not with all this hanging over me. The exams are in – what – four weeks?'

'Three,' Em corrected automatically.

'Can you really see me buckling down to a discussion of Greek vases while—'

I was interrupted by a sudden collective gasp of horror from the other side of the canteen.

'Oh my God!' I heard and 'My aunt works there.'

Emmaline and I exchanged a look and then we got up and hurried across.

A group of people were crowded round a laptop, hands pressed to faces, eyes wide with shock. As I craned over the top of their heads I saw the screen was playing live news footage of central London – and it looked like a bomb had gone off. Behind the commentator's urgent announcements there was the sound of wailing sirens and helicopters.

'Turn up the sound,' someone called and suddenly the canteen hubbub was drowned by the commentator's booming voice.

'. . . collapse of both Tower Bridge *and* Vauxhall Bridge, in a feared attack on the MI5 headquarters on the south bank of the Thames. All London Underground lines have been evacuated after reports of "a tide of gore" issuing from the deepest lines and the network is now closed while investigators try to ascertain the source. For people just tuning in, this is a report of the news that central London has been brought to a standstill by a series of devastating bridge collapses, following similar and still-unexplained events earlier this week in south London. A Whitehall source told the BBC that officials were treating the events as a potential terrorist attack, but environmental campaigners have pointed to evidence that last week's collapses in south London appear to have been spontaneous. All roads leading to and from Tower Bridge and Vauxhall Bridge are at a stand-still, the remaining central London bridges are being closed as a precautionary measure, and police are urging people *not* to travel to central London unless their journey is urgent. Once again, this is the news that . . .'

Emmaline turned to me, her face blank and white.

'What's happening?'

'I don't know.' I stared at her, wondering if my expression was as shocked and fearful as hers. 'I only know I have to go to London. Before . . .'

'Before you leave,' Emmaline said. There was none of her usual acidity in her voice, only fear.

The bell went for classes and Emmaline busied herself packing up her bag, avoiding my gaze. When she finally looked up, I was astonished to see her eyelashes were wet.

'Em, don't cry!' I put my arms around her and she held me tight as if she'd never let go.

'Don't go!' she said desperately. 'Please don't go.'

There was nothing I could say. I only hugged her, feeling all her bones against mine, thinking of everything I owed her, a huge debt of help and love.

At last the third bell went and she disentangled her arms from mine and wiped her eyes.

'I'm sorry, I didn't mean that.' She pulled her heavy bag to her shoulder. 'I know you have to do what you have to do. When will you go?'

'Soon.' I looked out of the window at the flawless sky and imagined the blood-soaked Thames beneath that same insouciant blue. 'As soon as I've been to London.'

I skived my last lesson and went straight to the station, leaving an answerphone message for Dad about a fictitious revision session with Emmaline.

On the train up to London I tried phone after phone – my grandmother's office, her home, her mobile, Marcus' mobile, my grandmother's home again – and in between I ran over and over what could have happened, imagining worse and worse scenarios. If Vauxhall Bridge had gone, did that mean the Effra was free too? Had another Chair . . . ? My mind flinched away, refusing to complete the sentence. But the question lurked, dark and unspoken.

As the train drew into London I got up and stood by the door, tensed and ready, not certain what I would find. I had my hand on the 'open' button, and my bag on my shoulder. I don't know what I expected – I'd lived in London through terrorist attacks and crises, but this was something different.

Whatever I expected, it wasn't what I found: Marcus, facing me exactly as the train slid to a halt, his black overcoat flapping in the wind, his face framed in the grimy window.

'Your grandmother's alive,' he said as the doors opened.

'Oh thank God.' I jumped on to the platform. I didn't know what to do, what to say. I wanted to kiss him for being alive and for having come to tell me about my grandmother. But instead I took a deep breath, trying to control my suddenly racing heart. 'Th-thank you. How did you . . . ?'

'I got your message. I tried to call back, but you must have been in a tunnel.'

'What happened?'

'Edward Throgmorton has died; natural causes or not, no one seems to know. But the Fleet and the Effra have broken free. The Chairs fought – fought hard. It was . . .' he stopped and for the first time he looked shaken, groping for words. 'Anna – your grandmother . . .'

163

'You said she's OK?' I grabbed his arm hard, harder than I'd meant, and he winced.

'I said she's alive. She's not OK.'

'Just *tell* me.'

'She's hurt. Badly.'

'Can I see her?'

'Yes, of course. I've got a taxi waiting.'

I heaved my bag on to my shoulder and followed him.

The cab was slow and Marcus sat, biting his thumbnail and staring out of the window. I could see the muscles moving in his jaw as he clenched his teeth with each delay. I wanted to ask him what had happened, but I didn't dare, with the cab driver just inches away and only thin plexi-glass between us.

'Sorry, mate,' the taxi driver said over his shoulder as we waited in yet another jam. 'It's gridlock – all these bombs or whatever it's supposed to be. They've shut all the bloody roads round Hyde Park and what with the underground being down . . . Oh here we go. Moving again.'

Marcus said nothing, only nodded without speaking, but as the taxi drew to yet another halt at a set of red lights I saw a vein tick in his temple. He looked at me and bit his lip, and then at the taxi driver, who was staring furiously out of the windscreen. With great caution, Marcus lifted his finger to the window, pointed at the closest set of lights and whispered a word under his breath.

The light turned green.

Marcus glanced at me and gave a slightly guilty shrug, but I didn't care. At this point I would have jumped on a broomstick if it got me there faster.

At last, after what seemed like an interminable crawl through Kensington, the cab turned into the broad terraced crescent where my grandmother lived and I jumped out and knocked at the gleaming black front door. It swung open to reveal Miss Vane.

'Is she here?' I asked. Miss Vane nodded. 'Can I see her?'

'Of course.' She stood aside and Marcus and I walked past her into the hall. 'She's in her bedroom.'

My heart started to thud again as we climbed the carpeted stairs. It wasn't just Miss Vane's expression, her worried look. It was the wrongness of it all – my grandmother, my indomitable grandmother, in bed in the day. I'd never seen her ill, never seen her succumb to tiredness or pain. And now . . .

At the landing I faced her tall, white-painted bedroom door and took a deep breath. Then I knocked.

'*Caaah* . . .' it was a harsh croak.

'Go in,' Miss Vane said.

My grandmother was lying on top of the high, white bed, her head lolling against the pillows. And she looked as if she were dying. That was my immediate, crippling thought. Her black hair was loosed from its rigid chignon and straggled across the pillow. And there was something wrong with her face: her expression was strange, lopsided. Her dark eyes watched me with quiet intensity, following

165

me as I crept across the room to kneel by her side, but her head did not turn.

'Grandmother?'

'A-aaah.'

'Wh-what's happened?' I tried to speak normally, but I found myself taking great gulping breaths between my teeth, forcing back my panic.

'She's had a stroke, I think.' Marcus' voice was level and dead. 'Is that right, ma'am?'

'Essss.' It was a hiss, no more. Accompanied by the faintest of lolling nods.

'Oh my God.' I pressed my hands to my mouth. My breath shuddered through my nose, before I could trust myself to speak. 'P-please, you should be in hospital.'

'No.' That word at least was intelligible and her eyes flashed fire as she said it.

'I'm sorry, Anna.' It was Miss Vane's quiet voice behind my shoulder. 'I did take her in, but she discharged herself.'

'But the doctors,' I cried, 'how could they let her go? Couldn't they declare her unfit – unsound – *something*?'

'She persuaded them.' Miss Vane held out her hands helplessly. 'She – she can be very persuasive.'

'Get back in there,' I said fiercely, ignoring Miss Vane, ignoring Marcus. I knelt by the bed and took my grandmother's thin, ringed hand in mine. 'Get back in hospital. You have to get well, do you hear me? You *have* to get well. I will not . . . You can't – another person can't die. You can't!'

Send them away . . . The voice spoke in my head, a thread, a whisper, so quiet I had to still everything, even my heart, to hear it. *Miss Vane. Marcus. I have something to say.*

I looked up.

'Can you give us a moment alone?'

They both nodded and turned to go, their feet silent on the thick carpet. I heard the door click shut and then the thin whisper filled my head.

We all die. I hope my time has not come yet. But if it has—

'No!' I shouted. I put my hands over my ears, knowing what was coming. But nothing could shut out my grandmother's insistence.

If it has, you must seize the Chair. Please, Anna. Please.

'No! You will *not* die! I won't let you.' Tears were running down my face, hot and angry. I pulled her limp, unresisting hand to my cheek and gripped it there, the stones of her rings cutting into my cheek. 'You can't. I'm going to stop this.'

Stop what?

'The traitor – the person who's doing this.' I put her hand very carefully back on the white linen cover and then stood, wiping my cheeks with my sleeve. 'Whoever's done this to you. Grandmother – you said the traitor could have been acting for another country.'

Yes . . . She closed her eyes. The voice in my head was almost gone, it was so faint.

'Which country? Which?'

No answer.

'Did you think –' I swiped my face fiercely and then pushed back my hair '– did you think it could be . . . Russia? The Others?'

No answer. I waited, watching the rise and fall of her chest beneath her nightgown and the restless movement of her eyes beneath the thin lavender lids.

'Grandmother?'

No answer.

I knelt again, resting my face on the covers, feeling the cool softness of the linen against my hot forehead.

'*Grandmother* . . .' I reached out with all my magic, reaching for her across the dark void where she'd retreated. 'Please . . . don't go. Did you ever think the spy might be – Isabella? Is that what you thought?'

It was like a cool sighing breath in my head, a relief, a surrender, a handing over of her burden of dark suspicions.

Yes, she said, inside my skull. And then she turned her face slowly to the wall. The only sound was the whisper of her breath on the pillow, and my footsteps on the carpet as I turned to go.

Outside the bedroom I stood with my back to the wall, struggling to keep a hold of myself. A fierce black wave broke over my head, drowning me, and I turned and pressed my cheek against the wall, digging my nails into the wallpaper as if it could anchor me to reality.

If you'd asked me the day before if I loved my grandmother I probably would have said yes. But only because it seemed like what you should say. How could you not love your grandmother? In reality, I wouldn't have known. My fierce, indomitable, iron-souled grandmother – how could you love something made of iron?

Marcus came up the stairs, his face full of concern, and he put his hand on my shoulder.

'Don't,' I said.

He took it away and stood watching me for a moment. Then he walked quietly back down the stairs towards the kitchen and I was alone.

I opened the kitchen door at the foot of the stairs and Marcus raised his head from where he was sitting at the table.

'I'm sorry,' I said. 'For before. I didn't mean . . .'

'Hey. It's fine. Truly.' He pushed a full jug of coffee towards me. 'Here. You look like you need something. Or would something stronger . . . ?' He nodded towards the door of the wine cellar and I shook my head.

'No, coffee's fine. Coffee's good.' I pushed back my tangled hair and suddenly realized how tired I was. 'It feels a bit early for wine. What time is it, anyway?'

'Only half-four. You can get back to Winter for supper, if you leave now.'

Leave? How could I leave, with my grandmother like this? But how could I stay knowing what I knew . . .

'Marcus,' I said. Then I stopped.

'Yes?' He looked at me over the rim of his cup, his eyes soft and liquid like melted chocolate, the lamplight glinting off his chestnut hair.

Was this stupid? Was I mad to go to Russia, plunge into the unknown? What could I do – one inexperienced girl against a swirling, shifting, malignant uncertainty?

'I . . .' I began again, then my courage failed me and I sighed. 'Nothing. Do – do you think she'll be OK? Elizabeth?'

'I don't know,' he said. 'I'm not going to make you false promises – you know the reality as well as I do. But she's as tough as they come and she's still holding the Falconbrook, which is pretty phenomenal, considering.'

'What about the other rivers?'

'The Tyburn was looking dicey at one stage, but it's calmed down a bit. Margot and Knyvet are doing what they can with the Fleet. The Neckinger and the Effra are still free. We're holding on.' *For now*, was the unspoken coda. Until the next explosion, the next disaster. Until the spy struck again.

'What do you think they're trying to do?' I asked. He sighed.

'I don't know. They've made no demands, so I can only think – they want to destroy us. Destroy the Ealdwitan. Take over. If that happens – well, it won't be pretty.'

There was silence and I stared down into the muddy depths of my cup. I swirled the last mouthful and the sooty dregs from the cafetiere rose up, like a cloud of tiny starlings swirling in a small dark sky.

'There's something I have to tell you,' I said at last.

'What?'

'I won't be here to help. I'm – I'm going to . . . Russia.'

For a minute he said nothing at all – the kitchen was completely still with astonishment. The only sound I could hear was the inexorable tick, tick of the clock, ticking down the time I had left. At last, as the silence stretched, I said, 'Marcus?'

'*Russia?*' His voice burst out, loud in the quiet room. 'With all this happening at home? Why?'

'Because I'm starting to think . . .' I ground to a halt, then forced myself on. 'I think that I may know the identity of the spy.'

Marcus leaned across the table, his fingers clenched around his cup. I could almost feel his shock reverberating through the wooden table top. Then he spoke and his voice was harsh with urgency.

'Who? For God's sake, tell me! W*ho?*'

I swallowed. Could I really do this? Could I really voice this horrible, disloyal, poisonous suspicion to Marcus?

'*Who?*' he shouted suddenly, so loud that I jumped and almost dropped my cup. 'My father was *killed* by that damn spy! Doesn't that give me some kind of right to your suspicions?'

He was right. Of course he was right. I gripped the cup hard, my fingers damp and clammy, slipping on the china.

'My . . . my mother.'

'*What?*' I don't know what he'd been expecting – but that threw him. There was no faking the blank astonishment on his face. Then his expression turned to outrage. 'No! Not Isabella – she loved . . . She'd never . . .'

He trailed off, his face blank with a shock too great to process all at once. I could almost see his thoughts whirring furiously, trying to piece together the missing parts of the past.

'I'm sorry, Marcus,' I said. 'I know you loved her – but she didn't kill herself, you know that. It was too planned, too calculated. She did everything she could to protect me – and I think she went too far. I think she gave herself up – to the Others. If I can track her down—'

'Then what?'

'I don't know,' I said. 'But I have to try. It's better than sitting here waiting for the axe to fall, waiting for another death.'

He said nothing, just sat opposite, staring down at his hands, his face like a mask. What was he thinking? I found Marcus so hard to read – he had the smooth inscrutability of all the Ealdwitan: a smooth, shining surface with fast currents beneath.

'I'm going,' I said. 'One way or another, I'm going. I'm fed up with waiting and looking over my shoulder. *I'm* taking control. Do you understand? If I go out to meet this – whatever it is – it's better, anything's better than being hunted down like an animal.'

'So you're really set on this?' he said. There was something odd in his voice: resignation perhaps. Defeat. 'There's nothing I can say?'

'Nothing. I'm going.'

'Good luck,' he said at last. He raised his gaze from the table, his brown eyes dark and troubled. 'You'll need it.'

The train drew into Winter station at dusk and I sat on the bench by the road, waiting for the bus in the rain. It was hard to believe it was almost summer, with the drizzling clouds shutting out the sky. I watched the drips pattering off the station canopy and the image of my grandmother's bleached, lopsided face rose up before me like a ghost. I shut my eyes – but it was still there, haunting me. And her voice in my head saying, *You must seize the Chair. Please Anna. Please.*

'Anna,' said a voice. 'Anna.'

It took me a moment to realize it was a real voice, not in my head – then I opened my eyes abruptly and found Caroline Flint standing in front of me.

'C-Caroline!' I was so surprised that my voice stammered and I wanted to kick myself. I didn't have to be afraid of her, not any more.

'Can I sit down?' she asked. I nodded and she sat, chewing a tress of golden hair. I realized, to my surprise, that she was as nervous as me, maybe more. She pulled out a packet of cigarettes and lit one, drawing the smoke down deep and exhaling it with a shuddery nervous breath.

'Sorry, you don't smoke. Do you – d'you mind?' she asked, her mouth lopsided around the cigarette.

'It's fine,' I said, but what I really wanted to ask was, *Why are you here?*

Caroline stared into the rain in a way that looked as if she was asking herself the same question. She took another long shaky drag and then spoke.

'Look, I heard what you said – to Emmaline in the canteen. I wasn't listening, I promise. I mean I wasn't trying to, but . . .'

'It's OK,' I said. My voice was level but my heart was sinking. I should have learned my damn lesson by now. What had we said? Anything compromising? I ran back over the conversation in my head but all I could remember was talking about Russia.

'You're leaving.'

'Yes.'

'Anna . . .' She stopped and then said in a rush, 'It's not because of me, is it? Because, if you knew how bad I feel about what I did to you – shopping you to those men, to the Malleus . . . I'm so, so sorry. If I'd known how they'd treat you, I'd never have done it – I was just so angry, about you and Seth.'

Oh. I shook my head.

'It's not because of you. It's lots of things: school, home – other stuff . . .' I trailed off and the last reason hung unspoken. Caroline knew though.

'We've both lost him now,' she said sadly.

'Yes,' I said. I swallowed. 'I'm – I'm sorry I came between you. I hope you know that.'

'I think I loved him,' she said slowly. 'I think I really did – but it was never like it was between the two of you. He . . . he'd *die* for you, even I can see that.'

I fought back the urge to snap that I didn't *want* him to die for me. What good would that do anyone?

'He still loves you,' she said. 'I saw you both at Bran's funeral. He looked . . . bad, didn't he?'

He looked broken, I thought. But I kept silent.

'Isn't there anything you can do?' Caroline asked.

'No.' I said. 'There's nothing either of us can do. We're . . .' Bran's harsh voice came suddenly into my head, as clear as if he was speaking over my shoulder. 'We're oil and water. We were never meant to be together.'

'But you love him!'

'It's not enough.'

'It has to be!' Caroline said desperately. 'If it's because of what I did . . .'

'It wasn't you,' I said. 'I promise. It was other stuff – problems between us.'

'You going away – are you going after him?'

'No. I'm going somewhere else. Russia.'

'Wow!' She blinked. 'Why there?'

'Because I think I've got family there.'

'You think?'

'I know it sounds nuts, but—'

'Anna,' said a voice behind us. I jumped and turned.

It was Abe. He was standing just outside the tiny station canopy, the rain running down his face and throat and soaking into his already soaked T-shirt. His body looked cold and drenched. But his face looked like he was planning to punch someone.

Something uneasy twisted inside me, but I only said, 'Hi, Abe. This is Caroline. Caroline – Abe.'

Abe ignored Caroline completely.

'Lift?'

I wavered, but Emmaline's words last week still echoed in my head. *Try being honest with yourself.* I shook my head.

'No, I'm fine, thanks, Abe. I'll get the bus.'

'You'll be waiting a while,' Caroline said. She looked at Abe under her lashes and blew a draught of smoke towards him. 'It's half-day closing today. The last bus went at four.'

'No! Are you sure?'

She nodded.

'Sorry, I would've said, but I thought you were waiting for a lift.'

'Oh crap.' I looked at my watch. 'I'd better phone Dad.'

'Don't be stupid,' Abe said crossly. 'I'm going your way right now.'

I knew when I was cornered. 'All right. Caroline, do you need a lift?'

'No, don't worry.' She stood and opened her umbrella. 'I'm only five minutes away. See you tomorrow.'

She walked away up the street and Abe watched her as

she rounded the corner. As she disappeared into the rainy dusk, he turned to me.

'What the hell are you on about?'

'I'm *sorry*? Where do you get off speaking to me like that!'

'Russia,' he spat. His fists were clenched and he wore an expression that would have made me quake, a few months ago. Now it only made me sigh.

'Abe—'

'You're going to *Russia*? Or do I need a hearing aid?'

'No, you heard right. I'm sorry, I wasn't planning to tell you like this—'

'So you *were* planning to tell me? Or were you just going to wait until I got your dog-tags in the mail?'

'Why would I wear dog-tags?'

'Don't change the subject. You know what I mean. How long have you been plotting this?'

'I haven't been plotting! Don't be so melodramatic.'

'So it's melodramatic to care whether you kill yourself chasing ghosts across—'

'It's none of your business!' I shouted. 'Why do you care anyway?'

'For Christ's sake, Anna! I care because . . .' He pushed his hands into his hair, the rain washing over his bare forearms and down his T-shirt. The thin material stuck to his ribs, showing every line from his throat to his belt. His chest was heaving.

We stood, facing each other and then he let his hands

fall to his sides. The rain dripped down his cheekbones and the bridge of his nose. If I hadn't known better I might have thought he was crying.

'I care because I'm your friend,' he said at last. He wiped the rain from his face with his forearm. Then he took my school bag and we walked in silence up the road to his car.

As we drove up the hill towards my house I tried to think what to say, how to explain, but it was easier to sit in silence, listening to the drumming of the rain and the squeak-swish of the wipers frantically swiping back and forth. Abe drove grimly, his face, in the reflected glow from the dashboard instruments, pale and bleak.

As we drew up outside Wicker House I was surprised to see it was in darkness. Dad must be out. The automatic light above the porch clicked on as Abe ground to a halt, but the rest of the house was still and black.

Abe was silent as we pulled up and for a minute I sat, waiting for him to say something. Then, realizing that he wasn't going to, I reached for the door handle.

'Thanks,' I said, not wanting to leave in silence. 'For the lift.'

'Wait.' His hand closed around mine. I swallowed.

'What?'

'Anna . . .' His eyes were black as oil, his face white and set. 'Do you remember saying once that you were grateful?'

'Of course. I was. I am. For everything.'

'And you asked me if there was something you could do for me, in return.'

I swallowed again, and tried half-heartedly to move my hand, but Abe's grip was firm; not painful, but strong.

'Abe—'

'Please, don't. Just let me speak for a second. I haven't ever asked you for anything – and I've done a lot; everyone's done a lot. Maya, Simon, Emmaline, Sienna – we've all helped you.'

Helped me? He'd risked his life and his magic for me. I owed him everything.

'I know.' I tried to keep my voice steady. 'Believe me I know, but—'

'I've never asked for anything in return – but I'm asking you for something now.'

'Abe—'

'I want to come. To Russia.'

For a second I was too shocked to speak. Then the surprise was drowned in a tidal wave of fear for him.

'No. It's too dangerous.'

'It'll be far less dangerous with two. Look, you're powerful but you've got no experience. Whatever you want to do there, you're more likely to succeed with my help. And I've never asked you for anything, you admit that. You owe me. You owe me this.'

'No.'

'I'm not going to stand by and watch you walk off into the unknown to kill yourself.'

'If I do, that's my business. I'm not dragging you into this, you can't ask me to.'

'You're not dragging me – and I'm not asking.'

'No! You're blackmailing me into this—'

'That's not fair!'

I wrenched my hand away from his. 'You're trying to be some kind of knight errant with a defenceless damsel – but I'm not defenceless and I'm *not* yours to protect.'

'I know!' he shouted. There was silence in the car, and I listened to our torn breathing, and tried to think what to say, how to make him see the stupidity of his request. Then, very quietly, as if the words hurt him, he said, 'I know. D'you think I don't know that?'

What could I say to that?

I was still groping for a reply when Abe spoke.

'I'm sorry.' His voice was very low. 'But I . . . I couldn't stand to lose someone else.'

And suddenly I wasn't angry any more. Only heart-sick at his pain, that what he wanted, I couldn't give.

We sat in silence, listening to the rain on the roof of the car and, as Abe's ragged breathing grew calmer, I took my courage in my hands.

'Abe – that girl. The one with the Ealdwitan. What happened?'

He didn't ask me which girl. He knew which one I meant. He leaned back in his seat and, as he did so, the automatic porch light clicked off, leaving the car and his face in darkness.

'Emmaline told you,' he said at last. I couldn't tell what the emotion was in his voice, only that he was holding it back, trying to keep level.

'Yes.'

'What did she say?'

'Not much. Only what I forced out of her – that there was a girl. That it ended, badly. That she died. That the Ealdwitan punished you.'

'Yes.'

'Did you . . . love her?'

'Yes.' He drew a breath; I heard the sharp intake, and then the shuddering sigh as he let it go.

'What happened?'

'It's over. She's gone.'

'It doesn't help, though, does it? Not to talk about the person you've lost.'

'No.' He was silent for a long while and I thought, *That's it, I won't press it. He won't say any more.* Then he began to speak. 'Her name was Rachel. She was . . . she was an outwith.'

'An outwith?' I couldn't keep the shock out of my voice. 'You? I never thought . . .'

'Thought what?'

'You . . .' I stumbled, trying not to hurt him. 'It's just – you've always seemed to think it was so impossible. To love someone without magic.'

'I don't think it's impossible,' he said softly. 'I just know it is. I learned that the hard way.'

'What do you mean?'

181

'She had cancer. She was dying.' He stopped, swallowed so that I heard the movement of his throat, and then forced himself on. 'I was stupid. I tried to prevent it. I should have known better. I poured all my magic into healing her – and it was futile. She died anyway and the Ealdwitan punished me.'

'How?' I whispered. 'Why?'

'Why? For interfering with the outwith, of course. For not being careful. I didn't bother to try to hide what I was doing – the doctors knew there was something up, they just didn't know what. I'd crossed a line, I knew that. As for how – well, the Ealdwitan knew there wasn't much they could do to *me*. I'd lost Rachel. I didn't care any more. So they punished my family.'

'And your family cut you off?'

'Completely. It was like I died. They mourned my death. I haven't spoken to any of them since the day they kicked me out. I have no family now, except Simon.'

'When . . . how old were you?' I whispered.

'It was a long time ago. I was sixteen when I met Rachel. Seventeen when she died.'

'Oh Abe.' I shut my eyes in the darkness, shutting out the picture of a seventeen-year-old boy alone with nothing but his grief and the clothes on his back, as he'd once told me.

'It was a long time ago,' he said again. And he put a hand up to his face, wiping something away.

I leaned across the car, awkwardly, and I put my arms

around him. At first it felt like holding a stone statue, but then his arms crept up, almost in spite of himself and his hands touched my back, uncertainly, as if he was feeling his way. I put my hand on his chest, feeling the hot skin beneath his still-damp shirt, the curve of his ribs, the thud of his heart. And I sent my magic down, deep into his skin and his bones and his heart, trying to heal the unhealable.

At last he spoke, his voice shaky.

'You should go. It's getting late. D'you want me to come in? You know, check the house?'

Ever since the night masked men had come to snatch me from my bed, I'd felt uneasy being alone in Wicker House. It was hard to fall asleep in the dark and silence, waiting for footsteps and the scrunch of gravel in the porch. But it wasn't going to get any easier if I relied on Abe to protect me.

'No – but thank you.' He let his arms drop and I sat up, raking the hair off my face. He watched me, his face bleak and sad. A lump rose in my throat and I kissed him gently on the cheek, and he sighed.

'All right. You know best. God shield me from an independent woman.'

'I'm sorry – for everything.'

Sorry about Rachel. About me. About this whole screwed up everything. I couldn't put it all into words, but I didn't have to. Abe knew. His eyes were sad as he leaned forward to return my kiss.

183

'Goodnight, Anna,' he said. 'But whatever else, I'm coming. OK?'

'To Russia?'

'You can't go to Russia alone. You'll be eaten alive. You want to find out about your mother? Well, don't cut off your nose about this – if you want to succeed, you stand a better chance with me.'

'I know.' I said. It was hard to admit, but it was the truth and we both knew it.

Abe nodded, just once. Then I opened the car door and climbed out, and he drove away.

CHAPTER TWELVE

'Emmaline! This is a nice surprise.' Dad looked up from reading the paper at the kitchen table as Emmaline slung her school bag on to the counter and slumped on to the settle. I hung my coat on the peg beside the back door and started up the coffee machine.

'Coffee, Dad? Em? Oh –' I dropped a sheaf of letters on to the table '– these were on the mat.'

'Yes please to coffee,' Dad said. He began to sort through the post. 'Haven't seen you over here for a while, Emmaline. Been busy?'

'Well, you know. Revision and all that – I hardly leave the house these days,' Emmaline said. Dad folded up his paper and shot me a look.

'Really? Anna seems to be barely home. She's up and down from London every other day. I'm amazed she's getting any revision done at all.'

'Look, Grandmother had a stroke. What do you want me to do?' I snapped. 'I'm sorry she timed her collapse so badly. I'll be sure to tell her to schedule her next stroke more considerately.'

'Hey, hey!' Dad held up a hand. 'I know you've had a lot on your plate. And of course you need to see Elizabeth. Just – you know. I worry. It's only a couple of weeks until your exams – I just want you to do yourself justice. Is that a crime?'

Guilt griped at my stomach. The exams *were* just a fortnight away – but I still hadn't told Dad that I wouldn't be here to take them. I hadn't been revising either – instead I'd used the time up in my room to scour the Internet for cheap flights and apply for visas. Abe knew the truth, of course. Emmaline knew, Marcus knew, my grandmother knew – it seemed like everyone knew except for Dad. And it was killing me – but I wanted to have everything in place before I told him. I didn't trust myself to hold firm in the face of his reaction. Telling Dad was going to take all the courage and resolve I possessed. I didn't want there to be even the slightest chink of an exit for me to back out.

The flights were booked for ten days' time. I was expecting my visa any day now. After that there would be nothing to do but tell Dad. Which was partly why I'd invited Emmaline over tonight. A kind of farewell dinner. Before everything hit the fan.

For the moment though, Dad was opening his post.

'Another bill,' he sighed. 'Bloody water board. It's a basic human right – shouldn't it be free?'

'Yeah,' agreed Emmaline. 'I'll tell those damn Ethiopians to send back that artesian well kit the school paid for; you clearly need it more than they do.'

'Sarcasm is the lowest form of wit,' Dad said loftily. 'Credit card bill – oh well, not too painful this month. Oh, thank you, sweetie.' He took the coffee I handed him and took a scalding gulp. 'Hmm, what's this?' He was looking at the back flap of the next envelope. 'Russian Embassy? That sounds a bit more exciting at least!'

My heart jumped into my throat and words stuck there, jostling to get free, but trapped. Dad's thumb moved to the flap and ripped open the envelope and, before I could do anything more than squeak a faint, 'Dad!' he was reading the letter. *My* letter.

'The embassy have approved my application for a visa to visit Russia?' Dad's face was blankly astonished. 'How very bizarre!' Then he looked more closely at the address line. 'Hang on – it says *Ms* Winterson. The embassy's approved *your* application, Anna? What's this about? You can't go to Russia – you've got exams!'

'Dad . . .' I croaked, but no more words came. One look at my face and he was round the table, standing in front of me, his hands on my shoulders.

'Anna?' He looked into my face, his expression alarmed. 'What is all this? Please, tell me this is some kind of mistake?'

'It's not a mistake,' I managed. 'I'm sorry, Dad, I was going to tell you—'

'What! When? You're trying to tell me you're planning to ditch exams you've been working towards for *two years* and swan off into the blue, alone?'

'Not alone,' I said, and then instantly realized that was a mistake.

'With who?'

'With Abe.'

'What?' Emmaline said, her voice a startled echo of Dad's shock.

'Yes, I'm going with Abe – not like that, Dad,' I said as I saw his face. 'As friends.'

'But you can't,' Dad said, shaking his head as if he could dislodge this crazy notion, shake it free. 'You've got exams! Why now? Why not in a couple of months, for the love of all that's reasonable?'

Because we might not be here in two months! Because at the current rate, Elizabeth would probably be dead. Because, left to run amok, the spy was going to bring the Ealdwitan to their knees, and London alongside.

But I couldn't say any of that – not to Dad. I could only shake my head, trying not to look at the bewildered, angry hurt in his face.

'I forbid it,' Dad said, and suddenly his voice was stony. 'I am your father and I will *not* allow this.'

'I'm an adult,' I said. 'I'm eighteen, remember? I can do what I want now. What are you going to do – lock me up?'

'You're a child! And that man – that bloody Goldsmith – he should know better. You are *not* going to Russia alone – and you're certainly not going alone with Abe Goldsmith. If he tries I'll . . . I'll . . . I'll have him prosecuted!'

'For what, Dad?' I said tiredly. 'For being my mate?'

'Anna, be reasonable!' Dad said, desperately. 'What do you want me to say? Yes, it's fine, jack in your exams, go to Russia with a man I barely know and trust less, here's my blessing?'

'First, I'm not going to pass my exams,' I said, trying to make my voice as steady as I could. 'Dad, you don't know what it's been like – I went off the rails a long while back. Seth . . . Grandmother . . . everything. It's all been too much. It's better this way. I'll come back –' at least, I hoped I would '– I'll resit next year with a clear head and I'll reapply for university. I won't gain anything by flunking out now. And second—'

'Second,' Emmaline interrupted, 'she's not going alone with Abe. I'm going too.'

'Em?' I gasped.

'Shut up,' Em said sternly. 'Thanks for not dropping me in it with your dad, but there's no point in keeping it a secret any longer. I'll tell my mum tonight. Anna didn't tell you because she didn't want me to get into trouble with my mum,' she said to Dad. 'We knew neither of you would be pleased. But you can rest easy because Abe's not going to be jumping anyone's bones. Anna and I will be sharing a room.'

'Emmaline, stop this,' I said desperately. I couldn't let her throw everything away, but how could I argue my point with Dad standing open-mouthed across the kitchen table? Dammit, Em had known I wouldn't let her do this – and she'd deliberately made it impossible for

189

me to fight my side. 'Please, Em . . .'

'Anna.' Em put her hand on my arm and I felt her magic prickle across my skin, trying to tell me that it would all be OK, wrapping her love and support and steadfastness around me like an invisible hug. 'I appreciate you trying to protect me, really I do, but it's better that your dad knows the score. He's not going to let you go alone with Abe, is he?' Her dark eyes beseeched me to keep quiet. 'So telling him this – it's the only way.'

Telling him? I spoke inside her head. *You're just telling him, right – to shut him up? Please tell me this is just a line to get me out of trouble and you're* not *actually coming. Em, you're* not *coming. That's my final word.*

'I'm coming,' she said firmly and aloud. 'I'm going to defer my place at LSE and do resits in the autumn. It's all settled.'

Dad looked from me, to Emmaline, and his face set into a kind of mulish determination. Then he stood and got down a frying pan. As he set it on the Aga, his whole back radiated obstinacy and denial. *We are not done here*, his posture said silently.

Well, I was his daughter. I could do silent obstinacy too.

After supper I walked Emmaline as far as the coast road and then started back. My watch said almost midnight and I had an automatic twinge of guilt as I remembered it was a school night. Then I laughed out loud feeling, for the first time in days, a lightening of my heart. It didn't matter any more.

The house was in darkness when I got back and for a moment, I thought I'd dodged the bullet and Dad had gone up to bed. But when I set my foot to the stairs, the kitchen door creaked open and Dad appeared, silhouetted against the light.

'Dad—' I began. He shook his head.

'No. Let me talk. I am *not* happy about this. And I'm going to be speaking to Maya about it tomorrow because frankly I can't believe she's going to let Emmaline get away with this. I've been thinking about what you said – that I can't stop you, that you're legally an adult. And it's true, I admit it. But you have to tell me *why*, Anna – why would you do this?'

I stopped, with my hand on the carved, blackened newel post, groping desperately for some explanation that would come close to the truth, but protect him at the same time. I couldn't think of anything.

'Is it Seth?' he asked at last. 'Because I know the break-up hit you pretty hard – but sweetie, running away isn't the answer. And throwing all your prospects away over some bloke who was too stupid to appreciate you . . .' He stopped and then started again. 'Listen, I know the move to Winter – I know it wasn't what you wanted. And I'm sorry if I seemed to take you for granted, you've always been so steady, so good at coping with stuff – I should have listened to you more, taken your problems more seriously. I just never thought . . .'

I wanted to say something; tell him it wasn't Seth, it

wasn't Winter, and most of all, it wasn't *him*. I wanted to say that I'd have given anything to stay, to be the daughter he wanted. But the hurt and bewilderment in his face tore at my heart and I couldn't reply. I thought of how he'd feel if I didn't come back and our last words had been angry. And for a moment my whole body yearned to cast a charm, one that would leave him happy memories instead of bitter ones.

But they'd be false. No better than happiness bought with drugs or alcohol. Not even my mother had done that – and she'd stopped at little else. She could have given him a happy ending, a story to tell to me, a memory of her that wasn't of heartbreak and betrayal. But she hadn't, and perhaps, after all, the heartbreak of real memories was better than a happy fog of false ones.

So what *could* I say? I couldn't promise him I'd come back and sit my exams. I couldn't even promise him that he'd see me again.

'Dad,' I said, 'you have to let me go. Please. You *have* to let me go to Russia.'

I could never tell him why. I could never inflict this darkness on him. I'd seen what the knowledge had done to Seth – the danger I'd put him in from the Ealdwitan, from the Malleus, and the bleak pain I'd inflicted on him with the understanding of my power and all it could do. Seth knew the gulf that lay between us. And I couldn't bear for Dad to look at me and see anything other than his daughter.

But as I looked at him, pleading with my eyes for him to understand, something in his gaze flickered. Some memory of my mother, perhaps. An understanding, even if he chose not to recognize it, name it.

He took a deep breath, opened his mouth to speak – and then he seemed to deflate, as though some fire in him had gone out.

'OK.' His face was sad and he put his hand to my cheek. 'If it means that much to you . . . I can't pretend I'm happy about it – but there's not much I can do. I'm not going to put you on house arrest, I know when I'm beaten. So . . . OK.'

He blinked and a tear ran down his cheek, on to his collar.

'Do you understand?' I asked. I wasn't sure what I wanted the answer to be.

'No,' he said sadly.

I hugged him very hard, completely unable to believe that I was about to let him go, let all of this good, comfortable life go. He hugged me back, his face in my hair, his breath ragged.

'Good night, sweetie,' he said at last.

'Good night, Dad,' I choked.

He kissed me on the forehead, very softly, both his hands either side of my face. It was a kiss goodnight. But it felt like goodbye.

CHAPTER THIRTEEN

We told Dad and Maya not to come to the airport. Emmaline and I said goodbye to them at the station, waving and waving as the train pulled away from the platform until they disappeared into the grey summer drizzle.

Neither of us spoke for the first half hour of the train journey. We just sat and looked out of the window. I wasn't sure what Em was thinking; my own mind was a mess of churning excitement, terror, guilt, and last minute practicalities – had I got my passport? If something happened to Emmaline, would Maya ever forgive me? When could I break the news about—

'Cheer up, love.' The ticket inspector's voice broke abruptly into my thoughts. 'It might never happen.'

Dick, I thought. But I only smiled thinly and held out my ticket.

'It's not too late,' I said to Em, after he'd gone. 'You can turn around at the airport. Catch the next train back.'

'Shut up,' Em said briefly.

And then she put her nose in her guidebook.

* * *

At the airport we checked in and then went to wait under the main departures board, where we'd all arranged to meet up.

'He's late,' Em said, looking at her watch for the fifth time and then up at the departures board. *Go to Gate* said the St Petersburg flight.

'Em,' I said nervously, 'there's something I haven't had a chance to mention.'

I still hadn't told her. Or Abe.

My excuse was that in the tearing rush of the last few days there'd been no time – and that Marcus hadn't actually *completely* confirmed anyway. But . . .

'Oh here he is,' Em said, relief in her voice.

'Sorry I'm late.' Abe swung his rucksack to the marbled floor with a resounding thump. It must have weighed as much as me. 'It won't take me two minutes to check this in and then we can go through security.'

'N-not quite,' I said, in a small voice.

'Why not?' Em said. Then, 'Oh Jeez, you didn't forget your passport, did you? I asked you!'

'It's not my passport,' I said. 'No . . . It's just that . . . We need to wait. For Marcus.'

'*Marcus?*' Emmaline said, at the same time as Abe said a very, very rude word.

'Yes.'

'Why?'

'B-because . . . he's coming.'

'*What?*' Emmaline said.

'Please.' Abe's face was suddenly dark. 'Please tell me this is a joke.'

'N-no.' Then as I saw their incredulous faces, bemused in Emmaline's case, unashamedly furious in Abe's, I began to stammer out explanations. 'Look – what was I supposed to do? I couldn't just tell him to sod off.'

'Yes you could!' Abe exploded. 'It's nothing to do with him!'

'Abe, his father was *killed* by the spy. How is that not to do with him?'

'You know nothing about him!'

'I know he speaks Russian – which can't be bad. And I know he wants to hunt this spy down even more than I do.'

'And what if the spy is your mother?' Abe spelled it out brutally, so that I flinched and looked away. 'What then?'

'He knew my mother,' I said in a low voice. 'He loved my mother. He has as many rights over her as I do. Abe, like it or not, Marcus has a right to be here.'

'So he emotionally blackmailed you into coming? Nice.'

'He didn't blackmail – he asked as a favour. Anyway, *you* can hardly talk about blackmail.'

Abe's face went closed and hard and, for a minute, I thought he was going to say something very ugly indeed. But then he looked over my shoulder. And his expression changed from fury to disgust.

'Anna!' Marcus called. He walked quickly through the

crowd to where we were standing and bent and kissed me on each cheek. Then, before she could object, he did the same to a slightly startled Emmaline. For the first time since I'd known him, he wasn't wearing a suit. Instead he was wearing a Barbour jacket and combats. 'Hello Abe,' he added. Was it my imagination or was there a touch of amusement in his voice at the sight of Abe's face?

'Well,' he said, after a short, fruitless wait for a reply, 'no point in hanging around I guess. Shall we get going?'

'Yes,' Abe said, through gritted teeth. 'You're right. There's no point in hanging around.'

I sighed. This was going to be a long flight.

The plane landed at some painfully early hour and we staggered out of the terminus and stood like sheep, yawning while Marcus paid off the porters and haggled in Russian with the taxi driver.

In the taxi itself we sat in silence. Marcus was silent because he was asleep, his head lolling against the passenger window. Em was silent because she was reading a book on Russian folklore, making notes in the margin with a pencil. Abe was silent because – well I didn't know why Abe was silent. Only that he was. He sat between Emmaline and me, his arms crossed, his face dark and uncompromising. When my attempts at conversation fizzled away, Emmaline gave me a look; it was a look that said 'Don't bother.'

I was silent because St Petersburg was so beautiful.

I don't know what I'd expected from Russia. Concrete blocks. Snow. Communist architecture.

Not this.

Not white stone, wrought-iron balconies, long vistas stretching like the Champs Elysées. Not golden domes, shining in the morning sun. Not this wide expanse of sky and water flashing past, dazzlingly bright even at this early hour.

The streets were all but deserted.

'It's so quiet,' I said to Emmaline, half under my breath.

'Is White Nights.' The driver caught my remark and spoke over his shoulder in heavily accented English. 'The people, we are dance, eat, drink until dawn. The sun, she does not setting. All night it is – what is the word?' He said something in Russian that sounded like 'sonyaky' and furrowed his brow. Then it cleared. 'Twilight. All night it is twilight. So we call the White Nights, when is never fully dark. We drink in the night and we sleep in the day. Today is Saturday. So. We sleep.'

We rounded a corner and I gasped. A cathedral towered in front of us, spiralled onion domes pointing to the sky, each one jewelled and gilded and bright blue as the morning sky. Then the driver swerved again down a side street and it was gone.

'What was that place?'

'The Church of the Saviour on Spilled Blood.' Emmaline

198

didn't raise her head. 'Built on the site of the assassination of Alexander the Second.'

'Nice,' I murmured.

'St Petersburg is town build on blood,' said our driver. 'It is build on bones, on bodies. It is beautiful – yes. But is beauty build upon death.'

'What do you mean?' I asked.

'It was built on the bones of serfs – that's what you mean, isn't it?' Emmaline asked. The driver nodded.

'Many thousands peasants died to raise St Petersburg from the mud. Ten, twenty thousands. Thirty thousands. History cannot to count. They are lost. Their bones lie beneath these streets, in the canals.' He waved a hand towards the shining skein of water running alongside the road and I couldn't suppress a shudder. Then we swung right, down another side street and across another bridge. The car slowed abruptly and the driver leaned out of the window, peering at the door numbers. At last we pulled to a halt and he consulted the piece of paper Marcus had handed him when we got in the cab.

'It is here. Hotel.'

'Wha—?' Marcus raised his head sleepily and rubbed his eyes. 'Oh, thank you.' He peeled more notes from the bundle in his wallet and I groaned. I was going to owe Marcus the national debt of a small country at this rate.

The room was small, dark and depressing with a double bed, two lamps (one not working), a small sink and a threadbare carpet. The walls seemed to be covered with some kind of brown corduroy and, when Emmaline threw her rucksack on the bed, it didn't bounce. She lay down beside it, took off her glasses and pressed her fingers to her eyes.

'What's the matter?' I asked.

She shook her head without replying.

'I don't know. Everything just feels . . . wrong. Strained. Forced. Do you know what I mean?'

'No.'

She sighed and tried again. 'I've been trying to, you know, *look*.' She had the half-defensive look she always adopted when talking about her ability to see unfolding events. 'Trying to see what we should be doing – what we should be looking out for. But everything feels weird. It's like . . . I can't explain, but it's like we're being – pulled. Pushed. Against the grain. Is this making any sense?'

'Kind of . . .' I sat beside her on the bed. 'Forced – how? By someone?'

'I don't know. That's what I can't work out. I can't tell whether we're going against the grain of what someone wants us to do, like we're on the track of something and they're trying to push us back, or if it's the opposite. If it's us being diverted, pushed into the wrong course and we *should* be turning back. But whatever it is, the pressure's making me ill. I've had a headache ever since we left London.'

'I'm sorry.' I didn't know what else to say. Emmaline sighed again.

'It's fine. I'll take a paracetamol. What's happening today, anyway?'

'I don't know . . .' I said slowly. 'All I can think is to follow the trail of the prophecy.'

'Which means?'

'Caradoc said the last reference he could find was to a copy in the library of Peter the Great. Which still exists – it's on Vasilievsky Island. And I know my mother tried to go there at least once. So I think we should go to the library. See what we can find out.'

'Sounds like a plan. Do you want to scry before we leave? See what's happening in London?'

'Um . . .'

The answer was no, not really. But I knew I was being stupid, cowardly. It was better to know. I nodded, reluctantly, and Emmaline undid her rucksack and got out a small silver bowl.

'You prefer water, don't you?' she asked.

I shrugged. 'I guess. I've never really done it any other way. I don't get runes and stuff.'

'They're an acquired taste.' Emmaline filled the bowl with water. 'Like olives. OK, shoot.'

'Don't look.'

'Jeez you're weird,' Emmaline stood up. 'But then aren't we all? All right then. I'll be down in Abe and Marcus' room, trying to break up the fight.'

201

I waited until the door clunked shut behind her, then I went and slid the chain across, put the bowl on the tiny bedside table and lowered my face to the water.

Grandmother, I told myself firmly. *Grandmother.* I thought of Elizabeth in the high white bed, of Miss Vane fussing round. *Don't think of Seth. Think of London. London.*

But the first thing I saw wasn't Elizabeth. It was Dad. He was sitting at a kitchen table and for a minute I didn't know where. Then I recognized it – he was in Elaine's little flat above the Anchor. Elaine was sitting next to him, her arm around Dad's shoulders, and Dad's head was down, his face buried in his hands. As I watched, he lifted his face and I saw he'd been crying.

My own eyes swam with tears. For a long moment I watched them both, fighting against the rising ache in my throat, and then a tear ran down my nose and dropped into the bowl. Then another. The water in the bowl shivered into ripples, the picture broke up, and when the surface smoothed again they were gone.

Instead – there was my grandmother. She was lying in her bed, just as she had been when I left. Her black hair straggled across the pillow and her eyes were closed. Beneath the thin lids, her eyes moved uneasily, roaming from side to side as if seeking something. Even asleep, she didn't look at rest. She looked as if she was fighting to control something, fighting to hold back the tide. But she was still alive – just.

Suddenly I couldn't do this any more. Watching

helplessly from across the ocean was too hard. I closed my eyes, shutting out the thin figure beneath the white sheets. Then I raised my head from the bowl and rubbed the tears fiercely from my eyes and nose.

When I opened my eyes, the sun had gone in, thick grey cloud was blanketing the sky and rain speckled the window. I jumped as a knock came at the door. It opened suddenly, crashing against the chain, and Emmaline's face peered through the gap.

'Can I come in? Why have you got the chain on?'

'Sorry, sorry.' I jumped up and pulled back the chain to let her in. 'Of course you can come in. I didn't mean to be weird earlier. I just can't . . .'

'It's fine. I get it. All OK on the home front?'

'No. Sort of. No worse, I guess. How are the boys?'

'Abe's asleep – Marcus has gone out. What shall we do?'

And suddenly I knew. No more waiting. No more brooding on what was going on in London. I had to do something concrete. Fearless.

'We're going to the library to get that book.'

'You think?' Em chewed at a piece of her hair uneasily. 'Shouldn't we wait for the others?'

'Why? What's the point in waiting?'

'Well . . . I don't know. We don't speak Russian for a start.'

'We'll give it a try,' I said firmly. 'If it doesn't work, we can come back with Marcus.'

'I really don't know,' Em said. She bit her lip and then

yanked off her glasses and polished the lenses crossly. 'It just seems a bit . . . I mean, people keep getting killed for God's sake!'

'Scared?' I said sweetly. 'We can wait for the boys if you prefer.'

Em's jaw set like concrete and I knew I'd hit the right button.

'Not on your bloody life. Get your coat, Anna Winterson.'

The wind whipped along the river, turning my hair into rats' tails and making my eyes water. It would take me hours to comb out the tangles. Emmaline had tied her scarf around her head and looked like a Russian Babushka doll. It didn't feel like early summer – nothing like it.

At last we reached a tall, columned entrance and Emmaline looked down at her map and up at the portico.

'I think this is it.'

We climbed the steps, the doors towering above us – ten, twenty feet high, like an entrance not for people, but for giants.

My breath came fast, the sound whipped away by the wind. I put my hand out to the brass knob and turned it.

Nothing happened. I tried turning it the other way.

'Is it locked?' Em asked.

'I don't know.' I peered through the window to one side of the door, but it was hard to see through the dirty panes. 'I think it's closed.'

A voice rang out from behind us in Russian and we both

jumped. A man in a security uniform was coming up the steps.

'I'm – I'm sorry,' I stammered. 'I don't . . . Do you speak English?'

The man said something else, more slowly, but equally incomprehensibly. Out of the corner of her mouth Emmaline muttered, 'Don't blame me. I said we should have waited for the others.'

'Oh shut up,' I growled. '*Spasiba*,' I said to the man and then I dragged Emmaline round the corner, out of sight of the entrance.

'Invisibility. Now.'

'Gawd . . .' Em groaned. 'Can't we do this the normal way?'

'No.' I didn't know why I felt so antsy about it – only that it was itching me to be so close to the end of the trail and not have the page in my hands. 'I'm not waiting. Come on, you were the one who was always telling me to embrace my witchcraft.'

'OK, OK.' Emmaline looked up and down the deserted street. There was a moment's pause and then she shivered out of view. I whispered a charm under my breath and looked down at my feet.

'Do I look all right?'

'I can't see you –' Em's disembodied voice was almost drowned by the sound of the wind '– if that's what you mean. Come on. I'm knackered. I don't want to keep this up too long.'

An alley led off from the side street into a courtyard behind the main building. We ducked down there and I looked around, searching for a door, a grille – anything. The courtyard was silent, empty. It was more sheltered from the wind here and papers and leaves danced in the trapped eddies.

Then I spotted a crumbling wooden door tucked away in the corner of the courtyard. I dragged Emmaline across and put my hand to the lock, feeling it click and grind beneath my fingers.

The door swung open, Emmaline and I glanced around, and then we ducked inside, out of the wind.

Inside it was hot – extremely hot – and I realized that we were in the basement of the building. Lagged pipes ran along a dimly lit corridor, clunking and groaning as we passed. We turned at random up another passage. After just a few minutes Emmaline's hand was hot and sweating, and I guessed mine must feel equally sticky in hers.

A wooden panelled door suddenly appeared on our left and I skidded to a halt. I looked at the door, then back at Emmaline's invisible presence in the air.

'Shall I?' I asked, my heart thudding with anticipation.

'Go on,' Em said.

I turned a handle. And suddenly – just like that – we were in the Library of Peter the Great.

We were standing at the edge of a huge galleried hall – shelves rising all around, twice as high as a man, and above that, a gallery with more tomes. The air was heavy with the smell of ancient books and crumbling leather bindings. I stood, looking in awe at the hundreds upon thousands of books that lined the walls of the vast library. One of them might contain 'The Riddle of the Epiphany'. But which?

There was not a single reader, not one person at the long rows of desks that stood beneath the high windows. Dust motes floated in a brief shaft of sunlight and then disappeared as another cloud drifted across. Beside me I heard Emmaline let out a sigh and I knew that, like me, she was gazing round at the vertiginous stacks of books and wondering where to start.

Then I felt her hand tug on mine and together we began to walk slowly through the reading rooms, looking for something – some clue. The rooms unfolded – mile, after mile, after mile of books. We walked through rooms of huge books, rooms of slim books, past shelves of pamphlets and maps. There were ancient books, modern ones, illustrated ones, and ones bound in gilt with huge ridged spines. Books with titles written in Cyrillic and ones in . . .

I stopped.

'Em, this room – it's all foreign editions. Not Russian books. Do you think it could be here?'

'Well, let's start looking,' Em said. There was a ripple in the air, like a heat haze, and she shimmered back into view.

'Is that a good idea?' I bit my lip.

'I'm bloody knackered. This is going to wear off soon one way or another. Anyway, there's no one around.'

'OK.'

I let myself come back into view, though I couldn't stop myself glancing nervously over my shoulder. Still, if anyone came in, it would look a lot better for them to see me and Em in plain view, rather than piles of books mysteriously unshelving and reading themselves.

I threw my bag on a desk by the door, then looked around at the stacked shelves, the thousands of volumes stretched around the room.

'Where shall we start?' Emmaline asked.

The scale of the task was overwhelming. It seemed ridiculous that out of all the spells I'd learned by rote, not one was for something as useful and sensible as finding a lost book. Bloody witches! Too busy messing around with the weather and each other's feelings to think of anything as useful as a spell to . . .

I stopped, remembering something my grandmother had shown me, almost light-heartedly, one time when she'd lost her keys.

We'd been in the kitchen and she'd used chopsticks, I remembered. I cast round for something equivalent. A couple of pencils were lying on a desk by the window and I hurried across and picked them up.

'What are you doing?' Emmaline said impatiently. 'I hardly think this is the time to start taking notes.'

'Hang on, let me just try something.'

I held them in my fingers, loosely, trying to clear my mind, chase away the panicky thought of someone coming in, asking us what we were doing here, throwing us out . . .

Slowly I turned in a circle, watching, watching . . .
I kept turning, trying not to lose concentration as I heard
a police car passing in the street, siren wailing. But it didn't
stop and I carried on turning . . . turning . . . ignoring
Emmaline's sceptical gaze, trying to focus my mind on the
poem's title, the heavy black type in the fragment I'd seen.

Nothing happened. I focussed harder, channelling every
nerve into visualizing the fragment ripped from Caradoc's
fingers. Then suddenly the pencils twitched. I took a step
forwards; they twitched again, more eagerly.

'It's working!' I called to Em. The pencils tugged
furiously and I hurried across the floor, back the way we'd
come, back towards the main reading room.

'Anna, you genius!' Em crowed. 'How did you think
of that?'

I didn't answer. I was too busy concentrating on the
pencils. I was almost back to the corner where we'd
shrugged off our coats when the pencils ripped themselves
furiously from my grip and flung themselves, clattering, to
the floor, right beneath the desk where my bag was lying.

For a minute we both just stared, nonplussed. And then
I groaned.

'The bit of paper. It's in there. That's what the pencils
found – the ripped corner Caradoc was holding.'

Emmaline said nothing; she just let out a long, frustrated
sigh. Then we began to search the shelves.

It was back-breaking, boring work, scouring the room,

volume by useless volume. I don't know how long we kept it up – hours, it felt like – but at last I straightened, rubbing my stiff neck.

'Em, this is pointless. Let's come back with Marcus tomorrow.'

'Ugh!' Emmaline stood and stretched so that her back and hips clicked horribly. 'I'm so effed off. This is ridiculous. It's here. It's got to be. I won't be defeated by a poxy filing system. I *will* find that poem, if it's the last thing I do.'

'Can I help you?' A voice came from behind us, female, softly accented.

Emmaline and I both froze, her horrified expression mirroring my feelings so exactly that I knew my own face must be stuck in the same mask of shock.

A slim, dark-haired woman was coming towards us across the parquet, her heels clicking softly. She held out a hand.

'I am Elena Bolshakov, the Foreign Collection Librarian,' she said. 'May I assist with your research?'

For a moment I only stood, gaping. Emmaline recovered first and took the woman's hand, with a kind of gulping noise.

'Th-thank you,' she said as they shook. 'That would be excellent.'

'Are you students here?' The woman shook my hand in turn and I felt a scarlet blush begin to creep up my throat and cheeks. God, I was a terrible liar.

'Yes,' I said. 'Sort of. It's a project. For school. A student project.'

Don't elaborate, Emmaline's voice said furiously in my head. *You're babbling. Stop babbling.*

'And . . . that's it . . .' I trailed off lamely. Luckily the woman didn't seem to notice anything strange. She only nodded.

'I see. And you are looking for a book? One in particular?'

'A p-poem, actually.' I managed. 'I was told that you had it, in translation. It's called "The Riddle of the Epiphany".'

'Ah,' the woman said. 'And you do not know the name of the collection?'

I shook my head and she frowned.

'I see. That will be difficult. Let me see what can be found on the computers. Wait one moment please, I will return.'

She disappeared and Emmaline sank on to a bench and let out a shaky breath of relief.

'Bloody hell! I thought we were goners.'

'I thought the place was closed,' I whispered back. 'Why hasn't she challenged us?'

'Maybe she thinks we got a special pass? Who knows? Don't knock it.'

'I won't.'

I sat down beside her and we waited and waited. My hands were wet with sweat and my palm slipped suddenly on the leather material of the bench, my arm skidding out from under me so that I lost my balance and jolted into Emmaline.

'For God's sake—' Emmaline snapped and then broke off. We both heard the cheerful click-clack of heels trotting down the corridor towards us.

I stood. I couldn't help it. My fingers twined together, mimicking the tight, griping knot in the pit of my stomach.

And? I wanted to shout. *Did you find it?*

'Alas,' she was holding something in her hand, but it wasn't a book. It looked like some kind of printout. 'It appears the volume in question, a volume of translated Old English poems and riddles, was victim to the 1988 fire.'

'The what?' Emmaline asked.

'The library was decimated by a very dreadful fire some years ago – many thousands of volumes were lost. It seems these poems were among them. The volume is gone.'

No. *No.*

My knees were suddenly weak and I groped for the leather bench and sat, the blood roaring in my ears.

Beneath it I could hear the woman's cheerful voice. She was saying something to Emmaline, but it was all so unimportant compared with that one, simple, immutable fact: the poem was gone.

'. . . no substitute for books of course, but in conservation terms they are extremely useful,' she was saying.

Emmaline took the piece of paper, her face blank, incredulous, as she turned to me.

'Th-thank you!' she stammered. There was something

strange about the way she held the paper – as if it might burst into flames or disintegrate in her hands. 'Thank you – this is incredible. Anna . . . Anna, did you hear?'

'Hear what?' I said dully.

'The book was destroyed, but they'd made a microfiche copy. Miss Bolshakov has printed us out a copy. Anna – we've got it. We've got the poem. Now let's get out of here.'

CHAPTER FOURTEEN

'I can't believe it.'

I looked again over my shoulder. The street was empty.

'Go on then – read it!' Em urged. I shook my head.

'Not now. I can't. Not here.'

'OK, well then, give the paper here,' Em said. I frowned and she clicked her fingers impatiently. 'Come on. This is the last known copy of the poem and possibly the answer to all our questions – aren't you even just *slightly* afraid it might go west?'

'Yes, of course. But are you sure—'

'*Psh.*' She made a snorting sound that was halfway between irritation and dismissal and twitched the paper out of my fingers. It fluttered in the wind and she began to prise off her boot.

'What are you . . . ?' I started, but then began to laugh shakily as Em folded the thin printout and slid it inside her shoe. 'Have you been watching too many spy movies?'

'Shut it, Winterson.' Em eased her boot back on and frowned. 'Ow, this is bloody uncomfortable actually. If I get a blister, I'm calling on you for a foot massage.'

We began to walk again, towards the grey expanse of river. In spite of the promises about near-twenty-four hour sun, we'd seen precious little sunlight since this morning. Black clouds had been pouring in from the sea, chased inland by the ceaseless wind. Now they were stacked across the skyline in towering mountainous ranges – like a thick, lead-grey duvet spread across the sky. A few more drops of rain spattered down as we stepped out on to the main road that ran alongside the Neva River. Em shivered and wrapped her coat more closely round herself.

'Well this is super miserable,' she said with faux-cheery bitterness. 'Bang goes coffee in the square.'

'I don't want to hang around anyway,' I said. 'I'd rather get the you-know-what back to the hotel.'

'Subtle, Anna, very subtle,' Emmaline drawled. 'Perhaps we could think of a code word. The Underpants, maybe. I've got to get the Underpants back to the hotel.'

'The Scotch Egg,' I said with a slightly hysterical nervous laugh.

'That's not embarrassing enough. How about, the Hot Stranger. I won't feel happy until I've got the Hot Stranger back to my room.'

'No wait,' I giggled, pulled in in spite of myself. 'I've got a better one—'

But before I could finish, a biting wind gusted down the road, bringing with it a cloud of dust and grit – crushed twigs and leaves and bits of debris. It swirled around our heads and we stopped, hunching our backs to the blast,

215

hands over our faces, trying to shield our eyes.

'Damn,' Emmaline had her glasses off, rubbing at her face. 'I can't see a thing.'

But I could – just. As my swimming vision cleared, I saw that the swirl of rubbish wasn't dispersing, but getting thicker and closer, and more defined. It seemed to have a shape, almost. The shape of a person, a woman – crouched as if to spring.

'Em!' I shouted. 'Run!'

But it was too late.

The woman stood in front of us – barring our way, her arms spread. She was beautiful, but dressed in rags and scraps stitched together into a threadbare shift and she didn't seem to feel the cold. Her eyes were speedwell-blue and her hair blew out behind her, a Medusa's mane of white serpents whipping in the wind.

She shouted something in Russian, followed by a word that sounded like 'Stop!'

Emmaline and I turned on our heel and began to pelt the other way. I glanced over my shoulder.

'Stop!' the witch screamed, running after us. She shouted a spell in Russian and suddenly my feet dragged on the pavement – I stumbled – they felt slow and impossibly heavy, as if my shoes had turned to lead. Beside me, Em tripped and fell and I grabbed her hand, dragging her back to her feet.

'Wiþræ!' I gasped. The heaviness lifted slightly and we staggered on, trying to run, but making nightmarishly slow progress. Worse – we were heading for a dead end, nothing but the sluggishly flowing river in front of us. I looked at the water, then at Em, and I saw the same terrified thought in her eyes. Jump or fight? Then I saw a gap between two buildings.

'Down here,' I gasped and we both swerved sideways, making for the alley.

The witch cried something again in Russian, her voice harsh and cracked. We took no notice and, as I glanced over my shoulder, I saw her point imperiously at a car, a shiny Mercedes. It gave a groan and slithered heavily across the tarmac, the tyres screaming as the rubber ground against the road. There was a horrible shriek of metal against stone and it crunched itself into the narrow alleyway, blocking our escape.

Frightened faces appeared at the windows of the apartment above – but the witch woman just opened her mouth and roared, like a lion. The blast of magic shook the walls of buildings all around – and the faces were no longer there; the occupants just seemed to disappear. I felt her breath like a searing wind against my face, her magic scouring like a snowstorm, biting through flesh and blood and bone.

'You bitch!' Emmaline yelled. She drew back her fist and flung a vicious blast of magic at the witch, a blow strong enough to kill an outwith, if one had stepped out at that moment. But the witch only laughed and buffeted her attack away like the blows of a child.

Then she blew.

Suddenly the air was as cold as a Siberian winter. When I tried to move my feet, they resisted. I looked down and realized the rain had frozen into a sheet of ice and my shoes were frozen to the concrete pavement. In a panic I yanked and yanked, and my shoes came away, but already I couldn't feel my fingers and my toes were numb. The Neva was icing over. Hoar-frost bristled from the cars and lamposts.

But the most terrifying thing, the thing that really made me shiver, was that the witch didn't seem to care who saw her, didn't care what the outwith might think. No rules seemed to bind her. What had she done with the faces at the window?

I looked at her mad, beautiful face, her wide blue eyes, her feet bare against the frozen ground. Her Medusa hair was matted with ice.

'Wh-who are y-y-you?' I asked. I almost couldn't speak, my teeth were chattering so much. Beside me I could feel Emmaline shaking violently, so hard it was almost not shivering at all, but more like a kind of convulsion.

'I . . . come . . . friend,' said the witch hoarsely. She smiled and I saw her teeth were black and jagged.

'Em,' I said, 'we have to run.'

'G-go,' Em said, her teeth gritted to stop them chattering.

We ripped our feet from the pavement, scrambled over the bonnet of the crumpled car, and then ran.

Our breath made white clouds in the frosted air. Our

feet slipped on the frozen paving stones, fingers freezing to metal railings as we tried to steady ourselves. And behind us I could hear the effortless thud, thud, thud of the witch in pursuit. We turned at random down side streets, feeling her chilly breath at our heels. It was cold – so cold. There was sweat on my spine but it only made me shiver harder as the cold wind screamed past us, bitter with frost.

My breath tore in my ears and beside me I could hear Emmaline panting desperately.

Then we rounded a corner and the Neva was in front of us again, a bridge spanning it. And I recognized it; our hotel was across that bridge.

'Come on!' I sobbed and we forced our tired legs to put on a burst of speed.

For a minute the air was warmer, we were outpacing her. Then I heard a scream of frustration from the witch and a huge gust of icy wind blasted at our backs. And the witch was on us. I felt a hand claw at my hair, my feet slipped from under me.

I fell headlong, crashing to the stone pavement with a force that knocked all the breath from my body. I clawed at the slippery, ice-covered flags, trying to get back to my feet, but the witch had me in her grip, her cold hands around me, her hair blowing across my face in the gale, blinding me. She was crushing me, crushing all the breath and warmth from my body.

'No!' Emmaline screamed. She drew back her hand and then flung a ball of fire. The witch flew into the air and then fell, sprawling on to the pavement. For a minute she lay gasping and Emmaline was running towards me, shrieking, 'Anna! Get up! Run!'

But before Emmaline could reach me, the witch sprang again – this time at her.

Magic swirled around our heads, snow and flame mixing together into a whirling, bewildering dance. The air filled with the sound of hissing and boiling, the smell of burning and fear. I saw Emmaline's face, flame-coloured and in agony, locked in a fierce embrace with the witch, and heard them both screaming curses at each other, their voices cracked and unintelligible.

Smoke and magic and steam wreathed around them.

'Stop,' I croaked, heaving myself to my hands and knees and trying to pull enough breath back into my body to cast a spell. 'Stop!'

I pulled my hand back, ready to fling a spell, but it was almost impossible to see who was who in the dizzying darkness. Then Emmaline shrieked something and the witch seemed to fly backwards off her, as if she'd been punched in the gut, straight into my arms. The force of the collision sent us both slithering unstoppably across the icy surface of the bridge, and my head cracked against a lampost with such force that for a long minute I couldn't see anything at all – just blackness and blood. I could hear Emmaline's terrified sobs, feel a hot, slippery wetness on my face. There was blood pouring down into my eyes, my own blood was blinding me.

Then I heard pounding footsteps and a voice screaming out a curse.

I clawed the bloodsoaked hair out of my eyes. Marcus – he was racing across the bridge, his face full of fear and fury.

'*Ábréoðe!*' he roared. The witch flew into the air, crashing into the other parapet of the bridge with a force that made the railings buckle. Marcus followed it up with another huge blast and the railings screamed in protest. One of the railings snapped with a sound like gunshot.

'*Smert!*' howled the witch. She drew back her hand and Marcus drew his, each ready to fling a crushing blow. But Marcus was faster. A bolt like white lightning shot from his palm and the witch screamed. Shards of ice flew on her breath, like frozen daggers, then the railings groaned and gave a metallic screech – and suddenly she was gone, just the twisted, mangled ends of the railings showing where she'd gone over.

There was a sickening crack as her body hit the frozen surface of the Neva.

For a minute I did nothing. Just sat, panting. But the silence stretched out and I crawled to the parapet to look over.

There was nothing there – only a black, swirling hole in the ice and something struggling, far downstream, beneath the icy surface. Then I couldn't see even that.

On the other side of the bridge Emmaline hauled herself shakily to her feet.

We stood, panting for a moment and then we staggered across the road into each other's arms.

'Oh my God, Em!'

'Your head!' she sobbed. 'Anna, your head!'

'It's fine.' I touched the back of my skull cautiously with my fingers, then winced. It wasn't fine. It felt horribly and ominously spongy. But I wasn't dead, which was the main thing.

We pulled back and looked at each other. I was checking Em's face for damage – she seemed to be, incredibly, OK.

'You look like you barely survived a bar brawl,' Em said.

I put my hand up to my face, feeling the crusting blood, then I spat on to my sleeve and scrubbed it across my face. God only knew what I looked like, but I didn't want to be arrested for GBH if I could possibly avoid it. At least my hair was dark – if I could just get the worst off my face, I could probably make it home without being spotted.

I was just about to ask Emmaline whether she had a tissue, when I heard a low snarling groan from behind us and we both turned in horror.

'Marcus!'

He was lying slumped against the railings of the bridge, his face grey. His eyes were open, but there was blood spreading across his shirt. A lot of blood.

I ran across and knelt beside him on the flagstones. They were still cold but already free from frost.

'Wh-what happened?' I stammered.

'Damn . . . icicle . . . that bloody witch . . .'

222

I looked down at his shirt, but whatever had been there had already melted. There was melt-water mixed with the pooling blood.

'We've got to stop the bleeding,' I said shakily. I started to peel back the bloodsoaked shirt to see what was beneath.

'Get off!' he growled, his voice twisted with pain. He shoved me away with one arm and shielded his body with the other, keeping me physically away. 'Don't touch me – please.'

There was sweat on his face and his skin was the colour of clay.

'Christ!' Emmaline looked at me, horrified. 'What do we do? Is he dying?'

'I'm not . . . bloody . . . dying . . .' Marcus said, his teeth gritted with pain. 'But we need to get out of here. Now.'

'You're not in any condition to move,' I said. 'Let me look, please. I can help heal you.'

'If you touch me,' he said, very low, 'I *will* kill you.'

I almost believed him. Then his eyelids fluttered shut and I realized that what looked like fury was actually extreme, unbearable pain – too much for anyone to deal with.

Emmaline was trying her phone, ringing Abe I guessed, but at last she shook her head and then looked up and down the bridge, biting her lip.

'Marcus is right, we can't stay here. That bitch didn't give a toss who saw her – probably half the KGB is on its way – not to mention whoever polices magic in this godforsaken place.'

'How can we get him home?'

'I can walk,' Marcus gasped.

I looked at him. He didn't look like he could walk. He looked like he was bleeding out. But he heaved himself to his feet with a sound like a sob and, leaning heavily on my shoulder, he did actually manage to take a step. Emmaline hurried to his other side; he took another. And then another.

Somehow we managed. Marcus hobbled, pitifully slowly, between me and Emmaline. We wound our arms beneath his shoulders and took as much of his weight as we could. After just a few feet my own muscles were screaming in protest. Marcus' weight felt like he'd crush me to my knees and my head had begun to throb as if there was a drum beating inside my skull. But I gritted my teeth and carried on doggedly putting one foot in front of the other. Whatever I was suffering, Marcus had it worse.

We were about half way to the hotel when we rounded a corner and almost ran into Abe. He skidded to a halt, his chest heaving.

'Anna, Em – what happened?' he panted. 'I came as fast as I could.'

'We were attacked,' Em said shortly. 'Anna and I nearly bought it. Marcus bailed us out. And he's bloody heavy.'

'Sorry, sorry,' Abe said hastily. He pushed Emmaline out of the way, intending to take her place at Marcus' side, but she shook her head.

'Take Anna's side. She's got incipient concussion or something.'

For the first time Abe seemed to register the streaks of drying blood on my face and his face went ashen.

'You weren't joking were you, when you said you nearly bought it?'

'Nope,' Em said shortly.

'Can you walk?' Abe asked.

'Yes,' I said. Not very well, it was true, but better than Marcus.

Abe pushed me aside and shouldered Marcus' weight, leaving Emmaline to support his other side. I trudged along beside them, listening to Emmaline's hoarse breathing beneath the sound of Marcus' tearing, agonized breaths. After a hundred yards I could see she was nearly done in, her feet stumbling and tripping on the pavement. I made her swap and we carried on our slow way. It was better with Abe taking Marcus' other shoulder; he was strong enough to carry most of the weight. But I was still unutterably thankful when we reached our hotel.

'I hope to God there's no one on the desk,' Abe muttered. He stuck his head around the door to reception and then nodded. 'We're fine. Let's go, quick.'

We hobbled across reception, but it took all three of us to heave Marcus' sweating, gasping body up the stairs and through the door to his room. Abe lowered him gently on to his back on the double bed and he lay still, his eyes closed, his skin glistening with a sick sheen.

'Will you let me take a look at that wound?' Abe asked. His black brows were drawn into a worried frown.

Marcus shook his head, his eyes still shut. 'No. Leave me alone.'

'I could help heal you,' Abe said. 'Look, I know we haven't got along – I've been a knob, I admit it. But you saved Anna and Em's lives. I owe you for that. Let me give you a hand.'

'No,' Marcus said. He opened his eyes and the fierceness in them made even me quail. 'No.'

'Marcus—' Abe began.

'*Go,*' Marcus hissed with such venom that in Abe's place I would have fled. But Abe only stood, his arms folded, his face worried. Then he shook his head.

'All right. I can't make you. I'll be up the corridor in the girls' room if you need anything.'

'Can I stay, Marcus?' I asked. But he shook his head.

'No. Leave me alone, please, all of you.'

'OK,' I said reluctantly. He closed his eyes and we turned towards the door and made our way up the corridor.

Back in our room I said, 'Take off your boot, Em.'

'When we've looked at your head,' Em said shortly.

'Please, just let me—'

'Anna, are you stupid or something? What good will a bit of paper do if you're dead from a brain haemorrhage?'

'Paper?' Abe said, looking from Emmaline to me.

'Don't ask,' Em said bitterly. 'Only the source of all

this bloodshed, folded up under my insole.'

'It's the prophecy!' I said desperately. 'Don't you understand? We found it – that's what she was after.'

'OK, I understand, but I think Em's right,' Abe said. 'The riddle's lasted this long – I think it'll last a few minutes longer. Let me look at your head.'

He bent my head forward, probing with gentle fingers at the top of my skull, but he didn't say anything, even when I swore and pulled away as his fingers touched a sore place.

'What do you think?' Em asked. Abe shrugged, but his eyes were worried.

'Hard to say. There's too much blood to tell.'

'I'm going to wash it out,' I said, moving to the sink.

'No!' Abe said, at the same time as Emmaline cried, 'Don't!'

'Why not?'

'Because if you've got something seriously wrong, I don't want you rinsing bits of your brain down into the sewers,' Abe said.

'Look, I'm conscious, I'm walking, I'm talking. I think I'll be fine. Just let me get the blood out of my hair and you can see what the damage is.'

Abe looked at Emmaline and they exchanged a glance that said, *What can you do with someone like her?*

'All right,' Abe said at last. 'But you'd better let me help. I don't want you sluicing away anything vital.'

We stood at the sink and Abe poured cup after cup of warm water over my hair, while the plughole ran red as a butcher's drain. While he washed my hair, Emmaline talked, filling him in on the discovery of the poem, the fight with the witch, our futile attempt to flee, and Marcus' rescue. Abe said nothing.

Every now and then I felt his fingers gently exploring the patch at the top of my head, checking that he wasn't making things worse. A gross smell filled the room; like an abattoir – blood and hot water mingling into a grim, iron-scented steam. But at last the sink was running pink and I could feel the huge clot at the top of my scalp was almost dissolved.

Em passed me a towel to wrap around my shoulders and I sat on a chair at the window, beneath the light, while she and Abe examined my skull.

'It's not as bad as it looks,' Abe said at last. 'I think you've just lost some skin and hair. But I'm seriously worried about concussion. From what Em said, that was quite a whack.'

'So? Do you think I should go to some Russian A&E and wait for the witch's mate to turn up?'

Abe's heavy black brows knitted together and he shoved his hands crossly into the pockets of his jeans.

'What do you suggest then?' Emmaline said.

'I've hit my head before,' I said. 'I remember what they said last time. I think I know what to look out for.'

'Oh you're impossible,' Em snapped. Then she sighed. 'OK. Well, I guess there's nothing for it.'

She sat down on the end of the bed, pulled off her boot,

and a piece of paper fluttered out on to the floor.

For a moment I didn't do anything – I couldn't. My heart was thudding too hard, my hands were cold and numb and, for a second, I wondered if perhaps Emmaline and Abe were right and I was on the brink of some kind of aneurysm.

Then I picked it up and opened it out.

CHAPTER FIFTEEN

A Rydelle

A childe shalle be born on the Feaft of Kynges
A childe of the Rook yet fowle she be not
And though she doth Fly, yet hath she no Wings
Born on a Chille Day but Merrie begot.

Sonne of the Wintere, yet stille she be Maide
Her Tongue speaks untruth, tho' she doth not lye
Her Brightest of Years shalle be fpent in the shade
And though she is Drownéd, yet she shalle not die.

She shalle walk Alone from her uery first Crie
Alone in this world from her first to last Breath
For, in this world where all Mortals must die,
She reigns alone: the Mistresse of Death.

We stared at the page, all three of us in silence.

'The Mistress of Death . . .' Abe said at last. 'Does that mean . . . ?'

He stopped and the sick foreboding that had been coiling in my stomach for so many months threatened to choke me. Death. Everything seemed to lead back to that word. All the deaths of the past few months pressed around me, drowning me in their shadows, and I felt the old, old fear wash over me again. The Mistress of Death. Was I some kind of horrendous WMD – a Typhoid Mary of witches? Was that what Corax had wanted from me?

I *had* the paper. And I still didn't know.

'Bloody witches!' I burst out furiously. 'Why can't anyone ever say what they mean? It's all smoke and mirrors and allusions. I'm sick of it!'

I clenched my fist, screwing the paper into a matted lump, and then stood, breathing hard, my fists pressed to my forehead. I felt like throwing the paper out of the window – the paper that had cost so much in lives and blood and suffering.

There was silence in the room. I could hear my own harsh breathing and a flutter as the paper fell to the floor.

Em bent and picked it up.

'Look, if you don't mind, I'm going to go to the Internet café downstairs and email this to Simon. He might be able to help. I'm extremely unhappy about being one of only three people who've seen this. I think the quicker we get this text back to England, the safer we'll all be. OK, Anna?'

I didn't trust myself to speak. I just nodded.

'Want me to go too?' Abe asked.

I squeezed my eyes tighter shut. I couldn't speak. The

231

lump in my throat choked me. If I'd tried, I don't know what would have come out – a great eviscerating howl of frustration and pain.

Instead, I just shrugged.

'Fine. Well I'll stay then,' Abe said in a *suit yourself* voice.

'See you in ten,' Em said. And then, with a laugh that tried just a little too hard to be relaxed, 'If I'm not back in fifteen, send out the search parties.'

After she'd gone I slumped on to the bed with my face in the pillow and tried to get a grip. *Stop being so bloody pathetic*, I snarled inside my head.

'It'll be OK,' Abe said, his voice low. I felt the bed springs shudder as he sat beside me.

I shook my head into the pillow and he said urgently, 'That line – the Mistress of Death – I know what you're thinking, but it could be something completely different. You're not evil, Anna, you're *not*.'

I didn't speak. My teeth were clenched against the despair. But when I felt Abe's hand touch the nape of my neck, I couldn't help it. A huge racking sob burst out.

He lay down beside me on the double bed and I rolled over and flung my arms around him, howling into the crook of his shoulder while he stroked his hands down my spine, one after the other, in a slow, comforting rhythm.

When I'd cried myself hoarse we lay with our foreheads touching. I felt his breath come and go on my face. His arms were around me. We were so close – as close as it was possible to get without being inside each other's skin.

His eyes were closed, but he must have felt my gaze, because he opened them and looked at me. His black eyes were steady, but full of a hunger I couldn't bear to see.

He touched my lip with his finger.

'Can I?'

It would be so easy. I wouldn't have to be careful with him. I wouldn't have to hold back.

He leaned forwards, slowly, giving me plenty of time to move or say something to stop him. But I didn't. I held my breath. And his lips touched mine, so gently I was almost unsure if I'd felt it at all.

Then he was kissing me. Hard. No uncertainty now. No holding back. His hands gripped at my shirt, at my waist, his breath coming hot and fast. His dark, heavy brows were drawn into a frown, but I couldn't tell from his face if it was of pain or pleasure. Perhaps some emotion too complex to skewer with a name.

His lips were at my jaw and my throat and his harsh three-day beard scraped the soft, almost unbearably tender skin beneath my ear. Then he held himself up on one arm and, still kissing me, he yanked off his shirt with his free hand, buttons ripping and clattering on the floor. I lay back, shivering with need, hearing my breath coming loud and harsh in the quiet of the room. Neither of us spoke. The room was silent, apart from the sound of our ragged breathing and my racing heart.

It was wrong. He wasn't Seth. And I wanted Seth –

I wanted his arms around me, his lips on my skin, his weight on me. But he wasn't here. And Abe was.

Seth, cried a voice in my heart.

He's gone, answered my head brutally. *You don't owe him anything. Why are you insisting on being faithful to him?*

He wasn't being faithful to me, that was for sure. I thought of the woman in the sarong and something hot and dark kindled inside me.

Abe's lips at my throat. My fingers, shaking, as they helped him with the buttons of my shirt.

It didn't take you long did it? From my bed to his.

I shook my head – shutting out the words, shutting out the memory. I owed him nothing. He'd left me. He wasn't here. Abe was here. Abe.

My heartbeat roared in my ears.

I tangled my fingers in Abe's hair.

'Abe.'

He didn't raise his head, but his lips moved against my skin.

'Anna . . .'

'Abe.' It was a gasp. He tightened his grip. 'Abe – Abe, *stop*.'

For a minute I wasn't sure if he would.

Then he flung himself on to his back, his breath coming fast and ragged and furious.

I lay, my heart pounding. Then I hauled myself on to my elbow.

'Abe . . .'

'Choose,' he said. His voice was hoarse, the word like an accusation.

'Abe . . .' I tried, but he cut me off.

'Choose!' he shouted. 'I'm sick of playing second fiddle to a ghost from the past. He's gone – he left you . . .'

I flinched as if I'd been slapped, but he ploughed viciously on, his words tearing at us both.

'You can't spend your life looking back! I'm here, Anna. I want you. I . . .' he stopped, his teeth ground together so that the tendons in his neck stood out. 'I *love* you.'

'Abe . . .' I wanted so much to say, *I love you too*. And I did. That was the worst thing. And I knew what this must be doing to him, what those words had cost him. But . . .

I wouldn't cry. I *wouldn't* cry. I pulled my knees up to my chest and buried my face in my hands.

The silence pulled out, so long that at last I scraped my cheeks on my sleeve and looked up.

Abe was staring down at my leg, where my jeans had ridden up my shin. When he looked up his face was blank with some emotion that might have been shock, or even fear.

'Abe,' I said huskily, 'Abe, you're scaring me.'

'Your scar.'

'My scar?' I echoed, confused.

'Your scar – from when you fell in the snow last winter. It's . . . gone.'

I pulled back my jeans and looked at my leg. He was right. It was gone. It seemed monumentally unimportant.

'Scars fade.'

'It's not faded, Anna. It's *gone*. In – what? Six months? That's not possible. I *saw* that scar. Marks like that don't just disappear. That cut was healed as far as it was ever going to be. No power on earth could've made that scar disappear – not natural, not magical.'

'W-what are you saying?' I said uneasily.

'I don't know.' He put his hand to his head. He looked suddenly sick with fear and I wrapped my arms around my body, shivering. 'I wish Emmaline hadn't taken that poem. I need to read it . . .'

'What are you *saying*?'

'It's not possible,' he whispered. 'There's a line in magic – a line you can't cross. You can't heal the unhealable. You *can't . . .*'

'What are you saying, Abe?'

But I knew. I knew before Emmaline burst into the room, her eyes wide, her breath panting.

'Simon messaged back,' she managed. 'He says . . .' Then she looked from my face, to Abe's, and then back again. 'You've worked it out.'

'No,' I said reflexively. I needed to hear her say it. Needed to hear her repeat Simon's cool, forensic analysis of the lines. I stood up, facing her.

'Why?' Em said.

'Say it, Em!' I cried.

'He says there's two possibilities,' Em said slowly, her eyes flickering from me, to Abe, then back again. 'But they both lead to the same thing. There's a reason you didn't die in that car crash with Seth. There's a reason why you've walked away from so many accidents that should have been fatal. You . . .'

She stopped.

'I – I can't be killed?' I choked out.

'You *can* be killed,' Emmaline corrected. 'But as long as you have a spark of witchcraft left in your body, you can will yourself back to life. And Simon thinks . . .'

She paused, as if suddenly doubting whether to go on.

'What?' Abe said sharply. His voice was hard and curt. 'Spit it out.'

'Simon thinks there's a strong possibility it's not just Anna. He thinks . . . she can do the same for others.'

'He thinks she can raise the *dead*?' Abe said. His naked chest rose and fell, and Em suddenly seemed to clock my rumpled clothes and Abe's missing shirt.

'What the hell's been going on here?' she asked thoughtlessly, and then flinched as she realized. 'No. Don't tell me.'

'Does this matter?' Abe shouted. 'Does any of this matter any more? Anna is the holy grail, for crying out loud – a witch who can raise the *dead*. Do you realize what this means?'

'It means I've got a massive target on my back,' I said, suddenly cold. 'That's what my mother knew, isn't it?'

I began pulling on a jumper. I had no idea what I was going to do – I just knew that whatever was coming, I didn't want to face it cold. There was a clap of thunder outside and the rain spattered again. It sounded like there was hail in the gusts that blew against the window.

Abe too was shrugging into his shirt.

'We have to go back,' I blurted. A picture of my grandmother – thin, spectral, dying – rose up in front of my face. Maybe it wasn't too late – for a witch who could heal the unhealable?

'Yes, we have to go back,' Abe said grimly. 'If this is right . . .'

'Oh God, that witch,' Emmaline said, her face suddenly white. 'She wasn't after the riddle, Anna. She was after *you*.'

'I'll call the airline,' Abe said. 'Em, you start packing. Anna—'

'I'll get Marcus,' I said.

'Anna,' Abe growled, and I knew he was going to start again, start on the stupidity of involving this unknown man in our plans.

'Abe,' I cried, 'just shut up. Please. He saved my life. Do you get that? And Emmaline's. He took a stab-wound to the chest to protect us. I am *not* leaving him bleeding in some seedy Russian hotel while we skip town. I'm just not.'

'Fine!' Abe held up his hands. His face was angry, but he knew when he was on a losing streak. 'Whatever. Tell him what you like. But if he's not ready to leave town by this evening, I don't want to know about it. Here,' he chucked a key fob across the room at me like a missile. 'Take this. Go.'

I went.

238

The cut on the back of my head was already healing as I knocked gently on the door. When I put my hand up to touch it, my hair was still damp, and the skin beneath was tender but unbroken. I shivered and knocked again.

No answer.

'Marcus!' I whispered through the crack.

Still no answer.

The door was locked, but Abe's key turned in the keyhole and I opened it quietly.

Marcus was lying on his back on the bed, the dim light from the rainy St Petersburg afternoon filtering across the room. His eyes were closed and his face, even in sleep, was twisted with pain. One side of his shirt had fallen open and what I saw beneath made me gasp: a huge puncture wound that split the skin below his ribs on the right, ugly with clotted blood and swelling.

I came closer and closer, watching the painful rise and fall of Marcus' chest, the gummy stretch and gape of the clotted wound beneath the cloth.

I felt sick – but perhaps . . . perhaps . . .

I put out my hand towards him and felt the magic gather and build and tingle in my fingers like fizzy water in my veins. I had never felt it so strongly – not since the first time I'd come to Winter, with seventeen years of pent-up magic trapped inside me, roaring to get out.

I sat beside him on the bed very carefully, trying not to disturb his sleep and hurt him any more than he was already. Then I laid one hand on the hot, squelching wound on his side, pouring all my magic into healing the gash. It looked dreadful. It looked unhealable.

But the hideous, maybe mortal, wound began to close. Underneath the blood I could see the skin was knitting together beneath my fingers and with my free hand I gently drew back the other side of his shirt, trying to expose the wound fully, work out what I was dealing with.

Beneath the other side of his shirt was something odd. A dressing, a magical one like the ones I'd seen Maya prepare. It was a white cloth, bound around a handful of twigs and herbs, and scrawled with a charm on top. Had he been hurt before?

The gash had half soaked the bandage, blurring the charms and turning the herbs to a bloody sludge, so I peeled it away.

In the very centre of his chest was a huge black hole. Around it was shiny melted skin, fused into a hard pink welt that covered half his chest. It looked – it looked like a *burn*. But the kind of burn that only a chemical weapon could inflict. The kind of burn that you couldn't – shouldn't – survive.

I froze, my hand still suspended over the half-healed gash.

'What the . . . ?' I whispered. 'Marcus?'

He opened his eyes and blinked blearily a few times. Then suddenly he seemed to focus and he was clutching, clawing at the sheets, desperate to cover himself. His

240

movements were animal, full of a bestial desperation – and then, just as abruptly, he gave up. He slumped back on the pillow, his breath coming fast, his lip curled in an involuntary snarl.

'Marcus,' I repeated, stupidly, 'what – what happened?'

He only stared at me, a creature at bay.

And then – I knew.

A picture filled my head: a huge black crow in vicious attack, its claws gashing at my eyes, and Seth, standing with a flare gun in his hand. He raised the gun, pointed it at the crow.

And fired.

A blue, blazing fire in the centre of the bird's chest.

The stench of burning feathers and scorched flesh.

And the crow wheeling desperately into the sky, spiralling away into the storm.

I'd always known that bird wasn't just a bird. It was a witch. One of the Ealdwitan. But I'd never stopped to wonder *who* at the Ealdwitan. I'd never asked myself whether that witch had survived, if he still bore the scar of Seth's attack.

Stupid.

Stupid, stupid Anna.

I felt very cold.

Marcus saw all this flicker across my face and his expression twisted into something halfway between amusement . . . and hate.

'Well . . .' he drawled. 'Now. This *is* rather inconvenient.'

'Marcus – please, tell me this is a mistake.'

'This is a mistake,' he said. But there was no conviction in his voice. Only an amused, ironic resignation that he'd been caught, just when he'd almost snagged the prize.

None of it made sense.

'Why?' I whispered.

'You don't know?' he laughed.

I shook my head angrily. 'That's not what I meant. I know what I am – I've found the riddle: "The Mistress of Death". But why did you hunt me, betray me, only to save me?'

'Because you were not the prize,' Marcus said softly. 'You were nothing but a chip. A bargaining piece. A means to an end.'

'What was the prize?' I asked, a crack in my voice. But even as he smiled, with a shrug that said, *Don't you know?* I realized.

The Ealdwitan.

He was the spy.

He was the one betraying secrets. In return for – what? Power? Being installed as the Head of the Chairs, what his father had fought for and failed to achieve?

'I was stupid in Winter,' he said softly. 'But you made me angry – with your arrogance and your ignorance of the pearl you held in the palm of your hand. When I found that you knew nothing of what you were, I realized that was your greatest strength – and your greatest weakness. I could use that against you. As long as you had no knowledge of what you were, I could bend you to my will. As long as you trusted me.'

'That was why you helped me,' I said. My voice cracked. 'It wasn't for my mother. It was to get my trust.'

'Yes.'

'And your father – d-did he know?'

'He had an idea – but he hadn't known Isabella like I did. I was the only person she kept in touch with, after she left. When she abandoned me, I traced her footsteps obsessively. It was easy to look up her dissertation, to realize what she'd stumbled upon. To realize what I could have, if I played my cards right. But I couldn't find you – her spells were too effective. Even with everything I knew, I couldn't track you down. And then one day, I had a call, from Winter. Vivian Brereton had no inkling of what he'd found, none at all. But a new witch? A new witch of the right age, with an apparently outwith father? I came to check you out, as I'd checked out every false lead for years and years. And it was you.'

'And the rest – did Thaddeus know about your plan to betray the Ealdwitan to the Others?'

'Him?' Marcus waved a dismissive hand. 'Of course not. He had no vision. He wasn't part of my plan. I'd always known he'd have to go, when the hour came. But you forced my hand with your demand for an interview. I couldn't afford for you to go and see him. It would have come out – what really happened in Winter. You see, *he* would have recognized your description of the crow you wounded. *He* would have put two and two together, and in the end he would have followed the trail through and realized who was at the bottom of all the conspiracies and betrayals: his own son. He was already suspicious, I think. But your grandmother was right. He couldn't bear to think the worst of one of his own camp. He was partisan. That was *his* weakness.'

Oh my God. Thaddeus. I put my face in my hands, thinking of his final moments, his son coming into his room, something in his hand. And then . . .

I felt sick.

'You bastard,' I choked out. There were tears running down my face. 'You traitor. You killed him – you killed your own father.'

I felt weak with hate, so overwhelmed by it that I could barely find the words.

'At least I don't have to pretend any more,' he said softly. 'It was getting rather trying, to be honest, feigning concern, feigning *interest*.'

Despair rose up in my gullet.

My mother. My grandmother. They'd both trusted him. Me. *I'd* trusted him.

It was hard to breathe, the tears constricting my throat.

And then suddenly it was *really* hard. Not just emotion choking me, but something real, as real as hands around my throat. I couldn't breathe.

'M—' I tried. Only a whimper came out.

My ribcage heaved like broken bellows. I could hear

244

pathetic squeaks from my lungs.

Everything was dissolving into black. I groped for a spell, trying to remember my grandmother's charms, but I didn't have the breath to say the words. I fell to my knees and felt the carpet rough against my cheek as my face thudded to the floor.

I couldn't see. I couldn't hear. There was a roaring in my ears and sparks of red and black in front of my eyes.

My fingers scratched at the short pile of the carpet, scrabbling uselessly for a hold, for a weapon.

Then very, very faint above the roaring in my ears I heard Marcus laugh.

The fury broke through like a scouring wave, brutally crashing away the threads of Marcus' spell.

I scrambled to my feet with a vicious slashing blast that sent Marcus flying backwards across the room, crashing into the window with a force that cracked the panes. He howled, a dreadful sound of fear and pain, and pressed his hand to the blackened hole in his chest. I should have followed it with another blow to send him spinning into the street, but at the sight of his agonized face I faltered for a second.

A second was all it took.

He lashed out with a smashing wall of light that left me blind and I stumbled to my knees, groping for something to hold on to, frantically gabbling out spells to clear my vision. Another blast caught me on my left side, sending me crashing into the wardrobe. The louvred door groaned and collapsed, the thin wooden slats splitting like matches.

'*Forescieldnes!*' I gasped, my arms clutched around my head, trying to protect myself from the blows raining down. How was he so strong? This was magic like I'd never encountered before. It felt like I was being battered by twenty people, not just one. I remembered the rumours I'd heard about the Others; the illegal procedures, the way they drained people . . .

Another blast rocked the cupboard, hangers and chunks of wood raining down. I couldn't see, I couldn't see how close he was, where he was. I couldn't see the next blast coming. I could only hear, above my own gasping, panicked breath.

'*Forescieldnes!*' I wept again, begging for protection more than invoking it. A weak shield enveloped me and in the moment's respite I tore at my eyes, too scared to remember a charm now, just working from blind instinct.

Somehow it worked – partly – and when I blinked I could see Marcus, dimly, over the far side of the room, as if through a fog. My eyes were watering as if I'd walked through mustard gas and I swiped again with my sleeve.

But he raised his hand and I cowered, prepared for another blinding blow, and flung a charm beneath his shield before he had time to protect himself.

It exploded in a hail of ice and snow, freezing him to the ground and, while he was cursing and shrieking charms to try to free his arms and legs, I scrambled out of the wardrobe and ran for the door.

I was almost there, when I felt his magic whip round me like a lasso, yanking my feet out from underneath me so that I fell with an agonising crash, sprawling across the floor. He pulled tighter and tighter, reeling me in across the floor, the carpet burning my face. I struggled, clawing at the carpet and sobbing charms over my shoulder, but it was impossible to think with the pain in my face and the pain in my head. The room was filled with a smoky swirling darkness: the darkness of too many spells gone wrong, of magic burned by magic. With a huge effort I managed to twist myself so that I was on my back, instead of face-down on the floor, and I could see him through the smoke.

'Don't fight me, Anna!' he said, between clenched teeth. 'Stop fighting, you stupid girl.'

He was standing with his back to the far wall, his muscles standing out with the effort of restraining me.

'What's the point in resisting?' he panted. 'If you get away, you'll just be condemning Abe and Emmaline along with you. Is that what you want?'

Four feet away . . . three feet . . . I thrashed in his grip, lashing out with spells that had no effect. This wasn't working. Fighting wasn't working.

But I'd *got* to get free.

I'd got to.

'I'll have no compunction about turning you in,' Marcus said. He grimaced and heaved again, the veins in his neck standing out like cords. 'And they'll come and get you. All of you.'

A foot away. There was no fight left in me. Only despair.

'You can't save yourself. But you can save them.'

And then he was hauling me to my feet, his muscles taut with the effort, even though I was no longer fighting him.

I stood in front of him, my arms bound, my legs bound, all the fight gone from my body, all my magic exhausted.

And he leaned down and towards me, his face very close, his lips just centimetres from mine.

'What do you want?' I asked, through gritted teeth.

'Perhaps . . .' I could feel his breath, soft on my face. Then he leaned even closer and put his cheek next to mine, so I could feel the warmth of his skin brushing my cheekbone and feel his lips moving next to my ear. My thighs were pressed against his, our bodies so close that I could feel the rise and fall of his chest against mine. My stomach heaved at the scent of his cologne.

'Perhaps . . .' he said again, very softly, 'the question is, what do *you* want?'

He pulled back.

And suddenly it was Seth staring at me.

Seth. His grey eyes dark as a winter sky. His lips so close to mine I could have leaned forwards and kissed him.

There was no anger in his face. Only the steadfast love I remembered so well.

I heard my breath whimper from my lips.

'Seth?'

'Anna . . .' he put out a hand to touch me. It brushed my cheek and for a moment I closed my eyes, melted into his touch, feeling the familiar painful desire explode within me like a consuming flame.

'Oh Seth . . .'

His hand stroked lovingly down my cheek, my jaw, my throat . . . I couldn't bear to move. I didn't even breathe.

His hand was smooth. Soft.

It had never done a day's work in its life, never hauled on a cable or struggled with an anchor.

I opened my eyes.

Seth's grey eyes looked steadily into mine.

And I kneed him viciously in the crotch.

There was a sound like the scream of an injured cat and he doubled up, weeping with pain. I smiled.

'Serves you right, you bastard.'

Marcus raised his head and his face, beneath the twisted mask of pain, was full of hate.

Then I really did run. Without waiting to see if he was OK. Without looking back. I just ran.

CHAPTER SIXTEEN

I crashed into the room I shared with Emmaline and slammed the door behind me, gasping. Emmaline wasn't there, but Abe was sitting on the bed, his head in his hands, staring at a photo.

As soon as he saw me in the doorway he twitched it back into his wallet.

Then he registered my wild gasping breath and my face, and his expression turned to alarm.

'What's the matter? Is Marcus OK?'

I shook my head, almost unable to speak, and then managed, 'It was him.'

'What was him?'

'He's the sp-spy. He was the crow – the one who attacked me last year. He k-killed Corax.' I took a huge shuddering lungful of air, trying to get control over my breathing. 'He's bargaining for control of the Ealdwitan. He's been selling secrets to the Russian witches and in return they're going to help him bring down the Ealdwitan and he'll be the new head.'

'No!' Abe's face was white with shock. 'And did you tell

him . . . ? Does he know . . . ?'

'About me? Oh yes. He knows. He's always known. I was the last thing to sell – he called me his "bargaining chip".' Nausea rose in my throat at the thought of his face leaning into mine, his smooth hands caressing my skin.

Abe made a noise that was close to a snarl, a wordless growl of hate and fury. Then he seemed to rein himself in.

'Did he hurt you?' he managed. 'What happened to your face?'

I glanced in the dark little mirror and saw there was a friction burn all down one side of my face where Marcus had dragged me across the carpet.

'We fought.'

'But he's injured – how could he fight?'

'I was stupid,' I said bitterly. 'I healed him.'

Abe shook his head, but he could see I didn't need his condemnation on top of everything else.

'Pity,' he said shortly. Then, 'Is he still there?'

'I don't know.' Fear prickled up and down my spine and I looked involuntarily at the door. Abe looked at me.

'How did you get away?' he asked.

'I kneed him in the crotch.' There was a grim satisfaction in the memory.

'Good,' Abe said. 'Can you bear to go back?'

'What – now?' I tried to keep the shudder out of my voice. 'Shouldn't we wait for Em?'

Abe shook his head.

'If he's still hurt, we need to get back before he's had a

chance to recover. Basic rule of fighting: if you've landed a blow that hurt, you land another one before your opponent recovers. The sooner we go back, the better. Ready?'

'OK,' I said, feeling sick.

Abe opened the door and we looked cautiously out into the corridor, our joint shield flickering faintly in the light from the dim bulb.

When we got to the door of the room, Abe looked at me and his voice spoke in my head.

I'm going to kick down the door. Ready? Five, four, three, two . . .

On 'one' he slammed his shoulder into the door along with a blast of magic. It gave with a crunch and we both stumbled into the room.

It was empty, the window swinging wide and the curtains blowing in a cold breeze.

'He's gone,' Abe said. There was a mix of relief and disappointment in his voice as he pushed the windows shut and latched them. I felt neither – only a chilly foreboding as I remembered Marcus' words: *They'll come and get you. All of you.*

'He'll be back,' I said. 'Probably with reinforcements. How soon until we can get home?'

'Well, that's proving a problem,' Abe's black brows furrowed in a frown and he ran his hand through his hair, rubbing his face distractedly so that his stubble rasped against his palm.

'Why?'

He didn't speak, just waved a hand at the window, and I saw what he meant. Outside, the afternoon was dark – very dark. Hail spattered in gusts down the street and I could hear the keening of the wind through the glass. I was cold, I realized suddenly. A shudder ran down the back of my neck.

'But – it's *May*,' I said stupidly. 'This isn't normal!'

Abe only shrugged. When was anything normal where witches were concerned?

'Is it real weather?' I asked. 'Or is someone messing with it?'

'I don't know,' he said shortly. 'I don't think it's real – but I can't alter it. I've tried. It's too big. This isn't just some little local flurry – this is an ice storm that's sweeping across half of northern Europe. It's coming from right across Finland, probably all the way down from Svalbad, for all I know. There's a weight behind this storm that's unstoppable. All the airports are closed. Em's been calling round but there's nothing from here to Moscow. Even the ferries are down. She's downstairs in the Internet café investigating transcontinental trains, but we don't think they'll be fast enough.'

'They're trying to stop us from getting away,' I said. The wind howled outside the window. 'They're hemming us in.'

'Maybe,' Abe said. Something hovered in his black, unreadable eyes. Some shadow of an emotion he was trying not to give way to. I thought it might be fear.

253

'Abe . . .' I said, and I couldn't help myself; my voice shook.

He put his arms around me and spoke into my hair. 'It'll be OK, I promise.'

His words didn't reassure me – he had no way of knowing that. But there was something in his fierce grip, in the hard strength of his shoulders and his arms around me, that was comforting. It was beyond logic. If they came for us, Abe's arms couldn't shelter me. But perhaps I wouldn't die alone.

The thought set a chill echo in my heart.

I *wouldn't* die alone.

Because Abe and Emmaline would die alongside me. Just as Marcus had promised.

Carefully, so that Abe wouldn't suspect my sudden panic, I eased myself out of his arms.

Think, Anna, think.

I walked to the window, pretending to look at the weather, but my heart was racing. The witches would come back. Abe and Emmaline would fight for me – like they always had. They would die. We'd all die.

Except – if Simon's theory was right . . .

My heart thumped in my chest so hard I felt sick. What were my choices? Walk away and face – what? Marcus and an army of crazed witches? Alone? I'd be captured. Captured, and imprisoned, and probably enslaved. But if Simon was right, I might not die.

Perhaps, though . . . I pushed the thought away, trying

not to let it taint my decision. But it forced its way back, a tiny frightened voice insisting, *Perhaps there are worse things than dying. Perhaps there'll come a time when you'll wish you could die.*

I ground my fists into my eye sockets, welcoming the flare of pain as my nails scratched at the tender burnt skin.

I had to think.

Abe and Emmaline would never let me face this alone. And we couldn't escape – at least, *I* couldn't escape.

Which meant – I had to go without telling them. I had to be the lure – distract the hunt from their scent, entice the pursuers somewhere else completely so Em and Abe could survive.

'Anna?' Abe's voice sounded from over my shoulder, suddenly wary. 'What's the matter? What just happened?'

'Nothing,' I said in a voice that sounded brittle and hard and untruthful, even to me. 'Just tired.'

He came over to the window and turned me to face him, studying my torn, bloodied face in the dim grey light. Snow filled the air now, gusting past at a dizzying speed, drifting up against the ledges and the sill. I tried to concentrate on the snow, tried not to look at Abe, at his face, his worried frown, his eyes, black as oil. But I felt his gaze on me.

'You're lying,' he said slowly. 'Why are you lying?'

'I'm not lying.'

'You are.' He laid his hand on my chest, feeling the racing of my heart, and then drew my hand to lie on his chest, where his own heart thudded with a strong, ceaseless beat. 'I can feel it in here. I know. I know something's wrong.'

'Of course something's wrong!' I burst out. 'It's all bloody wrong. We're trapped, like rats, and there's nothing we can do. And it's all my fault.'

He put his arms around me, trying to hug me, comfort me, but I had only one thought: I had to get away, before he worked out what I was trying to do. I had to betray him, both of them, in order to save them.

My heart gave a great broken thud and I shut my eyes, unable to look at him.

'Please let go of me,' I said.

'What?' His hands dropped. He took a step back.

'I'm sorry,' I tried to keep my voice steady, hard. 'I'm just . . . I want to get changed. I need to get out of these clothes.' They were stained with blood from my head wound and covered with chunks of plaster from my fight with Marcus.

Abe looked at me, his black brows drawn into a worried frown, but he only nodded.

'I'll come. I'll sit outside the door while you get changed.'

'No.' I shook my head, feeling numb and cold. 'I want some time on my own. Anyway you – *we* – should pack. We should find another hotel, I think.'

'OK . . .' he said reluctantly. His eyes followed me as I went out of the room. Something was wrong. He just didn't know what.

* * *

Back in the room I shared with Emmaline, I slammed and locked the door and then looked around, trying to work out what to do first. I didn't have long. Emmaline might be back any minute.

First I took the smallest of the two rucksacks, shoved in all the warm clothes I'd thought to bring, along with my wallet and my phone. Then I slung it on my back and picked up Em's pen from her bedside table.

There was nothing to write on except a printout of our airline tickets on the bed. I turned it over to the blank side – and got stuck.

Come on! I told myself. Write! *Write!* Em would be back any second, or Abe would be along to check. *Write* something.

But the words wouldn't come. They boiled up inside my heart – but my pen just hung in the air.

How could I put all the huge weight in my chest down on paper?

I couldn't. There were no words for this huge tearing love and sadness.

Goodbye, I wrote. *It's best I do this alone. I love you. I'm sorry. Anna.*

Then I whispered an invisibility charm and left, before my courage could fail.

CHAPTER SEVENTEEN

The receptionist didn't even raise his head when I tiptoed past. I waited until the phone rang and then I opened the door and slipped outside while his attention was on the call. The wind and snow hit me like a slap in the face.

The street was white with spiralling specks. The sky was grey as slate, and as dark, and the specks swirled and gusted in the light from the street lamps.

I pulled my thin summer coat around me and yanked the hood up to try to get some protection from the wind. What time was it? I glanced involuntarily at my wrist before I remembered the invisibility charm, but just then a clock struck: six loud, echoing notes.

Six o'clock. It would be night soon. Where would I sleep?

The thought gave me a shudder. At least I had money – not much, but Marcus had paid for the cab transfer and that had helped.

I turned my face to the wind and began to walk along the street. As I did, the lighted window of the Internet café drew my gaze and I caught a glimpse of Emmaline, hunched over a PC, her fingers flying furiously. Her back was to the window and I could see her screen. She was on a transcontinental rail site, running through lists of trains and destinations, trying to work out a way of getting out of Russia, fast.

Tears pricked at the back of my eyes and a huge longing came over me to run in and hug her, say goodbye. I could hardly bear to go like this – leaving them both without a word. It wasn't like I'd be coming back. I'd never get the chance to explain.

Em looked up from the keyboard, rubbing the back of her neck, and then slowly, very slowly, pulled by some witchy instinct, she began to turn around.

I felt as if something inside me was breaking in two.

Then I ducked my head inside my invisible hood and walked on.

I walked, and walked, and walked. Mainly to keep warm, because if I stopped I was going to freeze. The Russians around me were all dressed in boots and furs – winter clothes hastily dug out of storage, I guessed. The odd tourist hurried past with pathetic summer gear clutched around them, thin cardigans that showed blue arms – shivering children wrapped in rugs and their parents' jumpers.

'The g-guide b-book said average t-t-temperature f-f-fifteen!' shivered a British woman to her boyfriend as they huddled in the door of a museum. He shook his head and then took off his fleece and wrapped it around her shoulders.

'N-no,' she protested. 'You're as c-c-cold as m-me.'

But he said nothing, only tucked it tenderly around her and then wrapped her in his arms.

The gesture tore at my insides. I thought of Abe putting his jacket round me in the church, of all the times I'd warmed Seth with my arms and he'd warmed me.

I realized I was staring at them. I was invisible, but it still felt like spying, and I walked on.

The wind was at my back now and, as I trudged through the streets with the snow scudding along the pavements in front of me, I felt as if I were being blown along like the spiralling flakes. The roads became a meaningless blur, my shaky grasp of the city's geography slipping away. Each prospect was the same grey, swirling blank. The canals bled into each other. If I'd walked these streets before, I didn't recognize them now.

I had no plan. I'd have to find a place to spend the night, but for now all I could think was to get as far away from Emmaline and Abe as possible. Would they try to find me? Would they scry? I knew from Sienna that it was easier to find a still object than a moving one. So I didn't stop. I just kept walking, my invisible body making a flurrying eddy in the snow as I passed, my footsteps on the slush-covered pavements like the tracks of a ghost.

My feet were numb inside my shoes. My hands were numb inside my pockets. My insides felt hollow. When had I last eaten? I couldn't remember. It no longer seemed to matter.

All that mattered was to keep walking. If I stopped, they'd find me. If I stopped, I'd freeze to death.

Except I wouldn't. I almost wanted to laugh. Would it hurt, thawing my limbs? Was there a limit to what I could survive?

I was passing over a bridge and something made me stop. I put my hands onto the frost-thick railing and looked into the swirling black waters flowing sulkily beneath. Snow slushed the surface, making the water look thick and strange. I had the strangest urge to jump. I imagined myself letting go, sinking into the depths, lying there in the still and the silence while the river froze over and I slept in an ice coffin.

Would I survive even that?

But my fingers were sticking to the icy rail. It burned, pulling them off, and I put them in my mouth, trying to suck away the pain.

Then I saw something that made me forget even that. Something that felt like a punch in the gut.

Seth.

He was standing at the end of the bridge, looking down at something in his hand, and for a moment my heart gave that stupid involuntary leap, an agonising wrenching hope.

The perfection of the illusion was staggering. Everything – every detail. The rain-drenched hair plastered across his forehead. The sharpness of his cheekbones. The blue shadows around his eyes. The scars on his hands, the bruises on his face, the way his shoulder hunched inside his old sou'wester. The curve of his lips, lips that had kissed mine.

It was all just as I remembered.

And the pain inside my heart, the fish-hook ripping and tearing and my heart bleeding on to the snow – that too.

'You bastard.' I tried to speak, but the words were lost in a sob.

He looked up. His face was blank. And I realized I was still invisible.

I had one moment of advantage. I had to use it quick before Marcus saw through my spell.

I bowed my head and let all the agony and anger and sadness flood through me, drenching every cell in my body, calling out of me all the magic I possessed.

There were no charms for this.

There were no words for the way I hated him in that moment.

I clenched my fists, flung back my head, and let go.

The blast rippled out across the bridge: an enormous, unstoppable wall of fire – and time seemed to slow, like a river freezing as it flowed.

I saw his arm go up, as if he were trying to shield himself.

I saw a ring, silver bright in the light from the street lamp.

I saw the inferno engulf him and the ring burn impossibly bright.

I heard his scream.

And I felt the ring on my own finger, the seaglass ring, sear with a sudden, unbearable, burning heat. It scorched out from my hand, ripping through my body, flames burning through my skin, my clothes, my heart.

It was a forest fire. An atomic bomb. Molten gold.

I fell to the ground, convulsing in the hissing, steaming snow.

And then – nothing.

I was warm. That was something. I seemed to have been cold for ever.

I was lying down.

And I was – it came to me suddenly – I was on a boat.

I opened my eyes.

For a minute it was hard to focus, but then I blinked, and the shapes and lights resolved themselves into a blurry picture. Above me was a dark wood-panelled ceiling with an electric light, not a very bright one, and as I raised my head I saw I was lying on a bunk. There was a kettle on a locker and a table to my right with a half-drunk cup of tea and a sandwich.

And there was . . .

Seth.

It was *him*.

He was sitting on the bunk opposite, his head in his hands, and there was something about his utter weariness and despair that made me realize that it *was* him, had been him all along. He'd come back to me. And I'd tried to kill him.

A sound escaped my lips, like a whimper. His head shot up.

'You're awake.' His lip curled as he said the words and somehow he made them sound like an insult.

I struggled upright, but the blood rushed away from my head and I almost fell again. There was a moment's blackness and sickness, and the next thing I knew I was hunched over, Seth's hand on the back of my neck, pressing my head down between my knees.

'What have you been doing?' he said, almost angrily. 'When did you last eat?'

'I'm fine.' I clenched my teeth as if willpower could make the words true and then lifted my arm to push his hand away. This time, when I sat up, I kept it together, somehow. My hands were shaking and I had to prop myself on the table to keep upright, but I kept it together. 'Where are we? How did I get here?'

Seth sat on the bunk opposite, the table between us, and ran his hands through his hair. He looked emotionally and physically exhausted. Almost as tired as I felt.

'We're on my boat. In St Petersburg harbour. When did you last eat?' he repeated.

I couldn't remember. I just stared at him, stupidly, and he pushed the sandwich across the table towards me, and the mug of tea.

'Here.'

'But it's yours.'

'I'll make another one.'

I put the tea to my lips, feeling it scald against my hands. My fingertips were hot with the thawing pain that comes after extreme cold.

Seth stood up suddenly, as if he couldn't bear to look at me any more, and went to the hatch. When he opened it, a blast of frozen air whirled into the warm cabin, and outside there was nothing but dizzying white. I took a bite of sandwich and watched his back as he stood, his arms resting either side of the opening, staring into the night. His muscles were taut and too lean beneath his thin, faded shirt. I saw that he was favouring his bad leg, leaning his weight away from it as he stood. There was a stick – a crutch – propped against the locker. The sight made my stomach clench and the sandwich stuck in my throat.

'This weather, it's witches, right?' he said bitterly over his shoulder.

'I don't know.'

For a minute there was silence; neither of us spoke, we just listened to the scream of the wind and the sounds of the boats in the harbour: ropes whipping against the masts, the icy waves slushing against the hulls.

'Why did you do it?' Seth asked at last in a low voice, almost inaudible beneath the wind. His back was to me, his head bowed, but I could see his hands were clenched on the edge of the hatchway. They looked as if they might crunch through the wood at any moment.

'Do what?' I said hopelessly. I didn't know what he meant any more: the blast of fire, the weather, everything.

'If you wanted me so much, why did you try to kill me on the bridge? Why make me come all this way? To punish me? To show me you've still got me chained?'

'I . . . Seth . . .' I didn't know which accusation to start with.

'Why couldn't you just let me go?' he yelled suddenly, making me jump.

'I don't know what you mean!'

'This!' He grabbed something from a shelf and slammed it down on the table, so hard that the mug of tea jumped and drops spattered the melamine. 'This is what I mean!'

For a minute I had no idea what he was talking about. Then I recognized it. It was the brass compass I'd given him for Christmas – just six months ago, though it felt like a lifetime. The needle was pointing to me.

'I don't understand.'

Seth's jaw clenched. There was something close to fury in his expression, but he was keeping it reined in. I didn't know how long he could hold on to his temper for.

'Look,' he spat. He picked up the compass, moved it from left, to right. The needle swung, pointing always towards where I was sitting. I frowned. I didn't know much about navigation – but I did know that a compass should always point north.

'Is it broken?'

'Yes it's *broken*,' Seth ground out. 'Let me spell it out for

266

you. This compass no longer points to magnetic north. It points to *you*. Bloody fucking inconvenient if you're stuck in the middle of the Baltic sea. So I bought another one. That one points to you too. Every ship, every piece of navigational equipment I get near, they all home in on *you*. You've made me unemployable. No ship will have me on board. I'm a danger to myself. I can't plot a course. I can't steer into a harbour. I nearly died, trying to get back to Helsinki. Is this your idea of a *joke*?'

'I had no idea.' My blood was running cold. I remembered saying to Seth as I handed over the compass, *So you'll always find your way back to me*. And I thought of how I'd wished he *would* come back to me. Had *I* reset his compasses, just by the force of my longing? 'Seth, I never meant—'

'No,' he cut in brutally. 'You never mean it. You never mean to hurt anyone. But somehow I always end up bleeding when you're around. So you dragged me here only to – what? What happened on the bridge? Did you just think it would be fun to burn me alive?'

'No! Of course I—'

'So you got me there and then what? You lost your nerve?' he pursued, viciously. 'You've got the guts to plan a murder, but not to carry it out – is that right?'

'I didn't plan to murder you!' I cried. 'And if you hate me so much, why did you bring me here? Why didn't you just leave me to freeze on the bridge?'

'I don't know!' he shouted. He grabbed his hair, his eyes squeezed shut as if he couldn't bear to look at me.

'Because . . . Because . . . maybe I *am* tied to you.' His hands dropped and when he looked at me there was nothing in his face but bitterness and defeat. 'Just like Grandad said. I can't go on without you. God knows I've tried – but I can't. I love you. And it's killing me.' He fell to his knees on the wooden floor of the boat and I felt it rock with the movement. Then his head was in my lap, his clenched fists gripping my shirt, his face buried in my jeans. His shoulders shook, as if the sobs were ripping him apart from inside.

I slid awkwardly off the bench to kneel beside him and I put my arms around him, put my face in his hair, drawing huge shuddering breaths, remembering his smell, his body, the way we'd fitted together, still fitted.

We knelt for a long time, locked together like two pieces of a carved puzzle, shaped into a twisted symmetry with each other. His tears were wet on my shoulder. I could feel his chest shuddering in and out as if every breath tore at him and knew, too, that it was my own sobs shaking his body that I could feel echoed back to me.

'How could you do that?' he asked at last. His voice was broken. 'On the bridge. My God, Anna, I've hated you. But I would never – I could never . . .'

'I didn't.' I closed my eyes tight shut for a moment. 'Seth, you have to believe me. I thought you were Marcus.'

'Marcus? Who's Marcus?'

'Another witch. He – he knew about you. About us. And he pretended to be you one time. He used his magic to look like you. So when I saw you in St Petersburg . . .'

'But you knew I'd be here, you made me come here,' he said, bewildered. 'I don't understand. Wasn't it you, with the compass?'

'I think . . .' I rubbed my hand across my face, trying to make sense of it all. 'I think perhaps it was – but I'd never have done that deliberately. I never meant to.'

'So you were trying to kill this Marcus guy? Why? And why did I survive? I saw that wall of fire. It *should* have killed me.'

I didn't speak. I just took his hand and put it against mine. The silver ring was gone. In its place was a seared white mark on his ringfinger, like the silvered scar of a very old burn.

On my finger, where the seaglass ring had been, was the same scar.

'I put a spell on that ring,' I said. 'That was why I gave it to you.'

'What was the spell?' Seth's voice was very low.

'I enchanted it to protect you. I said –' I swallowed '– I said I would give anything to keep you from harm. Even my life. I just never thought . . .' I stopped; it was almost too hard to say the words. But I forced myself on. 'I never thought that harm would be from me.'

'So the fire . . . rebounded on you?'

'I think so. It should have killed me too.'

'But it didn't.'

But it didn't. The thought was cold and hard.

We sat for a long time in each other's arms, feeling the shift and rock of the boat beneath us. I knew I couldn't stay – but I knew there was no peace for me where Seth was not. Whatever had brought us together, whatever the rights and wrongs and reasons, it was set. We'd suffered and fought side by side. We'd hurt each other, and healed each other, and saved each other. And somehow, during it all, we'd grown to be part of each other, twisted together by what we'd been through, like two trees growing too close in a forest, twisted by the wind, so that being apart meant tearing out a living part of ourselves.

I knew I should go. And I knew I couldn't. Not tonight, anyway. Maybe tomorrow, when I was stronger, but tonight I couldn't do it to myself, to Seth . . .

At last Seth lifted his head and looked into my face, and his expression made my insides shiver with longing.

He took my hand and pulled me to my feet.

Then he turned out the lamp and together we walked slowly in the darkness, to the door at the far end of the boat, beneath the prow.

Seth pulled open the door and inside was a bed, no floor at all, just a tumbled sea of sheets from wooden wall to wooden wall.

We lay down together, side by side. Neither of us spoke. Seth closed his eyes and I traced one finger down the line of his forehead, the bridge of his nose, the curve of his lip, feeling the smoothness of his bones beneath the wind-roughened skin.

There was no light apart from a little moonlight filtering through a frosted porthole. In the moon-dappled darkness he was no longer an angry stranger. He was Seth. My Seth. The bitter, too-sharp lines softened into the face that I knew and loved, that still tugged at my heart.

'Seth . . .' I whispered.

'Yes.' He didn't open his eyes.

'I love you. I always have. I never stopped.'

His answer was so low I could hardly hear any words, but his lips moved and I felt his breath on my skin.

I shut my eyes and he pulled me into him, my head on his chest, his arms around me, and we lay in the quiet moonlight and slept in each other's arms.

When I awoke it was still dark, but the wind had dropped and it felt maybe a degree or two warmer.

I opened my eyes to look out of the porthole window, but there was nothing to see. Either it was too dark, or the snow was too thick on the pane. So I closed them again, feeling the warmth of Seth's chest beneath my cheek and the slow, steady beat of his heart. I should not have felt happy. There was no room for happiness in the middle of all this horror and uncertainty. And there would be no happy ending for Seth and me. Tomorrow I'd have to get up and go to meet whatever waited for me. And Seth – Seth would be free at last.

But it was still night. Dawn was a few hours away. And until it came, I could pretend.

I thought Seth was asleep, but then I felt his hand lift to his face and heard his shaking in-breath.

I opened my eyes and looked up at him. His face was wet.

'Seth,' I whispered, 'what's the matter?'

'Nothing,' he said huskily. 'I'm – I'm happy.'

'So am I.' I swallowed away the lump in my throat and hugged him tighter.

And then, I didn't mean to, but I couldn't help it: I kissed him, kissed his chest through the thin, worn material of his shirt. I heard the soft gasp of his breath and waited for him to tell me to stop. But he didn't. He said nothing, he only lay there, completely still, as if unable to move.

My lips were so close – too close. I kissed him again, in the hollow beneath his ribs. Then again, where his T-shirt had ridden up, and the skin stretched taut over his hip-bone, bare to the night air.

My hands pushed at his T-shirt, pushing it up and over his head, and then suddenly he was kissing me – his shaking hands pulling at my shirt, his lips hot against my skin, his breath shuddering against my shoulder.

I pulled, blindly, clumsily, struggling out of my jeans with fingers that trembled too hard to work the buttons. My belt clattered as it fell and Seth made a sound like a groan.

I reached for him in the dark – running my hands over the lean muscles of his shoulders, his chest, the dips

272

and hollows of his back, and he put his arms around me fiercely, turning in a tangle of sheets, pulling me with him so that I was on top of him, then beneath him, locked together.

'Anna . . .' His voice shook. 'Oh Anna.' He kissed me and then made a muffled sound against my shoulder, something like, 'Oh God!'

He sat up, pulling himself out of my arms.

'Wait – I can't think with you . . . Stop, please, stop.'

I heard his panting, trembling breath, coming fast in the darkness.

'Seth . . .' My breath was coming like sobs. 'I was wrong. That night, on Valentine's Day, when you asked . . .' I broke off; I couldn't say it, but he knew. He knew what I meant. That night, a night like this, he had asked if I believed that he loved me, and I'd been unable to answer. And he'd pushed me away and walked out of the house and out of my life. 'If you knew how I've wanted to turn back time, give a different answer . . . Please, I want you – I want *this*.'

'But maybe . . .' His breath caught in his throat. 'Maybe you were right.'

'What?'

It was like a slap. I sat up, pulling the sheets around me.

'I don't know any more.' He ran his hands through his hair, his face agonized. 'I thought this was love. But love shouldn't feel like this, should it? It shouldn't feel like you're being ripped in two. It shouldn't feel like someone

273

yanking your heart out between your ribs. It shouldn't *hurt* so much.'

I was silent. Was he right? My love for Seth had been the still centre of my life for so long it was hard to imagine how I'd existed without it. But . . . I thought of the fish-hook inside me, ripping and pulling at my heart. I thought of Seth's pain and mine. Perhaps this wasn't love. Perhaps love *shouldn't* hurt like this.

If so, what was it? Obsession? Addiction? Magic?

Seth spoke, his voice very low. 'You know what's the most fucked up thing of all?'

'What?' My voice cracked on the single word.

'I don't care. I don't care any more. I just want you, I *need* you. I don't care why – I don't care about the rights and wrongs. I can't live without you. I don't *want* to live without you.'

'I need you too.' It was the only thing I could think of to say.

He made a choking sound and then his arms found mine and his lips found mine and we were crushed together, clutching each other so hard that I whimpered. I lay back on the bed, pulling him with me.

And then, for a while, there were no words.

CHAPTER EIGHTEEN

I slept well and so deeply that when I woke it was with a sense of having slept for a week, or maybe a month. My limbs were stiff and sore and the ringfinger of my hand hurt.

I lifted it up and saw the scar, bone white. I twisted it from side to side, looking at the shallow dent in the pale sunshine. Would it heal, like the others?

The sunlight reminded me: however long I'd slept, it was morning now. And morning meant . . .

A sick feeling dropped down on me like a sudden weight. It was like re-entering a bad dream.

Morning meant facing reality.

It meant putting on my wet, snow-stained clothes and shouldering my pack. It meant leaving. It meant leaving Seth.

I turned to look at him. He was lying stretched out on his front, his legs sprawled across the bed, one arm flung protectively across my waist. His face, turned to one side, was perfectly peaceful, but I could see the effects of the last few weeks and months. He was no longer the beautiful boy

I'd fallen for when I first came to Winter. Instead his face was sharp with pain and lean, the bones too close beneath the skin. There were violet shadows beneath his eyes, as if he hadn't slept properly for a long, long time. And by the door of the boat was that crutch, like a reminder of what awaited him when he opened his eyes. My heart faltered.

I must have moved, for he shifted his arm very slightly, yawned, and then opened his eyes.

For a moment I thought he'd forgotten the night before, or was angry, or full of self-disgust.

But then his face split into his wide, incredible smile – the smile that never failed to make my heart lift and twist and beat a little faster. And even with his battered face and scarred hands, he was still Seth – my Seth – and the knowledge still filled me with the same joy.

'I love you,' I said softly.

He reached out and touched my face, as if hardly able to believe I was here, real.

'I half thought I'd dreamed all this. Last night –' he stroked my hair back from my face '– I've dreamed about it so often, but I always woke up alone. I thought I'd wake up and find you gone.'

It was too close to the truth and I flinched. A shadow crossed his face.

'What? Can't you stay?'

I opened my mouth – and then he shook his head, turning away.

'Don't tell me. I don't want to know. I'd rather pretend for a bit longer.'

'OK,' I said huskily. I stroked my hand down his ribs, feeling the too-sharp furrows beneath my hand, and then down his side, to rest over his hip-bone, where the pain was curled, waiting to ambush him when he stood.

'I could heal this,' I said, with a certainty I'd never felt before. A certainty in myself, in my magic.

But Seth shook his head.

'No.'

'Why not?'

'Because.'

'Because you don't trust me?' It hurt, though I couldn't blame him.

'I trust you,' he said slowly, as if trying to explain something he didn't fully understand himself. 'But I – I don't trust witchcraft. Not any more. And this pain, it's part of me. Do you understand?'

'No,' I said. Tears pricked at my eyes. 'I don't. I want you to be well again, whole.'

'I *am* whole, when I'm with you.'

He kissed me gently on the lips, and then harder, and I felt the desire welling up inside me. I let my arms go round him, then I lay back and the tiny room seemed to shiver and rock with the force of his longing and mine, like some kind of alchemical reaction that made the world fracture along fault lines too fine to see in everyday existence. I *felt* it move – physically shivering so

277

that a cup on a shelf rocked and fell.

Seth felt it too. He stopped, with his body poised over mine, half listening, half feeling the movement.

Then, abruptly, he swung his legs over the edge of the mattress, out into the galley, and picked up his jeans from the night before.

'What's the matter?' I asked.

'I don't know,' he said. 'Something doesn't feel right. I'm going to check the mooring.'

He pulled on his jeans and then stood. As his bad leg hit the floor he gave a sharp intake of breath that made my heart clench. I watched as he limped his way down the little galley.

He was halfway down the room when there was a sudden swell and he staggered, cracking his hand on a locker. He wrung his hand, swearing, and I jumped out of the bed.

'Your hand! Is it OK?'

'Sod my hand.' His face was really worried now. 'That was far too rough for a harbour wave.'

He opened the hatch and stuck his head out. And then he swore. Again. For a long time.

'What?' I asked. 'What is it?'

He didn't answer. He just stood, staring in disbelief at something I couldn't see. I grabbed a sheet from the bed and, winding it round myself, I shoved my way into the narrow space beside him in the doorway.

There was nothing there.

Nothing.

Nothing but the grey sky and the grey sea. No harbour. No city. No boats.

Somehow – impossibly – we'd come loose in the night and drifted out to sea. As we watched, another huge wave came rolling across from the horizon and under our hull, and the little boat lifted and slapped down, shaking the kettle on the stove.

'This is not possible,' I said, trying to suppress the edge of hysteria in my voice. 'It's *not* possible.'

'You're telling me! I don't understand it. I tied that mooring myself – I *know* there's no way those knots could have come undone. Did someone cut us loose, as a joke?'

'But why? Who'd do that?'

'Anna . . .' Seth stopped, and I could see the doubt in his face. 'It . . . it wasn't *you*, was it? By mistake?'

'No!' Anger bubbled up inside me, but I couldn't completely blame him for his suspicions. 'Honestly, Seth, it's not like that any more. I've got it under control. It's *months* since I've done any magic by mistake.'

'But the compass . . .'

'That's different – I gave that to you months and months ago. I must have done something to it then, without meaning to. But I promise you, I *didn't* do this. I'd know if I had.'

'OK . . .' he said. He didn't sound completely convinced, but there was nothing I could argue with. Anyway, our situation now was more important.

'What can we do?' I asked. 'Are we going to crash?' I couldn't remember what the proper boat word was. 'Will we find our way back?'

'We should be all right, I think,' Seth said, but he looked worried. 'We're in the Gulf of Finland – it isn't huge as seas go. It's not like being adrift in the Atlantic. We can't go for that long without seeing some kind of landmark and then we'll have a rough idea of where we are. As long as we don't drift too close to the shore in a fog, we'll be OK.' He looked at the sky. It was clear and cold, but I remembered the weather in St Petersburg and how fast the snow had blown in from nowhere. There was nothing to say that tonight there wouldn't be snow, or mist, or even a hurricane.

'But I don't understand,' he said again. He rubbed his hand over his face, his palms rasping against the stubble. 'I just don't get how we could drift out to sea like this – past all those boats, past the harbour arm – and all without feeling a thing! I swear when we woke in the night, we were still tied up. How could we get so far in a few hours?'

'Well . . .' A blush rose up my cheeks and I felt ridiculous. It was stupid to be embarrassed about this with Seth. 'We weren't really paying much attention to outside, were we?' The truth was that a tornado could have lifted the boat up like Dorothy's house in *The Wizard of Oz* and I wouldn't have known any better last night.

'N-no . . .' Seth said. He cracked a reluctant half-smile. 'It could be worse, I suppose. Adrift on a boat with you, with no clothes on. I can think of worse situations.'

'Oh really?' I attempted some mock outrage to hide my fears. 'You can *just* think of a worse situation? How flattering.'

Seth smiled properly then and he put his arm around me, kissing the top of my head. I leaned into him, thinking how screwed up this was. That we'd found each other like this, that the bleakest night of my life had also been the best, that the fear running through me now was mixed with such an impossible, irrepressible joy.

There was one silver lining at least: Emmaline and Abe would have a bloody hard time finding me here.

The thought gave me an idea.

'Seth, do you have a map?'

He looked at me like I'd lost the plot and then nodded.

'Er, yes. They tend to be quite useful in sailing, you know. But it's not much use without GPS, or even a compass. Without that, I can't take a proper bearing.'

'Can I see it? The map, I mean. I want to try something.'

Seth led me back into the cabin and I sat while he spread the table with charts. I didn't really understand them – some of the coastlines looked vaguely familiar, but the charts were covered with lines and shapes I didn't recognize at all. I guessed they must be currents, or depth readings, or shipping lanes.

Then I looked around.

'I need something like a chain or a bootlace, with a heavy object at the end.'

'How heavy?' Seth asked.

'Not very heavy – like a ring.' The thought made me look down at my finger again and I sighed. I'd loved the seaglass ring. But I couldn't regret it – it had saved Seth's life.

'Um . . .' Seth was searching round the cabin and at last he came up with a piece of string. He tied a keyring to the end of it. 'How's this?'

'It's a bit big, but it'll do.'

'What are you *doing*?'

'It's a form of divination. It's called cartomancy. I've never tried it before but I've seen Maya do it. Now shh, I need to concentrate if this is going to work.'

I stood up, over the spread-out charts, and held out the piece of string with the keys on the end. Then I shut my eyes and began to swing the makeshift pendulum in slow circles above the map, waiting for the pull.

'*Séce*,' I whispered, as the pendulum swung round and round in ever widening circles. '*Séce . . . Séce . . . Séce . . .*'

The tug came unexpectedly on the fourth and widest circle, far to the right. I let the pendulum complete another revolution and then felt it again, in just the same place, stronger than before. One last slow circle and the tug this time was a yank. The keys pulled from my grasp and chinked on to the map and I opened my eyes.

'Did it work?'

Seth looked down at the chart and then began to laugh.

'No, I can safely say it didn't.'

'Why not? It felt like it did. Are you sure?'

'The keys seem to think we're in the Kara Sea.'

'Which is . . . ?'

'Somewhere north of Siberia.'

'What's wrong with that?' I asked. Seth laughed again, slightly incredulously this time.

'Anna, tell me you didn't do Geography at GCSE? Have you got any idea *where* Siberia is?'

'Yes!' I said, slightly annoyed. 'It's in Russia. So are we. What's wrong with that?'

'Russia is the size of a continent. And St Petersburg is on the far western side, tucked into a long crevice under Finland and Sweden. Whereas Siberia is on the far eastern side. Look.'

He showed me with his finger, tracing the route the boat would have had to have drifted: along the Gulf of Finland, past Finland, Poland, Germany, north round Norway and over the top of Sweden, and then all the way along the immensely long coast of Russia, miles, and miles, and miles disappearing beneath his finger as it traced the route. Even I could see it was impossible. It was something like the equivalent to drifting from the UK to America and back. Twice. In a single night.

'There's absolutely no way we can have gone more than thirty or forty miles,' Seth said. 'And even that's unlikely given the wind.'

'Oh.' That was good – right? 'So what do we do now?'

'Well given your magical map thing didn't work so well –' Seth was suppressing a smile '– I guess we wait. I'll get the sails up and you can make us a cup of tea.'

'Can I get dressed first?' I asked meekly.

'As captain of this boat, if I said no, would you obey my order?'

'No. And I might have to give you two fingers as well.'

Another smile twitched Seth's mouth.

'Well, since you'd probably whip my arse if I tried to flog you for mutiny, I'd better say yes then.'

My clothes were still wet from the night before so I helped myself to some of Seth's. The shirts were OK – baggy but wearable – but he laughed out loud when I came on deck in his jeans. The waistband didn't meet around my hips so I'd threaded some string through the belt loops into a makeshift belt and the legs were so long I'd had to roll them into fat sausages around my ankles.

'Nice! Very nice.'

'Oh shut up,' I said and handed him a cup of tea. He kissed my cheek and then my lips.

'I meant it. You look –' he took a swallow of tea, his eyes smoke-dark over the rim of the cup '– I don't know. There's something about seeing a girl in your own clothes. It's – very sexy.'

'Don't get used to it,' I said grumpily, though a part of me melted inside at his words and the look in his eyes. 'As soon as my jeans are dry I'm putting them back on.'

'There's always an alternative,' he teased. I raised an eyebrow and he looked back at the bed with a shrug. 'I don't mind if you don't mind . . . ?'

'Drink your tea!' I said scoldingly. And he did, suppressing a smile and turning to watch the horizon.

For the next few hours we sailed slowly on. I watched Seth guiding the boat and occasionally pulled a rope or checked the barometer if he asked me to. The compass was still pointing to me, resolutely following me as I padded about the boat in my bare feet.

By late morning the wind was cold and there was sleet in the air. Seth was in his sou'wester and I was huddled below making lunch, sticking my head out of the hatch only occasionally to ask how to work the stove or where to find a knife.

At last lunch was ready and Seth came below to eat it. He wolfed it down, keeping one eye watchfully on the window.

'What's the matter?' I asked at last.

'I don't know.' He wiped his mouth and ducked his head to look out of the porthole again. 'This just – it all feels wrong. We should have seen something.'

'Land, you mean?'

'No, not necessarily land, but just *something*. This is a shipping lane – there should be boats, ferries, *something*.'

'They closed the ferries I think, last night, because of the weather,' I said. Seth shook his head.

'Makes no difference. There'd be people stranded in the wrong place, keen to get home. They'd be on the sea by now.' He looked over at the compass and his face was suddenly fierce with frustration. 'You don't think . . . Could you make it, you know, work again?'

'I don't know,' I said slowly. 'I could try, but . . .'

'Or even better, the GPS system?'

'I'm really not sure. I don't know how they work. I'm not very good with stuff like that . . .' I trailed off, remembering how I hadn't been able to fix my phone when it was waterlogged.

'Will you try?' Seth pushed his plate aside and looked out of the window at the rolling grey sea and then at the thermometer on the window, which was dropping steadily along with the barometer.

'I'll try.'

After he went back up on deck, I took the compass down off the shelf and stared at it. I had no idea how they worked; I knew that the needle was magnetized and pointed to magnetic north, but the physics behind the actual magnetism was a mystery. It was something to do with electrons, I thought – or was it protons? Either way, I was pretty sure I'd have even less success with the GPS system. It was a flashy-looking thing with a blue backlit display, on a console with the radio. The display showed numbers all right, but according to Seth they were completely meaningless. I had nowhere to begin with that – but the compass . . .

I held it in my hand and began tentatively probing it with my magic. There was definitely some kind of magic tangled up with its workings, I could feel that, but I couldn't see how or why. In the end I shut my eyes and opened my mind up cautiously. In the shadowy magical realm the room was dim, but the compass glowed with a white light, something like witchlight. It was enchanted – I could see it, feel it, clearly now. But with magic so pure, so elemental, I didn't even know how to begin disentangling it. It wasn't a spell, or a charm, or anything that could be explained or written down or solved. It throbbed with *need*. My need, but also Seth's. Our need to be together. The need to find each other.

Somehow, through me, through my power, the compass had become that simple, burning desire. There *was* no way of mending it, any more than you could 'mend' an ordinary compass to tell the time. It was what it was. To change it would be to destroy it. And destroying it wouldn't bring us any closer to finding out where we were.

With a sigh, I pushed the compass away and went up on deck to find Seth. He was standing at the tiller, staring out to sea. It was cold, very cold, and I shivered as I shut the hatch behind me.

'Seth . . .' I said and he turned.

'Did it work?'

'No. I can't fix it. I don't think it can be fixed.'

'Shit.' He sank on to a bench and put his head in his hands. 'I don't suppose you fancy trying that map thing again?' There was no mockery in his face now. In silence we went back down into the galley and in silence I watched as he spread the charts again. I picked up the keys and began to swing them, just as before.

This time the pull was almost unbearable; I tried for a second revolution but the keys wouldn't leave the spot they'd chosen and, when I opened my eyes, they were suspended at an unnatural angle, defying gravity.

I let go of the string and they fell to the map with an abrupt, dull chink, like a ball-bearing hitting a magnet.

Seth began shaking his head almost immediately.

'No. No, no, no.'

'What is it?'

'This is not possible.'

'What?' I begged. His face was pale.

'They seem to think we're in the Laptev Sea now. Which means we've travelled – what . . . ?' He looked at his charts and made a rapid calculation. 'Something like four hundred miles in about two hours.'

'Seth, I could be wrong. I don't know much about cartomancy. I could be completely wrong.'

But neither of us thought so any more. I could see that from the look on Seth's face as he stared at the charts and then out at the huge, featureless sea, with nothing between us and the horizon apart from the vast grey waves. I thought of all the times I'd spied on him in the water, the tiny boat scudding in the enormous, lonely waste of the ocean.

And now I was there.

'I should go back on deck,' Seth said. He stood, his face very bleak and reached for his sou'wester. Ice spattered on the porthole and suddenly I was calm.

'Seth, stay below.'

He shook his head, tried to speak, but I put out my hand to stop him.

'Listen, I think we're being pulled. I think *I'm* being pulled – reeled in, taken somewhere. I don't know where. But I don't think it matters if you steer this boat or not. I think we'll end up at the same place.'

'I'm not going to let you get pulled into some trap! We'll fight! Surely if I sail the opposite way . . .'

'But which way *is* the opposite way?'

Seth's gaze followed mine towards the window and we both stared out at the unending grey. There was no clue to where the danger lay. His shoulders seemed to slump.

'If I don't steer we could die.'

'I think . . .' I couldn't finish. But he knew. He bowed his head.

Then he held out his hand.

Perhaps we *should* have gone on deck, tried to turn the boat around, fought to the end.

But we didn't. I led him the other way, down the galley to the room with the bed. It felt like we had only a few hours left. If so, I didn't want to spend them fighting.

CHAPTER NINETEEN

It was late when Seth stirred in my arms.

'What?' I said softly.

'Can't you feel? The sea's changed. We're near land.'

We pushed back the covers, shivering at the bite of the cold air, and began to get dressed. My jeans were dry now and I pulled them on, along with my top and one of Seth's sweaters beneath my coat. Seth had on a thick cable-knit jumper under his sou'wester. It made him look huge, like a giant in yellow oilskins. I shivered as he limped down the galley towards the hatch; in silhouette he looked eerily like Bran.

On deck we stood staring across the sea. It was very late, but still not yet dark in spite of the thick clouds that blanketed the sky. Tiny flecks of snow fell from the greyness, disappearing into the sea. A few landed on Seth's dark curls, melting slowly into liquid diamonds.

'Look.' Seth pointed out towards the horizon. At first I couldn't see anything, but after I strained my eyes into the dim, shifting light, I thought I could see a new darkness between sea and sky. 'Land,' Seth said. He looked at me, his face uncertain. 'What shall we do?'

'What do you mean?'

'Well, whoever's bringing you here, "reeling you in", do you think they're a friend or not?'

'I . . . I don't know,' I said. Possibilities flickered through my head, hope and dread fighting in my imagination: Marcus; the mad Russian witch on the bridge; my mother . . .

'What I'm saying is, I can try to turn the boat around. Do you want me to?'

'They'll just come after us.' I felt fury and frustration boil up inside me and, most of all, fear for Seth. 'I'm so, so sorry. You should never have been mixed up in this. Listen –' I gripped the front of his sou'wester with fierce, numb hands '– I have to see this through to the end, but maybe you can get away.'

'What do you mean?' He frowned.

'As long as I'm in this boat they'll carry on pursuing us. But if I can get ashore, maybe you can make a run for it.'

'What?' His face was frank disbelief now. 'And leave you alone to face – that?'

'You *have* to. *Please.* If you're involved, it'll only make it harder. If I can hold on to just one thing – the idea that you might be OK—'

'Anna, you're crazy. Either that or you think I'm a total shit.'

'I'm not,' I cried. 'I don't. You were never meant to be involved in this. I dragged you in with that stupid spell;

please, cut yourself free. *Please*. For me.'

'I won't do it.'

'We could both be going to our deaths! Do you understand that?'

'Yes!' he shouted. His hands gripped my shoulders. 'Yes, I understand – of course I understand. But *you* need to understand – how could I live with myself if I sailed away now, not knowing what happened to you? I tried to leave you once and it nearly killed me.'

'But it *didn't* kill you – did it? No one ever died from a broken heart. You cut yourself free once, Seth – you *can* do it again.'

'Don't ask me again,' he said, his voice fierce. 'Do you understand? And don't you dare tell me what it was like for me to leave you. You don't know what it was like. You have no idea.'

'You left me!' I cried. 'Do you think that didn't hurt?'

We stood for a moment, staring at each other in the biting wind. Then his face crumpled and I hugged him, hard enough to crush him, it felt like, my fingernails digging into the tough rubber of his sou'wester.

'I'm sorry,' he gasped, his voice hoarse. He pulled back and his fingers swept the wet, salt-draggled hair from my face. His eyes were filled with tears. 'Why are we fighting?'

'I don't want you to die for me. Please turn back. You might have a chance.'

'There's no chance.' Seth swept an arm out, gesturing to the vast grey waste of sea. 'Look. I can't sail back – it would take weeks, months, even with a working compass. Anyway, how would you get to shore without me? I've got no dinghy, you know.'

'I could swim.'

'Are you mad?' He looked at me in disbelief. 'You'd die!'

'I wouldn't die. That's what this is all about.' I closed my eyes, suddenly weary of the futility of it all. Of running, of waiting, of hiding. If my mother hadn't succeeded in keeping my secret, how could I? 'As long as I have witchcraft, I can't die. That's what my mother knew. That's what she was trying to hide. That's what the Ealdwitan knew – or at least some of them did.'

'You can't *die*?' Seth's face was blank with shock. 'What does that even mean?'

'I've no idea,' I said tiredly. 'I can age – clearly. And I can be very badly hurt, to the point of death. So maybe I'll just carry on, horribly old, horribly crippled, until whatever spring feeds my witchcraft runs dry.'

'And the people who're bringing you here – is that what they want?'

'I guess so. But I don't know. I don't know anything for sure.'

Seth only stared at me, his face white. And then there was a grinding, shushing crunch, and the boat ran gently on to a shingle beach.

Seth and I both turned, still in each other's arms, and looked at the beach. My heart was beating like a drum and I felt Seth's hand press over it, feeling my panic.

293

'It's OK,' he whispered. But we both knew it was a lie.

In front of us was a black, shingle beach, studded with enormous rocks like teeth, and beyond that, tall black cliffs towering into the cloud. It was astonishingly beautiful – and the most barren place I had ever seen.

Seth lowered himself from the prow of the boat on to the black sand and then held out his arms. It looked horribly far from the deck to the beach and I stood for a moment, faltering on the deck.

'All this – and you're frightened to jump a few feet?' he said.

I clenched my teeth.

'I'm not frightened.'

Then I jumped. Seth steadied me on the sand and we looked around us.

'What now?' Seth asked. But before I could answer, a strange, hoarse cry rang out from further up the beach and we both whipped round, ready to face whatever was coming.

There was no one there. The beach stretched away, disappearing into the mist, empty of everything apart from rocks and breaking waves.

The sound came again – a low, resonant growl.

'What is it?' I whispered. 'Where's it coming from?'

Seth saw before I did and his laughter made an incongruous sound, echoing off the black cliffs.

'It's a walrus!'

He pointed and I saw it too, heaving itself off the rocks into the sea with that hoarse barking cry.

'A walrus!' I breathed.

We watched as first one, then another and another flopped into the water.

'They are beautiful, are they not?' A voice came from behind us, husky and cracked as if long unused. Seth and I wheeled round, the shingle hissing beneath our feet, and there, framed against the cliffs, was a woman.

Her hair was pitch-black and long, braided and coiled all over her head in intricate patterns, and her skin was very white – almost an eerie white. Bone-white, as if she hadn't seen sunlight in many years.

But she stood now, in the cloud-dimmed light, and she smiled. Her lips were almost as pale as her face, but her gums beneath were red and her eyes were red-rimmed too.

She spoke again, saying something in Russian and then smiled wider, showing her red mouth, and said, 'Welcome,' in a Russian accent. 'Ah-na.' She said my name slowly, making two words of it, letting her tongue dwell caressingly on each.

'Who are you?' I said, my voice a whisper above the sound of the waves on the beach. I swallowed and tried again, louder. 'Who are you?'

'My name is Tatiana.' She turned and nodded courteously at Seth. 'And you must be the man, Seth. You are welcome too, though you will be the first – how is it? *Čužestranec*,' she said slowly. 'One not of our kind.'

'Outwith,' I said uneasily.

'Yes. You will be the first outwith to enter our kingdom.

Come. Will you take bread and salt with us?'

I looked at Seth and he shrugged. Did we have a choice?

The woman turned without waiting for an answer and began to clamber up the cliff, moving at inhuman speed between the sharp black splinters of rock.

I took Seth's hand and we followed.

We walked, following the witch across rocks, and then into forest. Her feet were bare, but she didn't seem to feel the stones, or the pine needles, or the cold.

For the first few miles Seth and I kept up, but as the distance wore on we both began to struggle. Seth was limping badly, his face tight with pain. He'd forgotten his crutch and, at last, when we passed a long-fallen branch in the forest, he stopped.

'I can't keep walking on this leg,' he said shortly, his words clipped with the pain and the effort of speaking. 'I shouldn't have left my crutch on the boat. Hey, wait!' he yelled into the forest after the witch's disappearing shadow.

The witch stopped. She didn't return, but I could see her shadowy form far up among the trees, watching us. Seth pulled a penknife out of his pocket and began stripping away the leaves and twigs from the branch. At the top it divided into a fork and he whittled it out to make a curve. When he tried it, it fitted under his armpit. He made a face.

'Not very comfortable, but it's better than nothing.'

'Come,' the witch called urgently. 'It grows dark.'

I looked up, through the tall slender pines, stretching to the sky. It was hard to tell beneath their shadow – only a dim grey light filtered between the needles, the sky almost completely obscured by an intricate pattern of branches that disappeared into the cloud. But it had grown darker since we entered the forest and, as the witch began to walk again, I heard the far-off howl of a wolf, and felt Seth shudder beside me. I squeezed his free hand.

'Are you OK?' I whispered. Seth said nothing; he gave a sharp nod. But I knew from his face and from the shortness of his breath that he was in pain.

On we walked. The ground seemed to be rising and soon we were in thick cloud, hardly able to see the shape of the witch in front of us. She'd become just a dark wisp, shifting from tree to tree. Beside me Seth stumbled, grabbing at my arm to save himself. He made an involuntary sound of pain as he recovered his balance and my heart wrenched.

'Please,' I said urgently, 'let me try to heal it.'

He shook his head, a single movement, no words.

'Then can I at least help with the pain? I could do that—'

But he cut me off:

'No.'

'Come!' the witch shouted impatiently. At the sound of her voice the wolves howled again, the sound echoing mournfully through the cloud-wreathed trees. There were more of them now – different notes baying in harsh symphony with each other.

'Come on.' Seth gritted his teeth and began to walk again. 'I don't want to end up as wolf meat.'

The hours wore on and the forest grew darker, and darker, until at last it was full dark. It was colder too. The shrouding cloud did not lift, but now it was more like an ice mist and our breath made white ghosts in front of us, dispersing into the frozen fog. There was frost on the ground and my feet slipped on icy branches. But the witch ahead of us never broke stride, though she turned occasionally, exhorting us to 'Come!' over her shoulder in a voice that crackled with urgency.

I found myself wondering bitterly why they could pull us all this way in Seth's boat and yet these last few miles had to be so hard. Beside me I could hear Seth's breath, hear each hoarse involuntary whimper as he set his foot to the ground and the pain stabbed again and again.

At last I couldn't bear it any longer.

'Stop!' I cried out to the witch. 'Please stop! You're killing him.'

To my surprise she did stop and turned, her face glimmering bone-white in the darkness.

'Yes, we stop,' she said. 'We are here.'

I looked around us. There was nothing – nothing but the rough pine trunks and the cold, wreathing cloud.

'Where?' I said. I could hear the panic in my voice. Why had she brought us all this way, to the dark empty heart of the forest? The wolves howled and it sounded like they were echoing my plea, 'Where?'

'We descend,' said the witch. She pointed.

I looked in the direction of her finger but could see nothing – then the mist cleared a little and in front of us gaped a narrow muddy track, disappearing into the earth. Its mud walls were fortified with felled tree trunks, holding back the soil. And in the centre was a dark opening, a black mouth in the cold, wet mud. A cold breath exhaled from the opening and it smelled of blood.

Bile rose in my throat – and if it hadn't been for Seth I would have run, no matter how stupid it was, no matter that the forest was black and the place lonely, and the wolves howling all around. I would have run a hundred miles in the dark and the snow, with the wolves at my heels, rather than enter that place.

But Seth couldn't run. He couldn't even walk another mile. His breath hissed between his teeth and his hand in mine was cold and clammy with pain.

I'd brought him here. I couldn't leave him.

'Go,' said the witch. Her voice was sharp now. There was no hint of invitation any more. 'Descend.'

When we didn't move, she put a cold hand in the small of my back and pushed, and I stumbled forwards on to the rutted muddy track, towards the blackness below.

CHAPTER TWENTY

We walked into the darkness, Seth and I in front, the witch following. As the tunnel began to descend I heard a sound from behind us and turned around. The mouth of the tunnel had closed, its jaws shutting all but silently. All of a sudden we were in the complete, velvet blackness of the earth.

'Where are we?' Seth asked in a whisper. It echoed long, as if there were miles of tunnels in front of and beneath us, each reflecting back his voice.

'In the mines.' The witch's voice came from behind us. 'A gulag named Kalya. You have heard, in your country, of the gulag?'

I nodded, forgetting we were in the darkness.

'We were exiled, sentenced to be worked to death like the rest of the enemies of the state. But they underestimated our power. They confined us here together – and together, weak as we were, we rose up against our gaolers. We extinguished the lights, and without their sight they were helpless, and so we fell upon them in the dark.'

'What did you do to them?' I whispered. 'And the

other prisoners, the outwith, what happened to them?'

'Nothing was wasted,' the witch said. 'And afterwards there was nothing for us above but death and persecution. So we sealed ourselves in the earth to wait for better times. Now, perhaps, these times have come. It is time for us to return to the surface, to make Russia ours again.'

'How did you live all those years down here?'

'Cruelly,' said the witch; her voice sounded as if she was smiling in the darkness. 'With suffering. But suffering makes you strong, little Ah-na. It is like fire; if you can survive it, you come out tempered, hard as clay baked in the kiln, or steel from the furnace. We have been tempered by the fire of our suffering.'

Suffering, suffering, suffering . . . The sound echoed back at us from the tunnels, hissing and sibilant.

'Come,' said the witch. 'Walk.'

I felt her hand again, hard and cold between my shoulder blades, and I stumbled.

'But I can't see. How can you see in this dark?'

'There is no need for *us* to see,' she said scornfully. 'But at first we used our magic to light the paths. So . . . if you must . . .'

I held out my hand and the whiteish glow illuminated the walls. Beside me I could see Seth's face, his eyes huge and black. And behind us the beautiful, skull-white face of the witch. Tunnels led down and outwards – four, five branching off, maybe more. The witch pointed to one and said, 'Go. Bread and salt awaits.'

I glanced at Seth and together we began to walk.

As we descended the floor changed from mud to rock. The walls were stone too, marked with the chips from a thousand picks. In places there were veins of strange crystals and in others the rock glowed with a phosphorescent light, picking up the glow of my witchlight and reflecting it back.

At last we came into a vast echoing chamber, huge, like a cathedral. I let the light flare up, holding my hand up above my head like a torch – but it barely pricked the immensity of the place. I caught sight of the tips of stalactites, the wetness glinting, but the roof itself arched into shadow.

In the centre of the room were a dozen or so large stones, each about knee-height, arranged in a circle around a pile of charred bones. Around the bones was arranged an elaborate ring of smaller stones in intricate, geometric patterns; some of them pebbles; others huge lumps of crystal; or half-split geodes, the jewel-like centres glittering in the witchlight. It looked like the set-up for a macabre camp-fire.

'Sit,' said the witch. She gestured to the large stones. 'We bring you food.'

I exchanged a glance with Seth and a tiny shrug, and we both did as we'd been told. The witch disappeared with a rustle of garments and we were left alone. I looked at Seth, hunched next to me on the makeshift stone seat. His face was pale and glistened with sweat, in spite of the cold and he closed his eyes tight shut, the sockets bruised and blue in the pale witchlight.

I opened my mouth to say something, but before I could speak, a sound came from all the far corners of the chamber. It was an almost imperceptible whisper; the shush of bare feet, light on the stone. I let the witchlight flare, burning bright, and into the circle of light came face, after face, after face.

They were all white as bone, glimmering like ghosts in the pale light. And they were all thin and gaunt, with broad cheekbones that jutted through their skin. They crept forward into the circle of light, their faces full of a terrified yearning. At their head was the black-haired witch, Tatiana, and she was holding a rough wooden plate with two chunks of dark bread and a little mound of salt. In her other hand was a beaker of water.

Before she handed us the plate she took a pinch of salt and sprinkled it reverently on the pile of bones. Then she held out the food to us.

'Eat,' she said. 'You are our guests. You are welcome to Kalya, to our *sobor*.' She gestured grandly to the vast space.

Seth and I fell on the bread like starving animals. We'd neither of us eaten or drunk since that lunch in the galley. I didn't know what the time was now, but it felt like long gone midnight, and we'd walked without stopping for most of the evening and night.

I took a long gulp of the water – it was cold and sweet and very good – and then tore into the bread again.

The circle of faces watched in fascinated silence, their eyes following every bite, every sip. At last I paused and wiped my mouth. The bread had a strange aftertaste, not completely pleasant; slightly metallic. But at this point I didn't care. It was food, and it had filled my stomach and Seth's.

'What now?' I asked.

'Now, you sleep,' Tatiana said. 'For tomorrow is an important day. There is work to be done.'

My legs were stiff from walking and standing hurt. From the look on Seth's face as I helped him to his feet, I could see he was in more pain than I was. I waited while he gritted his teeth and manoeuvred the fir branch under his arm. But Tatiana was walking away. At the edge of the circle of light she paused. Her white, skeleton-thin hand beckoned.

'Come.'

We followed her, down passage after passage after passage, some so low that I had to crouch and Seth was almost bent double. We walked past rooms of huddled women, lying on mats in the dark, who looked up, blinking as we passed. Past a room where a fire burned low and the smell of burnt meat drifted into the corridor, together with choking smoke. Past rooms where stalactites dripped ceaselessly and rooms of carved patterns so lovely I might have stopped to marvel under other circumstances.

At last she stopped, at a room that was empty apart from a pile of rags.

'Please.' She gestured to the room – it was a cave really,

the roof too low for Seth to stand completely upright. 'Take sleep. Be rested. Tomorrow we work.'

'Wait,' I said desperately. 'Before you go – can I ask you a question—'

But she was gone, swallowed up into the darkness.

With a groan Seth lowered himself to the floor of the cave, his good leg curled under him, his bad leg stretched out on one of the ragged blankets. I was still staring around the little room, but after a while Seth looked up at me from the floor and held out his arms.

'Come here,' he said. I lay down beside him and we huddled together under the covers, locked in each other's arms, and I let the witchlight burn out. I couldn't keep it going indefinitely. I might need my strength tomorrow.

My mind was buzzing with fears, possibilities, but Seth's voice broke in on my thoughts.

'Where are all the men?'

'The men?' I echoed stupidly.

'The male witches – have you noticed, there aren't any?'

'N-no . . .' It was an oddly uncomfortable thought.

'What do you think happened to them?'

'I don't know.' I bit my lip. 'Maybe they were in a different camp?' But how had they survived without men for so many years? Had they been breeding with hapless, captured outwiths? I thought of my grandmother's words about Thaddeus Corax – about him extending his life with methods she couldn't bear to think about. I shuddered.

'What was the question you were going to ask?' Seth's voice broke in on my thoughts. 'Before that woman – before she left.'

'Oh.' I hunched my knees up to my chest, trying to get warm. 'I . . . I was going to ask about my mother.'

'Your *mother*?'

'She went to the Russian witches to buy protection for me. I think she might have come here, to Kalya.'

'But . . .' Seth's hand went up to rub his face. 'Anna, chasing a shadow – it's not going to bring her back, is it?'

I didn't answer.

I thought I'd never sleep. Eventually Seth fell into an exhausted doze in my arms, shifting even in his sleep to try to find a comfortable position for his leg against the hard, cold rock. But I stayed awake, staring into the darkness, trying to see through the blackness to the truth. I don't know how long I lay there, but at one point, as I was drifting in the strange halfway state between waking and sleep, I thought I heard a scream, the tearing, throbbing scream of someone in extreme pain. I jolted awake and scrambled upright in the dark, sweating and trembling, waiting for it to come again, but it never did and Seth slept on, untroubled.

At last I began to think I must have dreamed it and I lay back down. I put my arms around Seth, my lips against his forehead, and eventually I slept.

* * *

I woke with a start.

Someone was in the room, crouched over me.

I let my witchlight flash out like an electric spark and the witch fell back, shielding her eyes. It was Tatiana.

'What are you doing?' I hissed, furious with fear.

'It is morning,' she said.

My hammering heart slowed slightly and I sat up, looking around the little room. It was dark as ever; it could have been the middle of the night for all I knew. It certainly didn't feel like I'd slept long. My eyes scratched and my legs felt as weary as if I'd only just lain down. Beside me Seth stirred uneasily.

'Seth,' I said softly.

He moved again in his sleep but didn't wake.

'Let him sleep,' said the witch. 'His wound consumes him.'

Consumes him . . . I shuddered. It was such a horrible image: Seth being eaten away by the pain. And yet she was right; it *was* eating at him. Eating at his strength, and his happiness, and his ability to live. In ten, twenty years he'd be another Bran: bitter with constant pain.

I slid out from under Seth's arm and got slowly to my feet.

'While he sleeps we will show you our kingdom,' the witch said.

Kingdom. It seemed an odd word to use for a place inhabited solely by women. Where was the king?

'Come,' she said. 'Let us begin. Are you ready?'

'Yes.' I straightened my sleep-crumpled clothes. 'Only, I need to leave Seth a message for when he wakes.'

'I will call Svetlana,' the witch said. She said nothing, but a moment later a white, ghostly face appeared at the door and Tatiana spoke in Russian. The girl nodded and turned to me.

'Svetlana speaks English,' Tatiana said. 'Give to her your message. She will tell it to your Seth when he awakes.'

It wasn't what I'd had in mind – I'd thought of a pen and paper. But now I had no choice.

'All right,' I said slowly. 'Um . . . Tell him I went with Tatiana to – to look around . . . and I'll be back as soon as I can. Tell him . . .' *Tell him I love him*, was what I wanted to say. But I couldn't say it to this strange ghost-girl hovering in the doorway. 'Tell him I'll come back as fast as possible.'

Svetlana nodded and then pressed herself to the wall of the cave. Tatiana looked at me and I nodded and followed her out of the room.

My heart began to beat fast as I followed Tatiana down the mazelike corridors again. Faster, and faster, and painfully hard. As we passed caves I looked into each entrance. What was I looking for?

I knew the answer of course. I was looking for my mother. Perhaps I'd *always* been looking for her, ever since I first realized what the word meant. And perhaps I always would, until I knew for sure what had happened to her.

But as I scanned the faces that glimmered out of the

dark at me, I wondered. Did I really want to find my mother here, hidden in the dark for eighteen years, in the knowledge that somewhere her daughter was growing up alone? What would I say? What *could* I say?

'The bathing room . . .' Tatiana waved a hand as we passed a cave with a metal drum of water, glinting black in the witchlight. 'This is where we cook . . . here we weave cloth . . .' My witchlight lit up the dark chambers as we passed, showing white-faced women hunched over their tasks, their startled faces jerking up at the sight of my light passing the doorway.

'And now, our Cathedral,' Tatiana said, and she stood back to let me pass in front of her, into the room where we'd sat last night and eaten bread.

I walked into the huge cavern, my footsteps setting echoes ringing around the walls, and as I reached the circle of stones Tatiana held up her hand. A huge white light blazed out, dowsing my witchlight like the sun eclipsing a star. The stone walls blazed, white and luminous. I saw a roof stretching fifty, seventy, a hundred feet above our heads – arched like the roof of a cathedral and crusted with filigree white crystals that sparkled in the blaze, like quartz, or diamonds, almost blinding me with their brilliance.

'It's beautiful!' I gasped. 'What – what is it?'

'It is salt,' Tatiana said. 'It *is* beautiful and it grants a sort of . . . immortality to everything it touches.'

She let her light die down and the room dipped into shadow again.

'How?' I asked, suddenly unable to hold back. 'How are you so strong? I don't understand. That light – I've never seen anyone make a witchlight like that. I've never seen a power like yours.'

An echo jangled in my head, and I remembered Simon's words when we found the charm buried under my step: *This is power the likes of which I've never seen.*

'We have our secrets, little Ah-na.' She smiled, a strange and terrible smile, that showed her gums, red like the gums of the witch on the bridge. I shivered and she sat, patting the stone next to her in the circle. My heart was still beating hard in my chest and I'd never felt less like taking my courage in my hands, but I sat and took a deep breath.

'Can I ask you something?'

Tatiana inclined her head.

'Perhaps I will not answer, but you may ask.'

'Did you ever meet a woman – her name was Isabella, but she called herself Isla sometimes too? She looked . . .' I swallowed. 'They say, she looked a little like me.'

Tatiana said nothing; she only looked at me with her dark, dilated eyes. She had allowed her witchlight to burn out completely and it was only my dwindling strength illuminating the hall now, a glowing ember in the palm of my hand between us.

Then she spoke.

'Let me tell you a story, little Ah-na.' She looked at the pile of bones in the centre of the hall, as if gathering her strength, gathering her thoughts. 'Once there was a people.

They were good and bad, weak and strong, foolish and wise, as people will be. But they were also at war. The problem was, they did not know this. Over many years, centuries even, the war was waged and the people lost ground, a little more every year. Little by little they were driven to the brink. They were burned and imprisoned. They were persecuted and killed. Their numbers dwindled and at last they were forced into hiding, forced to pretend they were other than they were in order to survive. And still they did not know there was a war. Still they did not fight back.

'And then, one day, there came a man. He had a vision: a vision of peace and security for his people. But he knew, with a terrible certainty, that peace meant violence. That in order to secure peace for his people, there would be bloodshed. His enemies, and the enemies of his people, must be crushed: those without and those within.

'And so he began to fight. He fought stealthily and subtly. He used his magic to make his way into a position of great power, a position from which he could protect his people and smite his enemies. He told his people about the war. He showed them what they had to do to win their freedom. Some could not bear to hear the truth, but it *was* truth.

'At last, the fight became too violent to be hidden and the enemy realized what this man was and his intention. He was betrayed. He was struck down. Even then he did not die. Three times they killed him, by poison, and with bullets, and with drowning. At last they burned the flesh from his bones and his followers were imprisoned.'

She stopped, her eyes blazing with a fanatical love.

'But they did not forget him, his followers. They did not forget the man who had showed them the truth and a better way of life. They did not forget his dream, for a world that was pure and cleansed, where his people could live in peace without fear of persecution. They gathered his bones and took them deep beneath the ground to wait for better times. To wait for the coming of one who could return him to his throne.'

She took my hand, her fingers sharp as claws, and my heart leaped into my throat, choking me.

'Little Ah-na, do you know why you have been sent to us?'

'No,' I said. That one word was all I could manage.

'You have been sent to end the war. You have been sent to raise him, to raise our Master.'

She turned her skull-white face and we both looked at the pile of bleached, charred bones in the centre of the hall.

'There was a time when our people did not have to hide, Ah-na. That time will come again.'

'I don't understand . . .' I said. My voice was a whisper.

'With our Master at our head we will scour the world clean.'

'Clean? Clean – of what?'

'Clean of traitors, those of our kind who betray their own. And clean of *Čužestranec.*'

312

For a minute I didn't understand. Then I remembered her words on the beach: '*Čužestranec* – one not of our kind.'

My face froze. My heart froze. Something inside me seemed to break.

'Clean of outwith, you mean?' I managed.

Tatiana nodded.

'Then it will be time for a new kind of empire: the empire of witches, with our holy Master at its head.'

'You're mad.' My voice was small, so small it barely echoed in the great chamber. Tatiana shook her head, her face pitying and pitiless at the same time.

'No, little Ah-na. "Mad" is the word the *Čužestranec* use when they talk of those who see the truth behind the veil. We are a different kind to them. For centuries we have tried to live in harmony with the *Čužestranec* while they burned and persecuted and imprisoned us. No longer. Enough is enough. There is room for only one kind of being on this earth; it is a choice, us or them?'

'No!'

'It is they who have forced this, Ah-na. We never chose the war.'

'And you want me to raise that . . . that . . .' I couldn't speak – I just pointed at the pile of gnawed bones in the centre of the room, surrounded by the offerings of decades.

Tatiana nodded.

'It is what your mother knew, little Ah-na. It is what you were born for. It is your choice whether you die for it also.'

'No!' I shouted. The echoes bellowed the word back at

me from around the chamber: *No, no, no, no, no* . . . A dying fall of denial.

Tatiana stood, releasing my hand. She was quite still, but I had the impression of a huge fury rippling out from her like a wave.

Then she turned.

'Very well,' she said over her shoulder. 'If I cannot persuade you, perhaps there is one who can.'

And then she was gone.

For a long while I sat, shaking with fear and anger as the witchlight guttered and wavered in my palm. Where was Seth? How could I find my way back to him in the maze of tunnels?

I thought about running – trying to find him, breaking us both out of this hell-hole and not looking back. I crossed the hall to the exit Tatiana had taken and stood poised in the doorway. But I didn't know which way to go. I didn't even know if this was the right exit from the hall – there were five or six, all identical to my eyes. Beyond that, we'd walked for maybe ten minutes last night, taken ten or twenty turnings until we reached the cave where we slept. I'd never remember them all.

I'd been so stupid, allowing us to be separated. How could I undo my mistake?

'Seth!' I called quietly, with the pathetic, impossible hope that he would somehow hear me and call back. Nothing answered me. 'Seth!' I cried a little louder. I stood listening, trying to quiet even the pounding of my heart to listen for any sound at all.

Footsteps. Soft, halting footsteps that paused as if the walker was gathering their strength. They were coming from a different exit, one across the room from me. It couldn't be Seth – could it?

I turned to face them, my heart beating so hard with hope that I thought I might be sick. A shadowy figure filled the doorway – and for a minute my heart leaped. But it wasn't Seth. It was someone too slight, too short. A woman, hardly taller than me.

I forced the witchlight in my palm to flare, sending its blaze across the shadowy space to illuminate her face.

My gasp cut through the silence, the shocked echoes hissing and spitting.

The person in the door was . . . It was . . .

I stumbled across the rocky floor, tripping over stones and hollows, until at last I was standing just a metre or so away from the woman.

Except it wasn't just a woman.

It was my mother.

CHAPTER TWENTY-ONE

For a minute I didn't speak. I just stood, frozen, drinking in her face. It was older than the woman in the photographs I'd seen, but eerily, unmistakably like. But even without the photos I wouldn't have needed anyone to tell me. Her face – it was *my* face. My face twenty years on, framed by black silken hair so fine the threads floated in the still, unchanging air.

I found myself gasping, gulping, struggling to hold back tears. And then I ran. Across the few feet that separated us, into her arms, feeling her body firm in my grip – no mirage, but real, solid flesh. Her bones were sharp – too sharp – and her ribs felt as if they might crack in my fierce hug, but she was laughing and crying, hugging me back, the tears running down her face, mixing with mine as our cheeks pressed together.

'Anna,' she said, repeating my name as if she couldn't believe it, 'Anna, oh Anna, oh my little Anna, my darling Anna.'

'M—' I stumbled over the word. I'd never said it – not like this. I'd never called that name out in the night, after a bad dream. It was Dad I'd called for – I'd always known she was beyond my reach, out of my grasp. Until now.

'Anna,' she breathed again.

Then for a long time neither of us said anything, we just stood, holding each other, looking at each other's faces.

'What are you doing here?' I said at last. She led me to the stones and we sat, side by side, my hand enclosed in hers.

'Oh Anna, how can I explain?' She put her free hand to her face, as if pulling herself together, pulling the threads of her story from the frayed, tangled mess of our lives. 'Do you know why I left?'

'Yes,' I said. There was a hollow feeling in my stomach. 'Because of the prophecy. Because you thought . . . I might . . .'

'I thought you were the one, the witch who can break the only law that binds us: death. And I was right, wasn't I?' She searched my face.

'Yes.' No point in denying it now. No point in refusing to see the truth among all the lies. 'Yes, I think you were right. I should have died at least twice. Both times I came back. But that's not the end of it, is it?'

'No, it's not. Because your own life is only part of it. If I'm right,' she squeezed my hand, 'Anna, if the prophecy is right – you can raise others.'

Others.

I'd known it, but somehow hearing it in her voice made it real.

Caradoc. Bran. Bill. Even Thaddeus.

I thought of all the innocent people who'd died. All the people who'd laid down their lives to protect my secret. All the people whose lives had been taken in the fight over my power.

And all the others. All the good, ordinary people who'd died over the years, leaving the gaping hole of their loss bleeding grief into good, ordinary lives. Seth's dad. Abe's Rachel.

All gone, lost for ever, never to come back.

Except – she *had* come back.

'Why are you here?' I asked desperately. 'I don't understand. Why did you go through all this to protect me and then stand by while they brought me here?'

'Because I was weak, Anna.' She sighed. 'Because I was blind. And because I was wrong.'

'Wrong how?'

'I thought that your power could be hidden, or left unused. But it can't. I tried to fight fate and I couldn't. Fate brought you here, just like it brought me, though I thought I was acting to outwit it. I should have known better.'

'What do you mean?' I tried not to let my frustration boil over into tears, but it was hard, impossible, as she sat there talking in riddles, while somewhere Seth lay alone in the dark, wondering where I was, trying to ease the pain in his leg. Pain she'd caused.

She bowed her head as if trying to think, to work out how to begin. Then she drew a deep breath.

'The Ealdwitan – Anna, they're old, evil. You've seen their corruption – the way they fight amongst themselves for pre-eminence. They don't work for their people any more, they work for themselves. I came to the Others quite cynically – offering secrets to sell in return for their help. I didn't tell them the reason. I used them, just like the Ealdwitan used me, used you. I came expecting something even worse than the Ealdwitan – that was why I *chose* them, because they were the only people I could think of who might be even more unscrupulous and grasping and powerful. And afterwards, after I'd bargained away my knowledge, I was planning to leave, to run, to kill myself if I had to.'

'But you didn't,' I said. The fury was ebbing and I could feel the cold rock biting into my legs through my worn jeans.

'No, I didn't.' She fell silent for a moment, looking at the floor. Then she ran her hand through her fine dark hair and I saw the white hairs that glinted among the black. 'I didn't have the courage to face death. Instead, I stayed. And I found that though they are fierce and sometimes cruel, they have . . .' She stopped, struggling for the first time for words. 'They have a purity of purpose which the Ealdwitan lack. They have a mission. And it's that I think your gift is destined for.'

'What do you mean?' I dropped her hand and the cold shifted to the pit of my stomach, like a piece of ice twisting in my gut.

'He was the last great leader of our kind.'

'Not you,' I said. I felt weak with horror. 'They've sent you here to persuade me, haven't they? How *could* you? After all you did to protect me!'

'Anna, please, you don't understand. There's more at stake here than our lives.' Her hand holding mine was soft, but her grip was strong and her face was pleading, cowed, desperate. How could I have ever thought she looked like me?

'No,' I said. My voice cracked. My heart felt like it was turning into stone. I would not cry. I would *not* cry.

'Please, darling – please, for me. I don't have a lot of power here. I'll do what I can to keep you safe, but—'

'No,' I sobbed. It was all I could do, keep repeating it like a mantra, keep the soft, wheedling sound of her voice at bay.

'Anna you *must* do what they ask! You don't understand—'

'No!'

'Listen to me, if you don't do this thing voluntarily they will . . .' She stumbled, unable, for the first time, to speak.

'What?'

'They . . .'

'*What?*' I shouted.

A second voice spoke from the doorway.

'If you do not give this to us, we will take it.'

I turned, fast as my thrumming heart, to see Tatiana standing in the doorway.

320

'They have ways, Anna.' My mother's hand stroked my cheek, soft as silk against my skin. I shut my eyes. 'They have methods – extraction, *excision*. Please, darling – *please*. Resisting will only make this harder . . .'

'Harder for who? For you?'

My chest rose and fell and looked from Tatiana, proud and cruel and upright, to my mother, pleading, wheedling, pathetic. I had come so far. I had risked so much. For her. For this. For nothing.

'You traitor,' I managed. My voice was strange in my ears, a harsh croak. 'Traitor.'

Then something – something chinked inside me. A memory, struggling to get free.

A memory of Marcus – no, of my mother . . . What *was it*?

It came suddenly: hot, reeking with hate.

A crow's breath, scorching my cheek, laden with carrion stink.

Your mother died a traitor and a fool – and so will you.

It was like a slap to the face, waking me from a dream. I opened my eyes.

'He said she was dead.' I looked from Tatiana to my mother. I had the feeling of standing on the edge of a precipice; any false step could tip me into oblivion. 'Marcus: he said she was dead. He said my mother died a traitor. Why would he say that? Why would he say that if she was still alive?'

Tatiana's eyes flickered to the woman beside me – to my 'mother'. There was something there, some expression

I couldn't quite catch.

'I . . .' my mother said. Her eyes went to Tatiana – again that flicker. Consternation? Fear?

'What's my father's name?' I asked. My mother licked her lips. I could see her chest rising and falling.

'Don't answer her questions,' Tatiana said scornfully.

'No, wait,' my mother said. 'Wait. His name – I know this; his name is . . . Tim.'

'No,' I said. I stood suddenly, my heart pounding hard in my chest, pounding as if it would break. 'You are *not* my mother.'

'Anna,' she said, and there was a catch in her voice. She put out her hand towards me, pleadingly, and as she touched me a current went through me, like a jolt of static electricity, and I heard the unspoken words sizzle across the void between us: *Damn you, you stupid bitch, you'll get us both killed.*

'Marcus!' I hissed his name between my teeth and at the sound of his own name he staggered back, ripping his hand away from mine. A spasm of pure hate crossed his face – my mother's face – and then her image seemed to ripple in the air and it was Marcus standing there, his expression filled with utter loathing and contempt.

'You bloody stupid bitch,' he growled.

'*Mužčiny!*' Tatiana spat and she drew back her hand and slapped him, a ringing slap across the cheek that sent him staggering across the cave. 'Stupid? She was too clever for you!'

Then she took my arm and yanked me out of the cave.

'Where are we going?' I panted as I stumbled after her. My witchlight faltered as the fear and weariness threatened for a moment to overwhelm me, but Tatiana's step did not, even as we plunged into darkness. She led me unerringly along the dark maze of tunnels to a new chamber – one with nothing in it at all.

'Where's Seth? Take me to Seth!'

Tatiana said nothing; she just slammed the heavy door of the chamber with a resounding thud and I felt the stifling weight of a magical charm slapped over the lock.

God damn it!

I slumped in the corner and let my witchlight burn out. Keeping it up near-constantly was shattering and I began to realize why the witches down here had learned to live without it. I also realized how stupid I'd been to keep mine burning throughout the conversation with Marcus and Tatiana, draining *my* power instead of theirs. Stupid. *Stupid!*

My self-control broke and I began to sob.

I had been *so* naïve, so gullible. They'd lured me in with the one bait they knew how to dangle. I'd followed the retreating shadow of my mother all the way into a trap. If it hadn't been for Marcus it might even have worked. But he'd pushed too hard, his desperation too naked, too frightening. What had they promised him, if he succeeded? Or – perhaps – what threats had they held over him if he failed?

I shuddered. I understood, now, the strange pleading desperation in his voice. He was pleading for his soul, his magic.

As I sat in the dark I began to think about Seth. Would they give him a fire or a lamp? I thought of him sitting for hour after hour in that barren cell, waiting for me to come back.

What would happen to him, if something happened to me?

I thought of Tatiana's voice, cruel and slow.

Nothing is wasted.

I thought of her red gums and the strange, blood-tasting bread . . .

Stop it – stop being macabre.

I stood and went to the door, listening for a sound. None came, but I put my mouth to the crack and hollered, 'Seth!'

Silence: just the echoes of my own voice ringing through the tunnels.

'Seth!' I called again, straining my lungs to cracking. '*Seth!*'

My voice broke. 'Seth – please, Seth – if you can hear me, if you can't speak just make a sound, any sound . . .'

I stood listening, trying to hold back the sobs, trying to keep silent so I could listen. But there was no sound at all. Not even the long, throbbing scream of the night before. I might have been completely alone.

I sat with my back to the cold stone of the cave wall and

wrapped my anorak and Seth's jumper around me as tightly as I could. Then I sent my longing flowing out of the cave, beneath the crack under the door, out into the tunnels, far and wide. I hoped that somewhere, wherever he was, Seth could feel the heat of it in this chill underground tomb. I hoped that somewhere, he was warm, and not in pain, and not in fear. I hoped.

The hours passed slowly – I might even have slept or dozed. I had no idea what time it was. It felt like hours since Tatiana had woken me, telling me it was morning, but I was no longer certain whether it really had been morning, or just a few hours since I'd lain down at Seth's side. I'd left my watch on the boat, but since I didn't know what time zone we were in, it wouldn't have helped anyway. I had no idea where we were – no idea if we were in Siberia, or one of the islands, or somewhere else completely.

I could have conjured some light or some warmth, but I had to let my magic recover. I might need to fight. So instead I sat in the dark and I tried to think what to do.

I should scry: that was my first thought. Scry for Seth, and perhaps for Emmaline and Abe too. I thought of Abe, coming racing to London when I'd seen Caradoc's body: Emmaline's terse explanation that he'd *heard* my screams, felt my panic.

Could Abe feel my fear now? I stared into the blackness, wondering. Could I make contact with him?

For a minute, hope kindled in my chest and a flicker of

warmth began to spread through me – but then I realized what would happen next.

If I contacted them, they'd try to rescue me. And it would be a death sentence. What could Abe and Emmaline do alone against this army of witches? The Ealdwitan were in no position to offer help – even if my grandmother was still alive.

The spark of hope died. I put my hand to my forehead, pressing back the tears.

So that was it. I was condemned to die here – or worse, perhaps, *not* to die here, but to survive in darkness and fear. That thought was bad enough, but worst of all was the realization that I wasn't just condemning myself. I was condemning Seth. If I couldn't find a way out for myself, I *had* to find one for him, even if it meant I was chained here for ever.

I was still running the rats' maze of possibilities in my head, when I heard steps in the tunnel outside and I sprang upright. My witchlight blazed in the palm of my hand, my heart beat fast in my throat.

It was Tatiana.

'Where's Seth?' I demanded as soon as she entered the room. She bowed her head, hiding something, perhaps a smile.

'He is well taken care of.'

'I don't believe you! Take me to him.'

'In good time.'

'Now!' I cried. Tatiana shook her head, her ink-black

eyes glittering in the witchlight.

'Ah-na, Ah-na – you are in no position to make demands, little one.'

She was right, of course. I gritted my teeth.

'I'm sorry,' I said humbly. 'You're right. I'm not demanding – I'm begging. *Please* let me see him.'

'Perhaps,' Tatiana said imperturbably. 'If you help us, perhaps we will help you.'

I slumped and she looked at me, an amused smile at the corner of her lips.

'What happened . . . ?' A lump rose in my throat. Suddenly it was imperative that I knew, that I had one solid fact to hold onto. 'What *really* happened to my mother? All that stuff Marcus said in the cave. That was rubbish, wasn't it?'

Tatiana looked at me for a long moment, seeming to calculate something in her head. Then she relented.

'I will tell you.' She squatted on the floor on her heels and patted the rock beside her, gesturing to me to sit down. I sat, awkwardly, uncomfortably, and Tatiana said, 'Your mother came to us with a bargain: she asked for our help with a charm, in exchange for some information on our enemies. We obliged; we gave her the charm. And, as promised, she returned with information. But she did not give us all the information we wanted.'

'She gave you some?'

'Yes,' Tatiana nodded. 'Passwords, names, details we had asked her to obtain. But when we had more questions she declined. She said she had given us the information she promised and she refused to go further. But we had not rationed ourselves when we made her that charm; we had acted in faith, we had poured our all, our strength, our best endeavours into our work. It was strong and true – so strong that even we could not break it. In her cunning she had used our own spell to make you safe, even from us. And she did not repay us in the same coin. She gave grudgingly and held back her jewels.'

'So what did you do?' I asked, almost unwillingly.

'We attempted to persuade her. But she was brave.' Tatiana shrugged. 'Our persuasions, of one kind and another, did not flower into fruit. We cut her, but she gave us only blood, not words. At last, she had no more blood to give. And no more words.'

I felt a coldness run all over me, from the top of my head down my spine, into my heart and lungs and guts.

And then a huge, bursting dam of love.

All this. All this she had done for me.

All this she had given. Her love. Her blood. Her life.

For me.

I found I was crying and I spoke through sobs and tears, trying to make myself understood.

'And wh-what happened n-next? Her b-body, p-please tell me? Is she buried? C-can I see where she's buried?'

'Nothing was wasted,' Tatiana said soberly. 'We do not bury our dead for their blood to feed the earth. Child, your mother died in pain and futility. She saved no one – not you, not herself. Her life and magic was sacrificed to preserve yours. Now, I beg of you, for her sake, do not waste her sacrifice again. Come to the Cathedral. Raise our holy Master. Live yourself to see the wonder of his clean, new world.'

'If I refuse?' I whispered, wiping the tears from my face with my sleeve.

Tatiana sighed.

'Come, child. There is something you should see before you make up your mind. I will show you how we deal with traitors and those who falter on the path.'

She stood and I stood too, unwillingly, but unable to resist the power of her dark eyes.

'Come,' she said again and I began to walk. At least if I kept my eyes and ears open I might see something of Seth, find out where he was being held.

But although I stared in at every cave we passed, none of them was the cave with the blankets where we had slept in each other's arms. And none of them held Seth.

At last we came to a long corridor with a blaze of light at the end of it, a bright surgical light, unlike any I had seen down here. An electric light. It hurt my eyes after the long darkness and I put my hand up, shielding my face as we got closer.

Tatiana opened a door and we entered a square room lit with a dozen bulbs. The light was almost blinding and it took a while for my eyes to adjust. When they did, I looked around blinking, trying to take it in. We were in a large, square chamber, properly roomlike, its walls roughly plastered with concrete. In the middle was a grating, like a drain, and above it something like a cross between a cage, and a throne, and a dentist's chair. I had never seen anything like it. It looked like a child had created it from debris found around the mine, ornamented with objects scavenged from a museum of medical history. Here was part of an old office chair, the kind displayed in vintage shops selling twentieth-century antiques. There was a complicated web of coiling electrical wire, insulated with fabric and lead and ceramic fuses. There were makeshift shackles, hammered out from pieces of rusting metal. And on one side, on a rickety metal stand, was a huge, glass flagon, like the prototype intravenous drips I'd seen in old films.

There was one other incongruous touch: five or six huge iron rings set into the walls at intervals round the room, sunk deep into the concrete. They looked like the kind of thing you'd use to lock up a motorbike. I had no idea what they could be for.

Then I realized I could hear screams coming from down the corridor, from the opposite direction to the way we'd come.

For a moment I stood frozen, not certain who'd come through the door. The screams sounded completely hysterical: wild and desperate – and it was impossible to tell the identity of the screamer. Then a second pair of doors burst open and a group of people staggered into the room, carrying a struggling witch between them.

My first feeling was relief that it wasn't Seth. My second feeling was shock because, as they wrestled her into the chair and shackled her limbs, I realized: I had seen her before. It was the witch from the library, the one who had chased us on to the bridge. The mad, beautiful, wild-eyed witch. And one of the people wrestling her into the chair was Marcus.

'What are you doing to her?' I cried out, my voice shaking with panic.

No one answered, not even Marcus. I'm not sure they even heard me beneath the screams of the witch. She was shrieking: a high, inhuman sound, quite mad with fear. No one spoke in answer to her screams; they simply fought her in businesslike silence, subduing her until she was completely bound, shackled to the chair.

'No!' The witch found her tongue at last, her eyes darting round the room, speedwell-blue and shot with red. 'Danya, Tatiana, Yana! *Pozhalujsta!*'

'Sister.' Tatiana spoke comfortingly, soothingly. She walked to the witch's side and smoothed her hair back from her face with something like love. 'Irina, you betrayed us. You must pay the price.'

The witch began to gabble out a stream of Russian, her voice ragged with pleading. I didn't know what she was saying, but it sounded like she was begging for her life.

'It is too late, Irina,' Tatiana said sadly. Then she turned to the woman beside the chair, who had strapped the witch into the contraption. 'Danya, the needle.'

At her words Irina began to fight again, like a demon this time. She thrashed steadily and wildly in the chair, completely heedless of the metal biting into her skin and the blood running down her bare feet from the rusty shackles, flinging out useless spells right and left, spells that scorched and blistered the walls. One hit Marcus on the forehead, leaving a welt on his smooth tanned skin, but he ignored it as if it had been the bite of a midge.

It took all three of them to hold her while the witch called Danya approached with a long rubber tube. She bent over the chair, drew back her arm, and suddenly there was a long, agonized scream from Irina, a scream of complete despair. It went on, and on, a long throbbing sound of hopeless anguish. Danya stepped back and I saw that the thick tube had been stabbed into Irina's chest, right between her ribs.

Tatiana pressed a switch on the wall and the air filled with the thrum of an engine, a pump. Irina convulsed, suddenly rigid in her shackles. The tubing twisted and undulated gently, like a live thing feeding on her, and then a drop of yellow liquid stained the glass demijohn.

We stood completely still, watching as the machine pumped the golden liquid into the glass flagon. I was frozen with horror – unable to believe my eyes, unable to move. The witches stood in attitudes of resignation, as if this was an unpleasant task, something like slaughtering a family pet, but for the best in the end.

At last I found my voice.

'No!' I whispered. 'Marcus – please, stop this.'

'I can't,' Marcus said shortly. His face was not as resigned as the others. There was a kind of revulsion in his eyes, but he didn't look away.

'Tatiana,' I begged, 'please, please, what are you doing?'

'You cannot help her, little one.' Tatiana spoke kindly but firmly. 'It is too late. See, the glass is filling already. Irina betrayed her sisters. There must be punishment, in an ordered society. There must be consequences.'

'What did she do?' I cried. 'What could she possibly have done to deserve this?'

It was Marcus who answered, his face pitying.

'When she came for you, in St Petersburg, she wasn't trying to kidnap you. She was trying to warn you. But you wouldn't stop, you wouldn't listen. So she chased you. When Emmaline attacked her, she fought back – I don't know why. Perhaps she thought Emmaline was part of the plot.'

'That was why you fought her,' I whispered. 'You weren't saving us. You were stopping her from warning us.'

'Yes,' he said. One word. That was all.

'Please!' I cried. I turned to Tatiana – I don't know why, but it felt as if she had more humanity than Marcus. 'For God's sake, no! If you stop now—'

'If we stop now she would be too weak to survive,' Tatiana said. 'Her magic is all but gone, look at her.'

I looked, my eyes full of tears. Irina was grey, all her wild beauty withered, as if she'd been drained of life and love and spirit. She was still breathing – I could see the rise and fall of her thin chest – but only just.

She reminded me – suddenly it came to me with a cold horror – she reminded me of Abe, after he'd given his magic to me.

I looked at the flask, a quarter filled with yellow liquid, like thin pale honey. There was two, maybe three times as much as Abe had given me. Was this what they'd done to him? Had Maya and my grandmother had to hold him down while he screamed with pain?

My legs were suddenly unable to hold me and I groped to the wall and sank, slowly, to the ground, my back against the cold concrete, shivers running through and through me as I watched.

The flow of yellow magic had slowed to a drip and now the drip itself was slowing. Another drop fell. And another. And then a final drop hung, suspended from the top of the flask trembling in the electric light.

There was a click and a sudden silence as Tatiana turned off the engine pump.

Irina gave a last sighing breath and then her thin chest was still. Her beautiful blue eyes stared sightlessly at the ceiling, her fingers slowly uncurling as her muscles relaxed. There was a sudden stench of urine and her head slid to one side.

'It is done,' Tatiana said soberly. 'Take the body to the

room of blood. Then we gather in the Cathedral for the *pereraspredelenie*.'

There was a short struggle while the witches yanked at the tubing stuck into Irina's chest, wrenching it free with a grotesque slurp. They undid the shackles and the flagon of magic was taken off the stand and a metal lid screwed on top. At last Irina's body was slung on to a sheet and dragged away.

I vomited quietly on to the concrete floor, the bitter bile joining the swill of Irina's blood and urine, draining slowly into the grate in the floor.

Tatiana did not seem to notice; she only picked up the glass flask and moved to a table, where a syringe and some other instruments were laid out. Then she said something in Russian to Marcus and he moved to her side.

I sat watching them, wiping the sick and spit from my face with my sleeve. My stomach was empty, but my body still heaved, struggling to rid itself of the poisonous memory.

I knew now what my mother had probably suffered. I knew what Abe had gone through to save me. And I knew what awaited me if I didn't cooperate.

Tatiana was opening the jar of Irina's magic. It was beautiful, astonishingly beautiful. Even under the glare of the electric light it glowed like a small golden sun. Her bone-white face reflected back the glow, bright with longing.

I stood completely unnoticed with my back to the wall

and a thought came to me suddenly; I could make a break for it, run into the tunnels, call out for Seth while they were not expecting it. Could it work?

I took a single hesitant step sideways towards the door.

Tatiana picked up the old-fashioned metal syringe from the table beside the glass jar. She plunged it into the glowing yellow liquid and filled the syringe. Then she held out her arm, white and naked and glowing with the reflection of Irina's essence.

I took another step.

She plunged the syringe into her arm and pressed the plunger.

Suddenly I understood. I understood the source of their immense strength and I understood, too, their unity and their madness.

I watched, frozen with horror, as Tatiana refilled the syringe and passed it to Marcus. He pulled back his sleeve, rolling it so that it constricted the blood supply to his arm, and crunched his fist a few times until the veins stood out, clear and full. Then he pushed the needle into his vein, injecting himself with a portion of Irina's strength, absorbing her magic and her powers.

I found my breath was coming fast, in small gasps. And then suddenly, horribly, Tatiana turned, the syringe held out in her white, bony hand.

'Ah-na,' she said, 'will you share Irina's gift with us? You will be one of us; by one way or another you will be absorbed into our kin. Will you take her strength?'

'No,' I managed. My voice shook so much I wasn't sure if Tatiana could understand me. I could hardly hear it myself.

'Do not refuse this gift lightly,' Tatiana said. Her brow was furrowed.

This time I could not speak at all; I only shook my head, desperately trying not to give way to my creeping horror of the syringe, dark with blood and bright with drops of Irina's magic. If I did, I thought I might begin to scream and never stop.

There was a long silence.

'Very well,' Tatiana said at length. She called out something in Russian and a girl came into the room and took the full jar and the syringe out into the corridor. I saw its bright golden light glimmering as it headed into the darkness. I guessed she was heading out to share Irina's magic with the witches in the caves. *Nothing is wasted.*

Tatiana turned to me and her eyes were very cold.

'You have refused our gift, Ah-na. Am I to take it this means you do not ally your strength with ours?'

I nodded.

'Speak,' Tatiana said, her voice close to a snarl. 'Will you help us?'

'I will not,' I said, very low. 'I will never help you.'

She said nothing, her breath hissing long through her teeth as she looked at me, considering what to do.

'I will give you one last chance,' she said at last. 'One *last* chance, do you understand? After this, no more mercy.'

She turned, so quickly I felt the breeze from her movement ruffle my hair, and then she stalked out of the room.

'Come!' she snapped at Marcus. He followed, with a backward glance at me. The doors slammed behind them and I was alone.

First I ran to the other doors, the ones they'd brought Irina through. They were locked, physically and magically; I could see the bar across the gap and feel the weight of the charm on the door. Then I ran to the doors Tatiana and Marcus had used. They were locked as well. I wasn't surprised, but I still felt the sting of frustration.

I was trapped, condemned to wait for whatever last-ditch persuasion method they had in mind.

But it was with a drowning wave of dread that I realized what she'd gone to fetch. *Who* she'd gone to fetch.

Seth.

Seth would be the last method of persuading me.

I tried a spell against the door first, attempting to smash the charms on the lock, but it was useless. They were six-fold thick across the door and I was so tired my spells barely made the door rattle, let alone burst open.

So I gave up and began to scour the room, looking for a weapon – any weapon. I yanked open drawers and climbed up on to the table to look along the top of the shelves. There was nothing except empty syringes and spare glass flagons. For a minute I thought about smashing a glass jar and arming myself with a shard, but I didn't trust myself to use it properly. More likely I'd do myself more damage than the person I attacked. And anyway Tatiana would know as soon as she came back, from the smashed glass on the floor. It would have to be a syringe.

I picked one up and looked at it. It looked pathetic – the needle just a few centimetres long. It would make a nasty prick, but it wasn't going to slay any witches in their tracks.

Desperation rose inside me in a suffocating tide, but I fought it back down. Losing it now wouldn't help anyone. I put my head in my hands, willing myself to think of something. There must be a way out, there *must* be. But there wasn't. Or none that I could find.

Footsteps in the tunnel outside, coming closer, closer . . .

There was nothing for it but to fight. I backed up until my spine was pressed to the cold concrete wall and I screwed up every pathetic ounce of magic I had left into a ball. I only had one shot. I couldn't screw this up.

The door began to open.

CHAPTER TWENTY-TWO

I raised my free arm, ready to strike. I was shaking with fear, shaking so hard that the syringe in my other fist clattered against the concrete. I remembered Abe's lessons, remembered him forcing me to access that spring of fear and rage and love that seemed to be the key to my magic.

'Please . . .' I whispered. I don't know who I was begging: myself, the Russians – or something beyond all of us. 'Please . . .'

Then the door opened and three bodies catapulted into the room. They fell to the floor, the door crashing shut behind them with a noise that echoed along the tunnels like thunder.

For a moment I was frozen, not sure whether to waste my magic tearing them to shreds or if the real threat lay behind them, behind the door. But before I'd decided, the door lock came slapping down again – a leaden weight – and with a jolt of horror I recognized the long, black hair of the body nearest me.

'Emmaline!' I fell to my knees beside her and gently turned her face up. What I saw made me cry out. She was conscious, but only just. Her face was a bloodied mess, her right eye so swollen that I couldn't see if it was open or closed. Both her lips were split and I could see that one tooth was missing, knocked out by a particularly vicious blow.

Beside her lay Abe, curled on his side. His face was more or less unharmed apart from a few bruises, but his back and shoulders had been flayed to ribbons. His shirt was scorched and black, soaked with blood and crisscrossed with charred slashes.

The third body was Seth – but he was moving already, trying to haul himself upright.

'Seth!' I knelt beside him to try to help him, but he pushed my hand away.

'Don't worry about me.' His voice was hoarse. There was a cut across his cheekbone where it looked as if he'd been struck with something and his lip was bleeding. 'I'm OK, see to them.'

I crawled back on my hands and knees to Emmaline, tears running down my face now. Had I got enough magic left to heal such dreadful wounds? I didn't know. I had to try.

And then a horrible thought struck me. What if it wasn't Em? What if this was another trick, another mind-game?

'What are you waiting for?' Seth said thickly, around his bloodied lip. He'd pushed himself into a sitting position and now he leaned back against the concrete wall, his breath coming fast and painfully. 'Can't you do something for them?'

'Seth, I – I don't know. I don't know if it's them.' I looked from him to the bodies on the floor, fighting back the terror and the tears. Was it Em and Abe lying there, bleeding to death on the floor? Or strangers? Was it even Seth?

'Seth, this is going to sound crazy,' I said desperately, 'but I need to ask you something. What . . .' I stopped. What did they know? If this wasn't Seth, then what could they have beaten out of him before coming here? Marcus wouldn't make the same mistake twice. If it *was* him, he must know I'd be suspicious. I racked my brains for the right question – something the true Seth would know, but so odd and inconsequential, no one else would ever think of it. 'Seth, when we first met – do you remember what the lesson was?'

'What?' He looked at me like I was out of my mind. 'Anna, look at them! They're bleeding to death. I don't care what the lesson was, it could have been snorkelling.'

'This is important!' I cried. 'Please, just trust me. What was the lesson? Do you even remember?'

'Maths. We were doing differentiation.' His face was uncomprehending – angry. 'I said I should have taken Applied and Statistics. Of *course* I remember. It's burned into my goddam memory. What the hell is this about?'

'It's OK,' I said. Tears began to run down my face. 'I believe you. I'm sorry – but I had to check. Marcus – he's

342

really good at impersonating people. He made me believe—'
I choked. It was too hard – even to Seth I couldn't admit
what I'd thought, what I'd hoped. It sounded so stupid
now; the pathetic hope that my mother might still have
been alive. 'It doesn't matter. But listen, do you think this
is definitely Em and Abe?'

'I'm . . .' He started and then stopped, his face uncertain.
'I – I don't know. I can't be sure. I could hear them being
beaten up in the next cave and we talked through the
wall, but when they were brought in they were too . . . We
didn't speak.'

'Oh God.' I knelt beside them, not sure who was worse.
On the whole I thought Abe was. Emmaline's face was
pretty grim, but the marks looked like mainly swelling and
pain. Abe's injuries looked like they might possibly be life-
threatening. Should I take a chance and risk wasting my
magic on healing when it might all be an illusion?

Then Emmaline stirred.

'Anna . . .' she slurred through thick, bloodied lips. Her
good eye opened and she gazed at me for a long time before
letting it slip closed again. I made up my mind. I'd heal Abe
– just a bit – and try to get him to speak.

I put my hand over his body, feeling the emptiness
inside me, the hollow feeling of magic run almost completely
dry. But I forced myself and a little power trickled through
my fingers into Abe's torn back. He groaned as it entered
him and my heart twisted and hurt inside me. It felt like
him. I could feel the connection between us, strong as ever

– at least I thought I could. I no longer trusted anything any more.

'Abe,' I whispered. 'Abe, can you hear me?'

He moved his head very, very slightly, barely a nod.

'Abe,' I spoke very low, my lips close to his ear. 'I'm sorry but I have to ask you something, find out if it's you. Marcus has been impersonating people – I have to check.' He said nothing, but his face was resigned, accepting. I didn't know if he could speak. This would have to be a question with a very short answer.

'What's . . .' I paused. What could I ask? What would they both know, that no one else in the world would? Then an idea came. 'What's Sienna carrying at the moment?'

There was a moment. A moment when his eyes opened, flickered recognition.

Then he looked at Emmaline.

Something passed between them – and I couldn't tell what it was. There was a message there, something I didn't understand.

And then he closed his eyes.

'Abe,' I said desperately, 'Abe, please, just one word. What is it? You *know*, I can see you know.'

But he just shook his head, almost imperceptibly, wincing at the movement.

'Emmaline!' I said, turning to her. 'I'm begging you. *Please* tell me. I can heal you if you tell me. Can't you see? I can't –' I found I was on the verge of tears, my voice shaking '– I can't risk it. Please, just say it! What's she carrying?'

Emmaline's lips moved; her voice was thick, slurred.

'A handbag.' Blood welled from the sockets of her teeth as she spoke. I wanted to weep. They *knew*. Why were they doing this?

And then suddenly I realized. I realized what that look had been about. It *was* Emmaline and Abe. But they knew what their role was: hostages. Hostages to force me into doing what the Russian witches wanted.

And they knew that if I wasn't sure if it was really them lying bleeding on the floor, I'd hold out for longer. Maybe until the end.

'No,' I said, my voice suddenly fierce. 'I know what you're doing. Stop it.'

Neither of them said anything, they just lay there. Angry tears spilled down my cheeks.

'I don't understand,' Seth said, looking from the broken bodies on the floor to me. 'Is it them? Why won't they answer?'

'Because of their bloody stupid self-sacrifice!' I shouted. 'Because they don't want to be used against me. They think if I'm not sure, I'll let them die more easily. But I won't! Do you hear me?' I turned to Emmaline, to Abe, the tears running down my face now. 'I know it's you. I know it!'

They stayed silent. But then I saw Em's fingers move, almost imperceptibly. As I watched, she stretched out her hand towards Abe's, across the concrete floor, and I saw their fingers, slick with blood, gently interlock.

My heart felt like it was breaking.

'No!' I wept. 'I won't abandon you. I know it's you. I don't care – I'm going to heal you anyway.'

I put out my hands to them both, letting the tearing, suffocating love boil up and over, spilling out through my fingers into their souls.

'No!' Abe groaned as he felt his back begin to heal. 'No! Stop it, you stupid girl! Don't waste your power!'

'Keep it for fighting!' Em said painfully. She scrambled to her feet and stood in front of me, her face streaked with blood and tears, her cuts and bruises not healed, nothing like it, barely even *half* healed. But half healed was better than nothing – wasn't it?

'It's too late,' I said. I let my hands drop to my sides.

Abe gave a groan and rolled on to his knees. He crouched for a moment, gathering his strength, and then he sat up painfully.

'I've got nothing left,' he said bitterly. 'Nor has Em. They've beaten seven bells out of us. It was all Em and I could do to keep ourselves alive. All my magic's gone, spent. Otherwise we'd have healed ourselves.'

'What do they want you to do?' Emmaline asked. Over her shoulder I saw Seth's worried face and knew that he'd been wondering the same thing.

Cold prickled up and down my spine.

'Did they bring you through that big room, the one they call the Cathedral?' I asked. Em nodded. 'Did you see the bones in the middle?'

'The stuff that looked like old firewood?'

346

'Yes. They're the bones of their last leader. Some dead Russian. They want me to raise him.' I spat out the short sentences like pieces of glass, feeling them cut my mouth. 'Then he's going to lead them in a war against the outwith.'

'They're nuts!' Em said blankly. 'Surely? I mean – we're talking fruitcake crazy, right?'

'Does that matter?' I asked bitterly. 'When we're all dead we won't care if they were a little eccentric round the edges or bonafide bat-shit.'

'And your role in this?' Abe said.

'Aside from raising the Holy Master? Well I presume I'm supposed to go marching after them, healing them if they get a bit low, and raising the head dude at regular intervals if he gets slain again. Kind of like having your own personal "save and reload" button on life.'

We were all silent for a moment at the picture. It was not a pretty one.

'And if you say no?' Em said at last.

I couldn't say it.

But Abe knew. I could see it from his face, from the way his eyes went to the glass flagon, to the chair, and back to me.

'Anna?' Em prodded.

'Excision, right?' Abe said to me. I shrugged.

'Hang on.' Seth's face was baffled. 'Can someone please explain for the dumb outwith over here?'

'Excision is a process where . . .' Abe stopped. He looked

347

sick. For a moment I wasn't sure if he'd continue, if his wounds had got the better of him again. But he forced himself on. 'Magic is a physical substance – like blood, or bone marrow. And you can extract it. It's dangerous. If you lose too much, you go into shock. And if you go past a certain point, it's irrecoverable. The magic never replenishes itself. You're crippled for life. You're no longer a witch.'

'But,' Seth said slowly, 'that's what you did for Anna, wasn't it? You gave her some of your magic, so she could escape the Malleus. And you weren't crippled, right?'

'No,' Abe agreed. 'It wasn't fun, but I didn't suffer any lasting harm. But what they did to me wasn't an excision. With excision . . .' Abe swallowed and carried on. 'With excision they take *all* the magic. It's almost always fatal.'

'Fatal?' Seth said. His face was white and suddenly he looked as sick as Abe.

Abe's eyes met Seth's and in that moment their faces, so unlike, wore the same expression.

'But why?' Emmaline said furiously. 'What would it achieve? They want Anna alive, don't they, so she can raise their stack of holy firewood?'

'Ideally – yes, they want her alive,' Abe said. 'But failing that – they want her power. If they drain her magic and give it *all* to one single witch, that witch gets a shot with Anna's abilities. Only for a limited time, because they can't regenerate Anna's magic; when it's gone, it's gone. But one shot is better than none.'

348

'What are you saying?' Em demanded. 'Anna caves – they get to control her power. Or she holds out, we all die – and they still get a shot? *That's* the choice?'

'It's still better though, isn't it?' I said. I spoke to Abe, not to Emmaline. 'It's better they get just one try. They might not succeed.'

'No, they might not,' Abe said quietly. 'We don't know how this works, after all. Yours is a power no one else has ever had. We don't know if it will transplant.'

'So that's it?' Emmaline looked from me, to Abe, to Seth, and back to me. 'You're giving up? You're going to die?'

'I don't know what else to do!' I cried back. 'What can I do? You tell me!'

My voice rang round the room, shockingly loud. Then we all stopped, suddenly frozen, listening. There were footsteps in the corridor.

'Listen,' Abe said hurriedly. He grabbed my wrist. 'Anna, there's one thing – they can't extract your magic unless you use it.'

'What do you mean?' I stared at him.

'I know from when they took my magic – *you* have to unlock it. If you don't do a spell—'

But the door flew open and Tatiana stalked into the room, flanked by Danya and Marcus.

'*Udalit!*' Tatiana spat and Emmaline, Abe and Seth flew backwards across the room, crashing into the walls with a crunch that made me cry out. They hung there, immobilized by Tatiana's spell, and as the witches moved

349

across the room, I realized what the rings were for: shackles. For when the room was not used for a single operation, but for multiple drainings, the victims lined up like cattle.

'*Framdaþ!*' I shouted as they closed in on them, ropes and chains in their hands. '*Framdaþ!*' Begging them, *ordering* them to stop.

But there was nothing there. There was nothing left. I screamed and sobbed spells as they went about their task with businesslike determination. I might as well have been singing nursery rhymes. They didn't pause – they didn't even flinch. They just ignored my spells like they were flies buzzing around their heads.

I'd have to try something else.

I took a deep breath, gripped the syringe more tightly in my fist, and leapt towards Tatiana.

I never reached her. She didn't miss a beat, didn't even look around. She just shouted a curse over her shoulder in Russian. It hit me like a blow to the stomach, catapulting me across the room into the draining chair. The syringe skittered out of my hand across the concrete floor and lay useless in a corner.

For a minute I just lay in the chair, agonizingly winded. All the breath had been knocked out of my body and I couldn't seem to get it back.

But then I saw the witches straightening from their tasks and turn, and I realized I was next. I flung myself out of the chair, ready to fight, ready to bite and scratch and kick.

It was useless. I knew that even as I thrashed and

struggled, in a horrible re-enactment of Irina's last fight. They didn't even have to use magic to restrain me – without spells I was pathetically easy to subdue. Danya held me down while Tatiana closed the shackles on my wrists, my ankles, around my throat.

Marcus watched from the sidelines, his brown eyes meltingly soft, as I fought and wept.

At last every part of me was locked down and the only thing I could do was scream.

CHAPTER TWENTY-THREE

'Anna . . .' It was a whisper, soft in my ear. 'Anna, wake up.'

I turned my head away from the sound. I didn't want to. I didn't want to go back to a world where my friends were in chains and my mother was dead, once and for all.

'Anna, you can't ignore this. Look at me.'

I opened my eyes. Warm, brown eyes stared into mine. A hand stroked my face, smoothing back my sweaty, tangled hair.

I spat. And the face recoiled. Marcus wiped his cheek theatrically with his sleeve and then began to laugh.

'You really don't know when you're beaten, do you?'

'No,' I croaked. It was hard to speak with the shackle around my throat, crushing my windpipe.

'Tatiana?' Marcus said with a shrug.

She stepped forwards. Her face wasn't grim – there was too much sorrow in it for that. But it was uncompromising. And she held in her hand a long, steel needle. It was about the thickness of my thumb, dwindling to a blunt point. On the other end snaked a rubber tube.

I felt myself grow sick with fear. My heart began to beat so hard that I could hear it in my ears – a rushing thud of irrepressible blood and life. If I could have stopped it at that moment . . .

Tatiana raised her arm, holding the steel needle high in the air.

'No!' Seth shouted. His voice was cracked and his chains gave a rusty shriek as he struggled to his feet, yanking at them with vicious strength. 'For God's sake, are you mad? Don't! Please don't!'

'You can't help her, *Čužestranec*,' Tatiana said, but not unkindly.

And she brought the needle down with all her force.

There was an audible crack as the thing went through my ribs.

And then the sound of my own scream, echoing in the small room. And my panting breath, sobbing out inarticulate sounds of agony.

The temptation was to lash out, to protect myself, to stop it hurting – but somewhere in the hot red agony I heard Abe's voice. He was shouting.

'Remember what I said, Anna! Don't use your magic!'

Tatiana flung out a blast of magic that smacked him in the face and he fell silent, wiping blood on his sleeve – but I'd heard him.

It took every bit of control I had – but I kept it in. I wouldn't cast a spell. I *wouldn't*. I just had to hold on to that. I squeezed my eyes shut, feeling the hot tears stream down my face, listening to my own whimpering sounds of pain, and everything seemed to shrink down to this room, to this chair, to the burning pain in the centre of my chest.

'Listen to me . . .' I heard Marcus' voice through the red mist and when I opened my eyes he was squatting beside the chair. He ran his hands through his hair, the immaculate shining waves glimmering in the electric light from overhead. 'You can't get out of this – you do understand that? You're not going to get out of this place alive and with your magic intact. But your friends *can* walk away. If you cooperate. Are you selfish enough to put them through this?'

'Shut up!' Emmaline spat from across the room. 'I've always hated you, you smug upper-class cock. Anna, if you do as he says—'

Marcus took two quick steps across the room and punched her, hard, right across the cheekbone. Emmaline gasped and fell sideways, only the chains around her wrists stopping her from falling completely. Then she laughed. It was a horrible sound in the silence of the room.

'I'm going to make you beg,' Marcus said. 'Not for your own life – you'll be too far gone for that. But I'll make you beg Anna to do as I say. Do you understand?'

'Shut up,' Emmaline said contemptuously. 'You've watched too many Bond movies for your own good.'

Marcus took another step – but not towards Em. Towards Abe.

Em made a sound – halfway between a gasp and a cry.

Marcus looked at her and smiled. Then he drew back his fist and hit Abe, hard, in the gut.

I expected Abe to crash back against the wall with the force of the blow. But instead, Marcus' fist seemed to sink unnaturally into Abe's stomach – up to the knuckles . . . then up to the wrist.

Abe gave a strange, strangled whimper.

Then Marcus started to pull and Abe's face went completely white, sheened with cold sweat. He barely made a sound as Marcus withdrew his fist, slowly . . . slowly.

Marcus' hand was wet with blood to the shirt cuffs and he was holding something dark red and purple, which glistened in the electric light from above. Then, with a noise like a sigh, Abe slumped in his chains, unconscious.

It took me a moment to realize what Marcus was holding: Abe's guts. He'd reached inside Abe's body and pulled out a handful of his intestines.

Emmaline's face was almost as white and sick as Abe's and she watched in helpless horror as Marcus dropped the loops of flesh to hang loose against Abe's belly, where they rose and fell with his gasping, shallow breaths.

Marcus wiped his hand fastidiously on his trousers.

'Shall we try that again?' he said to Emmaline. 'Perhaps with his heart?'

Emmaline didn't speak; she just gasped and retched. Marcus put his face close to hers.

'I know. I know what you've tried to keep from him and

from Anna. I know you love him. You can hide it from them, but not from me.'

'No . . .' Em sobbed. But her eyes were fixed on Abe, fixed on his unconscious face, and I saw what I'd missed all these months. It was true.

'I know you've longed for his heart,' Marcus said softly. 'I know how you've wished it could be yours. I can give it to you. Wet and beating.'

Em retched again, a pool of spit and acid at Marcus' feet. When she looked up, her eyes were full of hate. But she didn't speak.

Marcus sighed.

'Don't think I've finished with you,' he said. 'This is a pause, not a reprieve.'

And then he turned and looked at Seth.

'Don't kill him,' Tatiana said casually. 'Not yet. If you kill him, the girl will only have less to lose.'

'I'll try not to,' Marcus said distastefully. He put his head on one side, thinking. I could see Seth's chest rising and falling beneath his shirt, his face wary and full of fury as he tried to work out what Marcus had in store for him.

Then – to my shock – he began to speak.

'There've been times when I hated you,' Seth said. His voice was strange, reluctant, almost thick, as if he was forcing the words out, or as if they were forcing themselves out, in spite of everything he could do to prevent it. He stopped, shook his head, bewildered, and then said, 'Anna, I'm so sorry – I never meant . . .' He stopped again and

356

then spat out, 'I slept with other people. Twice. Once in Morocco. Once in Helsinki.'

This time he clapped his manacled hand across his mouth. His eyes as they looked at me were full of mute horror. I longed to wrench my hands free of the chains, to cover my ears, to spare us both the torture of the truth. Because that was the worst thing. I knew it *was* the truth.

Marcus began to laugh and Seth turned to him, furious.

'You're doing this! You bastard – what are you doing? How are you . . . ? No!' He clamped his lips shut, trying to physically stop the words, but his face twisted and they spilled out like poison. 'It was like a revenge. I thought I could screw you out of my system – but it didn't work. The more I tried to forget you, the more I obsessed about you.'

I strained uselessly at the shackles, wondering hopelessly why we could close our eyes but not our ears. I would've given anything to be able to shut this out.

'I began to realize it was true,' Seth choked out. 'What Grandad said. This isn't love. It was never love . . . *No!*' he bellowed suddenly, ripping control back from Marcus, the veins in his neck and on his forehead standing out. 'It's *not* true – I won't do this to her!'

'Stop it, Marcus!' I knew it was pointless to beg, but I couldn't stop myself. The words spilled out, along with my tears. 'Please stop this.'

'I've hated you,' Seth said brokenly, his face wretched. He turned his face to the wall, speaking into the painted concrete, refusing to meet my eyes as Marcus tore the truth out from deep inside his heart. His voice cracked. 'I feel like you took my free will away. I feel like you've left me half a person, broken without you. I've had nights when I wanted to die. I've had nights when I wished *you'd* die, if it meant I could stop feeling like this. I want to be free. I don't want to hurt like this any more.' He stopped with a huge effort, his fists clenched against the concrete. When he spoke again, it was through clenched teeth. 'Anna, don't listen to me, this is not the truth, it's *not* how I feel – OK, it's a tiny part of the truth but . . .'

He stopped again, his forehead against the rough wall. His shoulders were rising and falling. His breath came quick, like pants of pain. I could see he was fighting Marcus' will, fighting to keep silent.

'What else have you got?' Marcus asked softly. 'What other secrets have you hidden from her?'

'Don't,' I sobbed. The hot tears scorched my face. I shut my eyes, shutting out the sight of the three of them, broken and bloodied and ashamed.

'I thought . . .' Seth whispered, 'I thought . . . when I left I thought that I'd convince you that you were wrong. I thought I'd show you that I *could* walk away . . . But I didn't.' He caught his breath. 'I only convinced myself. I'll never be free.'

'Stop it!' I screamed.

Seth's breathing was ragged in the silence of the room.

'Come on,' Marcus whispered. 'Tell her the truth. What

do you want? What do you *really* want?'

For a long moment Seth said nothing. Then the words came slowly, jerkily, torn from him by Marcus' magic.

'Anna . . . I want . . . you . . . to make . . . this . . . stop . . .'

And suddenly I couldn't hold back.

The magic pulsed through me like a flame.

I wanted it to stop. I wanted to blast Marcus into bloody cinders and annihilate Tatiana and Danya and and all the others. I wanted to bring this whole mine crashing down on our heads, bury us all, if that was what it took.

But none of that happened.

Instead the sharp pain in my chest exploded into a tearing, gaping agony. A pearl-white drop hovered at the lip of the glass flagon for a fraction of a second – and then it splashed into the jar. And from somewhere outside the room, the sound of a pump started up.

'No!' Seth shouted, at the same time as Emmaline wept, 'Oh, Anna – you fool!'

She lunged towards me, ripping uselessly at her chains as the magic began to flood out of me in great gouts, splashing up inside the glass jar, sending mother-of-pearl reflections dancing and shimmering across the room. And all I could think, above the roar of the pain, and Emmaline's furious impotent cries, was that it was beautiful. It was astonishingly beautiful.

I could feel it draining out of me, like that time Maya had taken my magic and used it to heal the town of Winter. But this was far faster, far more urgent – the magic was being sucked out of me with a terrible, hungry force, without my consent. I could hear Emmaline's shouts and cries above the sound of the pump, pleading with me to stop it, to fight it. And I tried to fight – I couldn't *not* fight. I felt myself convulse helplessly in the shackles, though I knew it couldn't do any good.

The pump droned on and above its noise I could hear Emmaline's screams and shouts, sobbing at me, at Marcus, begging him for a mercy he wouldn't – couldn't – grant.

But her voice seemed to be drifting away. I could feel my movements becoming weaker. My arms and legs wouldn't obey me any more.

Now, my fingers were numb. My arms were numb. My feet and legs were numb. I was cold, incredibly cold.

I closed my eyes. Waiting for the end. Waiting for it *all* to end.

Instead there was a grinding, clanking sound and the pump ground to a halt.

Tatiana said something that sounded like swearing in Russian.

'Marcus, I must mend the pump,' she said. Then she and Danya ran from the room.

Marcus stood with his arms folded by the door, watching, his foot tapping.

'For God's sake, Marcus, it's not too late . . .' I heard Emmaline's imploring voice, as if from a long way off. 'You know that, don't you? It's not too late. Please, for the love of all that's good, *please* change your mind. She's your cousin – your own cousin.'

'Do you really think I've come this far, to give up now?' Marcus said contemptuously.

'You fucking bastard!' Em shouted. I heard her voice change from pleading to fury. 'D'you realize what you're doing? To your own flesh and blood? Come on, admit it, part of you *must* be ashamed. You haven't even got the guts to look at me. Look me in the eye and tell me you're going to do this.'

And, through dim, blurry eyes, I saw Marcus turn slowly, mockingly, to look at her.

Em straightened; there was something in her hand.

She drew her fist back – and flung it.

It glittered as it flew through the air, quick and true. There was a sound like a skewer punching into meat and Marcus gave a roar of anguish. He staggered back, clawing at his face, and I saw the syringe sticking out of his eye socket. Blood was pouring down his face.

'You mad bitch!' he screamed.

'Now!' Em shouted at Seth, and Seth smashed his cuffs into the rivet on the wall until the white walls were flecked with blood.

'I can't,' he gasped. 'They're not . . . God damn it! . . . There!'

There was a crack and the chain broke, sending him staggering across the room. He groped along the shelves, searching for something, anything to use as a weapon. A metal box. It clanged horribly as he battered Em's chains – then he swore and tossed it aside and picked up a metal stand.

'I'll try not to hurt you,' he panted, 'but there's not much slack.'

He pushed a leg of the stand through one of the chain links and twisted, groaning with effort.

The chain tightened . . . tightened. Em screamed involuntarily and Seth faltered, but she sobbed, 'No! Carry on, I'm OK.'

There was a shriek as the links gave way and she stumbled over to me, wringing at her wrists.

'Free Abe,' she ordered Seth over her shoulder, and he nodded and began to lever at Abe's binding. I felt her hands touch my forehead, cool and smooth. 'Can you hear me Anna?'

I tried to nod, but my head wouldn't move. She must have seen something though, for she gave a sob of relief.

'Can you hold on while I help Seth free Abe and heal his stomach? I'm frightened to touch this.' She gestured to the tube sticking out of my chest. 'Abe will know what to do – he'll know how to get it out of you.'

'Go,' I managed and she kissed my cheek and then ran across to Abe.

Marcus was on the far side of the room, staggering along one wall, keening with pain, groping for the door and trying to pull the syringe out of his eye. Feathers prickled across his skin and his nose was suddenly sharp and beaked.

On the other side of the room Em was crouched over Abe, muttering spells. Her face was lit with a fierce flame.

'Don't die,' I heard her voice repeating, beneath Marcus' panting cries. 'Don't die, you bastard. Don't do this to me, Abe. Come back to me. Oh, Abe – please come back to me. Don't leave me, I'll never forgive you. Don't die.'

And then – Abe's hand seemed to shake. At the same time, Marcus lashed out with a spell, towards the sound of her voice.

'I'll kill you!' Marcus roared. 'I'll kill you all!'

A sheet of flame billowed across the room, towards where Seth was edging round Marcus' blind side, making for the door. He gasped, beating sparks from his shirt and hair, and Marcus caught the sound, lashing out with a spell that cracked like a whip, sending trays and syringes clattering across the tiled floor. Seth dodged, just in time – and then he reached the door. For a minute I thought he was going to escape, but instead he shot the bolt with his free hand.

What was he doing? Was he mad, shutting us up here with Marcus? Even wounded and half-blind Marcus was more dangerous than Seth could possibly imagine.

But on the other side of the room something was happening. I heard Em's gasp of relief and a croaking voice: 'Shove my bloody intestines back in, you stupid woman.'

Abe. His face was grey, his shirt was covered in blood, but somehow he was pulling himself upright. Emmaline pressed her hand to his stomach, her face white and sick

363

– she was physically pushing Abe's guts back inside him and Abe began to mutter spells, through teeth gritted with pain. To my amazement, he hauled himself to his feet on Emmaline's arm. His face was haggard, his skin the colour of clay – but he was walking.

And then there was a shuddering, clanking groan – and the pump started up again.

I felt it before I'd realized what it meant – the clattering groan, the dreadful sucking at my heart.

I turned my head, slowly, painfully, to look at the flask.

The splashing, dancing magic had slowed. There was a huge amount there – more than twice what they'd taken from Irina. But now the flood was slowing, just as hers had done before the end. It no longer gushed into the glass flagon, it dripped. Slowly.

Abe hobbled to the chair, supporting himself on Em's shoulder.

'Can you get it out of her?' Emmaline asked frantically. 'That bloody tube – do you know how to take it out?'

'Shit.' Abe looked at the pipes and the nozzle, his face drawn with pain. 'This isn't the same set up as they used for me. God! Em, what do I do? Do I just pull? What if I kill her?'

'Jesus!' Em cried frantically. 'Don't ask me. It's in her *heart*, Abe. I can see the bones of her ribs. What the hell do we do?'

'I don't know!' Abe ran his hands through his hair in an agony of indecision. 'If only we had more *time*. But she's almost gone. Anna!' He put his hand on my shoulder, his face fierce and frightened. 'Anna, listen, hang in there, OK? We're going to get you out of this thing. And then somehow we'll get your magic back into you. The Ealdwitan will know how, I swear it.'

He looked at the glass flask on its stand, full almost to overflowing with magic. The pump was almost dry. A single drop hovered at the lip of the jar.

But before it could fall, Marcus lashed out again. Jars and bottles smashed to the floor and Abe staggered as a coil of electrical wire struck him on the shoulder. The glass flagon rocked precariously on its stand.

'Abe!' Em grabbed his arm, holding him up and then lurched for the flagon of magic, steadying it before it could fall. Behind her I saw Seth reach down and snatch up the tangle of chains from the floor.

The single drop of magic quivered and fell, and the pump sucked and sucked at my heart. The room shivered.

'Tatiana!' Marcus roared at the top of his lungs. 'Help!'

Footsteps in the corridor – running.

And then Seth brought the chains down with all his strength.

Marcus crashed to the floor, enmeshed in the tangle of chains, flinging out curses left and right as he fell. The room began to fill with the black smoke of thwarted magic as he made one last, inhuman effort, his face suddenly dark with feathers, his shoulders hunching into wings. He lifted from the floor, his great black wings flapping uselessly against the encircling chains – and then his magic failed him. He fell back to earth, his head smashing against the concrete with a crack that sounded like he'd broken his skull. Blood began to gather in a dark, glittering pool beneath his head.

Smoke still swirled and gusted in eddies, but Abe, Em and Seth stood completely motionless, waiting for him to rise again. He didn't.

I closed my eyes, listening to the sounds that filled the room.

The sound of Seth, Abe and Emmaline's panting breath.

The dreadful dry suck of the pump at my heart.

And the noise of footsteps, terrifyingly close. Had the others even heard them? I tried to gasp a warning, but nothing came.

Then the pump gave a gasping death-rattle and they all turned.

'There's nothing left.' Em's voice was full of horror. 'There's no more magic coming out. Oh God, Abe. We're too late.'

'What?' Seth's shocked voice. 'She's not dead! You've got to try!'

'No one can lose that much magic and live.' Abe's voice, harsh. 'I didn't even give a tenth of that – but it nearly killed me.'

'Get her off that thing!' Seth shouted. 'Or will I do it myself?'

But before Abe could answer, the room shook with

a deafening crash – Tatiana and Danya had reached the locked door.

'I'll hold the door for as long as I can,' Seth said. I heard the rattle of the doors as he flung something across it. 'Abe – for God's sake, just do whatever you have to. Get her free.'

'Abe?' Em asked. 'Can you do it?'

'We've got no choice,' Abe said. His voice was grim. 'I'm going to pull it out.'

Emmaline made a sound like a retch and then managed, 'OK.'

There was another crash and the sound of screaming metal.

'Hurry up!' Seth shouted.

'Em – you hold the jar. For God's sake, don't let any spill. That's her only chance.'

And then something – somebody – seized hold of the pipe in my heart and pulled.

CHAPTER TWENTY-FOUR

I was gripped against someone's chest, my head lolling against a shoulder. I tried to lift my head, to see who it was, but I was so weak I couldn't manage it.

'She should be dead!' Abe's voice was incredulous. 'No one could survive that. No one.'

'Does it matter?' Em asked in an agony of impatience. 'Let's just get—'

But she never finished. There was a shriek of warping metal and the huge double doors burst off their hinges and into the room.

With an immense effort, I opened my eyes.

Tatiana stood in the doorway. Flames seemed to crackle from her, rippling across her shimmering bone-white skin. Her inky hair had escaped its plaits and streamed out behind her, alive with electricity. A cold, harsh light blazed from her.

'*Og*—' she roared, but before she had finished the spell, Em screamed:

'*Stop!*'

She held up the jar, gleaming pearl-white in Tatiana's

blazing light.

'If you take one step towards us – *one step* – this jar smashes on the floor.'

'NO!' Tatiana screeched and from beside me I heard Abe's echoing gasp of horror:

'Em, no! Are you crazy? That's Anna's only chance of getting any power back.'

'It's her only chance of getting out alive,' Em snapped back. 'What good is her magic if she's dead, along with the rest of us?'

She turned back to Tatiana.

'You want this magic? Well, don't come any closer. And tell your mates the same thing. One spell – one false move – this jar goes smash and so do your chances with that heap of firewood in the hall.'

Tatiana's face was twisted with hate, but she nodded, very slowly.

'Walk,' Em hissed to Seth. 'Keep behind me. If they can kill us without endangering the magic, they will. Abe, can you manage to walk without me? I need both hands for this.'

'I can manage,' Abe said shortly. 'Don't worry about me. Concentrate on finding the way.'

Slowly – very slowly – they began to walk. Into the darkness of the tunnels.

I was a dead weight against Seth's chest, my head lolling as he shifted me in his arms, trying to balance. I wanted to help – but I couldn't, I couldn't seem to lift a finger. The only thing I could move was my eyes, though they kept closing as I slipped in and out of the darkness. I dragged them open for a moment to see Em leading the way, turning, seemingly at random, down one tunnel after another. The jar of magic glittered in front of us, lighting up the caves we passed, filled with stalactites and witches. Their faces glimmered out of the darkness, a susurration of shock and anguish following us.

One witch reached out as if to stop us, but Em raised the jar above her head and shouted, 'Tatiana, I *will* drop it!'

Tatiana's voice came from a long way back, shrieking a command in Russian. The witch fell back and let us pass.

My eyes slid closed again. I could hear Abe's tearing breath behind us as he forced himself onwards, in spite of his injuries, and I could feel Seth's limp in his halting, painful progress. Holding me, he had no hand for his crutch, no way to spare his bad leg, and I could feel the pain in every step, hear it in the catch of breath each time he put down his foot.

At last the echoes changed and I opened my eyes. We were in the great hall, the cave they called the Cathedral.

'Stay close,' Em whispered under her breath. 'This is going to be the most difficult part.'

They began to edge across the vast shadowy space, Em holding the jar of magic – *my* magic – high, so that she could see if anyone was casting a spell.

'Abe, can you manage any extra light?' she whispered. Abe shook his head.

'I'm sorry.' His voice was clipped and curt with pain. 'I'm barely keeping myself upright.'

'OK, don't worry. Just keep your eyes open in case they try something – that goes for you too, Seth.'

I felt Seth nod.

We were almost at the centre of the hall now, close by the stones they used as seats. After that, the long walk upwards, to the exit, to the outside of the mine. And after that . . . But I couldn't think about that. If I saw daylight again before I died, that would be enough for me.

'Keep going,' Em whispered. Her voice was shaking. 'Come on, you can do it, I *know* you can. It's only a few hundred yards after this.'

And then – a shadow darted from behind one of the huge stones, straight into our path. It was a young witch – thin as a skeleton, pale as death. She stood, poised for a second in front of Em, and then she flung herself towards us, screaming a spell.

I heard Tatiana's shout of panic from far back across the cave.

I heard Em's cry, her voice shouting, 'Shield! Abe, help me shield!'

A huge shield sprang out to encompass us – Em's? Abe's? Tatiana's? It no longer mattered.

Everything seemed to happen very slowly.

The witch's spell ricocheted off the shield and flew upwards, into the vaulted space above our heads, where it exploded with a burst of white light and a sound like thunder.

For a moment nothing happened – and then there was a scream of rending rock and salt-crusted stalactites began to rain down around us like murderous, glittering spears. One crashed into the ground to our left, another exploded in our path, sending shards of salt spraying into our faces.

But it wasn't just stalactites. Rocks were following – enormous chunks of stone crashing down, skittering across the vast chamber. A great rent was opening in the rock above our heads and daylight glittered through – faint and pale and grey, but light.

Around us the witches screamed in horror, as if the light would burn them. Another huge piece of roof crashed down, so close I felt the blast of air as it smashed into the rocky floor. Only Em kept her head.

'Run!' she shouted at Seth and Abe. 'Run for the exit! We're going to die if we stay here.'

They ran – though it wasn't much like running, more like an agonising, hobbling limp. Em had one arm wrapped around the glass jar, the other round Abe's shoulder. Seth's hands gripped me painfully; his breath was hot against my forehead, his heart pounding beneath my cheek.

Over his shoulder I saw a piece of rock the size of a small car smash down on to the pile of bones at the centre of the hall. Thick, acrid smoke began to pour out from beneath it. It smelled of burning tyres, of industrial pollution, of charred meat and chemicals all mixed into one foul, black, choking stench. Screams went up from the witches around the cave – and suddenly they were running too. Not towards us, but towards the bones, hardly even noticing the murderous hail of rocks. One witch after another went down, smashed by the falling stones, but they didn't stop for each other. It was as if nothing else existed, nothing else mattered, but the bones crushed beneath the boulder.

And then we were in the tunnels beyond the Cathedral, inching painfully upwards, and the only thing left of the terror inside the hall was the sound of screams and the stench of burning bones.

'Come *on*,' Em said, her voice a sob. 'We're nearly there!'

We reached a crossroads I remembered, five tunnels all meeting, and Em pointed to the one that led upwards.

'This is it!' There was a terrified hope in her voice. 'This is *it*, the last tunnel!'

Something would stop us – wouldn't it? There would be a door, a guard – *something*.

But the door opened at Em's touch, yawning outwards – and we stumbled out of the black mouth of the tunnel, into the cool whiteness of the snow-covered forest.

Seth fell to his knees in the snow, his breath coming hard against my cheek, and then he laid me gently on the ground.

'Give me a moment,' he said, his words like ragged gasps.

Beside him I saw Abe slump against a tree trunk, a hand pressed over his stomach.

'I know you're tired,' Em said. There was a crack in her voice. 'But we've got to keep going. They still might come after us.'

'I know,' Abe said croakily. He drew his knees up to his chest, his face sick with pain. 'Anna, can you hear me?'

I tried to speak. No words came out and Abe glowered at me from beneath his black brows, as though he could bully me into surviving.

'You're going to be OK, Anna. D'you understand? We're going to get you home and get your magic back into you somehow.'

'Can they do that?' Em asked. 'What if it doesn't take? Don't all the rules say that once you've gone past a certain point . . . ?'

'All the rules say that Anna should be dead right now,' Abe said angrily. 'Anyway it's the only chance we've got; it's better than nothing. Once we get home—'

'But how *can* we get home?' Em said despairingly. She'd been so strong inside the caves – now her hot determination seemed to have evaporated.

'I can get us out of here.' Seth's voice was hoarse. 'If we can get down to the shore – that's where they left my boat – I can sail us. Maybe not home – but somewhere with an airport.' He turned to me, pushing the damp, matted hair off my face. 'Anna, can you hang on that long?'

I couldn't answer. I couldn't even nod. I just looked at him, at his wide grey eyes, his face cut and bruised and bloodied.

'Anna . . .' His voice cracked and he stroked my face. I saw there were tears in his eyes. 'All that stuff I said in that room – it wasn't true. It *wasn't*.'

But it was. Not the whole truth, maybe. But a part of it. Marcus had pulled out part of Seth's soul, in that room. Abe's guts would heal, with luck, but Seth – nothing could force those truths back where they came from. They'd always be there between us, dark and bloody.

'Come on,' Emmaline said. 'I'm sorry, Seth, Abe. I know you're both hurt but we've *got* to keep going. Seth, which way's your boat?'

Seth pulled me into his arms and then stood with a gasp of pain. He scanned the forest.

'It's hard – it was night when we came. Everything looked different. But I think –' he nodded towards a track in the forest '– I think it was that path. It's the right direction anyway – and if we can get to the shore, we can probably find the boat, so let's head down and worry about it when we get to the beach.'

'OK,' Em said. 'Abe, can you manage?'

'Yep,' Abe said. He heaved himself to his feet using Em's arm and I saw her face crumple as he began to hobble through the snow, towards the forest track. I recognized the look in her eyes: love, helpless in the face of suffering. How had I missed it for so long?

Then she turned and followed him, the heavy glass jar full of my life and magic clutched in her arms, and we began to walk . . .

'Stop.' Seth's voice cut through the night air, above the pounding of his heart beneath my cheek. As he spoke, something glittered through the trees ahead, and at first I thought it was the moon, strangely low in the sky, but then I realized it was Em, turning with the jar of my magic in her arms.

'What?'

'I can't go on.' His tearing breath made white clouds in the darkness. 'You have to give me a minute.'

'Come on, we *must* be nearly there,' Em pleaded. She came back up the track. 'I'm pretty sure I can hear the sea – can't you manage a few more metres?'

'I just . . . I can't. I need a second.' Seth let me slide awkwardly to the ground and then he slumped beside me, groaning with pain as he straightened his leg.

From somewhere further back up the track I heard a halting crunch, crunch of twigs and Abe came into the clearing. He slid to the ground beside Seth. His face, beneath its black stubble, was completely white, his eyes were closed, and his cheekbones were sharp and shadowed.

'Please!' Em begged. She set the jar of magic on the ground and knelt beside them, stroking Abe's hair back from his face. Then she took Seth's hand and squeezed it. 'Come on, I know you can do this, both of you. When we get to the boat we can rest—'

She broke off as a low howl echoed through the forest.

376

'Jesus, what was that?'

'Wolves,' Seth said hoarsely. 'They were howling on our way up too.'

'Great. Something else on our track.' She stood, scanning the forest, then crouched back down. 'Abe, I'm going to try to heal you again.'

'No,' Abe said, his voice short with pain. 'Not me – Seth. He's got to sail.'

'I don't want to be healed!' Seth snapped out. Then he spoke more calmly, but just as sure. 'I know you mean well, but I've had enough of magic. Never again.'

'You'd rather let us all die?' Em said angrily.

'I'm tired,' Seth said. 'And I'm in pain. But I can sail. Heal Abe. He needs it more than I do.'

Em looked at Abe, who shrugged as if to say, *What can you do?* Em nodded and lifted his shirt.

What she saw made her suck in her breath and Seth made a noise like a choke and turned away. There was a half-healed split across Abe's stomach, black and gummy with congealed blood.

'Oh my God,' Em managed. 'And you walked all this way – with that?'

Abe said nothing, he just closed his eyes. Em laid her hands on the oozing, gaping wound and I saw her lips move in silent pleading incantations.

I found I was cold, lying on the ground – cold, and wet, and there was a rock digging into my cheek. It was the first time I'd felt anything but numb since leaving the cave.

Snow had melted on my cheek and was trickling down my face. It tickled unbearably and I wished I could move to wipe it away. If I could have cast a spell to stop the feeling I would – but there was nothing there. Nothing. Just a terrifying hollow emptiness. My whole body yearned towards the jar that Emmaline had put down the ground. It felt like my heart had been pulled out of my body and imprisoned, just metres away, where I couldn't touch it.

I made a sound – a mew of despair – and Seth turned towards me, his face suddenly alight with a fierce hope.

'Anna?'

'S . . . Se . . .' I managed. His hands gripped my shoulders and then he pulled me on to his lap and into his arms, in a heavy, slithering rush.

'Anna!' He cupped my face with his free hand, the other arm holding me against his chest so hard I could barely breathe. 'You said something. You said . . . Did you say my name?'

I couldn't nod, my head lolled heavily against his chest, but he hugged me fiercely.

'Hey, Em!' he called hoarsely. 'Abe!'

'What?' Em turned from kneeling over Abe. Her face was white and drawn. I could see she was as tired as Seth, almost ready to drop.

'She said something.'

'What?' Her dark eyes stared into mine, full of hope. 'Anna, can you hear me?'

This time I managed a nod, just the smallest movement possible, but she caught it and her tired face broke into a smile.

'Abe,' she said over her shoulder, 'she's still there – Anna's still alive.'

'I never doubted it,' Abe croaked back. He stood, shakily, but his face was a better colour than before. 'Anna – we're going to get you back home and get your magic back. Do you understand?' Then he looked at Em. 'Thank you, Em,' he said quietly. He took her hand in his and pulled her to standing, bringing her clenched fingers up to his face. For a minute I thought he was going to kiss them, but he didn't, he just touched her knuckles gently to his cheek.

They stood for a moment, silent, Em's hand against his face, then there came another howl from the woods, a long drawn-out sobbing noise, and Emmaline shivered and dropped her hand from his.

'Come on,' she said. 'I can hear the sea – can't you?'

'I can see it,' Seth said. 'At least I think I can. See that glimmer through the trees?' He pointed towards a gap in the forest. It looked like every other gap to me, but Emmaline craned and then nodded her head excitedly.

'I think you're right. I can definitely see something. Can you manage? Anna, I mean – can you manage the last bit with her?'

'I can manage,' Seth said shortly. He stood and then heaved me into his arms with a little catch of breath. Abe looked at Emmaline and she nodded and then picked up the heavy jar of magic. Together they began to stumble slowly down the last few hundred yards of track, towards the cliff.

Snow flakes speckled the black rocks of the clifftop, stark white in the moonlight. At the edge Seth stopped and we looked out to sea.

The boat was there.

It was only when I heard Seth's shuddering sigh of relief that I realized how fragile it was, how easily something might have happened to it – destroyed by a storm while we were in the mines, or holed by the witches and sunk. But it was still there, floating on the dark waves. There was frost glittering on the rigging and it had drifted out a little way from the beach when the tide rose, but the anchor had held firm.

Seth set me carefully down on the cliff-top and this time I managed to stay sitting upright against a rock, supporting myself on shaking arms.

'Are you all right?' he asked. I managed to nod.

'I'm . . . OK.' My voice was cracked and hoarse, but it seemed like a miracle to be able to speak at all.

Seth's exhausted face broke into a smile.

'You can talk!' He crouched in front of me on his heels and touched my face. 'I was so frightened, Anna. I thought . . . I thought you were going to die.'

'Was it true . . . ?' It was hard to speak; the words felt like pebbles in my mouth, each one having to be spat out.

'W-what . . . you said . . . in the cave?'

'That I . . .' He stopped, looked away. 'That I wished . . .'

'You wished . . .' I took a deep breath. 'I'd die.'

'No.' His voice shook.

'Please . . . don't . . . l-lie,' I said painfully. He ran his hands through his hair, his face white and haggard. I knew that feeling: wanting to say the right thing, not wanting to lie.

'OK,' he said at last. 'It *was* true. But not – not like that. I thought about it – when I wanted the pain to stop. I wondered what would happen – if you died. I wondered – if I'd be free . . .' His voice broke and he knelt in front of me. 'But I don't want to be free – if freedom means being without you. That's what I realized in the cave . . . I . . .'

I was too tired to speak. We only looked at each other in the moonlight, full of pain and fear for each other's safety.

Then, over his shoulder, I saw Abe stumble out of the trees. His face was clay-coloured, his hand pressed to his side. He tripped on a rock and fell to his knees, and then just lay, slumped against a boulder.

'How will we get down to the shore?' Em said worriedly.

'We climb,' Seth said curtly. 'That's how we got up.'

Em said nothing. She looked at Abe and then down at the jar of magic in her arms. I knew what she was thinking. But there was no other way.

'How will we do this?' Em asked at last.

'You take the magic,' Seth said. 'I'll help Abe. Then I'll

come back for Anna.'

'No,' Abe said, his breathing panting white in the cold night air. 'I need – need to rest. Just for a minute.'

Seth looked at him, his face twisted with sympathy and worry. Then he nodded shortly.

'All right. Anna first. Then we'll come back for you. Ready, Anna?'

I nodded, steeling myself.

The descent was a nightmare. A grim, slithering nightmare of stumbling and swearing and scraped limbs. Seth carried me against his chest and he gasped with pain every time our combined weight landed on his bad leg. Once he slipped on a loose boulder and I thought we were going to fall to our deaths on the sharp black rocks below, but he managed to save himself, holding my weight on his arm and scrabbling with his fingertips for a hold while we teetered over the drop.

Em climbed in silence. Her face was grim and she clutched the jar of magic with cold determination, leaving no hand to save herself when she stumbled.

At last, after what seemed like hours of sweating agony, we reached the beach and I heard feet scrunching on the black shingle. Seth lowered me slowly to the ground. Then Emmaline slithered down the scree with a last rush and set the jar of magic down on the sand, wiping her face with her sleeve. She looked out towards the boat and her voice came drifting on the sea wind.

'So that's your boat. How are we going to get out to it?'

'I'll have to swim out and row it back.'

'Swim!' Em's voice was full of a horror that seemed almost comical after all we'd been through. 'It's snowing!'

'Well since I can't yet walk on water, got any other ideas?' Seth asked. Em looked out at the boat, floating on the black waves, and then she nodded, reluctantly.

'All right. You get the boat, I'll go back up to Abe.'

'He's too heavy for you.'

'We'll take it slowly,' Em promised. 'I'll stop, if I can't manage him, and wait for you to get back.'

Seth nodded and he began unlacing his boots.

'Seth,' Em said awkwardly. She twisted her fingers together. 'I wanted to say – you've been . . . I mean, I couldn't have . . .' She swallowed and then began again. 'I know we haven't always been very welcoming, Abe and me, but if we get out of here safely then it'll be down to—'

'Let's wait until we're out of here before we talk about getting back safely,' Seth said.

Em nodded. Then she turned and began clambering slowly back up the cliff.

Seth was prising off his boots, one after the other, and unbuttoning his shirt. The moonlight shone on his body, showing every scar and sinew in sharp relief, right down to the goosebumps that shivered across his skin as he put his shirt down on the black sand.

He looked at me for a moment and bent to kiss my forehead. Then he began to walk into the sea.

I heard his gasp as the icy water bit. But after that one sharp sound he just waded in grim silence into the dark, choppy sea. A few metres out he crouched and then dived into the waves. I watched the surface and saw his sleek, black head surface far out, halfway to the ship already.

Then a hoarse cry split the night and I looked up.

A crow was wheeling above the cliff top, huge and black against the moon, its wings spread to an impossible span.

I'd never seen a bird so huge, not even an eagle, and it flew so strangely, drunkenly almost, dipping and swooping and then recovering itself just before it hit. It swooped down towards the beach, so fast that I felt sure it would fall and smash on the rocks. But it flapped its wings furiously at the last moment, pulling back from its spiralling fall. I felt the wind from its wings ruffle my hair as it swooped across – then it thudded on to the black sand . . . and turned into Marcus.

He staggered towards me, naked, covered in blood and feathers, his one good eye still full of the inhuman blankness of the crow. The other was a bloody hole in his head.

'Anna,' he said. His voice was half human and half a rasping caw.

'Marcus,' I tried to keep the fear out of my voice – but it still shook. There was something so horrible about him, about his battered body and bloody face, full of hate and madness.

From far above, I heard Emmaline's cry of fear.

'Marcus,' she shouted down the cliff, 'Marcus, walk

away. There's three of us – you won't win this.'

'I don't want to win any longer.' He spoke to me, rather than Emmaline, as if I'd said the words. He coughed and spat blood. 'I've nothing left. I want revenge. Revenge for destroying me, destroying my plans. Revenge for wasting the greatest gift witchkind ever had.'

He lashed out suddenly, a spear of fire shooting across the dark rocks towards me – and there was nothing I could do. I had no shield, no spells, no defence.

'No!' Em shrieked. She flung out a spell from her precarious perch halfway up the cliff and somehow the spear ricocheted off her shield. It glanced away, towards the cliff-edge, smashing into the black rocks and sending a cascade down towards Em.

She screamed, clinging with her knuckles to a crevice as sharp stones showered down on her.

'Abe!' Her voice was half strangled with fear. She clung to the rocks with one hand, trying to protect her head with the other. There was the sound of more rocks rattling down and then one struck Emmaline full in the face. She gave a scream and let go, her body thumping horribly as it began to tumble slowly down the cliff, ricocheting off jutting outcrops of rock. Her hands clutched as she fell, desperately scrabbling for a hold, trying to save herself from the final, sheer drop. If she fell to the rocks on the beach, that would be it.

'Em!' Abe cried. He reached out towards her from the cliff-top – I saw his fingers stretching desperately across the space between them as he threw the last dregs of his magic into stopping her fall – and she did stop, her fingers clutching at the sharp stone, her legs dangling into space. Abe's magic held her there, the air seeming to shiver with the intensity of his effort. How long could he hold her? Long enough for Emmaline to scramble on to the ledge?

Marcus wasn't even watching. Instead he began to walk towards me.

'I've nothing left to lose,' he croaked. He pointed at his face and his heart, where the huge charred wound gaped and oozed. 'See this? You've broken me, Anna. You've broken everything.'

'I'm sorry,' I gasped. I pressed myself back against the rock, trying to conjure a shield. But there was nothing there. Just the terrifying emptiness. Nothing. Nothing. Nothing.

'I could have led the Ealdwitan to greatness. I could have fulfilled my father's dream: one man, a single vision . . .'

'You *killed* your father,' I sobbed.

'No, *you* killed him,' Marcus spat. 'With your questions, and your probing, and your stupidity. You were given a gift we've searched for for centuries – and you *wasted* it.'

He was very close now, his single eye locked on me, full of hate.

There was something in his hand. It shone in the moonlight. A knife.

'Marcus, *no* . . .'

386

'You've survived drowning, Anna. Having your head bashed in with a rock. Excision. But no witch, not even you, can survive having her heart cut out.'

He raised the knife, the moon and the black rocks reflecting off the long, hungry blade.

I pulled together all my strength and managed to move, dragging myself backwards, away from him, across the beach.

'Where are you going to go?' Marcus asked softly. Feathers shivered across his skin and his panting breath was a white cloud against the moon. 'There's no one left. No one to save you. You can't even save yourself.'

He raised the knife above his head. It flashed in the moonlight – cold and bright as death. His lips moved, but I could no longer hear what he was saying – I couldn't hear anything except for a roaring in my head, my blood pounding in my ears as if it had to use up all its beats in these last, dying seconds. My hands shook. I dug my fingers into the sand, hoping that from somewhere I could find the strength to pull myself upright and run.

But there was nothing.

Nothing but the silent scream in my head and the blinding whiteness of the blade as it flashed towards my heart.

Then something cold and wet crashed into me, flinging me sideways so that my head smashed against a stone and the whole night exploded in a blast of light and pain.

For a minute I was too blinded to see what had

happened. I lay on the sand, pain stabbing through my head, my eyes refusing to focus. Everything was a blur, but I could feel hands clutching at me – cold hands – wet, salty hair across my face, and there was the sound of breathing, hard and harsh against my ear and a cry of pain.

It was Seth – Seth lying across me, salt-wet from the sea, his breath tearing white in the darkness, his body shielding mine from Marcus' knife.

He hauled himself to his knees and then turned to Marcus.

They stood facing each other in the moonlight, Marcus naked, Seth stripped to the waist, both of them bloodied and battered and exhausted. There was a long slash across Seth's back where he'd taken the blow Marcus meant for me. Blood dripped to the sand, slow and dark.

'Go home,' Seth said. His voice was cracked with anger and exhaustion.

Marcus only laughed. He threw back his head and laughed, his throat bared to the moon, the knife slack in his hand. Then he looked at me.

'Things are pretty bleak, Anna, when you have to rely on an outwith for protection.'

He raised his knife hand high. But before he could take a step towards me, Seth grabbed him, wrestling him to the ground with a thump that shook the rocks around us.

For a long, horrible while they struggled, skin on skin, fingers tearing at each other, panting breaths and the smack of fist against muscle and bone. The knife flashed between them, catching the moonlight as they struggled.

Then suddenly Seth gave a gasp and sprawled backwards on to the sand. He pulled himself to his feet, his legs shaking with the effort, and stood, looking down at himself, at his naked chest.

At the knife that stuck out of his side, pushed hilt-deep beneath his ribs.

Then he looked at me. I tried to say something – but there were no words. My voice died in my throat as Marcus grabbed Seth's shoulder and yanked, dragging the knife out, pulling, pulling, inch after inch, until it came free and Marcus staggered back. Seth made a sound like a strangled, gargling gasp and blood began to gush from the wound.

Marcus held him by the shoulder and he thrust again, this time in the centre of Seth's belly, in and up and back out, with a squelching, grating suck.

'A—' Seth managed. His eyes were locked on mine.

He staggered, just one step, then he fell, twelve stone of muscle and bone and life crashing to the beach.

He lay, gasping, the blood pooling beneath him, and Marcus shoved the knife in one last time, ripping up through his ribcage, up to his heart.

Seth's body gave one, last convulsive heave – and then lay still on the black sand at Marcus' feet.

Fury and agony and grief exploded through me. From somewhere I found the strength to stagger forwards and I fell on my knees beside Seth, tears streaming down my face, falling on to his shoulders, into his hair. I kissed his cheeks and his lips and his forehead, the sobs ripping me up inside.

He reached out his fingers towards me.

And then his eyes left mine. He raised them, over my head, looking at something I couldn't see. His lips parted – but no sound came out.

I raised my head, following his gaze. It was Marcus, standing over us both, a smile on his lips, Seth's blood on his hands.

I reached for the knife.

It was stuck in Seth's ribs, and I sobbed helplessly as I pulled it out, feeling the bone grate against steel and the blood spew out beneath my hand.

I knew the action might kill him, if Marcus hadn't already done that. But I had nothing left to defend him with – no magic, no weapons of my own. It was the only weapon left.

I staggered to my feet and stood, facing Marcus.

'Leave us alone.'

'You stupid girl,' he said softly. 'Any power you ever had is in that jar over there.' He nodded to the fragile glass flagon glowing on the beach, white as a second moon. 'You think that knife gives you power? You don't even know what you've lost.'

A coldness spread into my fingers, up my arms, through my body. It was a chilling, hopeless, horrendous cold. The worst cold ever. Worse than death.

'*This* is power,' Marcus whispered. 'This is the only power that matters.'

My hands were suddenly locked to the hilt, but numb – so numb I couldn't feel anything. I wanted to stab Marcus in the heart, watch him die. But instead, slowly – very slowly – the point of the blade turned in, towards me, as Marcus forced my hands inwards.

Seth made a sound at my feet, a gargling rattling sound.

The point bit and a red blossom began to spread across my chest.

I was shaking. In spite of the cold, there was sweat on my lip and on the palms of my hands. My fingers slipped on the hilt of the knife, as the point dug deeper . . . deeper . . . God, it hurt!

A whimper came out of my lips.

Marcus smiled.

I took a breath, feeling my abdomen press agonisingly against the tip of the knife. Every breath, I impaled myself a little more. The point burrowed into my skin while I fought against it, my fingers refusing to obey, but my own muscles driving the knife deeper and deeper into myself – compelled by Marcus's magic and hate.

'*This is the only power that matters.*' Marcus stepped very close, his cheek next to mine, his hand over mine, ready to push the knife home if my hands faltered.

Was it true? Had I lost it – the only power that mattered in the world? What use was strength and honour and endurance against a power like this, a power that could force you to gut yourself while your friends watched, helpless, waiting for their own deaths.

While Seth died at my feet . . .

'Give up, Anna,' Marcus whispered in my ear, his breath a cold cloud of white, like a halo overhead. 'Give up.'

My hands slipped on the knife.

I closed my eyes.

It was not true. It was *not* true. There *were* other powers that mattered.

I wrenched the knife-tip out of my stomach, feeling warmth flood through my limbs, and with my other hand I pushed Marcus away with all my strength.

His face was white, blank with shock. Then he crouched and leapt at me, like a crow crouching to leap into the air. For a moment there was nothing but the sound of his breath in my ear, snapping beak, scratching claws, hands wrestling for the knife, wrestling to turn it back into my gut, his strength against mine, his breath hot on my cheek.

I fought like I'd never fought before, fighting for my life, for Seth's, for Emmaline and Abe – hands slippery with blood, face wet with tears and sweat. The knife flashed between us as our fingers slipped and clawed for control, first on the hilt, then the blade, then grabbing for each other's wrists, trying somehow, anyhow, to get possession of the knife.

Somehow I found the hilt and hung on to it, but Marcus' hands closed round my wrists, his grip painfully strong. He began to force my arms backwards, forcing the tip of the blade back towards my heart. I pushed against him with all my strength, but his grip was iron. The muscles on his arms stood out in the moonlight.

The knife-point bit into my skin and I knew this was it – I'd lost.

Then suddenly his hands, wet with blood, slipped from my wrists and he lost his grip. The blade flipped towards his gut.

I thrust, as hard as I could.

There was a sound like a scream – but worse. The worst scream you could imagine – high and harsh as a crow, keening as a man, with all the horror of death. And then it stopped.

Marcus staggered backwards, gasping. He looked up at me and then down at the hilt of the knife, buried fist-deep in his charred black wound.

He fell suddenly to his knees, then on to his side, convulsing in agony. Blood bubbled from his lips and a black stream, like hot tar, welled from the knife wound. His mouth tried to form words – but only blood came out. His head lolled to one side and darkness bubbled out from his eyes and mouth, covering his face and throat in a slick black shroud. It welled unstoppably, spilling out over his stomach and chest, until his whole body was covered, melting, consuming itself and soaking into the black sand.

At last there was nothing left – just a handful of feathers, drowning in tar.

I stood, looking down at my hands, soaked in blood

and streaked with black to the wrist, and I tried to feel something for him. I'd murdered my cousin. I'd murdered my own cousin, stabbed him to death. I ought to feel something: guilt, horror. I *wanted* to feel something, even if it was only the sick, fierce delight of victory.

But any other feelings lay buried beneath a huge suffocating weight of anguish.

Seth was dead.

CHAPTER TWENTY-FIVE

He lay at my feet. His face was completely untouched, his eyes wide and open, their calm grey expression unchanged by death. He was looking up at me and his lips seemed to smile, as if to say, *It's all right. Everything's all right.*

But it was not. Nothing could ever be right again. Seth was dead – his body broken, his blood spilled out all over the sand.

I don't know how long I stood, watching over his still, unmoving body. But I became aware after a while that Emmaline and Abe were there, had somehow dragged themselves down the cliff-face and were standing behind me.

'Anna . . .' Abe put his hands on my shoulders. 'For God's sake, don't look. You can't do anything for him now.'

He tried to pull me away, tried to turn my face away from the carnage, tried to take me in his arms. But I couldn't move. I couldn't look away from Seth's face. His eyes.

It'll be all right.

How could it be? I'd done this to him – from the first moment I laid eyes on him. In that moment I'd reached into his life and ripped out his heart, split him in two, just as surely as Marcus had. I'd brought him here, dragged him here in spite of his will.

I'd brought him to his death.

And there was nothing I could do. No spells left to cast. The emptiness inside me screamed.

I had no magic left.

Except . . .

The jar on the sand glowed white, shimmering like liquid pearl.

I pulled myself out of Abe's grip and took a faltering step.

'Anna . . .' Abe said. Then, as I bent towards the jar, 'Wait, what are you doing?'

I began to struggle with the lid.

'What are you *doing*?' Abe asked, a sudden fear in his voice. Then, as I carried on grappling with the lid, 'No! Don't do this. Wait, please wait. Maybe, if we take Seth's body home—'

'You were the one who told me I had to choose.'

'Not like this! How can you give this up? I won't let you! I won't let you do this to yourself. Em, for God's sake, say something! She's going to . . .' He choked, unable to finish.

'Anna!' Em lifted her head, her face white and blotched. 'Don't do this – don't destroy yourself like this! It won't work!'

'You don't know that.' The lid slipped in my stupid, weak fingers. I couldn't get it undone. 'It might work.'

'You can't give up your whole future for a chance!'

'I have to choose.'

'You don't!' Abe cried. He stood in front of me, the wind tearing at his hair, his black eyes full of agony. 'I didn't mean like this – not like this. I told you once, you could have both. Love *and* magic – you could have both. For God's sake . . .' His voice broke. '*I* could give you both. Please, please don't do this.'

'Will you help me open the jar?' I held it out to him and he shook his head, tears running down his cheeks.

'No!' His voice was cracked. 'I won't do this to you – I won't help you destroy your life like this. You're throwing your magic away, for God's sake. He's an outwith! His body will reject it – shut down. This isn't going to *work*.'

'Em?' I held it out to her. 'Em, *please*.'

'No.' She looked sick with fear. 'Please, no – you can't ask me. *Please* don't do this.'

'Anna . . .' Abe held me in his arms, his face white, his black eyes reflecting the jar's light. The agony in his voice tore at my heart. 'Please, I'm begging you. Give me a *chance*.'

'I love you.' I touched his cheek, where the tears lay wet and cold against his skin. 'I'll always love you. But Seth . . .' I swiped at my eyes with my free hand and took a shuddering breath. 'Seth never asked me to choose. Seth loved me no matter what – with magic or without.'

'Are you sure?' Abe said. He looked sick and I knew suddenly what he was about to say, but he forced himself on, forced himself to spell it out. 'Are you *sure* he did?

What if you give up your magic, only to find it's gone – his love is gone?'

'I—'

'I love you *now*,' he said. 'For real. No spells. No illusions.'

My hands trembled, the magic in the jar rippling and lapping at the glass. My heart hurt inside me.

'I will *always* love you,' Abe said.

I looked up at him. His face was shadowed and I remembered the feel of his hands, the softness of his lips, the combination of strength and gentleness and magic.

'Would you?' I asked. My voice shook. 'Could you love me without magic?'

His lips opened – and he didn't speak. Behind me I heard Em's stifled sob.

I leaned forwards and I kissed his lips, very gently.

'I have to choose,' I said. 'But you don't – you *can* have both. But not with me.'

I picked up a stone.

'No,' Abe said.

I held the jar out, over Seth's body, and smashed the stone into the glass.

'*No!*'

But it was too late.

The crack spread across the surface of the glass more swiftly than my eye could follow – and then the whole jar exploded in my hands, glass and magic raining down in a shower of light, spattering Seth's body in a fiery white blaze that lit up the beach and the black cliffs as if it were dawn.

It poured into the huge cavity at the centre of his chest, welling up out of the wound, bathing him in a glowing whiteness that flooded out across the sand.

And then . . . it was gone. And I had nothing.

'Anna, come away.' Emmaline pulled gently at my arm, her face worried. 'It's nearly dawn . . .'

'I can't leave him,' I said.

'Anna . . .' Emmaline let her voice trail away. She didn't need to say the rest. I knew.

I'd been so stupid – so pathetically stupid and hopeful. How could that gaping split in his chest possibly heal?

I lay down on the sand beside him and turned his face towards me. His neck was stiff, as if he was resisting, but I knew it was only rigor mortis setting in.

'Anna . . .' Em sounded really worried now. 'Are you listening?'

'Yes,' I said tiredly. 'Yes, I know. Can you give me a minute?'

'All right.' She rubbed beneath her glasses, at the sore place where they pinched her nose, then straightened. 'Abe!' she called. 'I'm going to try to swim out to the boat, like S . . .' she faltered. 'Like we talked about.'

'All right.' Abe stood stiffly from where he was slumped against a rock, his head in his hands. 'Can I do anything?'

'Hold my glasses,' Em said, with an attempt at a laugh.

Abe didn't smile back. He just nodded and they began to crunch towards the water, leaving me and Seth alone.

Seth's eyes stared into mine, grey and calm and full of love, and suddenly I couldn't bear it any more, I couldn't bear his unfaltering, unchanging, steadfast gaze. I reached out and put my two fingers on his lids, closing them. Then I let the tears come, running down my face and into the sand. They were silent. I didn't sob, or shake. Just my eyes – welling, and welling, and welling unstoppably.

'Don't be stupid.' Em's voice was hard with fear and exhaustion. She was shaking with cold. 'Anna, be reasonable. How are you going to get him to the boat?'

'I'm not leaving him,' I said, for the tenth time.

Abe said nothing. He just sat, crouched against a rock, his head in his hands.

'Christ!' Em cried. She clenched her fists, as if biting back something she didn't want to say, and turned to look across the cliffs again. I knew what she was looking for. Followers. Witches from the mine. We had to get out of here – and fast. But . . .

'I'm sorry,' I said. My voice cracked. 'I can't leave him. I can't.'

'He's dead.' Abe's voice was hard. He rose to his feet, his face dark with sudden anger. 'Don't you get it? He's dead. It's hard – God, I know how hard it is. But he's bloody dead!'

'I know!' I screamed at him. The words echoed back at

me from the cliffs, mocking me. The tears spilled down my cheeks. I swiped furiously at my eyes. 'But I can't leave him. I can't. Please, Abe – I have to do this. I can't leave him to rot in this place. Help me get him to the boat. *Please.*'

Abe put a hand over his face and rubbed his eyes wearily. He looked close to dropping. I didn't know if he could get *himself* to the boat, let alone Seth's body. But at last he nodded.

'All right.'

'Abe . . .' Em started and I knew what she was going to say. The impossibility of it – three knackered people, all wounded, with barely a spark of magic between us. How could we wrestle a cold, stiffening body through the icy waves and up the side of the boat? But then she stopped. 'OK,' was all she said. 'OK.'

I don't know how long it took. A long time. It felt like hours of cold struggle in the buffeting waves, while our fingers slipped and the boat crashed against our shoulders and skulls and knuckles, and Seth's heavy body slipped from our grip and slithered and refused to leave the water. But at last we were all shivering like drowned rats in the galley, dripping salt water on to the boards as we tried to work out what to do next.

'Where . . . ?' Em looked at Seth's body and then at Abe.

'On deck?' Abe asked. 'We could lash him down in case of storms.'

'No,' I said stubbornly. 'In the bedroom.'

'Anna . . .' Emmaline bit her lip. She looked close to losing it. 'I know you don't want to believe this but he's going to . . . to start to smell.'

'Then Abe has to keep the room cold . . .' My voice cracked.

'I can't,' Abe said desperately. 'For God's sake, none of us know how to steer this boat – do you know how to sail?'

I shook my head, feeling the stupid, welling tears spill down my cheeks again. Not really. Not without Seth telling me which rope to pull and when to go about.

'So how are we going to get home,' Abe spelled it out, 'unless I force the wind to do it? I can't do both, I'm barely keeping it together here.'

'Then I'll keep the window open. It's cold.'

'Where will we all sleep?' Emmaline said despairingly.

'There's another berth under the cockpit. You can have that.'

'What about you?'

'I'll stay with Seth.' I wiped my cheeks with my arm. *Stop crying*, I begged my eyes. *Please, stop crying.*

'With the window open?' Em exclaimed incredulously. 'Are you nuts? You'll freeze!'

'Will you help me get him into the bedroom?' I asked fiercely.

They said nothing. Then Abe moved to take Seth's shoulders. As he lifted, Seth's heavy lifeless body slipped from his fingers, his head thudding against the floor like a stone. Abe's face twisted.

'How could you?' The words were wrung out of him, full of bitterness. 'You could have been anything, done anything. How could you throw it away like that?'

'She didn't throw it away,' Emmaline cut in angrily. 'She *gave* it away. It was her choice, Abe. Hers.'

But Abe just looked at me, his face stiff with grief. Then he shook his head and lifted Seth's shoulders again. His eyes were full of tears.

Together we manoeuvred the body along the narrow gangway between the bunks. As we passed the table I saw the big brass binnacle compass. Its needle was swinging wide – back to magnetic north, where it belonged.

Somehow that small thing, a needle returning to its true home, undid me. It was proof – proof that Seth was gone and my magic was no more. I felt a great pain in my heart, as if Marcus' knife had gone deep, as deep as he'd intended.

In a way, Marcus really had cut out my heart, just as he'd promised. I almost wished he had. At least that pain would have stopped, in the end.

CHAPTER TWENTY-SIX

It was quiet in the little bedroom, and cold. I could hear Emmaline and Abe pacing in the galley, talking in low whispers. I couldn't hear what they were saying – I didn't try. I knew what it would be. Worry about the boat. About whether Abe, in his shattered, exhausted state, could control the weather enough to get us home. About me – about whether I'd lost my reason along with everything else.

The cool wind blew through the porthole and I shivered and moved as close to Seth as I possibly could, turning his stiff, cold body so that his arm flopped over my waist and his cheek rested on the pillow.

Like that, you could almost believe he was just asleep. The gaping wound in his chest was pressed closed, the drench of gore hidden in the shadows between us. His eyes were closed and his lips still curved in that half-smile. If I wanted, I could almost pretend . . .

I shut my eyes, pressed my forehead to his lips.

'Oh Seth,' I whispered. 'I'm so sorry.'

'Don't be.'

I squeezed my eyes tighter shut, the hot tears cooling as they traced across my skin. I wanted so much to believe . . .

'Anna, don't cry.'

His voice in my head was so real – *so* real. A whimper of pain came from my lips.

I pressed my eyes shut, so hard that lights and darkness exploded inside my skull, a blaze of pain in the blackness.

'I love you,' I whispered. I felt the tears roll across my nose and down my cheek. But there was no answer. There never would be an answer, in spite of all I'd given up.

Abe's words in the galley came back to me, making me ache inside, thinking of everything that I'd poured into that hole in Seth's chest. The soaring sensation of flying through the air, with nothing to hold me up but my own willpower. The intoxicating feeling that anything, anything was possible. The chance of being something more, something . . . remarkable.

But I thought I knew what he'd really meant. Him. I'd given up Abe.

And it was true. But more than that, I'd given up my mother. The chance of ever knowing the truth, of ever seeing her again. Ever since I'd grasped the meaning of the riddle I'd hoped. Hoped that even if my mother *were* dead, it might not be the end. Because with a power that could conquer death . . .

For a moment it had flared inside me: a tiny spark of possibility, even if I never had the courage to ignite it. And now it was gone. And for what? Seth's body lay in my arms, still and cold. I'd given it all up – for nothing.

I lay, with my eyes closed, listening to the sound of the waves, feeling the emptiness inside my heart, and Seth's body, pressed against mine, becoming faintly warm with borrowed heat from my skin.

I couldn't stay like this for long. He'd have to stay cold, if I were going to get his body back to Winter. But I didn't want to move.

Up on deck I could hear Emmaline and Abe moving around, wrestling with the sails. I knew I should get up, go and help them.

I opened my eyes.

Seth's cool, cloud-grey eyes gazed into mine.

'Seth . . . ?' I put up a hand to touch his face, cool beneath my fingers. '*Seth?*'

God, how I wanted to believe. The emptiness roared and screamed inside me.

And then he smiled.

My heart gave a great thump – and seemed to stop.

I scrambled to my knees, dragging him upright by his bloodstained shirt, my hands touching his face, running over the naked skin of his shoulders and chest; trying to look for the wound beneath the clotted blood; frantically searching his body for a sign, a sign that he was real.

'Am I going mad?' I found I was sobbing. 'Seth?'

'You're not going mad!' He took my hands in his, trapping my desperate movements. 'I'm real – stop with the strip-search. Why all the panic?'

'You *died!*' I put my forehead against his, my tears running down his face, mingling with the blood and the sweat. 'Don't you remember?'

'What?' His face was blank with shock. 'Is this a joke?'

'You *died*,' I wept. 'Marcus stabbed you in the heart. You bled out all over the sand. Don't you remember?'

Seth sat, his face pale.

'I don't remember,' he said blankly. Then he looked down at his chest. The skin was black and streaked with blood from his ribs down to his belly, the dark hair above his belt matted and crusted.

He touched it, his fingers turning sticky and red.

'Christ, what happened? The last thing I remember . . .' He rubbed his hand over his face, leaving a stripe of blood and then stopped. 'This is so weird. I remember the caves . . . I remember walking through the forest . . . I remember . . .'

He put his hand to his side and then to his chest, to his heart. He stopped, abruptly, frozen.

'What?' I was suddenly frightened by his expression. His face blazed.

'I can't feel it any more, it's gone.'

I stared at him, my face blank with shock.

'It's *gone*. There's just – nothing . . .'

Gone.

It was gone.

I felt suddenly cold – incredibly cold – and the hollow space inside me that my magic had once filled felt like a roaring barren emptiness.

'What did you do?' He moved towards me, grabbing me by the shoulders. 'Anna, where's your magic?'

It was gone.

I tried to say, 'You're free,' I tried to feel glad. But I couldn't speak and I couldn't feel anything apart from the tearing emptiness that seemed to be spreading out from my heart.

Seth caught me, holding me in his arms, his grip frantic and painful.

'What did you do?' he cried, his voice fierce. 'Where's the jar – your magic? What did you *do*?'

'I gave it . . .' I swallowed. My hands were shaking with tiredness. I felt if Seth relaxed his fierce grip on my shoulders I might fall. 'I gave it – to you.'

'No.' His face was sick, blank. He began to shake his head. 'No. No! How could you? How?'

'How? I poured it into . . .' I felt sick. 'Into the hole. In your chest.'

'That's not what I meant! I meant, how could you *do* that? How could you sacrifice your magic for me?'

'It wasn't a sacrifice.' My throat felt raw with tears. 'It was selfish. I didn't want you to die.'

'But your magic!' He put his head in his hands, his face agonized. 'What have you done? Oh my God, what have you done?'

'I'm glad,' I tried to say. I swallowed against the pain. It felt like a thorn in my throat, choking me, making it almost impossible to speak. 'I'm glad. Glad you're free.'

'What do you mean?'

'You're free,' I said again. And then I couldn't stop it – the tears came, welling up, hot and angry and full of pain.

I knew this was wrong – Seth was alive, nothing else mattered. And hadn't I always *wanted* to know for sure? Hadn't I always *wanted* him to be free, if his love wasn't real?

I'd still hoped. I'd always hoped. Hoped that one of my attempts had broken the spell. Hoped that it was real.

But his words: *I can't feel it any more . . . It's gone . . . There's just – nothing . . .*

I *should* be glad. But I couldn't feel anything apart from despair, as I realized that it had all been a lie. It wasn't just the knowledge that Seth didn't love me. It was the knowledge that *none* of it had been true. The times he'd said he loved me weren't true. Our first date wasn't true. The kisses weren't true. The night we'd spent together in this boat, in this *bed* . . .

I couldn't go any further. I turned away and a huge sob ripped from my throat.

'Anna . . .' He touched my shoulder. 'Sweetheart . . .'

'Don't call me that!' I cried. How could he say that? The word he'd always used, back when he thought he loved me, back when I hoped it was true. It felt like a violation – proof that it had all been nothing but words, lies, illusions.

'For God's sake!' His voice was a mixture of frustration and pain. 'What are you talking about? Don't call you what?

Is it over? Is that what you're trying to say?'

'Is it *over*?' I began to sob and laugh at the same time, a strange bubbling hysteria. 'You should know! Didn't you say it just now?'

'Say what?' Seth's eyes were the colour of thunder clouds. His fists were clenched.

'You said,' I felt suddenly calm, empty, drained of everything – not just magic, but all feeling as well, 'you said, "I can't feel it any more, it's gone. There's just nothing".'

'Yes.' His face blazed, fierce, full of an emotion so strong I couldn't name it, but it looked close to joy. It made the emptiness inside me howl with pain. 'Yes. It's gone. The pain is gone. My leg, Anna – I can walk again.'

I wanted to speak. But I couldn't.

He swung himself to his knees in an easy, fluid movement, without a flinch, and knelt in front of me.

'I don't know what your magic did, but it doesn't hurt. I feel . . . normal again. I feel whole.'

I stared at him, at his face, his eyes, his lips that I'd kissed, and loved, and kissed again.

'It's all gone,' he said softly. 'Every ache. Every pain. Even—' he turned his wrist, so that I could see the soft skin on the inside, where his scar had always snaked, the long rope burn '– even this.'

It was gone. The skin was smooth.

I turned his hand over wonderingly and then fitted it to mine. There was one scar left – the white mark of a very old burn on his right ringfinger, matching mine. The mark of my love for him, my need for him, my desperation to save him, and the pain I'd inflicted on us both.

'Anna . . .' He laced his fingers with mine, kneeling in front of me on the bed, his voice low and urgent. 'Anna, I love you. I've *always* loved you. Yesterday, today, tomorrow . . . Do you understand?'

I couldn't speak. I only looked at him.

'Do you believe me, Anna?'

'Yes,' I said. 'I believe you.'

And I did. I finally did.

The magic was gone, for ever. But in its place – this huge welling certainty, a sureness I'd never felt before, never hoped for. So this was what it felt like – love. Love without magic. Without spells. Just love.

And then I was kissing him, my arms around him, my fingers clutching at the muscles of his back, tracing the ridges of his ribs, his spine.

His lips were against mine, his fingers in my hair.

'I love you,' he said, again and again, his lips on my throat, my collarbone, the soft skin beneath my ear. 'I love you. I love you. I love you.'

EPILOGUE

Once there was a girl.

No, that's not right.

Once there was a witch.

And yet . . .

How can I tell it, this last part? Who am I?

I remember Emmaline's words, long ago: There's no such thing as half-outwith. If you've got magic, that's it. If you haven't, you're an outwith.

So what does that make me? An outwith? A witch? A murderer? A nobody?

'Anna, are you awake?'

Seth's voice broke in on my thoughts and I opened my eyes to see us drawing to a halt beside the tall, white house.

I nodded and began to unclip my seatbelt with numb fingers.

'Do you want me to come in?' Seth asked.

'I don't know,' I said. Then I sighed. 'No, I'm being cowardly. I know the answer – you should stay here. This is between me and Elizabeth. I'm just . . .' I swallowed. 'I'm scared to face her.'

'You've nothing to be ashamed of,' Seth said. 'You did what you had to do. He was a murderer. A murderer and a traitor, and he'd have sold you like a slave to the highest bidder.'

'He was my *cousin*.'

Seth sighed.

'I'll wait here. If you need me, I've got my phone, OK?'

'Yes.' I said. I climbed out of the car and stood, taking a couple of deep breaths to try to calm my thudding heart. Then I took my courage in my hands, climbed the wide, white steps and rang the bell.

To my surprise she was sitting in the drawing room, a tray of tea on the table by the window. She turned as I entered and her face broke into a smile.

'Anna!'

She opened her arms, but I didn't go to her.

'Wait,' I said. 'Please – there's something I have to tell you.'

She looked at me quizzically for a moment, then her face went quite grey. For a minute I thought it was another stroke and my hand went to the bell, to summon Miss Vane, but she pulled herself half out of her chair, the knuckles on the hand that clutched the head of her cane white with the effort.

'Anna, what happened?'

'W-what do you mean?'

'What's happened to you!' She put out her hand, her grip on my arm so tight it was almost painful. 'Your magic. Oh dear God, Anna. What happened to your magic?'

And so I told her. The whole story. Every detail.

When I finished I waited for her to speak, but she didn't. She simply sat, her hand gripped over her cane, her face unreadable as stone.

'I suppose you think I'm a failure,' I managed. 'Someone who threw her chances away for an outwith – like my mother. And worse. I'm a murderer.'

There was a long silence. Then she nodded.

'Anna, I am not one to mince words. Yes, you killed him. Nothing I can say will change that fact – you murdered my sister's child and you will have to live with that blood on your hands for the rest of your life.'

I felt cold, very cold. Hearing it from her lips . . .

'But,' she continued, 'it was him or you. And moreover, it was him or the Ealdwitan. If he'd lived, free to continue his betrayal . . .'

'But you loved him,' I said huskily. 'I know that.'

'More fool me,' Elizabeth said grimly. 'If I had not been such a trusting old simpleton . . .' She sighed and passed a hand over her face, the rings winking as they caught the light. 'You have paid, Anna. God knows, you've paid. And, if I know you, you'll continue to pay for the rest of your life. The guilt – the loss of your magic . . .' Her voice cracked. 'If someone had to shoulder the burden for this, it should have been me. The Ealdwitan was *my* burden; it should have been my price to pay, not yours.'

'I didn't do it for the Ealdwitan,' I said. She shook her head and started to speak, but I forced myself on. There was no honour in accepting her gratitude for something I hadn't done. 'No, listen, Grandmother. I can't let you think that. Yes, I killed Marcus. Yes, I laid down my magic. But it wasn't *for* the Chairs. I can't let you—'

'Nevertheless, you did it,' she broke in fiercely. 'It does not matter why. You paid the price. You could have turned away, but you did not. And for that reason alone, if for no other, you will always be my granddaughter. There will always be a room for you here. There will always be a seat for you in the chamber.'

'Though not a Chair?' I said, with a twisted smile.

'I don't know.' She turned to look out at the garden and I saw the white streaks in her hair, more white now than black. 'It was my dearest wish, but without magic . . . Is there really nothing – nothing there at all?'

'Nothing,' I said huskily. 'I've tried and tried. I can't even get a witchlight. And anyway, I can *feel* there's nothing there. It's just . . . empty.'

Elizabeth made a small sound, barely a sigh.

'I never wanted the Chair,' I said. 'I couldn't have done it, Grandmother, truly. I couldn't live your life – I couldn't carry that weight of responsibility.'

'You have a far heavier weight to carry,' she said sadly, and she sank back into her chair, letting her head rest

415

wearily against one wing. For a moment she looked far, far smaller than I'd remembered and impossibly frail. Her wrists looked as if they might snap. Her throat, in its heavy collar of gold, was like the brittle branch of an ageing tree. Then she straightened her back and reached for the teapot.

'No more of this,' she said firmly. 'Anna, please ring for more hot water and we will have tea, and talk of less maudlin things.'

Elizabeth came to the door to say goodbye, when I left. Her footsteps were slow and dragged on the polished parquet, but she was up and walking. Her strength of will astonished me. I thought of the frail, slurring skeleton under the covers just a few short weeks before, and it was hard to believe she was walking and talking beside me. Her steps were faltering, but she was bearing her own weight, and her eyes were bright and snapping as ever.

At the door she kissed me.

'Goodbye, my darling.'

Then she looked over my shoulder. Seth stood against the bonnet of the car, his dark hair tousled by the wind, his grey eyes watching us.

'So this is the one, is it?' she said under her breath. 'One outwith: the source of all this chaos and grief. Well, Lord knows I've made mistakes in my time . . .'

She straightened her spine, let go of my arm, and then slowly – very slowly – she descended the steps towards the car. I went to help her, but she held out an imperious hand, keeping me in my place.

At the car she put her hand on Seth's arm and he bent his head low, listening to words too faint for me to hear.

My stomach clenched with sudden nerves. I don't know what I thought she might say – something awful, something unforgiveable, perhaps. After all, she'd never forgiven my mother, nor my father.

But Seth only nodded and said something quietly in return. And when he straightened to meet my eyes, there was a smile on his lips.

'Go on,' my grandmother said firmly. 'Be off with you back to Winter, Anna. I'm too old to stand around on the street.'

I kissed her again and climbed into the car and we drove away.

'So what now?' Seth asked, as we drove over Hammersmith Bridge, and began the long, slow weave out towards the M25.

'What now?' I looked over my shoulder for the *A-Z*. 'I'm not completely sure, but I'd take signs for Richmond if I were you. Or Twickenham maybe.'

'No, I meant, what happens next. For you. For . . . us.'

'Oh.' I bit the inside of my lip. 'I don't know. Dad thinks I'm going back to school, but . . .'

'I know,' Seth said. He knew what I meant – the impossibility of going through all we'd seen and done and

417

suffered, and then going back to the old life we'd left. He drove for a while, his face set and unreadable. Then he spoke.

'D'you remember once, I said we could run away?'

'Yes,' I smiled at the memory. 'Sail away on your boat. Catch fish for food.'

'Because, I still have to take that boat to Helsinki and somehow I've got to earn enough to pay off the harbour fines and stuff.' He took a breath, his fingers tight on the wheel. 'And if you wanted, you could – well . . . come. I know!' He hurried on, before I could answer. 'I know what you're thinking. Everything that's happened, everything that's gone wrong. I wouldn't blame you if you never wanted to set foot on a boat again. But the sea will always be part of me. I can't tear that out. And you could learn how to sail, to navigate. With two people crewing we'd make better time. Who knows, you might even learn how to fish.'

I thought about it while we drove through the streets of London, past the places I'd lived and loved, past the Thames, with all its hidden secrets.

Then something occurred to me.

'What did she say, Seth? My grandmother, I mean. What did she tell you when we were leaving?'

'Oh!' Seth said. Then he smiled. 'She said, "Look after her, young man. She's even more remarkable than you know".'

'And what did you say?'

'I said, "I know. But she doesn't need me to look after her, she's stronger than both of us." And your grandmother nodded.'

Poor Dad. He was horrified of course. He wanted to know what would happen to my A-levels, my poor, stuffed-up A-levels. But I told him it would be OK. There were always retakes. I could revise from the boat, take a year out, apply next year. He was still unpersuaded though, even when I told him how good it would look on an Oxbridge application form. It was Elaine who talked him round in the end, I think. And, as I told him, I wasn't giving up on uni, just taking the long way round.

The quay was full of faces when we left: Dad, Elaine, Maya, Emmaline, Sienna with her bump just starting to show, Simon with his arm around her – all smiling, though there were tears in Dad's eyes and in mine.

I shouldn't have been crying. I didn't cry when I left for Russia. But perhaps it was because one person wasn't there: Abe.

'He's wrong,' Emmaline said fiercely, as she hugged me goodbye. 'You're still one of us, magic or no magic. You always will be. He'll come round, I promise.'

'I don't know. I don't think he'll ever forgive me,' I said. She hugged me hard, fierce, and all of a sudden I couldn't hold back. 'Em, you have to say something. To Abe. *Please* say something – what have you got to lose?'

'What have I got to lose?' Her laugh was bitter. 'Christ!

Only his friendship. Only my self-respect. Only a very happy status quo, thanks very much.'

'But – you *love* him. I know you do.'

She pulled back, her face rueful.

'I'm not promising anything. I'm not as tough as you are. There are some sacrifices I won't make, not even for that. What you did . . . What you gave up . . .' She shook her head.

Then Seth loosed the painter, Em took a step back, and we began to move out, between the closely crowded boats lining the quay.

'Goodbye, darlings!' Elaine shouted, over the flapping of the sails.

'I've made a charm!' Em called. She held up a plait, blowing in the wind, her hair and mine, twisted into one. 'You'll have to come back.'

'Be safe!' Dad shouted. 'Don't forget to email!'

As Seth's sure hands guided us out into the deep water I watched the faces lining the quay, thinking about Em's words, about Abe, about what I'd given up, and whether it was worth it.

And as the little figures on the quay grew smaller and smaller, still waving, still smiling, I realized something: I didn't give anything up, not really. I just chose a different path. All the remarkable people I know – my mother, my grandmother, Emmaline, Abe and all the others – they're not remarkable because of their magic, they're remarkable in spite of it. Their strength, their determination, their capacity to love and be loved – none of that came from magic. That came from something else. Something you can't take away.

And then there's Dad of course, who is pretty remarkable himself, in his own quiet way. He could have held on to the past and grown as bitter and introspective as the witches in the mine. But he didn't. He learned to live with questions unasked, and answered, and to be happy. He let the past go. He let my mother go. And, in the end, he let me go too.

And there's Seth. Seth, who gave up his life for me, without asking anything in return. Perhaps he's the most remarkable person of all.

'Can you feel it?' I called across to Seth, over the sound of the waves splashing against the hull.

'Feel what?' he shouted back.

'My magic.' I'd been watching him as we sailed. His shirt was off and I could see the veins on his arms standing out as he pulled on the ropes and turned the rudder this way and that, steering us across the open sea. And I'd been thinking of Abe's magic – the way it had coursed through *my* veins, making me see life differently, changing me, linking us. 'Can you feel me inside you, inside your heart?'

Seth only looked out to sea, his hair blowing in the breeze, his eyes as grey as the chalky channel sea on a stormy day, though today was clear and bright, full summer.

Then he looked at me.

'You were always inside my heart,' he said. 'Always.'

And then he kissed me.

And the world rocked beneath my feet, as it always did, as it always does. So that my heart beat faster, and my skin shivered beneath my clothes, and my fingers curled and uncurled against his back.

When we broke apart Seth stood and cast his net out across the sea, as the waves sparkled and glinted and danced in the summer sun.

But I leaned back against the boards of the boat, my head back, and I looked up at the sky, at the endless sunny blue. The sun leaped off the waves, dazzling me, and for a moment, just a moment, I thought I might have seen a handful of snowflakes flutter on the wind.

Then they were gone, melted into the sea and its infinite possibilities.